MONTANA
TERRITORY

MONTANA TERRITORY

A JOHN HAWK WESTERN

CHARLES G. WEST

PINNACLE BOOKS
Kensington Publishing Corp.
www.kensingtonbooks.com

PINNACLE BOOKS are published by

Kensington Publishing Corp.
119 West 40th Street
New York, NY 10018

All Kensington titles, imprints, and distributed lines are available at special quantity discounts for bulk purchases for sales promotions, premiums, fund-raising, educational, or institutional use. Special book excerpts or customized printings can also be created to fit specific needs. For details, write or phone the office of the Kensington sales manager: Kensington Publishing Corp., 119 West 40th Street, New York, NY 10018, attn: Sales Department; phone 1-800-221-2647.

PINNACLE BOOKS and the Pinnacle logo are Reg. U.S. Pat. & TM Off.

ISBN-13: 978-0-7860-4560-0
ISBN-10: 0-7860-4560-4

First printing: August 2020

10 9 8 7 6 5 4 3 2 1

Printed in the United States of America

Electronic edition:

ISBN-13: 978-0-7860-4561-7 (e-book)
ISBN-10: 0-7860-4561-2 (e-book)

FOR RONDA

CHAPTER 1

Army scout John Hawk stood on the bank of Sweet Grass Creek, waiting for the fifteen-man cavalry patrol to catch up to him. While he waited, he poked with his boot at a scorched bone from the ashes of a campfire. It required no scouting of the creek bank to tell him this was where the party of Indians had camped the night before. He knew it was the night just past because digging with his fingers in the ashes told him they were still warm from that morning. He could easily form a mental picture of the small party of Indian hunters gathered around the fire, enjoying a breakfast of fresh beef. His guess was Blackfoot, because he knew that his old friend Walking Owl and his village of old men and women were still trying to survive in this area below the Musselshell. His small band was all that was left of his village after the young warriors headed north to escape the army's efforts to send them to the reservation. The village must have been desperate for food to have come down this far to butcher a cow from one of the ranches in the valley. In Hawk's mind, the problem was that the ranchers had gotten to the point where they contacted the army at Fort Ellis every time they lost one cow to a group of starving Indians. And when they contacted the fort, that stolen cow was reported as a large part of their herd.

Hawk wasn't enthusiastic about riding scout for these patrols, and Lieutenant Meade knew it, so he was surprised that Meade had assigned him to scout on this one. Meade was commander of all scouts, so he could pick anyone he wanted. He and Hawk had already established a condition of mutual dislike that had resulted in Meade being openly opposed to working with the tall scout with the hawk's feather stuck in his hatband. They had had a couple of disagreements in the past, the last of which took place about twenty miles south of where Hawk presently stood. The incident came to mind now. It occurred at the Big Timber Hog Ranch when Hawk had tracked three outlaws to that compound on the Yellowstone River. The soldiers searched the cluster of small houses next to the main saloon but found no trace of the outlaws. Meade ordered the patrol back to Fort Ellis over Hawk's argument that the three outlaws were there. Meade informed him that he had done a poor job of tracking and the patrol's mission was impossible to complete. Hawk, in turn, informed the lieutenant that he knew damn well the three outlaws were in the compound, and he was just too anxious to call it quits and go home. Recalling it now got Hawk's dander up. The fact that it was later found that he had been right was of no solace. In view of all this, he had to again wonder why Meade had assigned him to a patrol he was commanding. His thoughts on the matter were distracted then when he saw Ben Mullins emerge from the screen of trees beside the creek. The patrol was not far behind.

Sitting tall and erect in the saddle, as if on parade, Lieutenant Harvey Meade led his patrol into the clearing where Hawk waited. "Like you figured," Ben commented when he pulled his horse up beside Rascal. He stepped down while Meade gave his men the order to dismount. "One bunch of poor-devil Injuns dropped down to get some fresh steaks," Ben continued. "Where you reckon they're headin'?"

"Yes, Hawk," Lieutenant Meade interrupted. "Where do you think they're driving those cattle?"

"Like I told you from the start," Hawk answered, "they ain't drivin' any cattle. There ain't any tracks of any more cattle." He nodded toward the ashes. "You're lookin' at the cow they stole, and it 'pears like they ate a good bit of it right here. To answer your question, though, it looks to me like they headed toward the Crazy Mountains with what they've got left."

Meade considered that for a few moments before commenting, "I suppose that could be, or it could be a war party that just happened to stop here to eat before they swung south to raid again."

Hawk shrugged. "It could be," he said, "but it ain't. They ain't lookin' to raid nobody. They ain't in any shape to raid anybody. They're just hungry, and there ain't no more buffalo to hunt, thanks to us."

"If they're hungry, they should report to the reservation," Meade snapped. "It's our job to drive them there, if they don't go willingly."

"That's one way of lookin' at it," Hawk allowed. "But it ain't always turnin' out for 'em like that. Judgin' by what's happened to some of their brothers, the reservation just gives them a place to sit around while they starve to death."

Meade fixed on him with an expression of disgust. "Sometimes I forget your love for your Blackfoot friends. I was willing to give you the opportunity to demonstrate your loyalty to the people who pay your salary as a scout. But I can plainly see that your loyalty continues to ride with the Indians. In view of that, I'm telling you, as of this instant, you are no longer employed by the U.S. Army." He waited for Hawk's reaction, half expecting to have to have him restrained.

Hawk didn't say anything for a long moment. He was not really surprised, but somewhat stunned by the incredibly simple excuse to fire him. He had known for a long time that it was Meade's desire to fire him. But because of Hawk's popularity with all the other officers, it had been difficult for him to find good reason. When Hawk finally responded, it was to say, "Well, you're the boss. I figured you'd come up with something sooner or later." He turned to Ben Mullins, who appeared to be more in shock than Hawk was. "There are tracks on the other side of the creek where they headed back west toward the Crazy Mountains. They'll most likely give you a good time tryin' to find 'em up in those mountains." With that, he turned, took Rascal's reins, and led the big buckskin gelding toward the rear of the column, exchanging nods of good luck with several of the soldiers as he passed. Behind him, he heard Meade giving orders to rest the horses. Rascal deserved a rest as well, so to avoid any further conflict with the lieutenant, he walked a few dozen yards upstream before letting his horse go to water.

Hawk's firing caused an awkward silence among

the troopers. John Hawk had proven himself the most capable scout at Fort Ellis in the estimation of every soldier who had ever ridden with him. That opinion was shared by most of the other scouts who rode out of Fort Ellis. Soon the silence was breached by several whispered discussions about the unexpected firing, as several small fires were built to boil coffee. Off in his exile, Hawk decided a cup of coffee would taste pretty good right then as well. He gathered some dead limbs and soon had a fire going. He was down by the creek filling his coffeepot when he heard Ben Mullins behind him. "Put enough water in it for me."

Hawk looked over his shoulder and smiled. "All right, I'll fill it up, but ain't you worried the lieutenant will see you drinkin' coffee with me?"

"Well, he didn't order me not to," Ben said, "and me and you share a campfire most of the time, anyway." He shrugged. "I don't know, maybe he'll fire me, too. Then he can scout for himself." He picked up a few sticks for the fire on his way back with Hawk and the coffeepot. Getting serious then, he said, "Damn, Hawk, that was a raw deal that son of a bitch just gave you. What the hell did you do to deserve that?"

"I don't know, Ben. Some folks just have a natural dislike for other folks. Meade and I ain't ever got along real good." He paused to think about it. "And there was that time on the Yellowstone when I told him he was a damn fool for givin' up on a patrol." The thought of that brought a chuckle from him. "Meade don't take criticism too well."

Ben shook his head, still finding it hard to believe. "Can he fire you from your job like that? Without goin' through Major Brisbin or anybody?"

"I reckon so," Hawk said, placing the coffeepot on

the edge of the fire, so it wouldn't boil too fast. "He's in command of all the scouts at Fort Ellis, so you'd best mind your p's and q's when you ride with him."

"Maybe you can still scout at one of the other forts," Ben suggested, genuinely worried for Hawk.

"Maybe I could," Hawk allowed, "but I ain't sure I even want to. I might just decide to give up scoutin' for a livin'."

"And do what?" Ben scoffed, thinking Hawk was born to be a scout.

"I don't know, rob banks, I reckon." He appreciated Ben's concern over his loss of a job, but he was not greatly upset about it. He'd find something else to do—he always had.

When the horses were rested, the fires were put out, and the troopers were ordered to mount up. Hawk stood upstream and watched them move out as they crossed the creek and started toward the Crazy Mountains. He hoped that Ben would point out to the stubborn lieutenant that there were no tracks to support the rancher's claims that the Indians were driving a sizable portion of his herd away. He gave a little whistle, and the buckskin came up from the edge of the creek at once. Hawk climbed on board, already thinking about some things he hadn't gotten around to doing back at his cabin on the Boulder River. He would have time to replace some of the mud chinking on his stone chimney now that he was a free man. And he would need to do some hunting to make sure he had enough meat smoke-cured. First, however, he would have to return to Fort Ellis to get his packhorse and pick up the possibles he kept in one of the stables there. It was a day and a half back to Fort Ellis. Rascal could make it in a day if he had to, but now, with all the time in the world at Hawk's disposal, there was no need to push the buckskin.

As he rode, moving comfortably with Rascal's easy rhythm, he thought about the patrol he had just left, and it occurred to him that he was relieved to have been fired. Old Walking Owl and his people had long been friends of his, and he wasn't really comfortable leading a patrol to capture him. In fact, he sincerely hoped the old chief successfully escaped into the mountains. Ben Mullins was a good scout, but Walking Owl was a pretty shrewd old bird, and he had been avoiding army patrols for quite some time. Hawk was glad to be relieved of the task of finding the small village of Blackfeet, because he was confident that he could have tracked them down. Unlike Ben, he had lived with the Crow and the Blackfeet. He knew how they thought. He also suspected he knew Lieutenant Meade's lack of determination. And if Walking Owl could manage to stay ahead of the cavalry patrol, he thought there was a good chance Meade would call it quits. It had been Hawk's experience that Meade wasn't comfortable when he reached the exhaustion of the rations drawn for an estimated number of days and would recall the patrol. So, with the chance of that possibility in mind, Hawk headed southwest, intending to strike the Yellowstone west of Big Timber and follow it in to Fort Ellis.

Over 150 miles northwest of Hawk's position as he rode toward the Yellowstone River, an important meeting was taking place near the Missouri River at the farmhouse of Donald Lewis. Lewis, a quiet young man, was the pastor of a small religious community of the Society of Friends. The meeting today was not the usual weekly meeting for worship, as they called their church service. This meeting was called to discuss the final plans for the entire church to leave their farms and homes in this uncivilized territory downriver from Fort Benton. Just two nights before, Brother William Boston's farm had been struck by the same raiders who had struck several of the other farms, running off stock and destroying gardens, even setting fires in some of the outbuildings. The little group of Friends had decided to migrate to more peaceful lands close to Helena, land enough to parcel off tracts for all of the seven families who had decided to go. A recent convert to the society, Brother David Booth had been instrumental in locating the new land near Helena and had volunteered to lead the party west along the Mullan Road. Everything the Friends owned, primarily their farms, but everything else other than their basic possessions, had been sold, the money from which would be used to buy what they needed in their new home. There had been some objections to selling their wagons, but Brother Booth had persuaded them to go by mule train and leave the cumbersome wagons behind. That way, he said, they could get to Helena much quicker with fewer stops for rest.

It had taken some time, and quite a few Indian raids, to persuade some of the Friends that this exodus was a sensible thing to do. But the promise of a nonviolent land at a very attractive price was enough to finally bring everyone around. Brother Lewis was convinced that David Booth had been sent to help them as a result of their fervent prayers. Though not a man of violence, he was obviously a strong man, and he was very familiar with the land they would buy near Helena. One of the purposes of this meeting tonight was to announce it was time to start out to their new homes. A general sum of cash had been accumulated through the sales of everyone's property, enough to buy a tract of land large enough to accommodate every family, with enough left over to build a meeting-house. It was time to go. As was their custom, at the end of the meeting there was a period of quiet contemplation, during which an occasional member voiced an inspirational thought that had come to him. On this night, all of those who saw fit to share their thoughts spoke in favor of going. And everyone agreed, all signs pointed toward a new beginning in the territory Brother Booth had suggested.

Half a day's ride found Hawk at the Yellowstone, where he turned Rascal to the west. Riding about three miles to a spot where the river bowed around a rocky area, he left the road to continue straight ahead. Hawk had camped there before and found that, once past the rocky crags, there was a grassy clearing in the trees that lined the river and provided a secluded campsite over a hundred yards from the road. After pulling Rascal's saddle off, he released the buckskin to go to the water, then he gathered some limbs to start a fire. With jerky, bacon, and hardtack enough to last him for a ten-day patrol, there was no shortage of food.

So, when he got his fire going, he went to the edge of the river to fill his coffeepot. "What are you snortin' about?" he asked Rascal when he walked down the bank where the buckskin was drinking. The horse issued a few inquisitive whinnies as Hawk walked past him to fill his pot upstream from the spot where Rascal was stirring up the water. The horse whinnied again, causing him to stop and take a good look around him before deciding Rascal must have seen a muskrat or something. Thinking it was nothing, Hawk squatted on his heels and reached out to fill his coffeepot. It was then that he discovered what Rascal had been trying to tell him. Kneeling close to the ground, he could see a small moccasin under the low-hanging branches of a large chokecherry bush. He was surprised but gave no sign of having seen whoever was hiding in the bushes. If it was an ambush, he figured he'd be dead by now, so he continued filling his coffeepot. When it was full, he stood up and said, "I'm fixin' to have me a cup of coffee and something to eat here in a few minutes. If you want some, you'll have to come outta that bush to get it."

There was no response from the owner of the moccasin, even though it was drawn quickly back when Hawk spoke. Judging by the size of the foot, he figured it to belong to either a young boy or a woman. From the glimpse he got of the beaded design on the moccasin before it was suddenly drawn back in the bushes, he guessed it to be Crow. "Suit yourself," he said, after another few moments with no response. "I've got an extra cup and some food to cook. If you change your mind, come on out." He turned and walked back toward his fire, which was burning nicely now.

It occurred to him that he should have spoken in the Crow tongue. He was about to do that, but he heard the rustle of bushes behind him, so he stopped and waited. A young Indian woman emerged, still trying to free herself from the chokecherry branches that held on to her. Her dress was wet. When she looked up to see him watching her efforts, she stopped as if she thought she might have made the wrong decision to come out of her hiding place. "Come on," he said, "and you can help me cook some of this meat." Then he turned his back on her again and continued toward his fire. Still undecided, she paused a few moments more, then decided to follow the strange white man. He was tall, with broad shoulders, and wearing a buckskin shirt and a flat-crowned hat with a feather stuck in the band. She wondered if he might be the white man her tribesmen called Hawk. If he was, he was a friend to the Crow. Even if he was not that man, he seemed to have no evil intent toward her, so she decided to follow him.

She walked up to within ten feet of the fire, where he busied himself situating his coffeepot in the flames. She stopped then to ask a question. "Are you the white man they call Hawk?"

"Yes, I'm Hawk," he answered. "What is your name?"

"My name is Winter Flower," she replied.

"Crow?" Hawk asked, and she nodded vigorously. "Well, Winter Flower, why are you here in this place? Are you alone?" She said that she was alone and that she was trying to get back to her family on the Crow Reservation. "On the Stillwater River?" Hawk asked.

She nodded vigorously again and began to explain her presence there on the Yellowstone. Soon the story poured out of her. When she and her younger sister left their father's cabin to dig up wild turnips, they were accosted by two white men on horseback. She recognized the two men as evil men who came to the reservation to sell whiskey to the young men of her village. "One of them asked me if I wanted to go with him," she said. "When I said no, he tried to grab me, but my sister and I ran. He ran me down on his horse and knocked me to the ground. Then he tied me up. The man who took me asked his friend if he wanted my sister and he said 'No, she is too young.' They didn't tie her up, and I was afraid they were going to shoot her, so I told her to run to tell our father what had happened to me. The man who held me tried to grab her, but she was too quick, and she ran into the forest. The other man was still on his horse, but he didn't try to run her down. He shot at her, instead, but he missed her. Morning Sky can run very fast, and the man's horse would not hold still, so he missed when he shot at her again."

"So, she got away," Hawk said, and Winter Flower nodded. "But you got away, too. It looks like you were in the river."

"Yes, they drank much whiskey and got sleepy. They didn't tie me very good, so I got away while they slept. They have been looking for me since this morning, and I think if they find me, they will kill me. The one called Luke said that he would kill me if I tried to run away. So, I slipped out of their camp and crossed the river, hoping they would not follow me. But they must have seen footprints where I went into the river because I heard them on the other side behind me. So, I crossed back to this side and found a place to hide."

Based on what she had just told him, Hawk had a clear picture of what she had been through. He had no idea where the two men might be now, on this side of the river, or the other, how far behind her they might be, or how strong their determination to find

her was. Without knowing any of this, it was difficult
to decide what to do. So, he decided to do nothing.
"You'll have to trust me," he told her. "I'll take you
home to your village, but first, we'll stay right here
and see if they figured out where you went. I've got a
blanket in my bedroll. You can go back in the bushes
there and get out of that wet buckskin dress and leg-
gings and we'll dry 'em out by the fire. I'll keep watch
while you change. Then you can drink some of this
coffee to warm you up a little." She looked at him as
if astonished. He guessed that she expected him to
quickly pack up his things and gallop away on his
horse with her behind him. "Trust me," he repeated.
"I promise I won't let them take you, if they find us."

Feeling that he might not understand how dangerous the two men were, she was not sure if he was
making the right decision or if maybe he was with
them. But at this point, her options were limited, so
she decided to trust the man called Hawk. From what
she had heard in her village, Hawk was a man to be
trusted. She nodded obediently when he handed her
his blanket, then took it and went behind the closest
patch of bushes from the fire. "Whatever you want,"
she answered when he asked if she wanted deer meat
or bacon.

"We'll have some deer jerky," he announced. Then
thinking he had plenty of provisions, he said, "And
some bacon, too." He doubted that she had been
given anything to eat by the two men who had captured her.

CHAPTER 2

"Luke!" Bud Jenkins yelled. "Over here!" He stepped down from the saddle to take a closer look, then he waited for his partner to catch up to him. They had found the girl's tracks leading into the water, so they had crossed over and found her tracks where she came out on that side. But she had been more careful from that point on. When Luke Ivey pulled his horse up beside his partner's, Bud pointed to a broken branch between two berry bushes growing on the edge of a low bluff. "That's what she did," he said, looking over the low bluff at the water below. "She pushed through this here bush and jumped in the river, thought we wouldn't see no tracks, so we wouldn't know she went back across the river. She's smart, but she ain't as smart as me and you, right, Luke?"

"I 'spect not," Luke said. "Come on." He wheeled his horse and loped past the bluff to a point where the bank was not so steep and entered the water there. When Bud caught up to him on the other side, he said, "You look upstream, I'll look downstream. We oughta find some tracks where she came out." As he expected, it wasn't long before he discovered Winter Flower's tracks where she had come out of the water. "Down here, Bud," he called out, and waited for him. When he caught up to him, Luke chuckled and pointed to the footprints coming out of the river. "Looks like she tried to brush her tracks out with a branch or somethin'. I reckon she was in too big a hurry to do a good job. Let's see which way she ran."

They scouted the riverbank for only a short while before finding a single footprint heading downstream. "She can't be far," Bud speculated. "She mighta found her a place to hole up and hide. Best keep a sharp eye." They went on foot, leading their horses, so as not to miss any other signs of her escape route, and after a distance of about fifty yards, they discovered another footprint in the moss at the base of a cottonwood tree. "She's runnin' straight down the river," he said with a laugh. "Reckon she's figurin' on runnin' all the way back home?" They continued along the river until Bud suddenly stopped and exclaimed, "Whoa!" When Luke came up beside him, Bud pointed to a column of smoke drifting up through the trees ahead.

"What the hell?" Luke puzzled, "You reckon she stopped to build a fire?"

"No, jackass, we done run up on somebody's camp," Bud replied. "Best leave the horses here and slip up a little closer, so we can take a look-see." They tied their horses there and moved cautiously up closer to the source of the smoke. Parting the branches of a large laurel bush, he peeked through to see the small camp.

Pushing up beside him, Luke said, "I don't see but one horse down by the water, and there ain't but one man I can see, and he's settin' up close to that big cottonwood."

"On the other side of him," Bud whispered, excitedly. "That looks like a woman settin' next to him with a robe on."

"It's her!" Luke blurted, although with the blanket covering her head and shoulders, he could not be absolutely sure. "It's gotta be her. The little bitch has took up with another man. Well, I'll take care of that real quick," he declared as he drew the .44 riding on his hip.

"That might not be too smart," Bud cautioned. "We shoulda brung our rifles. With him settin' up close against that tree like he is, he ain't givin' you much of a target. And that far away, you'd be lucky to hit the damn tree with your pistol."

"Well, he don't look like he's goin' anywhere," Luke said. "Let's go back and get our rifles."

"There ain't no use in takin' a chance on pluggin' that tree instead of him," Bud suggested. "Why don't we go back and get the horses, then just ride on into his camp peaceable-like?" Luke cocked his head to the side, a sign that told Bud he wasn't too sure that was a good idea, so Bud explained his reasoning. "If we just ride on in like we're peaceful travelers and don't give him any idea we're lookin' for trouble, we'll be able to ride to the right of that campfire so there won't be none of him behind the tree. As soon as we get the angle on him, we can blast away. That way, we can get a better look at who's under that blanket." He punched Luke playfully on the shoulder and commented, "That might be his old granny under there."

They both chuckled over that and Luke said, "Then

I reckon that'd be a woman for you, since you said my gal's sister was too young for you."

Sitting close by the trunk of the large cottonwood, Hawk heard Rascal nicker. He had been watching the big buckskin near the edge of the water, the horse's ears constantly twitching, and knew their company was near. "They're gettin' pretty close," he said, and Winter Flower moved even tighter up to the tree behind his shoulder. He cocked the hammer back on the Winchester lying on the ground right beside his hand. "You know how to shoot a gun?" She answered with a nod of her head. He reached down and eased the .44 out of his holster. "Here, use this only if you have to. That's just in case I ain't as smart as I think I am." He gave her a reassuring smile and said, "All we gotta do now is wait and let 'em come to us." In a matter of minutes, the two men slow-walked their horses into the little grassy clearing. "When the shootin' starts, you roll over all the way behind this tree, understand?" She nodded.

"Hello, the camp!" Bud sang out. "Saw your smoke. Mind if we come in?"

"Not if you're peaceful," Hawk answered. He didn't move to get to his feet, sitting where he was as the two men continued walking their horses to the other side of his fire. He figured they were intent upon getting a better angle to shoot at him. He wondered if he considered the fact that it also made them a better target and that his rifle was already aimed at the spot where he guessed they would stop.

"No matter, friend," Bud replied. "We ain't lookin' to stop. We're searchin' for a little Injun woman that's been travelin' with us, and I'm afraid she's gone off and got herself lost."

"Is that a fact?" Hawk asked.

"Yes, sir, it is," Bud answered. "We'd be awful worried if we thought we'd lost her. Ya see, she's tetched in the head and we're tryin' to get her to her folks on the reservation. I don't reckon she wandered by here, did she?"

"Not since we've been here," Hawk replied. "We just got here a little while ago, though, just me and my woman. We ain't seen anybody else."

"I reckon that's your woman settin' there beside you," Luke said, "all huddled up under that blanket."

"Yep, that's her. She'd come out and say howdy, but she's kinda shy, don't you know?"

Luke was rapidly losing his patience in the game of verbal sparring. "I'm thinkin' you might be makin' a big mistake and that ain't your woman a-tall."

Hawk sensed that they were about to make their move, but he maintained his casual front, even while his finger slowly eased onto the trigger. "No, no mistake," he said. "I'm pretty sure I can tell my woman from all the others. Maybe you boys have been lookin' in the wrong direction." To Winter Flower, he whispered, "Remember what I told you." She nodded, clutching the pistol with both hands.

Bud was convinced that their bluff wasn't working, and he saw the Winchester lying conveniently looking in their direction. He decided it best to respect the other man's bluff and ride on out of the camp. There was no doubt the woman huddled between the man and the tree was the Indian girl they had stolen. Their best bet was to ride on out, then return that night and shoot him, take the girl and everything the man had. He was about to say as much to Luke, but he had waited too long. Exhausted of the tiny amount of patience he normally had and frustrated by the game of casual the stranger was playing, he reached for his six-gun. The peace of the riverside was shattered by the crack of the Winchester as Luke rolled backward off his horse. Bud had no choice but to go for his gun and managed to get off a shot, but the sudden crack of the rifle caused both horses to jump, spoiling his aim. Before he had time to cock the .44 again, he joined Luke on the ground, both men dead from shots in their chests.

"Are you all right?" Hawk asked, and turned to look at her. She had remembered what he had told her to do, so she had rolled over behind the tree. And now she was pressing her back tightly against the trunk, holding his .44 against her breast with both hands. "Here," he said, "you can give it back now." She released it, realizing only then that she had been clutching it with the muzzle aimed up under her chin. "I reckon I'd best clean up our campsite if you're gonna feel like havin' any of that deer meat I was talkin' about." She could only nod in response, her emotions not sufficiently recovered from the sudden shooting.

Except for their weapons, horses, and saddles, the two kidnappers had very little of value between them. Hawk dragged the bodies away from the camp, then unsaddled their horses. "If it's all right with you," he told her, "we'll eat some supper and sleep here tonight. Then, in the mornin', I'll take you back to your family. My horse needs a rest, and maybe theirs might, too. At least, you'll have your own horse to ride. I know your family is mighty sick about what happened to you, so we won't waste any time gettin' you home." He suspected there was a good chance there might be another issue of great concern to her, so he thought to reassure her. "I won't ask you if those men violated you, but I'll tell your father that I rescued you before they had any chance to hurt you."

She said nothing at first, but big tears welled up in her eyes as she nodded her thanks. Then she tearfully admitted, "The one called Luke tried to lie with me, but I fought him and he was too drunk to do anything."

"Your father will be glad to know that you ain't been harmed in any way," Hawk continued. "And he'll be happy when you bring him two good horses and saddles." This surprised her, for she assumed that he would take all of the two men's possessions for himself.

Finally convinced that she was safe now, she thanked him for her rescue and volunteered to take over the cooking of their meager supper, tending the sizzling meat with one hand while holding the blanket around her with the other. Amused by her attempts, he cut a three-foot length of rope from one of the kidnappers' saddles and gave it to her to use as a sash for her robe. With both hands free, she gave him a great big smile with a nod of her head. He was sorry he didn't have any fresh-killed game to cook, instead of his meager rations of jerky and bacon, but she seemed grateful for what he offered.

They got an early start the following morning, delaying breakfast until it was time to rest the horses. The Crow agency was in the opposite direction from where Hawk had been going, but it was only a ride of about thirty-five miles, not even a full day's travel. So it wasn't really much out of his way, especially since he was in no particular hurry to reach Fort Ellis. To the contrary, since he had been fired, he was beginning to enjoy the feeling of being free of the discipline of an army patrol. With Winter Flower perched on the back of a yellow dun gelding, formerly the ride of the late Bud Jenkins, they left the Yellowstone and started out to the southeast to strike the Stillwater River and Winter Flower's home. Following a game trail Hawk had traveled before, they made their way across an expanse of rolling hills, devoid of trees, except along the occasional streams they came upon. One such stream, a little healthier-looking than most, was selected as the stop for breakfast, although they had ridden no more than about fifteen or sixteen miles. It would leave them only about twenty miles to the Crow agency. It would still be early when they arrived at Winter Flower's village. After he took care of the horses, he sat down by the fire Winter Flower had made and watched her as she fashioned a spit for the meat out of a green cottonwood branch. When the coffee was made, she filled his cup for him.

She had said nothing about her sister to that point, so he thought it time to ask. "How old is your sister?"

"Morning Sky has seen ten summers," she replied.

"How far were you and Mornin' Sky from your village when those two men took you?" He had some concern that her sister might have lost her way, if the distance was great, and he could possibly find himself searching for her.

"It was not far," she answered, "not even a half a day's walk. I'm sure she got home all right." She smiled at him, aware of his concern. Feeling safe now that the nightmare of her abduction was past, she sought to learn more about the man who had saved her. "They call you Hawk. Is it because you wear that feather in your hatband?"

"No," he answered. "Hawk is my name—John Hawk. So, I reckon it's more the other way around. I wear the feather because that's my name." She looked puzzled, so he said, "It's not so unusual, is it? I mean, the men of your tribe wear feathers in their hair, right?"

"Yes, but you are a white man, and white men don't wear feathers," she insisted.

"Maybe I wear one because I lived in a Crow village until I was nineteen, so I adopted the ways of the Crow, and the hawk feather is big medicine to me." He left it at that, since it seemed to please her, thinking it would be best not to tell her of his time living with the Blackfeet for a couple of years after that.

She paused to study his face for a moment. "I am lucky you found me, John Hawk. I think your medicine is strong." She paused again, this time a few moments longer before confessing her thoughts. "I have a feather, too." She got up from the fire, so she could reach down in the deep pocket of her skirt and pull a feather from it. She held it up for him to see. "It is a hawk feather, like yours." Again, she paused, not sure if she should tell him or not. Finally, she decided she had gone this far, and she should continue. "When the evil man named Luke threw me down on the ground and tied my hands behind my back, he was drunk from drinking the firewater they carried and didn't do a good job tying the knots. He told me he would kill me if I tried to run while he went to get some more firewater from his saddle. I prayed that I would die before I was forced to lie with him. I found

that he had not tied my hands tight enough, so I tried
very hard to loosen the rope. I got one hand free, but
I was afraid he would come back before I could run
away. Then I heard the sound of a hawk and another
bird fighting in the sky above and the two white men
started to shoot their guns at the birds. They did not
hit them, but I felt something lightly touch my one
bound wrist, and then I saw that it was this feather."
She held it up again. "While the men ran around like
crazy men, trying to shoot at the birds, I saw that it was
my chance to run, so I did, and I held on to the hawk
feather and prayed as I ran that the spirit of the hawk
would come and save me. I ran until I could run no
more, so I found a place to hide." She looked at him
and smiled. "When you discovered my hiding place, I
thought I had run into one of their friends. And when
you said we would just sit there and wait for those two
devils, I was almost sure they were your friends then.
But now I know that the medicine feather sent a hawk
to save me. It was just another kind of hawk."

He wasn't sure of the best way to respond to her
theory. Young Indian boys, as a ritual of coming of
age, went out in the wilderness alone with no food or
water to fast for days seeking the source of their medicine. But what might be normal for boys was not the
custom for girls. He had to admit she had created a
good story, and he supposed there was no harm in
letting her believe in it. He had made up different
stories about the reason he wore the feather in his
hatband, but the truth of it was he just happened to
find a stray hawk feather now and again. And when he
did, he would swap the one in his hat for it, if it was in
better shape, and it was simply because his name was

Hawk. He was reluctant to tell her that, because her eyes were literally shining as she looked into his eyes, waiting for him to tell her she was right, and he had been sent to her by the spirit of the hawk. She continued to look to him as if waiting for him to confirm her belief, and he didn't have the heart to tell her he wasn't sent to the banks of the Yellowstone by anyone, bird or man. He just liked that particular spot to camp in. He thought for a minute before he responded to her story.

"How old are you, Winter Flower?"

"I have fourteen summers," she answered, "but my mother says I am very wise for my age."

"Well, I can believe that with no trouble a-tall." He could not help thinking about another young girl close to her age, whose memory he kept in a safe place in the depths of his mind. "No one of us can hope to learn the secrets of this life we're given. They are too many for a man or a woman to understand. But once in a while, we may be given just a little glimpse of a secret. I think that's what happened to you yesterday. I think somebody thinks you've got too much more to do in your life to be stopped by the likes of those two. And I'm glad that somebody sent me to help you. I think it would be good if we swapped feathers. You take mine and I'll wear your feather in my hat. Whaddaya think?" That seemed to please her very much, so that's what they did. Judging by the expression on her face, he could imagine that she was convinced that the hawk was truly her guardian. He took her feather and placed it in his hatband. "I don't know," he said, "that feather might be prettier than the one I had." He gave her a smile, put his hat on, and said, "Whaddaya say we take you back home now?"

* * *

It was shortly after noon when they rode into the Crow village and Winter Flower pushed ahead on her horse to lead Hawk to her father's house. Her father, hearing sounds of joyful greetings from the people of the village, opened the door of the crude log cabin to see what was going on. "Winter Flower!" he exclaimed moments before being pushed aside by his wife in her excitement to see for herself. When she saw her daughter in the saddle of the yellow roan, she ran to meet her, with Winter Flower's younger sister following close behind. Winter Flower literally flew out of the saddle to greet her parents. Hawk reined Rascal to a stop a few yards back to give them plenty of room. He was already thinking about how quickly he could turn Rascal back toward Fort Ellis, but he knew he would have to do Winter Flower's family the courtesy of at least a short visit. It was a joyous reunion as other people of the village came to welcome her home. It was obvious that they had never expected to see her again, and all their attention was focused on her, except one. As Hawk sat there in the saddle, his gaze drifted across the barren front yard of the cabin, then stopped and came back to focus on one little girl, who was staring at him. They locked gazes for a short while before the little girl started pulling at her sister's skirt until she captured her attention. "What is it, Morning Sky?" Winter Flower asked.

"Who's he?" Morning Sky asked, and pointed at Hawk. "He is not one of the men who chased you and me."

"His name is Hawk," Winter Flower replied. Then loud enough for everyone to hear, she said, "He

is the man who saved me and brought me home."
This immediately shifted the attention to the man on
the buckskin horse.

Already curious about the horse his daughter rode,
as well as the extra horse and saddle, Black Shirt
turned to Hawk. "Forgive us for not welcoming you
properly," he said. "We were just so happy to see our
daughter again. I thought she was dead. Please step
down and we will fix some food for you." Hawk dismounted, but declined the food, insisting that he and
Winter Flower had eaten when they rested the horses.
Black Shirt studied Hawk's face for a long moment. "I
have heard of a man called Hawk who rides with the
soldiers. Are you that man?" Hawk said that he was.
Black Shirt continued to question him. "These two
horses, did they belong to the two men who stole my
daughter?"

"They did," Hawk answered, "but those two men
are dead, so the horses belong to Winter Flower, and
I think she wants to give them to you." He saw Black
Shirt's eyes widen when he heard that, and he immediately took a closer look at them. "One other thing I
should tell you," Hawk said. "I was lucky to kill the two
men before they had a chance to take out their lust on
her. She's got some bruises and cuts, but that happened
when they first grabbed her. She's still a maiden." As
soon as he said it, he hoped that was the case, recalling what she had told him, but she would have been
damn lucky for it to be so, judging by the likes of the two
men who stole her. More than likely, that would have
been the first thought in their twisted minds. However,
her father's eyes were filled with gratitude to hear it.
Hawk could imagine how badly the girl's father and
mother wanted to believe their daughter had escaped

permanent harm. It occurred to Hawk that if Winter Flower swelled up pregnant for nine months, Black Shirt would probably think he was the father.

Unable to think of any reason to linger, now that Winter Flower was safely home, Hawk declared that he was expected to report to Fort Ellis yesterday, so he must regretfully take his leave now. It was not the case, of course, since he had been fired from his position as scout, but he was not inclined to hang around any longer. Overhearing him telling her father that he had to leave, Winter Flower broke free of her mother and sister long enough to come to him and express her thanks once again. She reached in her skirt pocket and drew Hawk's feather out. "I will always keep this close to my heart, and I will always be grateful to you." She beamed up at him. "We are children of the hawk, you and I."

"Reckon so," he said, and stepped up into the saddle, wheeled Rascal, and headed back the way he had come. It was not for him to question the ways of the spiritual world, having lived with the Indians as long as he had. A lot of things had happened in his life that he could not explain, sometimes good, sometimes bad. Maybe his getting fired by Lieutenant Meade happened so he could be in the right place and time to save Winter Flower. Why question it? He reached up and touched the feather in his hatband.

CHAPTER 3

He took two full days to ride to Fort Ellis, pushing Rascal a little because he wanted to make it to Bozeman, about three miles west of the fort. He had been living on bacon and jerky, and he hoped to get there in time to catch supper at Sadie's. When he rode up to the front of the little dining room, the CLOSED sign was not hung out as yet, so he tied Rascal at the rail and hurried inside. "Well, you just did make it in time," Sadie declared. "I reckon you want coffee." He said that he did, and she went to fetch him a cup. When she came back with it, she asked, "Where in the world have you been? You ain't been in here in I don't know when."

"Oh, I don't know, round and about, I reckon—been outta town most of the time, ridin' patrol." He was talking to Sadie, but he was looking at a couple sitting at a table in the back corner of the dining room. "I had to get back here to get a decent meal. Whatcha pushin' tonight?" While she told him what his choices were, he still concentrated on the back of the man seated at the table with a young lady. He was a soldier, and Hawk was almost sure who he was.

"I'll take the stew," he told Sadie. Then certain that he recognized the back of the soldier, he raised his voice and declared, "But I don't know if I wanna eat in here with any army riffraff."

Hearing the comment, Lieutenant Mathew Conner turned to see who the troublemaker was. "Hawk!" Conner exclaimed. "Where have you been?"

"That's what Sadie just asked me," Hawk replied. "Ain't nobody lookin' for me, is there?"

Conner turned his chair halfway around to better see him. "Harvey Meade's patrol came back early yesterday, and you weren't with 'em. I asked him why you didn't come back with the patrol, and he just said it wasn't your choice."

"That's what he said, huh?" Hawk responded. "He came back mighty early, gave up on findin' that party of Indians, I suppose."

"Come back here and join us," Conner said. "Meet my lovely dining companion. This is Miss Dora Carpenter. Dora, this half-wild-looking man is John Hawk."

"Pleased to meet you, Miss Carpenter," Hawk said. "I'll just sit down over here at this table. I don't wanna disturb your supper." She smiled sweetly at him as he pulled a chair back and sat down at a table across from theirs.

"Come out with it," Conner demanded. "You and Harvey got into it again, right? So, you left the patrol, but you didn't come back to the fort."

"Well, we had a little disagreement," Hawk admitted. "Didn't seem like that much to me, but Meade fired me, so I reckon it was more important to him."

Conner shook his head as if exasperated. "Kicked you off the patrol, huh?"

"Kicked me out of the scoutin' service," Hawk said.

"The army would no longer require my services, is what he said."

"Why, that pompous ass," Conner blurted, then quickly apologized to Dora for his outburst. "He can't do that. I'll talk to Brisbin. I need you on my patrols." He glanced at Dora and explained. "Hawk's the best scout on the post."

Hawk glanced at her and said, "There's some that disagree." Back to Conner then, he said, "He wasn't without a scout when I left. Ben Mullins was with us. He's a good man. We were trackin' a little group of old Walkin' Owl's village. They stole one cow and ate it. Meade insisted that they were drivin' a small herd. If that had been the case, all but one of 'em woulda had wings on their feet, either that, or the Indians were flyin' 'em like kites."

This whole fiasco with Meade was upsetting to Mathew Conner. Hawk was a friend of his, in addition to being his most trusted scout. "What are you going to do now?" he asked. "You going to talk to Major Brisbin?"

"Don't know if there's any sense in that. Meade is the commander of all the scouts on the post. And if the major told him who he can fire and who he can't, then he's countermanding Meade's authority. Don't get yourself all worked up about it, I've got a lot of work I need to do on my cabin up on the Boulder— been puttin' it off for months. Winter's gonna be comin' in before you know it, and I need to have my place ready. I need to do a lot of huntin', too, lay in a supply of meat."

"I'm gonna go talk to Brisbin," Conner insisted. "He needs to do something about Harvey Meade."

"Don't get involved in this," Hawk said. He looked

again at the young lady. "I apologize, ma'am. You most likely know that the lieutenant here can get pretty excited about a lot of things. I just hope I haven't spoiled your supper." He got up just as Sadie was bringing his supper out of the kitchen. "Put it on that table near the front," he said, thinking Conner and Miss Carpenter could use a little more privacy. Then he quickly walked to intercept Sadie and his supper.

He attacked the large plate of beef stew she placed before him and stayed with it until he had cleaned the plate. "I reckon that's all I can hold," he said to Sadie when she approached with the coffeepot again. He paid her, got to his feet, and headed for the door. "It's still far and away the best cookin' in all Montana Territory," he said, bringing a smile to her face.

Before he reached the door, Conner called after him. "I'll see you later tonight," he said. "You are going back to the fort, aren't you?"

"Yep, I'm headin' there now. I've got some packs I need to pick up and get my packhorse from the stable." It was Hawk's guess that whether or not he saw Conner later that night would be determined by how much time the young lieutenant might spend with Miss Carpenter. At any rate, he was not going to wait around for Conner. There was a bright full moon illuminating the street outside the dining room, so there was no reason to wait around for morning. He could get in a half day's ride that night and reach his camp early the next day. He liked Conner and appreciated the fact that he would go over Meade's head in an attempt to save his job. But he was afraid his young friend was going to succeed only in getting himself in trouble. "Pleased to meet you, ma'am," he called out as he went out the door.

* * *

As he had anticipated, there was no sign of Mathew Conner, even after Hawk had packed his possibles on the sorrel packhorse. He could sleep in the barracks and eat breakfast with the soldiers, if he chose to, but he could see no point in staying there overnight when he could just as well be on the Boulder River at sunup. The decision was easy to make, so he rode out of the fort, following a familiar trail in the moonlight that would take him to a point where that trail struck the Boulder before following the river up into the rugged mountains of the Absaroka Range.

By the time he struck the river, the moon had dropped below some of the higher mountains of the Absaroka Range. He decided to stop there by the river for the night and take the narrow trail to his cabin in the morning. He figured Rascal would appreciate it, and he thought they could both use a little sleep, so he unloaded his horses and made camp. Up with the sun the next morning, he loaded his horses again and crossed over the river to the east side, since it was easier to cross there instead of farther upstream. The trail up to his cabin was on that side of the river, anyway, and by the time he would reach that point, the river would be a lot more difficult to cross. Once across, he set off up the river trail, which soon became a narrow, rocky path the closer he got to the point where the rushing waterway left the mountains. Spruce, fir, and lodgepole pines came right down to the crystal-clear water, making the trail even more of a challenge. He continued on until reaching a large pie-shaped rock on the eastern bank. He had to give Rascal no more than a gentle nudge and the big buckskin dutifully started up the little creek rushing beneath the rock to empty into the river. A steep climb of almost three hundred yards brought him to his cabin.

As he always did, when he had been away for any length of time, he stopped a short distance from the log structure built underneath the overhang of the thickly wooded ridge above it. From where he sat, he could see no sign of anything having changed since he had left it. There were no horses in the small clearing in front of the cabin, and he could see his padlock still on the door. There was always the chance that someone might have stumbled onto his cabin, but it was not likely. The narrow stream that flowed under the rock by the river was not likely to be taken as a path. Even if they did explore it, they would have to travel three hundred yards to reach his camp. Consequently, he had never found anyone in his cabin upon returning after an extended absence. The cabin's location was an oft-repeated complaint by Lieutenant Mathew Conner on the few occasions when he had attempted to find it, even with explicit instructions from Hawk.

Confident that nothing had been disturbed, he continued on to the clearing and stepped down from the saddle. The only change he could see was the grass in the clearing, which was almost a foot high. He stood there for a few minutes, inspecting the outside of his cabin, thinking about any work that needed to be done to ready it for the coming winter. The cabin, itself, was sound. His main concern was the stone fireplace and chimney. There was some work to be done there to replace some of the chinking between the stones. At last, he had some time to work on it, thanks to Harvey Meade. He was going to have to do some hunting, too—lay in enough meat to last him a winter.

He had coffee and flour in the packs he picked up, and salt and sugar, too. "I think we're all right for a while," he announced to Rascal, as he loosened the cinch and pulled his saddle off. "Okay, you're home now, so start eatin' some of this grass." That reminded him that he would need to go to Big Timber and buy some grain for his horses. Rascal promptly walked back to the rough shed that served as his stable. After relieving the sorrel of his packs, he looked in his saddlebags to find the key to the padlock. "Now we'll see what kinda critters are livin' inside." When he brought his saddle and packs in, he discovered that a raccoon had taken up residence inside. *I knew I should have fixed that hole by the back door,* he thought. It was on his list of things to do. Backed into a corner near the fireplace, the critter bared its teeth and hissed. "That ain't very polite," Hawk said, "when I'm fixin' to invite you to breakfast." He pulled his .44 handgun and shot the raccoon. *That'll be a change in my diet,* he thought. *Didn't think I'd have breakfast waiting for me when I got here.*

The peace and quiet of his little retreat from the scouting business did not last long. Late in the afternoon of his third day at his cabin, he was in the process of butchering a deer when he heard the sound of gunfire. It was coming from somewhere down the mountain, and anytime he heard shooting on his mountain it was cause for concern. Of further concern, the shots sounded to be from a pistol, and they came in bursts of two or three shots at a time. It was definitely not a hunter, so he decided it was in his best interest to investigate. Whatever the shooting, it was too close to his camp. He washed his hands in the stream to clean the deer blood off them, picked up his rifle, and started down the stream on foot. The shooting stopped for a short while but started again when he was a little farther down. He realized then that whoever it was, they had evidently found his stream. More cautious now, he moved carefully, his rifle ready to fire. He stopped when he detected movement through the branches of the trees, then moved forward again, his rifle cocked, until he discovered the cause of the trouble.

"Conner, what the hell are you doin' here?"

Just before aiming his pistol up in the air to fire off a couple more shots, Lieutenant Conner jumped, startled. "Hawk?" he asked.

"Who else would you expect it to be?" Hawk answered. "What are you doin' up here doin' all that shootin'? What are you shootin' at?"

"Hawk," Conner repeated, this time with a tone of satisfaction. "I knew you'd find me. I know this is the way you told me to come to your place—pie-shaped rock on the river, follow the stream up the mountain. I did that, but I climbed up this stream so far that I was beginning to wonder if I was on the right stream."

"You ain't but about halfway there. What are you lookin' for me for?"

Without answering his question, Conner complained, "The other night in town, you didn't wait for me to come back to the fort."

"And you came all the way up here to complain because I wasn't there?" Hawk asked.

"No, I came here on official business. I need you for a search patrol," Conner answered. "I woulda told you that night at Sadie's, but I didn't think it polite to talk about it in front of Miss Carpenter. She's a very delicate young lady, and it might have upset her to hear talk about Indians, and outlaws, and such."

"Ain't you heard? I don't work for the army anymore," Hawk responded. "Does Lieutenant Meade know you've come all the way up here to see me?"

Conner grinned. "He knows it, but he doesn't like it. I convinced Major Brisbin that you're the man I've got to have on this patrol."

"And what makes you think that? What about Ben Mullins or Raymond Red Coyote? They're both good scouts." He paused and shrugged. "Don't get me wrong, I appreciate your efforts to try to get me back on the payroll, but I've still got a lot of work to do on my cabin."

"Ah, that cabin ain't gonna go anywhere," Conner replied, "and you know you couldn't stand sitting around up here in these damn woods very long. You'd be back in Bozeman, begging Harvey to let you go back to work. I'm giving you a chance to come back under your terms, and you won't have to beg Harvey Meade."

Hawk had to admit that Conner might have a point there, and it was always nice to know he had a job. "What's so special about this patrol?"

"Why don't you show some manners and invite me up to your cabin, instead of standing here in the middle of this little stream? Have you got any coffee and something to eat? It's already suppertime and I'll tell you all about it while we eat. I know I ain't going back tonight. It's already getting dark under these trees."

Hawk couldn't help laughing at his good friend. Sometimes he acted like a young kid, but he never came up short when it was time to fight, and Hawk had seen that in more than one engagement. "All right," he said. "I reckon I can spare a little bit of venison and coffee. Come on." He turned and started back up the mountain.

Conner followed him, leading his horse. "Venison?" he asked. "Are you talking about old deer jerky you've smoked about six months ago? Or are you talking about fresh-killed deer meat?"

"For someone who just invited himself to share my food, you sure are mighty picky. I killed a deer not two hours ago. I was workin' on it when I heard you shootin' up the trees."

"I had to get your attention," Conner said in defense of his actions. "Hot damn, I haven't had any fresh venison since the last patrol we were on together."

As he had said, Conner didn't start to tell Hawk of the mission until they were both sitting by the fire, eating. Finally, he became serious. "Hawk, there's a whole mule train gone missing for about five days now." He went on to explain that a party of immigrants had last been seen when they left Fort Benton. "They're a church group," he said, "maybe Mormons, I don't know for sure, about thirty folks, counting women and children. They never showed up at Great Falls, not hide nor hair of them. And they were carrying a large amount of money to build a new church in Helena."

"That's a pretty good reason they might be missin'," Hawk said. "Why did you need me to guide the patrol? They were most likely followin' the Mullan Road, so I don't reckon I'd do any different than Ben or Raymond would have. You probably don't even need a scout."

"Like I told Major Brisbin, you were up in that part

of the territory just recently, and you probably know it better than they do."

"Well, that's true, I was up that way not long ago, but it wasn't on an army patrol. I was doing some personal business."

"That's right," Conner insisted. "You told me about it. You were gone from the fort for a long time and you said you scouted the Mullan Road, from Great Falls all the way to the Bitterroot Valley. You found the three men you were looking for, so you know that country a lot better than the other scouts. Hell, you lived up in that part of the territory for a couple of years with the Blackfoot Indians. Ain't that right?"

Hawk shrugged modestly. "Maybe, but that ain't no guarantee I'll find those folks. A mule train of that size had to leave some tracks. Are you tellin' me nobody saw where they left the road?"

"Guess not," Conner replied. "They said a detachment of soldiers was sent down to Great Falls from Fort Benton. They looked around for a day or two, said they could find no trace of 'em, and went on back to Fort Benton."

"A party that big had to leave some tracks," Hawk insisted.

"Right," Conner was quick to agree. "And that's why I need you to ride scout on this patrol. So, what about it, will you go?"

"I reckon." His curiosity was finally aroused.

"Good man," Conner said. "I told Major Brisbin you'd do the job. I knew you wouldn't let me down."

"All I'm agreein' to do is go up there to see if I can find out what happened to 'em. Most likely all we'll find is a bunch of dead bodies. You said they left Fort Benton five days ago. That ain't much more'n thirty miles from Great Falls, so that gives 'em four days to wander off to who knows where right there. It's three and a half days' ride from Fort Ellis to Great Falls for us, so that makes it well over a week, and that's not countin' the time it'll take for us to get back to Fort Ellis and get a patrol on the road."

"Well, I suppose that's right," Conner allowed. "But the patrol is already scheduled to move out tomorrow at noon, so we'll save a little time there." He grinned sheepishly. "I knew you wouldn't let me down."

Hawk shook his head as if exasperated. "You know there ain't a chance in hell we'll find any of those folks alive, and we'll sure as hell never recover the money. How in the world did you talk Brisbin into lettin' you take a patrol up there?"

"The fellow who was leading the mule train was Major Brisbin's nephew, Donald."

"Oh," Hawk replied, and raised an eyebrow. "So, this big mission to save the mule train wasn't your idea at all." When Conner merely responded with another sheepish grin and a shrug of his shoulders, Hawk said, "Well, I reckon we can try to find out what happened to the major's nephew. Brisbin's always been a fair man with me." He paused to think about it. "How did you get the job of leadin' a patrol up there?" As important as it was to the major, he would have thought his ranking lieutenant, Harvey Meade, would had drawn the assignment.

"Because Brisbin knew I could persuade you to go as scout," Conner said, in answer to Hawk's question.

The rest of that evening was spent on preparing Hawk's cabin to be left again. He finished up the butchering of the deer and kept a small portion to cook in the morning. The rest was staked out to be

smoke-cured that night. The next morning, Hawk
carried some smoked meat and other supplies up the
mountain to his cache. Then he closed his cabin up
and padlocked it, and as always, hoped no one would
find it before he got back.

They rode into Fort Ellis shortly before noon and
went straight to the headquarters building. When his
clerk alerted him that Lieutenant Conner was heading his way, with Hawk riding beside him, the major
got up from his desk and came out to meet them at
the door. "Hawk," Brisbin greeted him. "I appreciate
you coming to help us on this thing. I expect Lieutenant Conner filled you in on all the details. I agree
with Lieutenant Conner that no one would be better
qualified to scout on this mission than you. My sister's
only son organized a party of religious people to go to
Helena to build a church. Donald was always a little
shy when it came to being a man, and I know my sister
wishes he hadn't involved himself in this church
business. I tried to talk him into joining the army,
but he said he could not bring himself to take up
arms against his fellow man." He slowly shook his
head as soon as he said it, then realizing he was
drifting off point, he said, "I apologize for that mis-
understanding about you being fired. Lieutenant
Meade and I have talked about that."

"There wasn't any misunderstandin' on my part,"
Hawk said, finally able to get a word in. "The lieutenant said I was no longer employed in any capacity
at Fort Ellis. He made it pretty clear." He looked
around at the open doors to the two inner offices, but
he didn't see Meade anywhere. From his experience

trying to work with the man, he wasn't surprised. He
speculated that he might be off somewhere choking
on his pride. "But I'd always be ready to help you in
any way I can." He felt he had to discourage the major
from expecting any results other than sorrowful ones,
however, since the group had been missing so long
already. Just as he had advised Conner, he told Brisbin
that it seemed totally unlikely that anyone escaped.
But, since no one had showed up to tell what had
happened, it was hard not to assume them all dead.

"I understand what you're saying," Brisbin said,
"and I have to admit that I share your expectations.
But, man, this is my sister's only son! Not that I
wouldn't send a patrol up there to search if I didn't
have a personal interest," he quickly added. "So you
just tell Lieutenant Conner what you need and we'll
get it for you. I've authorized a patrol of fifteen men,
with rations for ten days. They're ready to leave when
you are."

"I'll need some grain for my horse," Hawk answered,
"maybe some extra coffee from your food stores,
some hardtack, some .44 cartridges. I've got meat.
That's about all I need, and I'll be ready to start as
soon as I pack it on the horse."

"Excellent!" the major said. "Conner, make sure he
gets what he wants."

"When did that mule train leave Fort Benton?"
Hawk asked, even though Conner had already told
him. The major said they had left there more than six
days ago and had expected to reach Great Falls the
afternoon of that day, but never showed up. It was
the same as Conner had told him, but he thought
it wouldn't hurt to double-check. That meant they
would have departed Fort Benton about ten days

before Conner's patrol could even reach Fort Benton, maybe more, if there were any delays along the way. It would be a miracle if there were any tracks to follow after that amount of time. The patrol was beginning to sound more and more like a lost cause. They weren't likely to find any survivors, but maybe they could find out what had happened to the mule train.

Major Brisbin walked Hawk and Conner to the door. "Thank you again, Hawk, and good hunting."

So far, things were moving right along, as far as Hawk was concerned. When Conner scheduled the patrol, he didn't allow much time to find Hawk and start back the next day. Even so, they were less than an hour behind the scheduled departure time Conner had informed him of the night before. With the horses of the patrol standing saddled and ready, Hawk was happy there had been no chance meeting with Lieutenant Meade. That feeling was only temporary, however, for as the patrol was about to mount, the lieutenant came out of the powder magazine and walked directly toward the head of the column where Hawk and Conner stood. As Hawk expected, it was an ego visit on the part of Meade to make sure Hawk, as well as Conner, understood his higher ranking. "Good luck on your patrol," Meade said, addressing Conner. "There's been no hostile activity reported by any of the patrols in that area. I think you'll find a pretty simple reason for the disappearance of that mule train in the short distance between Fort Benton and Great Falls. They most likely changed their minds, turned around, and headed back to their homes."

"Sounds like you've got the whole thing figured

out, Harvey," Conner said. "Might not be any use for us to even go up there, although I heard they had all sold their homes."

Meade did not miss the sarcasm in Conner's reply. He responded with a knowing smile. "At least it'll give you something to do for a few days. Hawk should be able to find Great Falls for you." The sarcasm was too obvious to miss, and he paused in case there was a response from the solemn scout. "I was happy to allow his reinstatement as a favor to the major, for this one mission, at least." He turned to address Hawk at last. "See that you take advantage of this second chance. I don't make it a rule to grant very many." He nodded to Conner, turned, and headed for the post headquarters.

Conner said nothing more, but turned to look at Hawk, who showed no evidence of animosity toward the pompous first lieutenant. It relieved Conner's mind, for he had been a little concerned that if Meade made it a point to come out and chastise Hawk, the rugged scout might decide to tell him to go to hell. And if he did, that would give Meade reason to fire him again. But that didn't happen. Hawk didn't react, so there was nothing for Meade to base any punishment on. "Thanks, Hawk," Conner said, then told Corporal Johnson to order the men to mount up.

"Thanks for what?" Hawk asked.

"You know what," Conner said.

Hawk laughed and stepped up into the saddle. "Rascal wanted to answer him. I told him to hold his comments until we got off the parade ground, but he couldn't resist leaving one little pile of comments."

With the men in the saddle, Conner gave the order to march and they left the post, heading to the north, planning to travel with the Big Belt Mountains to their west and make their first night's camp somewhere along Cottonwood Creek. As the horses settled into the pace, Corporal Johnson pulled up alongside Hawk and commented, "Maybe we'll get a chance to shoot a deer or two, headin' up this way. Right, Hawk?"

Hawk smiled at him. "Might at that," he answered. Most of the men on the post knew that it was the best duty possible when riding on a patrol commanded by Lieutenant Mathew Conner and scouted by Hawk. Even though grousing with Conner the night before about the work he needed to do to put his cabin in order, Hawk had to admit that it felt good to be in the saddle again, heading out to see what tomorrow held in store.

CHAPTER 4

Following the Smith River, north, between the Big Belt Mountains to the west and the Little Belts to the east, it was an uneventful scouting mission during the three and a half days it took to get to Great Falls. Near the north end of the Little Belts at Hound Creek, the patrol frightened a herd of deer as they approached the bank of the creek. Corporal Johnson was quick to suggest it was an opportunity to supplement their rations. But Conner, knowing their time was short enough to complete their mission as it was, refused permission. Hawk had to laugh at Johnson's disappointment because there did seem to be deer aplenty.

At Hawk's suggestion, they went into camp close to Luther Trotter's trading post, which was located on the Missouri River at its confluence with the Sun River. Hawk figured if anyone knew anything about the mule train, it would most likely be Luther. So, while the patrol began the process of going into camp, Hawk continued a little farther down the river to the trading post. As often happened, Luther was sitting on the porch in his rocking chair, smoking his pipe.

"I declare, it's gettin' to where you're comin' by right regular," Luther greeted him when Hawk pulled Rascal up at the rail. "If I recollect right, that's twice in the last six months."

"Maybe so," Hawk replied. "Have you been outta that chair since I saw you last?"

"A time or two, maybe," Luther said with a chuckle. "Come on inside and I'll pour you a drink, and you can tell me what brings you up our way this time." He got up from his chair, banged his pipe on his boot heel to knock the ashes out, and led Hawk into the store. "This got anythin' to do with those folks gone missin' on their mules?"

"Matter of fact," Hawk answered. "I left a cavalry patrol about half a mile back up the river, sent up here from Fort Ellis to see if we could find out what happened to those folks. They're goin' into camp now, gettin' ready to eat supper, so I thought I'd give you some warnin' that you're liable to see some of 'em here tonight."

"'Preciate the business," Luther said as he poured Hawk a shot of whiskey. Fully aware of the real courtesy the big scout was extending, he added, "It's a good time for the army to call. There ain't no riffraff hangin' around right now. Always happy to do business with the U.S. Army."

Hawk downed the shot of whiskey and paused a moment to feel the burn. Then he waved Luther off when he started to pour another. "That'll do," Hawk said. "I've gotta get back to camp for supper. Like I said, you might see some thirsty souls in here tonight, but the lieutenant and I'll be back in the mornin', for sure."

"There ain't a helluva lot I can tell you about those

Mormons," Luther claimed. "I don't know any more than everybody else around Great Falls knows. A party of religious folks left Fort Benton, headed this way, but they never showed up. End of story." He threw his hands up and shrugged. "Maybe they can tell you somethin' more than that up at Fort Benton. Looks to me like, whatever happened to 'em, your soldiers are too late to save 'em."

"Everybody's pretty much figured the same thing," Hawk said. "We're just hopin' we can find out just what did happen. I'll see you in the mornin'."

When he returned to the campsite, Hawk pulled his saddle off Rascal and turned the buckskin loose to join the cavalry horses at the edge of the river. There were three healthy fires going, all with coffeepots and a few frying pans resting in the edges. He got his coffeepot and some deer jerky from his packs and joined Conner at one of the fires. "What did you find out?" Conner asked when Hawk walked up.

"I know every bit as much as I did before we got here," Hawk answered. "Luther hasn't got any idea what happened to those people, because they never got this far." When Johnson got up to tend to some bacon he was frying, Hawk asked, "Are you goin' to tell the men about Trotter's place right down the river?"

Conner grinned. "No, I'll let 'em find out in the morning when we ride by there. I'll let 'em get one good night and a little food in their bellies before they start sneaking off to get drunk."

"Hell, you might as well let 'em go and get all their money spent tonight," Hawk said. "Then you won't have to worry about 'em the rest of the time we're up here."

"Mr. Hawk," Conner announced grandly, "your wisdom is always appreciated, but I think I'll settle for one more sober night before I turn 'em loose."

As Conner had hoped, the patrol's first night in camp by the Missouri was a quiet and peaceful one. At Conner's request, Hawk didn't inform any of the men of the existence of a saloon a short distance down the river. At sunup the next morning, the fires were revived and breakfast was under way. Although Hawk had already established the fact that Luther Trotter was not in possession of any information helpful to their mission, Conner planned to stop there briefly before heading to Fort Benton. He figured the distance from Great Falls to Fort Benton was about forty miles, one day's march up the Mullan Road. "Might as well start where they were last seen and go on up to Fort Benton," he said to Hawk.

"I don't see as how there's any other place to start," Hawk replied. "Maybe somebody up there can tell us a little bit more about these folks we're tryin' to find. Right now, we're not even sure of the exact number of folks in that train. But if they were all ridin' mules and, I expect, leadin' pack mules behind 'em, they can't have just disappeared. 'Course, you said they were a religious group of folks, so I reckon we have to allow for the possibility that they were suddenly called home to heaven. And that's gonna make trackin' 'em that much harder."

"Maybe I shoulda brought one of the other scouts and left you back on the Boulder to work on your cabin," Conner responded in like sarcasm. "We might as well get started." They walked over to where the men were preparing to saddle up and Conner informed them of the day's schedule. "We'll make a day's ride up to Fort Benton. There's a trading post about half a mile downstream from here, and we'll stop there briefly while I talk to the owner. If you want to, and if you have any money, you can take that opportunity to buy any food or whatever to supplement your rations." It took a moment of silence before his soldiers thought to add two and two to realize they could have used that information the night before. Some low mumbling could soon be heard near the back of the column. Conner looked at Hawk and grinned.

"Ain't you afraid you're gonna ruin your reputation as the most popular patrol leader at Fort Ellis?" Hawk asked.

Conner suddenly looked serious. "I'm afraid I'm *not* gonna lose it," he said, and Hawk realized that he meant it. He was glad to see his friend was aware of the importance of maintaining military discipline. It was something that Mathew Conner had little respect for. At the present time, when there was no real fighting going on, it was especially important to maintain a strong command. Hawk had often worried that Conner might not realize that he ran a very loose command, and one day it might cost him. As if to reassure his friend, Conner called out a command to Johnson, loud enough for everyone to hear it. "Corporal Johnson! Order the men 'To Horse.' I don't intend to spend the entire day dragging ass around here."

As he promised, Conner gave the men twenty minutes to go into the store while he and Hawk talked to Trotter. When they walked in, Trotter met them with

a wide smile for Hawk. "You shoulda hung around
and took that second drink last night."

"That so?" Hawk responded. "Why is that?"

"Not thirty minutes after you left, Barney Mayfield
rode in, drivin' a freight wagon, headin' for Helena,
and you and the lieutenant there would be tickled to
hear what he was talkin' about."

"You reckon you could get around to tellin' us what
he told you?" Hawk asked.

"He said some of them folks on that missin' mule
train showed up day before yesterday back at Fort
Benton." When Trotter saw that he had both Hawk's
and Conner's complete interest, he went on to ex-
pound on the news. "He said they said they was robbed,
and most of 'em got killed." Other than that broad
statement, Luther had little additional information
with which to answer Hawk's and Conner's questions.
More anxious than before to get started, Conner ordered the men to get mounted and they were soon
under way again.

Originally built as a trading post, primarily for the
Blackfoot Indians, the American Fur Company sold
Fort Benton to the military after the demise of the fur-
trading industry. The army moved into the fort in
1870, but in the years since, the number of troops
were reduced to the present-day skeleton garrison of
custodians, commanded by Lieutenant Robert Sessions. The fifteen-man patrol from Fort Ellis arrived
in Fort Benton at suppertime. It had been several
years since Hawk had actually been inside the gates

of the fort. Even so, he found it hard to believe the decline of what had been the most important fort on the upper Missouri for so many years.

Checking his railroad pocket watch, Conner commented that it was five o'clock on the nose, but there was no sign of a bugler sounding out mess call. Surprisingly, the appearance of a fifteen-man patrol attracted very little interest from the soldiers casually walking toward what Hawk guessed was the mess hall. Conner pointed out the headquarters building and led his patrol directly toward it. The troopers were still dismounting when an officer walked outside to meet them. "Robert Sessions," the lieutenant greeted Conner, and extended his hand. "What brings you to Fort Benton?"

"Mathew Conner," he returned. "We're out of Fort Ellis, trying to find out what we can about your missing mule train."

Sessions didn't hide his surprise. "You came up here from Bozeman to investigate the trouble with those Mormons? You must not have any more to do than we do up here."

"Well, we haven't run outta work to do at Ellis, but your problem with the mule train was of interest to our post commander." He went on to explain Major Brisbin's personal interest in the welfare of his nephew, prompting the major to extend a helping hand to the Fort Benton garrison.

"We sent a patrol all the way down to Great Falls to look for those people and we couldn't find a clue as to what happened to them. But a few days ago, six survivors showed up here and said they were ambushed, the rest of the party were killed, and the outlaws got away with all their money for the church."

"Six survived?" Conner asked. "How many were killed?"

"Twenty-eight, counting women and children," Sessions answered. "They said the only reason they got away was because they got pushed in the river when they started shooting. There was no warning, they just suddenly started executing everybody."

"Who was it?" Hawk asked. "Indians, white men, who?"

"They said it was white men, there weren't no Indians." He paused while that sank in. "Listen, those six survivors are staying in town at the First Baptist Church. Why don't you go talk to them? The fellow you want to talk to is Donald Lewis. He's the man who organized the whole trip." Hawk and Conner exchanged glances in reaction to the mention of the name.

It didn't take long to determine there was not much more information to come from Lieutenant Sessions. And it was obvious that he had no interest in following the matter further, so they thanked him for his help and bade him a good evening. Outside the gate, Conner decided to let the patrol go into camp, so they could cook their supper while he and Hawk went in search of Donald Lewis. Conner had hoped to have the men eat supper in the Fort Benton mess hall, but Sessions said there would not be food enough for seventeen extra men. "If I'd known you were coming, I could have made provisions." Conner was not pleased with the lieutenant's lack of hospitality but thanked him for his information. In the saddle again, they rode upstream from the town until a suitable place to camp was found. Then, leaving Corporal Johnson to take charge of the camp, Hawk and Conner rode back to town.

The Baptist church was easy enough to spot, even from the edge of town. It was sitting on a grassy bluff close by the river, with a well-traveled wagon track leading up to it from the main street. When they got up to the churchyard, they could see a large fire burning behind the church and a small group of people gathered around it. "Looks like they're fixing supper," Conner commented. They stepped down and tied their horses at the hitching rail in front, then walked around back.

"Evenin', gentlemen," the Reverend Henry Bridger greeted them as he walked to meet them. "Can I be of service to you?"

"Evenin'," Conner returned. "I understand the survivors of that tragedy with the Mormon mule train are staying here. Are you Donald Lewis?"

"No, sir, I'm Henry Bridger. I'm the pastor of this church." He turned to point toward the fire. "Those people around the fire are the people you're lookin' for. The tall, thin fellow is Donald Lewis. I oughta point out one thing. Ever since this terrible thing happened to these poor folks, everybody's been callin' them Mormons. They ain't Mormons, they're Quakers, or Friends, as they refer to themselves." He smiled broadly. "Other'n that, they're just like you and me. I hope you're bringin' good news 'bout the evil scoundrels who took their money."

"Well, thank you very much for telling us," Conner said. "I don't wanna start off on the wrong foot, but I'm afraid I don't have any good news." He and Hawk followed the preacher over to the fire, where four men, one woman, and a young boy were gathered. There was a large iron pot on the fire, and the woman was tending it.

"Donald," Bridger called out. "This officer here was lookin' for you."

The tall willowy young man looked up from the fire and immediately came to meet them. "Have you come with any news about those men who murdered our people?" Donald asked at once.

"No, sir, I have not," Conner answered. "I'm commanding a patrol out of Fort Ellis to try to find out what happened to you folks. But we just arrived here this evening. I'm hoping we can be of some help, but I need to have you tell me everything you can remember about your attack. Hopefully, you can take us to the place where they did the executions." Donald was plainly confused that a single patrol had ridden all the way up there from a fort on the Yellowstone, when the soldiers there at Fort Benton decided there was nothing they could do to help. Conner told him that his uncle, Major Brisbin, the post commander, had received word of the tragedy that had befallen him. This, too, came as quite a surprise to young Lewis and he admitted that he knew that his uncle was now a major, but he had no idea where he was stationed.

While Conner and Lewis were talking, Hawk studied the other folks at the fire. When there was a pause in the conversation, Hawk commented, "The preacher said the survivors were around the fire. I make it seven, countin' you."

Lewis glanced back at the fire. "You musta counted the little fellow sitting on that side by himself. That's Frog. He came back from the river with us, but he wasn't in our original party." Hawk took a closer look at the little, elflike man, dressed in animal skins, sitting close by the fire. His knees pulled up under his chin, he seemed fascinated by the flames that licked the iron stewpot as he rocked gently back and forth in time with some rhythm obviously he alone could hear. "Don't mind him," Lewis said. "I don't know where he came from. He's tetched in the head, but he's harmless." He paused a moment before deciding to say, "As a matter of fact, I kinda believe Frog was placed in our path by God." When that statement caused Conner to raise an eyebrow, Lewis continued, "I don't know how he wound up with us after we floated down that river, but when we came out, he was with us. I was pretty much confused after half drownin' in that cold water. I don't think any of us knew for sure which way to go and we started in the wrong direction. But he came up and kept tuggin' on my shirtsleeve and pointin' in the opposite direction, till I gave in and went the way he pointed. We didn't walk a quarter of a mile before we came to a farmhouse and the people who took us in and cared for us till we were all well enough to go back to Fort Benton."

Hawk and Conner both took another look at the little man huddled by the fire. Conner saw fit to say, "The Lord moves in mysterious ways."

Hawk asked, "Why do you call him Frog?"

Lewis shook his head as if apologizing. He nodded toward the young boy. "Lemuel started callin' him that because he hops around like a frog. Like I said, he's tetched. We don't know his real name."

"How far from here is that place where you went into the river, where they shot all the rest of your party?" Hawk asked. Lewis said he wasn't sure, but that he would guess about halfway to Great Falls. "How did it happen that so many of you were ambushed? How many were in the gang that attacked you?"

"You have to understand," Lewis stressed, "we were deceived by one we had welcomed into our family of Friends. David Booth had been coming to our Sunday meetings since the beginning of summer. He wanted to know more about our religious beliefs and soon became a member of our society. When we talked about our plans to take our church to some other part of the country, David was the one who urged us to build it in the new lands west of Great Falls and told us that he had seen these unclaimed lands, ripe for farming. He even talked of dreams he had when he was sure that Jesus was telling him to find us and lead us to our new home."

The rest of the story was not hard to assume. "So this fellow, Booth, acted as your guide and led you to a place where a gang of outlaws were waitin' for you," Hawk summed it up. "And that's when you found out he was one of them." The outright robbery was easy enough to understand, but the massacre didn't make sense to Hawk. "Why did they start shootin'? Did some of your party put up a fight?"

"No," Lewis replied. "Brother Adams was leading the mule with our money, and when he saw what was about to happen, he tried to keep them from stealing the money we had saved up to buy our land and build our church. He turned and tried to escape. That's when the shooting started. They shot him, then everyone started shooting, especially this one fellow with them. Men, women, the children, even the mules were massacred. We survivors escaped only because our brothers in front of us pushed us back until we fell into the river." He shook his head slowly as the pain of that memory returned.

"How many were the bandits?" Conner asked.

"I don't know for certain," Donald apologized. "Five, I think. Right now, I find it hard to remember for sure."

Conner looked at Hawk and shook his head. It was a tragic picture of highway robbery gone bad. At worst, the religious group should have lost their money but not their lives. Instead, it turned into a senseless massacre of innocent folks. "I don't know how much we can do after this amount of time," Conner said to Lewis. "But if I can rent a horse and wagon, can I ask you and maybe the other four men to take us back up the river to the place where all this occurred?"

"If it will help you to catch those men and maybe recover the church's money, of course we will," Donald replied.

The Reverend Henry Bridger, who had been listening to the interrogation, volunteered then. "You can take my wagon and horses, Lieutenant. You don't have to rent one."

"Let's take him along, too," Hawk said, and pointed to the little man still huddling up to the fire.

"What for?" Conner asked.

"'Cause there's a lot of things flyin' around in his brain that the rest of us don't even know exist," Hawk answered. "Besides, it doesn't look like he's too busy to go for a little ride."

"Whatever makes you happy, Hawk." Conner shrugged. "Thank you for the use of your wagon, Reverend Bridger. We'll take good care of your horses," he said to the preacher, then turned back to Lewis. "We'll start back right after breakfast. All right?" When

Donald agreed, Conner said, "We'll let you get back to your supper now and we'll see you in the morning."

Hawk had one more question for Lewis. "Did you tell Lieutenant Sessions everything you just told us?"

"Yes, we told the lieutenant, and he said he was real happy that the six of us made it back. But he said there was no use thinking about catching the murderers now. It had been too long, he said. They would be out of the territory already. Out of his field of jurisdiction, I think he put it."

Hawk and Conner exchanged glances of contempt. "Well, it's not out of our jurisdiction," Conner promptly declared. "We'll do our best to try to find those men."

As if only then aware of their presence when Hawk and Conner started to leave, the elflike little man got up from the fire and walked over to stand in front of them. Straining to look up from the posture his curved spine allowed, he glanced at Conner, then fixed his gaze upon Hawk. He continued to stare up at the tall, broad-shouldered scout in the buckskin shirt. Finally, he uttered one word: "Hawk."

"That's right," Hawk answered, and the little man Lemuel had nicknamed Frog hopped back over by the fire, contented.

"How the hell did he know your name?" Conner asked as soon as they were out of earshot of the others.

"He doesn't," Hawk said. "He just said that's a hawk feather in my hatband. He notices things. That's why I want him to come with us."

"How do you know he notices things?" Conner asked, not ready to accept Hawk's reasoning.

"I don't," Hawk answered. "Sometimes you just have to hope, I reckon."

CHAPTER 5

When Conner led his patrol back to the church the next morning, he found Donald Lewis and the three other men ready to leave. The preacher's horses were hitched up, and the wagon was loaded with a pick and shovel as well as some food for a day or two. He hadn't thought to offer it before, so Conner volunteered the services of his men to dig graves for the bodies of the slain Quakers. "There were some shovels and other tools packed on some of the mules," Lewis said, "but we thought we'd bring the Reverend Bridger's as well."

It was a trip of about ten miles down a wagon road that led them to the farm of Adam Wylie, the farmer who took the survivors to Fort Benton after they came out of the river. As gracious as before, Wylie and his wife welcomed them back and offered to feed everyone, including the patrol of sixteen soldiers plus a scout. The offer was declined, of course, much to Mrs. Wylie's relief, when Conner explained that they were working to save as much daylight as possible for their investigation. Thinking Mr. Wylie probably had a better idea how far the Quakers had walked from the river, Hawk asked him the distance and was told about three quarters of a mile. "We're closer to the river than that," Wylie said, "but they came outta the water a little farther up the river. My boy can take you to the spot."

"That won't be necessary," Conner said, after an inquisitive look in Hawk's direction. "We'll be moving right along up the river after we rest these horses a little while. We're just trying to get an idea of how far they drifted in the river before they got here."

The only reason to pause there was to rest the team of horses pulling the wagon, so Hawk saw no reason to wait there, too, so he made a suggestion. "Rascal doesn't need any rest yet, so why don't I go on ahead of you. I can ride down along the riverbank and I might see where the massacre happened." His point was well taken, since the terrain along the river was too rugged for the wagon. It would have to stay on the road. "If Donald was floatin' in the water as long as he thought, I might be able to find the place it happened, then I'll come out to the road to wait for you to catch up." That sounded like a good plan to Conner, so Hawk stepped back up into the saddle and wheeled Rascal back toward the road. "Don't forget to bring Frog," he said in parting.

Back on the road, Hawk headed west, continuing on the rough wagon road for a distance he figured to be a reasonable gamble. When he came to a bend in the river that brought it within about a couple dozen yards of the road, he guided Rascal off the road and rode down along the water's edge. It was a rough trail to ride, especially in some spots where rocks or trees extended out over the water, causing him to have to detour around them. Each time, he would get back to the water's edge as soon as he could. After an hour or so, he determined that he had been wasting his time and tiring Rascal out needlessly. Ahead of him, the river cut through a high hill, leaving steep bluffs on each side. At the top of the bluff, he could see a large flock of buzzards circling over it. "Hell," he said to Rascal, "I coulda seen that from the road." He guided the buckskin up from the water and climbed the hill. When he reached the top of the hill, he suddenly pulled the gelding to a stop. "Another day or two, and I could smell it from the road," he muttered when he discovered the grisly scene before him. The odor from the putrefying bodies caused him to pull his bandanna up to cover his mouth and nose.

He walked Rascal slowly through a grass-covered hilltop, surrounded by a thick belt of fir trees and strewn with the bodies of the late Quaker mule train. The magnitude of the vicious slaughter was beyond his belief in the depth of evil man was capable of. Adding to the revulsion of the scene was the raucous squawking of the competing vultures as they fought over the rotting feast. Riding close to the edge of the steep bluff, he could see where Donald and the others had been forced over the edge to drop fifty feet or more to the river below. He turned to look back toward the road but could see no sign of it through the thick trees. He continued to slow-walk Rascal around the circle, looking for any sign that might tell him which way the killers left the hilltop. The only obvious path was the one where the mule train had entered the circle. He followed that down the hill to the road, where he prepared to wait for Conner and the wagon to show up. There were tracks that told of the meeting between the killers and the Quaker party where they were stopped on the road, then climbed the hill on the path he had just come down. He could not understand how the patrol sent out from Fort Benton had not found the tracks he was looking at. He could only assume they had not continued their search for very long, perhaps not riding as far down the road to Great Falls as Lieutenant Sessions had said.

By his estimation, it was sometime after noon when he caught sight of the wagon rounding the bend in the road as it wound around the hill. "You find 'em?" Conner asked after he rode around the wagon and loped up ahead. Hawk held his thumb up and motioned toward the sky. Conner looked up to see the buzzards circling. "Oh," he said, and dismounted. "Pretty bad, huh?"

"It might be pretty hard for those men in the wagon to take," Hawk answered. "Now that we're here, I'm wonderin' if it was a good idea to haul those poor souls back here to see this. It ain't just the sight of it, it's also the smell of it. I can't see as how they're gonna be of any help in tellin' us which way they went, anyway. Hell, they were pushed off a damn cliff up there. They don't have any notion what the bastards did after that."

"Well, they've been talking about feeling obligated to give their friends a decent burial," Conner said, and looked over his shoulder at the wagon pulling up to them. "I guess we can see how they feel about it now."

"This is the place!" Lewis exclaimed, and hopped down as the wagon rolled to a stop. "This is it, ain't it, Corey?" The man named Corey said that it was. Lewis turned to Conner and started to explain. "They were waiting here in the middle of the road, I remember now. There were four of 'em, just sitting on their horses, waiting for us. David Booth said there was no need to fear them, he knew who they were. He rode on up ahead to talk to them. When he came back he said they told him there was a big war party of Blackfoot Indians coming this way, and we needed to ride up through the trees there to hide on top of the hill." He paused only briefly to look at the other three men for verification, then he continued, "When we got up on the hill, they suddenly pulled their guns and one of them handed a gun belt to David. He put it on and pulled the pistol out of the holster and said if nobody did anything foolish, nobody would get hurt. Brother Adams was leading the mule carrying all our money, and he tried to run with it, and that's when they all went crazy. They shot poor Brother Adams down, and then they all started shooting. I can't remember much of what happened after that. There was just so much noise, the shooting and the screaming, and the next thing I knew, I was falling. When I hit the water, it musta knocked the wind outta me, 'cause I couldn't breathe. I thought I was drowning."

Hawk looked at the faces of Donald's fellow survivors and he could tell they were reliving the horrible experience along with him. He nudged Conner and said softly, "I don't know if we oughta take them up to see that scene or not." Even as he said it, the little elf called Frog hopped down from the wagon and started up through the trees toward the top of the hill.

When Donald turned as if to start up the hill after Frog, Conner stopped him. "Mr. Lewis, I'm not sure you and your friends oughta go up that hill. Hawk, here, says it's a pretty grim scene up there. Nothing but bodies lying everywhere, and the buzzards are already working on them."

It was enough to cause Donald to hesitate, then turn to the other three survivors before deciding. They talked briefly, then Donald turned back to Conner. "We know it's something we don't really want to see, but we owe it to our friends to drive the vultures away and bury our people." He gestured toward one of the three. "Brother James lost his wife and two sons, and he wants to bury them, himself." So, they unhitched the horses from the wagon and Corporal Johnson detailed three of the men to take all the horses around the base of the hill to water them in the river. The rest of the party climbed up through the trees to the grisly scene at the top. The rest of the day was consumed with the work of digging deep trenches, using the few tools they'd brought with them, plus some found on the bodies of the pack mules. After battling the buzzards for what was left of the bodies of their fellow church members, they decided to let the fierce birds have the mules for their feast. Sick with grief, Brother James was unable to continue when he could not identify his wife and children after the buzzards had mutilated all the bodies. It was almost dark when the last mound was tamped down over the mass graves, and Donald gave a brief eulogy for the departed souls.

"Well, I guess that's about all we can do up here for these poor folks," Conner commented to Hawk. "I'm thinking I'll have the men set up camp back down the road by that little stream we crossed on the way here, since it's too much trouble to get to the river from here. That way, we can let the Quakers sleep in the wagon. Then we'll go back to Fort Benton in the morning. Whatcha think?" Hawk said it was as good a plan as any, then another thought occurred to Conner. "What the hell happened to that little fellow? He just disappeared after we got up here on the hill."

Hawk had to chuckle. "He was here all day. This is where he lives." When Conner looked confused, Hawk explained, "I wondered about him, myself, earlier this afternoon, so I did a little scoutin'. He's got a cave in the face of that cliff, hangin' over the river. He crawls up and down a rope to get in and out of it. I found his rope tied around the foot of a pine where the trees run right up to the edge of the bluff. He had it covered up pretty good to keep anybody from seein' it."

"Well, I'll be . . ." Conner started. "So that's why he just appeared, and nobody knew where he came from. He ain't a goblin after all," he announced, laughing as he did. Then another thought occurred. "I wonder why he jumped in the river with Lewis and the others."

"I expect he decided things were gettin' too hot to stay here," Hawk speculated. "And after he showed 'em how to get to Adam Wylie's farm, he decided he might as well go with 'em to Fort Benton and get a good meal, especially after those outlaws made such a mess of his homeplace."

"Maybe we should take him back to Fort Benton," Conner said. "It doesn't seem right to leave him out here in this wilderness."

"I don't know," Hawk said. "I expect he's been livin' like this for most of his life. I reckon he's just another wild thing livin' in the woods—most likely prefers it to livin' with people. If it was up to me, I'd say leave it up to him."

"I guess you're right," Conner said. "At any rate, we'll find out in the morning, because I expect he'll just hop on the wagon if he wants to go back with the others." He turned to follow the rest of his soldiers back down the trail to the road. "You coming?"

"I'll be along directly," Hawk answered. "I wanna check a few things first." He waited until Conner was on his way back down before turning and going to the edge of the cliff where he had found the rope tied around the tree. He stepped back into the trees and sat down where he could watch the tree with the rope tied to it. After a little while, when the last sounds of the men moving down through the forest to the road faded away and all was quiet on the hilltop, he saw what he expected. At first, there was a slight movement in the pine straw covering the rope, then it was followed by the appearance of a gray, woolly head over the edge of the cliff. Hawk waited until the little man was all the way up and onto the top of the bluff before speaking. On a hunch, he spoke in the Blackfoot tongue. "Your home is quiet now." The little man nicknamed Frog jerked upright, looking all around him, much like a squirrel when startled. "Have no fear," Hawk said, "I am a friend."

Then locating the source of the voice, the little man focused his gaze upon the man seated, Indian fashion, among the trees. "Hawk," he said, also in the Blackfoot tongue.

"My name is Hawk," Hawk said. "You are a white man?"

"I am Siksika," he replied, claiming to be Blackfoot.

Hawk was not surprised. He had figured Frog to have possibly been captured by the Indians when he was a small boy. "These men who attacked these people, had they been here before?" He thought it possible that David Booth's outlaw partners might have been looking for a good place to hide bodies, should it become a necessity. Frog nodded anxiously in response. "Did you see them when they left?" Again, Frog nodded rapidly. "Will you show me?" Hawk asked. With no hesitation, Frog started toward the path back down to the road. Hawk followed right behind him.

When they reached the road, the little man turned to the west. Moving rapidly, even though unable to stand up straight, Frog limped along the side of the road until he came to a deep gully. He stopped and pointed to hoofprints, some leading down into a gully, others coming up from it. Hawk hopped down into the gully, interested more in the fresher tracks leaving the road. Looking as closely as he could in the fading light of day, he was able to make out the smaller tracks of a mule, mixed in with those of the horses. *That would be the mule carrying all the Quakers' money,* he thought. He paused to look around him at the growing darkness, knowing it would be better to follow the tracks in daylight. At least, it gave him a start. He looked back at the road, where Frog stood watching him. When he caught his eye, the little man grinned and began nodding rapidly again. "Choteau," he said, and repeated, "Choteau." Then he asked, "Good?"

"Good," Hawk answered, not really understanding what he meant by *Choteau.* "Let's go get something to eat now," he said. Together, they walked back down the road to the campsite, where a couple of healthy fires were already burning. He went to his packhorse and got some deer jerky and hardtack, which he gave to Frog and motioned for him to eat.

"Looks like you made a friend," Conner commented

when Hawk walked up to the fire. "How'd you get him outta his hole?"

Hawk responded with a question of his own. "What are you plannin' to do in the mornin'?"

"We'll take all these folks back to Fort Benton," Conner said, surprised that he had asked. "What did you think?"

"Well, I've got a trail I can follow outta here. It ain't as fresh as I'd like it, but it's pretty plain to see. It's the same one Booth's partners rode in on, so there's a good chance it might lead us to 'em." He imagined he could see the wheels turning in Conner's brain, but knew his friend was obligated to see that Lewis and his friends were escorted safely back to Fort Benton. "What I want to know is, are you goin' after those murderin' bastards, once you take the preacher's wagon back?"

"Well, sure, I'm gonna see if we can catch up with them, although I know we'll most likely be too far behind to have much chance of doing it," Conner said. "How many days ago did this thing happen? I'm not really sure."

Hawk was halfway convinced that Conner was really feeling as if his mission had been completed, now that Major Brisbin's nephew was safe. "You don't need me to show you how to get back to Fort Benton, so I'm thinkin' it's a good idea if I start out on their trail. And maybe by the time you and your soldiers show up I might have an idea where they're holed up." He paused, waiting for a show of commitment. When Conner failed to comment right away, he said, "I just wanna be sure you'll be comin' along behind me."

"Damn, I don't know, Hawk. What if we lose your trail?" Conner responded.

"I'll make sure you don't. I'll mark it enough so even you can follow it," he japed. "Maybe, if we're lucky, they're headed for a hideout somewhere. I can't abide the notion of lettin' that bunch get away with the murder of all those good folks back up on that hill."

"You're right, of course," Conner said. "All right, we'll do it your way, but you'll have to show me where to start out after you in the morning."

"By the way," Hawk said, "that little fellow they call Frog is the one who showed me where to pick up their trail. Otherwise, I wouldn't know where to start lookin'."

At sunup the next morning, the fires were revived, but only enough to afford a cup of coffee for everyone. Conner planned to stop for breakfast when the horses were in need of rest, and Hawk was of the same mind. Before leaving the patrol, Hawk asked Donald if there was some way he could recognize David Booth, if he was lucky enough to find him. Donald, with Corey's help, tried to paint a detailed description of the man who had appeared to be such a devout Christian. A big man, they said, dark of hair and features, his seeming vanity would have to be his heavy mustache, which he groomed to curl up at the ends. Other than that, they said, his clothes were plain, like those of all the other men of their church. Hawk tried to form the image of Booth's face in his mind and promised he would do his best to track him down. When the horses were saddled, he led Conner to the gully where Booth and his partners had left the wagon road and headed north. Conner stood for a few moments, staring down the narrow gully, thinking he should advise his friend. "You know I'm ordered to lead a ten-day patrol, so I can't keep the men up here indefinitely. I'll come after you as soon as I can take those folks back to Fort Benton. But if we don't find Booth and his gang after a day or so, I'm gonna have to head back."

"I understand," Hawk assured him. They wished each other good luck and parted ways.

"I was damn glad to see that store," Tater Thompson repeated what he had said when they had caught sight of the little trading post owned by Grover Dean on the Teton River. "I was needin' a drink of likker bad." It was now several days since they had slaughtered the train of Quakers, then killed Dean and his wife at the trading post, and it appeared that no one was on their trail. Feeling confident he had pulled it off, Booth Corbin thought back to remember the chain of events.

"Maybe we won't have to keep moving so fast," his brother, Jesse, had remarked when they had left the scene of the massacre behind them. "Whaddaya think, Booth?" He always asked his brother's opinion. He was older than Booth by a good two years, but it was his brother who had formed the small gang of outlaws and was unchallenged as the boss. They had operated quite successfully in Wyoming Territory until the law became too hot on their trail. It was Booth's idea to leave Wyoming and head for Montana with a purpose to simply lie low until the pressure eased up in Wyoming. And it was Booth who stumbled upon a meeting of the Friends one Sunday and came up with the idea of fleecing those innocent folks out of their life savings. "We've put a good bit of distance between us and that hill by the Missouri," Jesse continued. "After all this time, I don't think there's anybody comin' after us, anyway."

"Yeah, Booth," Blue Davis had said, "who the hell's gonna know anything's happened to those damn Quakers? Most likely nobody even knows they're missin'. I don't know why we even worried about it. Who's gonna come after us? Nobody, that's who."

Booth had held the same opinion at the time, but he had still felt the need for caution. And now that they were back in their hideout, he was satisfied that they had gotten away with the assault, free and clear. He had invested a lot of time and sacrifice in setting up the robbery of the Society of Friends. He had joined the society, under the name of David Booth, gone to a lot of meetings, said a lot of *amen*s, even volunteered to help with some of the crops. Now that it had paid off, he didn't want anything to go wrong, just because of carelessness by any of them. They were probably right in thinking they had pulled off the perfect crime, even though there was no way of knowing if those few who were pushed off the cliff survived. He trusted the reasoning of his brother, and Jesse was of the opinion that they were free and clear. As for the massacre that took place on that hilltop, he had not foreseen the slaughter of the whole group of people. He had planned to take all the mules and leave the people on foot. The shooting had happened spontaneously, when Trip Dawson had suddenly pumped three shots into Brother Adams when Adams tried to save the money. Trip was always quick to use his gun, and maybe the death of all those people could have been avoided, as Booth had planned. Looking back on the incident, however, Booth decided it was better than his original plan, when he realized that it had ensured their getting away and leaving no witnesses. When the massacre started, there were people— men, women, children—running in every direction. Without thinking, he had reacted like the others, shooting to be sure no one escaped to report what was happening there. When all was said and done, things had worked even better than he expected. That mule they led back with them was carrying over thirty thousand dollars. He would not know the exact amount until he had a chance to count all of it. But that was a hell of a lot more than their average bank robbery yielded, with no risk of retaliation. To satisfy his impatient partners, he had counted out a hundred dollars to each man when they had stopped to camp the first night after the shooting. They seemed to have needed some evidence of the reward coming to them, so he gave them a little cash to hold.

Returning his thoughts to the day of his biggest robbery, Booth remembered announcing to his impatient men, "Yes, sir, I think we've all earned a little whiskey and a good supper. We'll see what that Injun bitch of Grover Dean's can cook up for five wealthy gentlemen."

He remembered how his declaration was met with grunts of enthusiasm. "Now you're talkin'," Tater had exclaimed. "If I don't get some whiskey pretty soon, I'm gonna die!" His testimony was met with guffaws from the others and a race down the bluff to the store.

Like the murdered Quakers, it had been a fateful night for the unfortunate storekeeper and his wife when Booth decided to stop there that night. Inside the combination store and saloon, Grover Dean heard them when they pulled up in front, so he walked over to the window to see. "There's that Wyomin' bunch back here again," he said to Beulah. "I hope to hell they've got some money to spend this time." Like her husband, Beulah, whose Blackfoot name was Walks Behind, was not enthusiastic about another visit from the rough group of outlaws. She had been with Grover ever since he built his trading post almost ten years ago, doing his bidding like any good wife would do. He called her Beulah because he had a sister with that name, who had died as a child, and he liked that more than Walks Behind. "You might better see if you've got anythin' to cook," Grover suggested. "They might be lookin' for somethin' to eat." He opened the door and stepped out on the porch to meet them.

"Didn't expect to see you boys back so soon," Grover said in greeting. Then noticing one extra, he said, "Looks like you picked up another rider since you left here."

"Howdy, Grover," Jesse Corbin responded. "Yep, we picked up my brother, Booth, and he's needin' a drink of whiskey, same as the rest of us."

"Only this time, we want the good stuff," Blue Davis informed him, "instead of that watered-down trash you sell the Injuns."

"I don't know why you'd say that," Grover replied, as Blue pushed by him and went inside. "I ain't got no watered-down whiskey," he claimed, and hurried to get behind the bar. "I've got some high-priced rye whiskey I sell by the bottle. It costs more than the regular corn whiskey I sell a drink at a time."

"We'll take a bottle of that rye whiskey," Booth called out as he walked in the door behind them.

"And how 'bout some food," Trip Dawson ordered. "Where's that squaw you're livin' with? Get her ass in the kitchen. I need some decent food."

"Sure thing, boys," Grover responded. "That's what I'm in business for, but last week when you were here, you were pretty tight with your money."

"Yeah?" Tater responded. "Well, that was last week." He pulled a wad of money out of his vest pocket and slammed it on the bar. "Now get me a drink of that rye whiskey, before I throw a fit." His antics drew a round of laughter from his partners, prompting a couple of them to slam some money down on the bar as well.

Grover was properly astonished by their behavior. "Looks like you boys musta held up a bank or some-thin' since you was last in here."

His comment had caused Booth to realize the picture they were creating with their frivolous display of money. "It might look that way, at that," he said. "We're just celebratin' 'cause I just got back from Wyomin' with some money we had buried down there." From the skeptical expression on Grover's face, he was afraid he leaned more toward the bank robbery explanation. *I wish I had warned them to keep their mouths shut,* he thought.

"Well, in that case, I'd best go tell Beulah to rustle up some food," Grover said, and reached under the bar and brought out an unopened bottle of rye whiskey.

The celebration had extended past suppertime and on into the night, keeping Grover busy supplying the whiskey and Beulah frying ham and baking biscuits.

Finally, a point was reached when the party began to settle into an alcoholic stupor for the most part, punctuated by the sawmill-like snoring of Tater Thompson, as it reverberated off the hard tabletop. The only sober man in the saloon, Grover Dean, was content to enjoy the financial windfall that had come his way, unaware of a confrontation that was to follow. Sitting at the table with the sleeping Tater, Blue Davis sat in a stupor that morphed into a drunken fantasy as he eyed Beulah while the weary Indian woman picked up the dirty dishes from the tables. When she bent over to pull a dirty plate from under Tater's arm, Blue pointed to her behind. "Now, I'm buyin' me some of that," he stated confidently.

His statement drew an instant response from Grover. "That ain't for sale."

"It is tonight," Blue said, and started to reach for the startled woman.

"She ain't for sale," Grover repeated, but this time he backed up his words with the double-barreled shotgun he kept under the counter. Just as he had on the hilltop by the Missouri, Trip Dawson had been the quickest to react. He drew his .44 and pumped two rounds into Grover's chest. Horrified, the Blackfoot woman screamed, then launched an attack upon Trip, only to receive his third shot in her stomach.

As Beulah collapsed to the floor, everyone seemed stunned except Trip and Tater, who continued to snore. After a moment when no one could think what to say, Booth finally demanded, "What the hell is wrong with you?"

"He was fixin' to shoot Blue," Trip replied as he casually replaced the three spent cartridges.

"You damn fool," Booth said. "He wouldn't have

shot that gun. Blue's too damn drunk to get up from that chair. Now we got ourselves into another mess."

"Least we're gonna save ourselves a lot of money we spent here tonight," Jesse said, seemingly not that concerned about the murder of Grover and his wife.

Rapidly sobering up at this turn of events, Booth got to his feet. "All right," he ordered. "Let's drag them outta here in case somebody happens by. We can put 'em in the storeroom." They did as he instructed, dragging the bodies out of the saloon, although no one really thought there was much chance of anybody else showing up at the trading post at this late hour. When Jesse said as much to his brother, Booth had to admit that he was probably right. They talked about the best thing to do, since it was now pretty late to think about saddling the horses and starting out to find a place to camp.

"Everything we need is right here," Jesse said. "We might as well stay here tonight and leave in the mornin'. Ain't nobody liable to turn up here before we leave. We can take what we need and burn the rest. Hell, Booth, this turned out to be a gold mine, and just like the Quaker business, we'll leave no witnesses."

At the time, Booth had thought it over for a few moments but couldn't come up with any reason not to do as Jesse advised, now that the killing was already done. "All right," he agreed. "Let's get all the ammunition and supplies we can carry ready to pack up in the mornin'. And let's see if we can find where Grover's secret hiding place for his money is." With that decision, the two brothers roused their companions out of their drunken states to help with the robbing of the trading post. All but Tater sobered up enough to help. Even after Blue kicked Tater's chair out from under him, he hung on the table by his arms until finally dropping to his knees to then roll over on his side, where he slept till morning.

Booth had seen to it that everyone was awake early when the next morning dawned, and they were soon packed up, including a generous quantity of supplies and ammunition, courtesy of the late Grover Dean. As a final touch, Booth set fire to the building and waited to watch it until satisfied it would continue to burn after they had gone. With heads still fragile from their celebration, the band of outlaws had started out to complete the final day's ride to the hideout they were now occupying. From Grover Dean's trading post, their hideout was a full day's ride, with a tiny settlement about halfway. They had ridden around the settlement, so they wouldn't all be seen together. In the eight months they had used this hideout, they had been careful not to come to town together. Booth thought it best to quell any curiosity the folks there might have about them. When buying supplies from the store there, Jesse or Blue would go in alone most of the time. There were marshals in Wyoming who would be interested to know a gang of five men were living in a cabin half a day's ride from the settlement. There was another man more than a little interested in their whereabouts. And on this particular morning, that man was setting out to follow their trail, even though it was already pretty old.

CHAPTER 6

From the beginning, the outlaws were careless in leaving a trail, taking no pains to cover their tracks. Hawk figured they weren't worried about anyone following them and probably thought it a good chance that no one would even know if the mule train of Quakers was missing. He had gone no farther than half a mile when the tracks struck an old trail. He figured it most likely an old Indian trail and the party he was tracking followed it. To make tracking easier, a light rain had fallen on the day of the massacre, or maybe the day after, and it helped to leave solid hoof imprints, especially where there was little grass. He rode on into midday over a treeless plain with the jagged peaks of the Rocky Mountains standing on the western horizon, never seeming to get closer. Water was scarce, so he was glad to see a line of trees after he estimated he had ridden close to thirty miles, about ten miles more than he liked to run his horse. Judging by the growth of trees and vegetation, he guessed that he was near a river. The trail he followed led toward the thickest part of the trees and then turned to follow the river west. It was plain to see that the men he followed had left the trail here and later returned to take it up again. So, he turned Rascal toward the water and rode down into the trees. As he anticipated, the remains of a campfire told him that the outlaws had stopped there as well. His immediate thought, after taking care of his horses, would have been to examine the ashes of the campfire to try to get an idea how far behind he was. This time, he didn't bother, since he was so far behind them. "Nothin' to do but keep ridin'," he said to Rascal.

After his horse was rested, he started out again on the trail that now followed close beside the river, wondering if he might be taking on a pointless mission. If the outlaws didn't hole up somewhere before much longer, he wasn't confident that Conner and his patrol could ever catch up to him. Conner was not as inclined to abort a mission as Harvey Meade was, but Hawk realized there would come a time when Conner would deem it no longer advisable to continue a search without foreseeable results. These thoughts were interrupted when he spotted half a dozen buzzards circling overhead, so he nudged Rascal into a gentle lope.

He rode for what he estimated to be about a quarter of a mile before he could see the reason for the buzzards. He pulled Rascal up short of a clearing on the riverbank and stared at what he guessed to be the charred remains of a house or store. A barn with a corral stood unscathed off to the side of the burned remnants that Hawk decided had been a trading post. He nudged Rascal forward and rode on down into the yard. The story required little thought to determine what had happened here when he saw the buzzards plucking away at the two scorched, half-burned bodies lying among the fallen roof beams. If there had been any doubt before, after the brutal massacre of the Quakers, this new evidence was proof enough that the men he trailed were without the first trace of human compassion. And there was no question who was responsible for this evil act of violence, for the hoof-prints left by the little mule were there plain to see at the hitching post, even after this amount of time.

Judging by the burned timbers, it would seem that he was not that far behind Booth and his gang, which didn't make sense, since they were more than a few days ahead of him. It could only mean they had stayed overnight at the trading post, possibly two nights. Everything was now a guess on Hawk's part, so he spent no more than a short time at the burned-out store. He chased the buzzards away from the two charred bodies, but there was little left to worry about burying, so he backed away and let the raucous birds return to clean up the remains of their feast. With ever increasing determination to bring Booth and his gang to face their vicious crimes, he returned to the river trail.

Back on the road, he rode for another twenty-five miles or so before spotting a small gathering of buildings up ahead. He followed the trail into the settlement, which consisted of a general store, a stable, a blacksmith, and a tent with a crude sign that claimed it to be a saloon. He directed Rascal toward the general store, dismounted, and looped the buckskin's reins around the hitching post. He was met with a genuine look of surprise by the owner when he walked inside. "Well, howdy, stranger," Franklin Pierce exclaimed, as he looked the tall, broad-shouldered man up and down. "What brings you to Choteau?"

"Where'd you say this was?" Hawk asked, not sure he had heard him correctly.

"Well, we call it Choteau," Pierce answered. "It ain't really got an official name, I reckon. What I was told, they called it that 'cause some Frenchman named Pierre Chouteau had a camp here. What can I do for you?"

Choteau, Hawk repeated to himself. That was what the little man called Frog had said when he showed him the trail the five men had taken from the Quaker massacre. He had pointed to the tracks and said, "Choteau." *He was trying to tell me that trail led to Choteau. I should have brought him with me,* he thought, *because he probably knows the whole country hereabouts.* He realized then that the storekeeper was waiting for him to reply. "I reckon I could use some coffee, if you've got any," Hawk said, "and some salt." Those were the only two items he was really short of.

"I've got both of them," Pierce said, "and I've got a coffee grinder, if you want me to grind up the beans for you." Hawk said that would be appreciated and Pierce continued talking. "I reckon you're just passin' through," he said. "Don't hardly ever see folks who are comin' to Choteau." As he was weighing out the coffee beans, a short, stocky woman came in from the back room to see whom Pierce was talking to. "This is my wife," Pierce said. "Flo, say howdy to the only customer we've had today. Pardon my manners," he said, returning his attention to Hawk. "My name's Franklin Pierce, and this is my wife, Flo." He extended his hand.

Hawk shook his hand. "John Hawk," he said.

"Is that why you got that in your hat?" Flo asked, pointing to the hawk feather in his hatband. Her husband chuckled and said he should have guessed that, himself.

"You guessed it. Sounds like business ain't so good in Choteau," Hawk said in response to Pierce's comment that he was the only customer that day.

"You can say that again," Pierce said. "Me and the missus are thinkin' about pullin' up stakes and headin' back to the farm in Minnesota. Things looked good here for a little while, had some farm families come in, and some miners lookin' for gold in the hills about twenty miles west of here. The farmers found out that the land ain't much good for raisin' anything but grass, and there evidently ain't no gold in the mountains. We've been hopin' the cattle ranchers would move in, but we've about give up on that now."

"All the miners ain't give up yet," Flo commented. "At least, I reckon they're prospectin'. Anyway, they still come into town to get supplies, always just one or two of 'em, but it ain't always the same two. So, I figure they're workin' a big claim somewhere, 'cause they sure don't look like farmers."

Her comment caused Hawk to ask, "Did you see any of 'em in the last few days?"

"Nope," Flo answered. "Ain't seen hide nor hair of 'em in a while."

Since she seemed to be free-flowing with information, he asked another question. "How 'bout anybody else? Did you happen to see a party of five men ride through here in the last couple of days?"

"No, like I said, we ain't seen anybody," Flo answered.

Finished with the grinding of the coffee beans, her husband's curiosity was piqued by Hawk's questions. "Are you a lawman, by any chance?"

Hawk saw no reason not to tell them whom he was trailing. "No, I'm not a lawman. I'm ridin' scout for a cavalry patrol outta Fort Ellis. They're a day or two behind me. We're on the trail of five outlaws that murdered a group of church folks back down on the Missouri. They killed twenty-eight people, includin' women and children. I've been trackin' 'em, and they came this way."

"Well, forever more . . ." Flo started. "I hope they didn't make it this far."

"We'da seen 'em if they had," Franklin said. "As dead as this town is, nobody can hardly ride through here without somebody noticin'." He paused but a second before continuing. "Fort Ellis, that's way down on the Yellowstone, ain't it?" When Hawk nodded, Franklin asked, "You and that cavalry patrol are a long way from home, ain't you?"

"That's a fact," Hawk said. "Just tryin' to give the garrison at Fort Benton a little help." He paid for his coffee and salt, then headed for the door. "Well, it was nice meetin' you folks. I reckon I'll be on my way." They thanked him for the business and said they hoped he'd come back to see them. Outside, he tied his purchases on his horse, thinking his situation over while he did. Booth and his men had definitely come to this town. He had seen the tracks to prove it. They must have ridden around the town, not wishing to be seen. There was nothing to do now but go back the way he had come and try to find the place where they left the road. So, he climbed up into the saddle and turned Rascal back to the east, thinking about what Flo Pierce had said about the men she assumed to be prospectors. He had a feeling he was close to their destination. There must be a hideout not too far from this little town. Her description of the men who some- times came in the store—one or two at a time, and not always the same men—seemed like what they would do if they didn't want it known there was a gang holed up near there. He encouraged Rascal to pick up his pace with a nudge of his heels, anxious to find the trail he had lost.

He was almost out of sight of the town when he found the place. The tracks were not that hard to see where the horses had left the wagon road and rode off to the south at a wide angle. He had just been careless. Since it happened at a point when the buildings of Choteau just came into view, he blamed it on that, thinking he must have been distracted by the appearance of a town when his eyes should have been on the trail. Now, with a trail to follow again, he hesitated to start out on it, in spite of his prior feeling of purpose. To be honest with himself, he had to admit that the tracks he had been following were so old by now that they might be somebody else's tracks. Still, he kept finding that smaller hoofprint of a mule, and there were never any fresh tracks on the road. So he had to figure he was still on their trail.

Another thought came to concern him, as well. He was afraid he had gotten too far ahead of Conner and the patrol at this point. They might have already turned back, and if they had, what should he do? He felt he was still on Booth's trail, but he had figured to have a cavalry patrol to take on the five ruthless gunmen. In all good conscience, he could not simply break off his tracking and call it a lost cause. The crimes these five murderers had committed were too atrocious to write off as too difficult to pursue. If he couldn't capture them on his own, he must at least find them, so they might still be brought to justice by some agency, either civilian or military. He made up his mind that he would make it his business to find

them, but there was still the question of Conner and
the patrol. It wasn't fair to Conner to leave him lost in
this wilderness, either. After laboring over the issue
for a few more moments, he decided the proper thing
to do was to ride back in hopes of meeting the patrol
before having to ride too far. Maybe, he hoped, they
might have reached the burned-out trading post,
thinking even then that the soldiers would have had
to ride like hell to have gotten that far. But if they had,
then that would mean only another half a day lost to
the outlaws. To satisfy his anxiety, he followed the
tracks leaving the road for about half a mile before
pulling up to stare out ahead in the general direction
they led. *They rode around that low mesa,* he thought,
*so nobody in Choteau could see them as they bypassed it.
That could account for Franklin and Flo failing to see them
in town.* Feeling now that he had saved himself some
time for when he returned, he turned Rascal around
and started back toward Grover Dean's trading post.

By the time he reached the blackened ruins of the
trading post, his horse was ready for some water and
rest. Thinking this as good a place as any to eat something, himself, he decided to try out some of the
coffee he had just purchased. If luck was riding with
him, maybe Mathew Conner and the fifteen-man
patrol would catch up to him there. After relieving his
horse of his burdens, he gathered enough wood to
build a fire in front of the barn. He figured it would
be seen from the road up above, if the patrol did get
that far. With water from the river, he made his coffee
and roasted some deer jerky over the fire. It would be
perfect, he thought, if the patrol caught up to him
here. There was still an hour or so before dark, and if
Conner was pushing his men to catch up, they might

not have gone into camp for the night. Knowing it was wishful thinking, he nonetheless hoped they would show up. When darkness finally engulfed the clearing by the river, he unrolled his bedroll inside the barn door and crawled in, wondering how far behind Booth he now was. Before many minutes passed, he was asleep, almost as peacefully as the man and woman sleeping beneath the burned timbers in the ashes of the trading post. He hadn't bothered to look to see if the buzzards left anything other than a couple of skeletons.

When he awoke early the next morning, he found that he was still troubled over what he should do in regard to the patrol. Thinking of the killers he was following, he felt that he had a tiger by the tail, and he was reluctant to let it go. He needed Conner and his soldiers, if that gang was to be apprehended. And if he didn't wait for the patrol, it would leave Conner with no idea what had happened to his scout. In the end, he decided he had to find the patrol, so he saddled up and started to backtrack again, planning to have breakfast when Rascal needed rest.

"Want me to get 'em mounted up, Lieutenant?" Corporal Johnson asked when he walked up from the creek.

"Yes, go ahead and get 'em ready to move out," Conner answered, even though he hadn't made up his mind in which direction he was going to take them. They had been out over a week on what was supposed to be a ten-day patrol. And he knew he was a lot farther from Fort Ellis than a three-day march.

How much farther, he wasn't really sure. *Damn it, Hawk,* he thought, *where the hell are you?*

In answer to his question, he heard one of the men call out, "Rider comin' in!"

Anxious to see if it was his scout, Conner hurried to the edge of the clearing to see. Even at a distance, there was no mistaking the identity of the rider. The sight of the tall figure, riding in perfect rhythm with the buckskin's gait, was enough to relieve the anxiety that had been building in his brain. He remained there and waited for Hawk to ride in. "I was about to give up on you," he said when Hawk pulled up before him. "Did you have any luck?"

"Some," Hawk answered, then gave him a complete report on what he had found. "I followed 'em as far as that little settlement I told you about, and I've got a trail to follow from there. But I figured I'd best come back and find you."

"I'm glad you did," Conner said. "We're already gonna be out longer than we were scheduled to be, and I was getting ready to turn this patrol back toward home. I'd like to catch up with that gang of murderers, but we're already running short of supplies." He turned and pointed toward the Rocky Mountains. "And it looks like this bunch is heading for the mountains. There ain't any way of telling how long we might search in those mountains without finding a trace of them." He shrugged apologetically. "As far as my mission's objective, I've found what I was sent to find out. Major Brisbin's nephew is safe and that's about all that matters as far as this patrol is concerned." Before Hawk could comment, Conner hurried to continue. "I know this was a terrible thing, killing all those innocent people . . ."

"Plus the man and woman in the store between here and the town of Choteau," Hawk interrupted.

"Right, right," Conner was quick to agree. "But, damn it, Hawk, I can't take a fifteen-man patrol and roam all over the Rocky Mountains with it. I've got to take these men back to the post."

"I understand your position," Hawk said. "You need to get your men back to Fort Ellis. But I don't need to get back there. Hell, I've already been fired, anyway, so I think I'll get back on that trail I just left and see if I can find those bastards. Then maybe I can tell somebody, either the military or the marshal service, where to look for 'em." He paused when Conner's reaction to his proposal didn't seem positive. "You don't need me to get you home," Hawk went on. "The way I figure it, you ain't but about a day's ride to Great Falls, almost straight south from where you are right now, and you know how to get to Ellis from there. As a matter of fact, I remember crossin' a north–south trail a few miles short of here, looked like an old Indian trail. I'd say it's a good chance it would take you right to Great Falls. If you're runnin' short of food, I've seen plenty of sign of deer and antelope at just about every place I've camped. Corporal Johnson is always itchin' to go huntin'. You could let him find a deer or something."

Conner shook his head as if amazed. "You really wanna find those outlaws that bad?" Hawk shrugged in response. "I hope you've got better sense than to try to take any action against them."

"I don't plan to," Hawk said. "I just wanna find out where they're holed up, so a posse can go after 'em. It'd be a damn sin to let men like that get away with what they did."

Conner hesitated, taking a long moment to study his friend's face. He was somewhat surprised by the compassion shown by the normally imperturbable scout and was feeling some guilt about the position he felt he had to take. "All right, if you feel that's what you need to do," Conner said. "I'm gonna turn back to Fort Ellis. I wish you good luck in scouting those killers, but damn it, Hawk, be careful they don't add you to the list of people they've already slaughtered." Hawk nodded in response and Conner asked, "You gonna start back right away, or do you need to rest your horse?"

"My horse is all right, but I'm gonna boil me a little coffee and chew on some bacon, since I see you ain't put out all your fires yet."

"I'll have a cup with you," Conner said, and told Johnson to hold up on the order to mount.

The patrol was delayed about forty-five minutes before departing for Great Falls and since the men really were running short of supplies, Hawk donated the coffee he had just bought from Franklin Pierce to the patrol. He figured he would replace it in Choteau, knowing Pierce would be glad to get the business. "I'll see you back at Fort Ellis," Conner said as they prepared to ride. When Hawk only nodded in reply, Conner added, "And you'd better report in or you won't get paid for this scout." Hawk nodded again and turned Rascal back toward Grover Dean's store, not particularly concerned if he got paid or not.

It was a full day's ride back to Choteau, but Hawk decided to go straight back to the little town, in hopes of getting there before Pierce closed his store. It was important to get back on Booth's trail, but it was more important to restock his coffee supply, because once back on the trail, there was no telling when there might be another opportunity to buy coffee. *And I've got to have coffee,* he told himself. As it turned out, the store was closed when he arrived, but he could see Franklin and his wife still inside, so he tapped on the door. Obviously surprised, Pierce unlocked the door. "Well, howdy, Mr. Hawk. Didn't expect to see you back so soon. Matter of fact, I didn't expect to see you back at all. Was there somethin' you forgot?"

"I'm gonna need to buy some more coffee," Hawk answered. "I'm glad I caught you before you left for the night."

"You sure must drink a lot of coffee," Flo saw fit to comment. "You ain't sayin' you've already run out, are you? 'Cause if you have, I'd say you're making it too doggone strong." She chuckled in appreciation of her own humor.

"Yes, ma'am," Hawk replied, japing as well. "I used it all up. Maybe you'd best show me how much you put in a pot of water." They all laughed then with Franklin and Flo still waiting for the real explanation. So, Hawk told them what had happened to his sack of freshly ground coffee. "And I reckon I can get by without air to breathe, but I need coffee to live," he said in conclusion.

When the joking was over, Franklin asked the question he was really interested in knowing an answer for. "That cavalry patrol you gave your coffee to, are they likely comin' to Choteau?" He glanced at his wife. "Because if they are, we might better take stock of what kind of supplies we've got in the storeroom."

"No, they won't be comin' here," Hawk replied,

and saw the immediate disappointment in Pierce's face. He figured that business must really be as dead as he had complained before. "No, they're already on their way back to Fort Ellis. They're way outta their usual territory, and the officer commanding the patrol said he's gotta take 'em back."

"But you're still here," Flo pointed out. "Don't you have to go back with 'em?"

"No, ma'am," Hawk replied. "I work for the army, but I ain't in the army." Not wanting to get into a discussion about why he was staying, he paid for his coffee and said, "Well, I'd best let you folks close up, so you can get on home." He picked up his coffee and started for the door.

"It ain't a long trip," Flo saw fit to remark, "since we live in the back of the store."

In the saddle again, Hawk rode down the short street to take a look at the stable in case he decided to put his horses up for the night where they might get some oats. One look at the shabby building made his decision for him. He'd camp on the riverbank—the stable looked as poor as Franklin Pierce claimed the whole town to be. He turned Rascal back up the road to the place where he had spotted Booth's tracks leaving the trail. When he reached that point, he rode down to the river and made his camp.

He was awakened the next morning by a light rain, thankful that he had decided to fashion a half tent with a piece of canvas he had brought with him for just such occasions. After taking a good look at the clouds rolling in off the mountains the night before, he had decided there was a good chance of rain. So, he awoke only half-wet, thinking he should have paid to sleep in the stable. With no inclination to try to

revive his campfire, he rolled up his bedroll inside
his piece of canvas and saddled Rascal. He wished at
that point that he had brought his packhorse, but he
had taken only the rations he thought he might need
for the ten-day patrol, just as the soldiers had.

He returned to the place where Booth and his
gang had left the road. The tracks were still there to
verify the outlaws had set out to circle around a low
mesa south of the town, but he was afraid the tracks
might disappear if it continued to rain. Once past
the long mesa, he could see the buildings in town in
the distance, and he found some tracks that led back
to the north. He continued in that direction, even
though tracks were harder to find. It promised to be
harder to track them once they returned to the road,
which he expected to strike before long. To his surprise, he came back to the river without crossing the
wagon road. The road had evidently ended at Choteau
and that meant there were probably no farms or
homesteaders of any kind west of the town. He reined
Rascal to a stop beside the river while he tried to
determine if he had overrun the gang's trail. While
there was no longer a road, there was a narrow path
that followed the winding river, that now looked more
like a creek, toward the mountains that suddenly
seemed closer. Looking in the opposite direction, he
could see that the path led toward town and was most
likely the path the strangers Flo Pierce told him about
had used to come to town. That thought caused him
to again consider the possibility the strangers she
talked about and the gang he was tracking were one
and the same.

He climbed down out of the saddle and began
walking along the river path, leading his horse. He

had walked about fifteen yards before he discovered
the first tracks he'd seen since rounding the foot of
the mesa, so he knew he was still on their trail. He
climbed back on Rascal and continued to follow the
path into the foothills. A few minutes more and the
rain tapered off and the sun began to peek through
holes in the clouds above him. When the rain stopped
completely, he decided he'd waited long enough for
his breakfast. So, when he came to a little grassy clearing between the willow trees, he dismounted and let
his horse drink while he searched for some usable
firewood. When he found enough for his fire, he got
a small canvas bag from his saddle. The bag contained
nothing more than dry grass and leaves to make starting a fire easier when his firewood was wet. Using it as
his kindling, he soon had a healthy fire going, and his
ever-necessary coffee boiling. Some deer tracks at the
edge of the river told him that a small herd had
crossed there that morning. It was enough to remind
him that he was going to have to do some hunting
before very much longer. But for now, he would settle
for bacon and hardtack.

After breakfast, he continued on along the path,
following the river. It became more and more narrow
as he moved up into the foothills, which were thick
with fir and pines. *Pretty soon, this river ain't gonna be
much more than a stream,* he thought. Another quarter
of a mile found him on a much steeper climb and
there were no longer any tracks to be seen. The path
he followed ended abruptly at a fork where two
streams joined to form the river that had led him to
this point. Looking up the steep mountainside before
him, he could see no sign that anyone had tried to
ride up it. And five riders, leading packhorses—and

one mule—could hardly have gone up the mountain without leaving an obvious trail. They had managed to lose him, that much was certain, so he turned around and began backtracking, hoping to find some sign. Most of the rest of the day was spent riding up one ravine after another, searching for some sign of the five killers. It was as if they had just disappeared. Certain that wasn't possible, he decided he'd search every canyon, stream, and ravine until he cut sign again.

The place he chose to set up his camp was in a narrow canyon between two mountains, divided by a rapidly flowing stream about twenty yards wide. Earlier in the day, when riding up the canyon, he had discovered numerous deer tracks along the stream, telling him the trail he found was a popular crossing, so he decided to make his camp about seventy-five yards upstream from the spot. Seeing what appeared to be a small clearing in the heavily forested hillside a little way up the slope, he led Rascal up through the trees and found a perfect spot for his camp. The clearing afforded a little grass for his horse, and the trees around the clearing would make it difficult to see smoke from his campfire. If it really turned out to be the perfect spot, maybe he might get a deer at that crossing in the morning. He didn't like to take time out to hunt, but he was getting low on meat.

CHAPTER 7

Four anxious souls were gathered around Booth Corbin, watching every bill he peeled off the packs of cash, as he counted the Quaker treasure that had been meant to build a new Friends community near Helena. He had managed to delay the official split of the money for several days in an effort to keep them from storming into Choteau to flash it around. The only reason he had been successful in holding them back was the fact that there wasn't much in Choteau to spend it on. Finally, however, it had gotten to the point where they threatened to take it away from him and he wasn't sure if they were serious or not. So, he decided he might as well deal the fortune out.

He had told them that the total was estimated to be around thirty thousand dollars and it represented the sales of six separate farms, plus the savings of all the members of the church. For most of the five bandits, it was difficult to imagine such a large payday, and they were eager to see exactly how much it was for each of them. Booth had started to simply deal the money in five separate piles, but his partners wanted him to count out the whole treasure in one pile first, so they could gloat over the score they had pulled off. With his brother, Jesse, helping him count, Booth laid the last bill down for a total of $30,800. None of the five had been schooled in arithmetic, but all knew they got six thousand each. Then Jesse called on his basic knowledge of long division and figured out that each man's share of the extra eight hundred was $160. With the one hundred dollars Booth gave everyone the first night after the massacre, each man's payday amounted to a total of $6,260. The whooping and hollering that followed his summation might have been heard by Hawk, had he been within a mile of the log cabin perched at the top of a ravine. At this particular time, he was closer to three miles from the ravine.

Tater Thompson's first response, as everyone expected, was that he was going to ride down to Choteau and buy all the whiskey the fellow in the tent-saloon had. He had already drunk up almost all the whiskey he had taken from Grover Dean's store. "That's just what we need, you damned old fool," Blue Davis scolded. "Let everybody in that little town know we're all suddenly rich. That would really give 'em somethin' to talk about in that dried-up little town."

"Blue's right," Booth said. "This ain't the time to show off your money. Before you know it, there'd be a bunch of soldiers or a posse of lawmen up here, combin' these hills."

"That woman down at the store thinks we're prospectors," Tater replied. "Maybe they'd just think we struck it rich."

"If we struck pay dirt up in these hills, it'd be gold

dust," Blue told him. "It don't come outta the ground as paper money."

"Hell, Tater," Trip Dawson japed, while everybody was laughing at Tater's stupidity, "that feller in that tent ain't likely got more'n twenty dollars' worth, anyway."

"I told you when I laid this job out," Booth reminded him, "we've gotta be smart about this and don't go showin' off our money. Like I said in the beginnin', we need to lay low up here in this cabin awhile, till we're sure ain't nobody talkin' about that bunch of Quakers gettin' killed. If I can go to church meetin's and sing hallelujah for eight straight months, you can sure as hell hole up here for a couple of weeks. Then we'll all head for someplace where we can spend our money."

"Booth's right," Blue said. "We need to lay low for a little while. And I'll tell you what I'm gonna do in the mornin'. I'm gonna ride down in that canyon and shoot one of them deer that likes to go down there in that stream. I'm damn sick of bacon. Anybody wanna go with me?"

"No, but I'll sure help you eat him," Tater said. "Might even help you butcher him."

"I knew I could count on you," Blue joked. "Nobody wanna do a little huntin'?" When no one showed any enthusiasm for going with him, he continued, "All right, but I'll tell you one thing, that's gonna be some mighty expensive venison. It's a good thing you've all got some money if you're thinkin' you might want some of that fresh meat."

"I ain't sure how much longer I can sit around this little cabin," Trip declared. "It's gonna get cold up here pretty soon and I'm thinkin' I need to get outta these mountains before it starts in to snowin'."

"I've been thinkin' about that, myself," Jesse said. "But Booth's right, we'd do well to lay low for at least a week or two, long enough to make sure there ain't nobody lookin' to find out what happened to those Quakers." He was well aware of his brother's concern that the men wouldn't be able to keep from displaying their sudden wealth. "Besides, it'll most likely be a month before the weather starts gettin' really cold." He turned toward his brother. "Right, Booth? And we'll be long gone by then."

"That's right, boys," Booth responded. "Just hold your horses for a little while and enjoy bein' rich. Then we'll go on down to one of those Kansas towns, Dodge City, or Wichita, where the gamblin' and the women are runnin' hot all winter long."

"That sounds good to me," Tater said. "And, hell, Blue. I'll even go huntin' with you in the mornin'. Some fresh deer meat would suit my taste right now. And if I go with you, we won't have to worry about missin' the damn deer 'cause I'm a better shot than you are."

"Ha," Blue barked. "That'll be the day when you can outshoot me." That was the start of a playful discussion about who was the best shot. "I remember when ol' Booth was settin' in the meetin'house, singin' and prayin' with them Friends, and we were out there raidin' their farms and scarin' the hell out of 'em. Remember that one time, when you shot at a hog big as a cow, and missed him?"

"I wasn't shootin' to kill it," Tater insisted. "I told you I was just tryin' to scare him."

"Yeah, right," Blue japed, "but you're gonna have

to drag your lazy bones outta your blanket in the mornin', if you're goin' huntin' with me."

It's about time, Hawk thought when he saw the four deer break from the trees on the far side of the narrow canyon. A buck and three does headed for the shallow stream, but they didn't stop to drink, which surprised him. Instead, they splashed on across the stream. *Something must have spooked them,* he thought. There wasn't much time before they would reach the trees on the other side, so he quickly raised his rifle and placed a shot right behind the front leg of the hindmost doe. The deer collapsed a few yards short of the trees as the others disappeared into the thick growth of trees along the base of the canyon.

"What the hell?" Blue blurted when they heard the rifle shot ahead of them. "Who the hell . . . ?" He looked at Tater, who was just as surprised as he was. "Somebody just took a shot at our deer."

"I'll be damned," Tater swore. "We sprung them deer and I ain't aimin' to let no damn Injun have 'em." On foot, they hurried through the trees, leading their horses, until they came to the stream. They stopped abruptly when they saw the tall hunter on the other side, some forty yards away. Hawk saw them at the same time. Both parties were obviously startled.

No one spoke for a few moments. Then Blue called across the stream, "That there's our deer you just shot, friend. We run 'em outta a thicket back up the side of this canyon. We 'preciate you stoppin' that one for us. Maybe if you hustle on after the rest of 'em, you can get another shot at 'em and get one for yourself." As an aside to Tater, he said, "If he puts up any fuss, we'll shoot the son of a bitch."

Hawk was still surprised. He had not expected to run into any other deer hunters, and their attitude toward ownership of the one slain doe was a little awkward as well. "Well, I reckon that's one way of lookin' at it," he called back to them. "I figure it's my bullet that brought the deer down, so that kinda makes it my deer. If you don't think you can follow the other three and get a shot, yourself, I could share this one with you."

"I don't think you understand," Blue said. "That deer was ours, and we need the whole damn deer, so I ain't thinkin' about sharin'."

"That ain't very neighborly of you," Hawk said. "Maybe that doe didn't know she belonged to you. Maybe if she had known that, she mighta ducked when I shot at her."

"You're a pretty funny feller," Blue replied. "I'm tellin' you plain as I can make it. We've been chasin' them deer for over a mile, and I ain't about to give one of 'em up just because you happened to get a lucky shot at it. And I ain't got no notion of sharin' that deer with nobody. We need the whole deer."

"That's right," Tater chimed in then. "There's five of us. We need the whole deer."

Blue flinched as soon as Tater said it, and he turned to give him a quick scowl before calling out to Hawk again. "That's a fact," he said. "We've got women and children to feed."

Hawk's suspicions about the two deer hunters were already growing, and the comment the one made about there being five of them to feed triggered a strong warning, especially after the one doing most of the talking tried to silence him with a frown. What were the odds that the men he searched for would come to him? Not likely, he decided, still he couldn't deny the possibility. "You shoulda said that in the first place," Hawk said. "I don't wanna take any food away from your women and children. You're welcome to that deer. I'll find another one." He backed slowly away, his rifle cocked, ready to fire at the first wrong move either of the two men made. If he could withdraw without trouble, he would then follow them in hopes he really had met with two of the men he hunted.

"This don't smell right to me," Blue murmured to Tater. To Hawk, he called out, "'Preciate it, friend, the young'uns will be mighty happy to get the meat." When Hawk continued to move toward the protection of the trees, Blue said, "Hold on a minute, I'd like to shake your hand."

"All the same to you," Hawk answered, "I think I'd best get goin', if I'm gonna catch up with those deer." He was almost in the cover of the trees when Blue suddenly jerked his rifle to his shoulder and fired. Anticipating just such a move, Hawk dropped to one knee at the same time he heard Blue's shot rip into the bark of the large tree beside him. Without thinking, he automatically returned fire, his shot catching Blue in the side. By the time Tater brought his rifle to bear, there was no target to shoot at, for Hawk disappeared in the thick forest of firs behind him. So Tater wisely took cover behind a sizable rock.

"Damn it, damn it, damn it," Tater heard Blue moaning as he lay wounded at the rocky edge of the stream. "Tater, I'm shot," he gasped. "I need help."

"How bad is it?" Tater responded. "Can you crawl?"

"No, damn it, I need help," Blue pleaded. "I don't think I can move."

"Just hang on as best you can. If I get out in the open to help you, I'm liable to get shot, too. Might be best for me to go back to the hideout and get the other boys to make sure that jasper ain't settin' there waitin' to pick another one of us off."

"You can't leave me here!" Blue wailed, as he frantically held his side, trying to stop the bleeding that was already forming a shallow scarlet pool in the wet rocks he lay upon. "It's a half hour's ride back to the cabin. I might be dead before you get back."

"You just hang in there, Blue," Tater said, all the while looking right and left for any sign of the man who shot him. He knew he could not stay there behind that rock, in case the man might be moving around in those trees to get a better angle to shoot at him. "He's got us in a tight spot, but I'm gonna go get some help. You just lay low. He'll think you're dead. You've got your rifle handy, so you can shoot him if he comes back. I'll go get the other boys." He started backing away from the rock, intent upon getting back to the horses.

"Tater! You son of a bitch!" Blue cried out, and fired his rifle in Tater's direction, but Tater was already sprinting toward the horses at that point and Blue's shot was nowhere close. The effort he expended caused him to fall back in pain as he grabbed desperately at the wound in his side, trying to stop the bleeding.

On the other side of the creek, Hawk watched Tater's retreat, and when he was sure it was safe, he ran across the stream, leading Rascal, in an attempt to follow him out of the canyon. It was not difficult to follow his trail through the thick growth of trees, because the path of broken branches was obvious enough, especially in Tater's haste to flee. It became more difficult, however, when he came to the edge of the band of trees that wrapped around the mountain and came to a wide meadow. He stopped to look for hoofprints that would tell him in which direction Tater had ridden after leaving the trees. The tracks from two horses led toward another band of trees farther around the mountain. He followed the tracks into the trees until reaching a flat rock ledge that led up to another stream coming down the mountain, and that was where he lost him. There were no tracks on the other side. Did he go upstream or downstream? That was what he had to determine. Maybe, he thought, he may have remained in the water for a long way before coming out again in an effort to lose anyone tailing him. With no option other than to ride up and down the stream, looking for tracks that would tell him where Tater had left the water, Hawk began searching. Unfortunately, the fleeing man had succeeded in disguising his trail, and eventually Hawk had to admit that he had lost him. He turned Rascal back the way they had come, thinking to check on the man Tater had left behind.

As he rode back toward the band of trees on the other side of the meadow, he remembered that the wounded man had cried out that it was half an hour back to the cabin. If that was true, it at least gave him a general area in which to look for this cabin. He was almost certain now that he had, in fact, caught up with two of the five murderers of the group of Friends. Maybe, he hoped, he could get some additional information out of the wounded man back in the stream.

When he approached the edge of the stream, he stopped and dismounted, leaving Rascal in the trees where Blue and Tater had left their horses before. Pausing in the cover of the trees, he watched the still figure lying on the edge of the shallow stream. After a few minutes without any sign of movement, he walked carefully toward the man, ready to react should Blue suddenly raise his rifle to shoot. Still there was no sign of life, so he walked up beside him, then reached down and took the rifle from his dead hands. He had bled to death. "Well, Blue, there's nothin' you can tell me, I reckon," Hawk said softly. Then as a matter of general principle, he took hold of the back of Blue's coat and dragged his body out of the stream, so as not to contaminate the water. From listening to the two men talking back and forth after Blue was shot, he knew that the dead one was Blue, and the one who deserted him was Tater. "That was more than I knew before," he said, then whistled softly and waited for the big buckskin horse to trot up to him. "We've got one more body to take care of," he said to Rascal, and turned to look at the carcass of the doe he had shot. "I still need food."

"What tha . . . ?" Jesse Corbin blurted when Tater rode up to the cabin, leading Blue's horse. "Where's Blue?"

"Blue's dead, or maybe he ain't. I don't know," Tater replied as he stepped down from his horse. He was not inclined to confess that he felt pretty sure that Blue was dead by now. He figured Blue was fading fast when he left. And even if he wasn't, the man in the buckskin shirt would most likely finish him off, probably as soon as he had run off with the horses. "He got shot," he went on, "by some feller down in the canyon. We was chasin' some deer we ran up on, and when we got ready to cross over a stream we saw this feller. Him and Blue shot at each other. He caught Blue in the side, but Blue missed with his shot."

"Booth!" Jesse called for his brother, who was inside the cabin, then turned back to Tater. "What happened to that feller? What about you, did you get him?" His first thought was that somehow, they already had a lawman on their trail.

Tater shook his head as Booth and Trip came out to see what the noise was about. "I couldn't get a shot at him," Tater answered. "He got back in the woods where I couldn't see him."

"Where's Blue?" Booth asked when he saw the horse with an empty saddle. Tater repeated his version of the confrontation with the mysterious man in the canyon. "Why didn't you bring Blue back with you?" Booth asked.

"He didn't wanna be moved," Tater lied. "He was hurt too bad to be moved. Told me to ride back here to get you, said he was dyin', so I did what he wanted me to."

"Damn," Booth swore. This was a situation he hadn't counted on. "Did you get a good look at the man who shot him?" Tater said there wasn't time to get much of a look at him, but he was a big fellow, wearing a buckskin shirt. "White man?" Booth asked, and Tater said that he was. That was not especially good news. Booth would rather have heard it was an Indian Tater and Blue had run into. But it was a white man, so now the question he had was, was the man a lone hunter or a lawman? And if he was a lawman, was he alone, or part of a posse?

"I know what you're thinkin', Booth," Jesse said. "I'm thinkin' the same thing. But I don't see no way a posse could be on our trail this soon—probably not at all. That feller coulda been anybody from that town, just out tryin' to get a deer. It was just bad luck, most likely. Let's saddle up and go get Blue. If that feller's still around, we'll settle up with him. If I had to bet on it, I'd bet he's long gone from that canyon."

"Maybe you're right," Booth allowed, although he was still thinking of other possibilities. He looked back at Tater, frowning as he asked, "What do you think, Tater? You think Blue's gonna make it?"

Tater hesitated a moment before answering. "I swear, Booth, I think ol' Blue's dead. He was dyin' when I came back to tell you. If he wasn't, I'da brought him back somehow."

When Booth hesitated for several moments, his brother asked, "What are you thinkin', Booth?"

"I'm thinkin' about the possibility that there might be a posse settin' out in those woods hopin' we'll come back to get Blue." When Jesse looked as if about to question that possibility, Booth continued, "I know what we just said about the odds against a posse gettin' on our trail, but if Blue's done for already, why even take the chance? I feel bad about Blue, but this is a risky business we're in, and the only way to win is to make sure you don't take risky chances." He asked Tater again, "You feel pretty sure Blue's dead, right?"

"I'm pretty sure," Tater answered. He decided it best to leave out the part of the incident that had really caused the shooting, the part where Hawk had shot the deer. If they thought the man was no more than a lone deer hunter, there might be more questions about his lack of action against the killer. Blue might not be dead, but Tater believed he was in the process. He didn't want to take the chance that Blue might have just enough life left to tell them that Tater had run off and left him.

"Then I reckon it's just as well we play it safe and leave Blue where he is," Booth said.

Having said nothing while he listened to the discussion, Trip Dawson spoke up then. "We might better go back there," he said. Then he walked over to Blue's horse and started searching through his saddlebags. "Never mind," he announced, and held up a canvas sack with Blue's share of the money in it. "I expect we might as well go ahead and split it four ways." Although Trip was the first to say it, the thought of splitting Blue's share of the money was definitely on everyone's mind. There was no further talk of going back to check on him.

"Too bad ol' Blue didn't get to eat any of that deer meat he was cravin'," Tater said, already trying to figure out the answer in his head when four was divided into six thousand.

"What's got you worried, Booth?" Jesse Corbin sat down at the table opposite his brother. He knew Booth well enough to know when there was something eating away at him. "You thinkin' maybe we oughta go back and get Blue?"

Booth met his brother's intense gaze and shook his head. "Nah, I don't give a damn about Blue. If Tater thinks he's dead, then he probably is. It's the feller that shot him I'm worried about. Accordin' to what Tater says, they were crossin' a stream and Blue took a shot at him, and the feller cut Blue down.

What for? That's what I wanna know. Was that feller huntin' deer, or was he huntin' us? The next thing I'm thinkin' is whether or not Tater's led that feller and whoever's with him right here to us."

His speculating planted a seed of doubt in Jesse's mind then. "What are you sayin', Booth? You thinkin' we oughta be gettin' ready in case we're gonna have to stand off a posse?"

Now that Jesse seemed to be concerned as well, Booth answered. "I'm thinkin' a posse, or a bunch of soldiers, could set on both paths to this cabin and catch us like a coon up a tree." When Jesse seemed to be thinking about that, Booth continued, "Oh, we could hold out awhile, but I went to a lot of trouble to get my hands on that money. I'd like to make sure I get to spend some of it. I ain't thinkin' about gettin' ready to hold off a bunch of lawmen in this cabin. I'm thinkin' that the smart thing to do is pack up right now and get the hell outta here before the door's closed on us."

Booth's words had a sobering effect on his brother. The scene he described was not beyond belief. Up until this incident with Blue and Tater, all of them had felt they had gotten away with the massacre of the group of Quakers, with nothing to tie it to them. Then right away, a stranger shows up and one of them is dead. Jesse had always believed in Booth's intuition about making decisions. He saw no reason to go against it now. "Maybe you're right," he decided. "But if we leave right now, where do we go?"

"Well, for right now, we could go to Wolf Creek, to Bodine's. He's made a livin' outta hidin' outlaws. That ain't more'n about sixty miles from here. If we just stop to rest the horses a couple of times, we could ride straight through and be there tomorrow. We can lay around there a day or two and decide where we wanna go to spend some of our money, where there ain't nobody lookin' for us."

"I reckon that might be the smart thing to do," Jesse said. "We might as well pack up right now." He got up from the table. "Listen up, boys. Me and Booth have decided to leave this cabin right now, and head down to Wolf Creek." His announcement caused a look of astonishment on the faces of their two partners, so he explained the reason, just as Booth had convinced him.

"You mean right now?" Trip asked, still confused.

"Just as fast as you can get all your stuff loaded on your horse," Booth answered. "Course, you're free to make your own decision. If you wanna stay here, in case I'm wrong, that's up to you."

"I'm goin' with you," Tater quickly decided.

Trip shrugged. "I reckon I might as well, too."

CHAPTER 8

Hawk's search for the place where the four remaining members of Booth's gang had holed up was now narrowed down somewhat, but still quite a challenge in this remote wilderness. In fact, he could not be certain they were not still on the move. But the conversation he had overheard between Blue and Tater led him to believe they were holed up somewhere for a while. For the time being, however, he had to wait where he was to see if the outlaws came to check on the man Tater had left to die. Things were not working out as he had foreseen. His plan from the beginning was to find the gang's hideout and report it to the military at Fort Benton and leave it to them to make the arrest. But that plan was already upside-down, as a result of his encounter that morning. If the plan was to be followed, he would have to trail them when they came to get Blue and let them lead him to their hideout. He would not hesitate to shoot if he had to, just as he had not hesitated that morning, but he wasn't sure he wanted to take on the role of executioner and try to stalk them individually with the intention of killing all of them.

All these thoughts were making his mind spin, so he decided he would do the one thing he knew was necessary, and that was to take care of the deer he had killed. He couldn't take the time to skin and butcher the animal, but he could at least move the carcass seventy-five yards upstream to his camp, hang it upside down, and gut it. That wouldn't take long, then he could finish the job when he had time later.

After hanging the deer and gutting it, he returned to the crossing to find a place to wait for Booth and his men. After almost three hours waiting on the side of the mountain, watching Blue's body, he decided they were not planning to come after him. It was hard to imagine they wouldn't come back to look for one of their gang, but apparently, they had no interest in that. He still found it hard to believe that, if the two were part of the gang, they wouldn't come looking for him. He reminded himself then of the obvious disregard the gang had for human life and the strong probability that there was no concern even for the loss of one of their number. So, it was beginning to look like he was going to be searching every stream and gully after all, a conclusion he had reached before he shot the deer. Being a practical man, he decided he would go ahead and spend the rest of the day taking care of his meat supply and start his search in the morning. He had the feeling he might be quite some time in finding their hideout.

He decided the place to start his search was at the stream where he had lost Tater the day before. His plan was simple, knowing the cabin he looked for was going to be on a stream, because they had to have water. So, to start, he rode Rascal up the stream, past the point where he had lost Tater's tracks before. He climbed only a couple hundred feet before reaching a rock-faced cliff with a hole where the stream came from underground. He dismounted and examined the ground up to the rocky opening. There was no evidence hinting that Tater had come out of the water there to continue up the mountain. And there would have been plenty of sign left by the two horses had that been the case. There was bare ground on both sides of the stream—their tracks would have been difficult to hide. He stood for a few moments, gazing at the cliff, and he knew for sure the two horses didn't jump thirty feet from the water to the rocky face of the cliff. He turned around and went back down the stream. After riding down the stream until it reached the valley, he gave up on it and continued on around the mountain, looking for another stream.

After weaving his way through the thick band of trees along the base of the chain of foothills without striking what could be considered a healthy stream, he stopped to consider. He reminded himself that he had overheard Blue crying out that it was a thirty-minute ride back to the cabin. If that was true, then the stream he had just left had to be the only one the cabin was on. He had to figure he had missed the tracks he was looking for, so he decided to turn back and look again. He had a strong feeling now that the cabin he looked for was high up the mountain before the stream went underground. One thing for sure, when he had been standing there, watching the water splash out of the face of that cliff, there was no way to climb up that way. The challenge was to find out how Tater had ridden up to the cabin. There was evidently an easier way up. So, Hawk turned around and went back the way he had come. Upon reaching the creek again, he rode up it until coming to the spot where he had lost Tater's trail. Just before reaching the cliff, the trail had crossed a rocky shelf that stopped at the stream. He had assumed that Tater had continued on across the shelf to the stream. But he had found no tracks on the other side of the stream. On foot now, he backtracked the trail, looking for some sign that would tell him Tater had left the trail before he reached the stream.

While Rascal drank from the stream, Hawk walked back across the rocks once again looking for sign he felt had to be there. Walking almost to the start of the rocky ledge, he stopped short when he saw it, a narrow path that started between two boulders. When he first glanced at it, it appeared to be nothing more than a path into the solid face of the rock wall. When he walked over to stand inside the boulders, he discovered a passage that led around the rock wall. *Well, I'll be . . .* he thought, because he knew he had found the path to the hideout. There were no tracks on the flat rock shelf. He whistled softly, and the big buckskin came to him at once. Due to the narrowness of the path, he thought it better to lead Rascal. Even then, it was a tight fit for a horse. He tried to imagine five men with packhorses negotiating the constricting double turns before reaching the upper end of the rock formation. Once clear of the rocks, the path, though not so confining, was still well hidden as it climbed up through the trees and away from the stream.

Since he had no idea how far the path led, he

stopped to listen when he heard the sound of gushing water. It came from a source about fifty feet to his right, and he realized then that he was even with the spot where the stream emerged from under the ground. It was the sound of the water splashing on the rocky shelf at the foot of the cliff. The thought occurred to him that he might be in one hell of a spot if he suddenly met the four outlaws coming down from the cabin. With that in mind, he carried his rifle in his right hand, ready to drop Rascal's reins from his left, should the meeting occur. Aware that the path was angling back toward the stream now, he continued for another thirty yards when he caught a glimpse of the cabin through the trees ahead. He stopped immediately, lest they might hear him climbing up the trail. He dropped Rascal's reins to the ground and gave the buckskin a few reassuring pats to keep him quiet. Then he continued the climb toward the cabin, moving carefully in case there was a surprise encounter, hoping, if there were one, they might be more surprised than he.

So far, so good, he thought when there were no inquisitive whinnies from any horses above him. Able to see most of the cabin now, he paused to consider what his situation really was. There was no apparent activity outside the rough log cabin and no sign of any horses, but from where he stood, he couldn't see what was behind the cabin. There was no smoke coming from the chimney, and as chilly as it was, there should have been. To make sure they were all inside, he thought it best to leave the path and make his way a little higher up, so he could see the back of the cabin. After climbing a little farther up the mountain, he moved in a little closer, where he could see the stream running

beside the cabin to form a little pool just before it went
underground. He could also see there was no one
there, since there were no horses anywhere about.

Reasonably sure the cabin was empty, but cautious
nevertheless, he moved down through the trees, his
gaze focused on the door, ready to open fire if suddenly surprised. With his rifle leveled before him, he
opened the door to find the cabin deserted. They were
gone, but for how long? Looking around the rough
structure, he saw no clothes, bedding, or anything that
would indicate the occupants would be coming back.
He went to the fireplace and tested the ashes. They
told him that there had been no fire rekindled that
morning, that the fire had been allowed to go out
during the night. *So, they either left last night or before
breakfast this morning,* he thought. And from the looks
of the cabin, they weren't planning to come back. *Good
thing I didn't ride back to Fort Benton and tell them where
they could find Booth and his gang.* As soon as he thought
it, he decided that his plan to find the killers for the
army to arrest was not likely to have resulted in bringing the guilty parties to trial, anyway. So now, standing
in an empty hideout, it was time to make a decision.
As Conner would advise, should he forget about something that was not his responsibility in the first place,
and go home? Or should he make it his business to
see that the four remaining members of the gang paid
for their atrocious crimes? "Hell, I shot one of the son
of a bitches," he announced to the cold fireplace. It
wasn't enough to satisfy him that justice had come to
only one of them, however. The problem now, if he decided to continue to tail them, was the fact that they were
gone and he had no idea where they might be heading.

Thinking all good hideouts had a backdoor escape

route, he decided to look for this one. Surely there was an easier way up and down this mountain, he thought, after just having climbed the almost impossible trail up. He went back outside and whistled Rascal up from the path below. Leading the buckskin, he walked around to the back of the cabin, where he immediately saw a path leading down the mountain. There was no evidence that they had tried to hide the path, for hoofprints were obvious. "Might as well see where this comes out," he said to Rascal. Again thinking of the tight crooks and turns of the rocky passage he had followed up from the stream, he figured this back path was not the way the gang had come up the mountain. The way he had come up was most likely the back door and an escape route.

He had descended for no more than thirty-five or forty yards when Rascal nickered several times. Well accustomed to being alerted by the buckskin when another horse was near, Hawk stopped at once. Thinking Booth was coming back, he led Rascal off the path far enough so as not to be seen right away, then he drew his rifle and went back to kneel beside the path. In a couple of minutes, he saw him coming up the path. A bowlegged, gray-bearded little man, dressed from head to foot in animal hides, was leading a horse. Behind the horse, on a lead rope, a mule followed. It was easy for Hawk to make a quick assumption that he was not looking at a member of Booth's gang. With his rifle ready to fire, just in case, Hawk rose to his feet and stepped onto the path.

"Whoa!" The little man stopped abruptly and threw up his hands. "Don't shoot! I was just bringin' your mule back! I found him runnin' through the woods down at the foot of the hill. Figured he musta got loose."

Hawk lowered his rifle and walked toward the man. Hawk had a pretty good idea why the mule was running loose. "Sorry," he said, "didn't mean to startle you. That ain't my mule."

Relieved to see that he might not be in any trouble, the man looked Hawk up and down. "I ain't never seen you before. You wasn't with them other fellers up at the cabin, was you? You thinkin' 'bout movin' in up there?"

"Nope," Hawk answered, "I'm just tryin' to catch up with them." He could see by the expression on the man's face that his answer was good news.

"Are you a lawman?" Again, Hawk said no, so the odd little man started talking. "I've had my eye on that cabin up there for a long time. My name's Davey Crabb, and I've been trappin', huntin', and prospectin' in these mountains for a helluva long time. The feller that built that cabin was kilt by a bear, and I kilt the bear that et him. I figured he'd want me to have his cabin, so I decided to move in, but I had to go get all my possibles from my shack over near Signal Mountain. This place here is closer to a town and the tradin' post I trade with. And don't you know, by the time I got back, there was four fellers holed up in that cabin. Where they came from, I don't know, but I knew they weren't there permanent. Hell, they didn't do no mining or trappin', just laid around doin' nothin'. So, I figured they was outlaws, hidin' out. Feller that built the shack, name of Sam Davis, had a brother that was an outlaw. I know that for a fact. So I figured that one of 'em mighta been his brother. I kept my eye on 'em, even came back to the cabin a couple of times when they were gone. But they still had their stuff there, so I was afraid to move in. Good thing I didn't, too, 'cause this time when they came back there was five of 'em." He finally stopped to take a breath then. "I reckon I've been runnin' off at the mouth," he said. "What's your name, young feller? Are you a lawman?" he asked again.

"My name's Hawk," he said. "No, I ain't a lawman. I'm just tryin' to catch up with the men you've been talkin' about. And I can tell you that the cabin is empty, looks like they ain't plannin' to come back. Maybe you can help me out." He figured Crabb must have seen Booth and the others ride out, or he would hardly be riding up the back trail to the cabin. "How'd you know they were gone for good this time?"

"'Cause this time they were leading all their pack-horses behind 'em and they was loaded down," Crabb declared. "I still weren't sure, though, 'cause there weren't but four of 'em. I thought the other'un musta stayed up there, but I thought I'd take a look—tell him I was bringin' his mule back, if he was still there. You liked to scare the pee outta me when you stepped outta the bushes."

"When did you see 'em leave?"

"Yesterday 'bout noon," Crabb answered.

That would mean they had left soon after Tater got back. "You have any idea which way those four men were headin'?"

"I can't say where they're headin'," Crabb replied. "But when I saw 'em, they were goin' down the trail that'll take you to Alvin Peavy's tradin' post on the Sun River. That's where I trade my pelts."

"I'd be obliged if you'd show me where I can strike that trail," Hawk said.

"No trouble findin' that trail," Crabb said. "You

take this one on down to the valley. You'll see where the trail comin' around the mountain forks, one headin' east to Choteau, the other'un headin' south. That south trail goes right to Alvin's place."

"How far is it to the Sun River?" Hawk asked.

"From here, I make it a long half day, about thirty miles, I expect."

That was pretty close to what Hawk would have guessed. "Much obliged, Davey. I hope you don't have any more visitors up here."

"You best be careful, Mr. Hawk," Crabb replied. "Those fellers look like they could give a man all the trouble he can handle."

Hawk whistled for Rascal, and as always, the buckskin responded immediately, suddenly emerging from the thicket of pines beside the path and coming to a stop beside Hawk. "I'll do that, Davey. You take care of yourself."

"Always do," the little man said softly as he watched Hawk disappear down the path.

Coming out of the trees at the base of the mountain, Hawk saw the obvious trail, just as Crabb had said it would be. Since it was leading in the direction he needed to go to get back to his camp, he followed it around to the fork, then took the trail heading almost straight south. He stayed on that trail until reaching the stream that ran through the canyon where he had made his camp. He left the trail then and followed the stream up past the crossing where he shot Blue Davis. He continued on to his camp, where he was happy to see his supply of meat, wrapped in the hide and still hanging undisturbed from a tree limb. With apologies to Rascal for the extra weight, he loaded the horse with the meat and his other supplies, then rode back down the creek to the Sun River trail. There was still half a day's worth of daylight left, so he figured he might as well start out for Peavy's trading post.

Close to the same time Hawk was setting out for Alvin Peavy's trading post on the Sun River, the four men he chased arrived at Rufus Bodine's store at Wolf Creek, sixty miles away. Ready for a drink of the rotgut Bodine sold for whiskey, Tater led them inside and headed straight for the saloon side of the room. Standing behind the counter in the general store half of the building, Bodine gave him no more than a nod for a welcome, having never seen Tater before. He followed Tater over to the saloon side, and when he looked back to see the three men following, he at once recognized two of them. He stopped and scowled, which was his version of a smile. "Well, well, if it ain't the Corbin boys," he greeted them then. "It's been a right long spell since you two passed this way."

"About two years, I expect," Booth responded. "How you makin' out, Bodine?"

"Better'n ever," Bodine answered. "I see you're travelin' with a couple of friends. Tell you the truth, I figured you boys had finally got yourselves caught, figured you might be in prison. I'm right glad to see you again. Figure you've come back to pay me for them forty-eight dollars' worth of horse feed and supplies you forgot you owed when you left that morning."

Remembering only then that he and Jesse had sneaked out early that morning two years ago, Booth was quick to reply. "That's exactly right. Me and Jesse said we had to get back here as soon as we could to

settle that bill with you. Matter of fact, we was thinkin'
we oughta pay you double that amount, since it took
us so long to get back to this part of the territory. Or,
I'll tell you what, knowin' you're a sportin' man, I'll
give us a hundred dollars and you pour us all one
drink of likker. How's that?"

"By God, that's fair enough, all right." Bodine was
surprised, to say the least, when Booth counted out
the money from a sizable roll in his pocket. Bodine
hurried over behind the bar and pulled a bottle from
a shelf underneath. "This is the good stuff," he said as
he poured four shots. He paused to watch Booth's
men toss the whiskey back. "You boys musta been
havin' a little luck lately."

"I reckon you could say that, wouldn't you say,
Jesse?" He looked at his brother and grinned. Back to
Bodine, he said, "You know Jesse. Say howdy to Trip
Dawson and Tater Thompson."

Bodine nodded to each of them in turn. "Glad to
have you boys come by. You plannin' on stayin' awhile?
I've still got them two cabins back down the creek.
Ain't nobody in 'em right now. Or, I've got two rooms
upstairs over the saloon that ain't occupied right now."

Booth watched Bodine pour another shot in the
four glasses before answering. "Don't know for sure, a
couple of days, I reckon, till we decide where we wanna
go. I reckon we'd rather take one of the cabins."

Almost drooling after seeing the roll of money that
came out of Booth's pocket, Bodine was eager to persuade the four outlaws to stay longer. "The big cabin's
in pretty good shape and there's a good-sized stack of
firewood ready for the fireplace, good grass for your
horses, and room in the back room for your saddles

and such. I've got me a gal workin' here since you've been here—name's Josie Johnson. She's a lot younger'n she looks." When Tater and Trip looked around the room to see her, Bodine said, "She ain't here right now. And you ain't likely to get no better vittles than comes outta my kitchen. My wife, Dinah Belle, is still doin' the cookin'."

Booth remembered Dinah Belle's cooking. It was fit to eat. That was about the most you could say for it. With a name like that, it was only natural that all the boys called her Dinner Bell. "Well, you talked me into it," Booth joked. "We'll move in the big cabin for a while, give you a little business."

"You'll get your money's worth," Bodine boasted. "I'll tell Dinah Belle she's gonna need to fix enough supper for four hungry fellers. She'll be tickled to do it."

"Good," Booth said. "Is that cabin locked?" When told that the door was open, he said, "All right, we'll move in and take care of our horses, then I expect we'll be back pretty quick for supper." He grabbed the bottle off the bar and the four walked out.

Bodine stood there, grinning to himself with antici- pation at the thought of separating Booth and his gang from their money, then he turned and went into the kitchen. Before he could speak, Dinah Belle blurted, "I heard. It's gonna take me a little time to fix enough for that bunch. It's a good thing I've got a helluva lot of cornmeal. I'll fill 'em up on corn bread."

"Do the best you can, honeypot, those jaspers are carryin' a lot of money. They musta hit a bank or somethin', if they're all totin' money like ol' Booth flashed. And that's just what he was totin' in his pocket. We need to get Josie on her feet again to keep those ol' boys buyin' whiskey."

"She's been huggin' that bed long enough," Dinah Belle said. "She claimed she was havin' female problems, but I know she ain't had any of them problems in years. She just don't wanna help out in the kitchen. I'll get her up."

"Reckon you'd better. Those boys will be back here lookin' for whiskey and supper."

CHAPTER 9

Although carrying a heavier load than usual, Rascal was willing and gave no sign of fatigue. It was not the first time on this patrol that Hawk wished he had his packhorse. Whether the horse was weary or not, Hawk was glad to see the trees that bordered the Sun River, because he was tired of riding. Then it occurred to him that he had eaten nothing all day, even though Rascal was carrying a bundle of deer meat. As Hawk neared what appeared to be a bend in the river, he caught sight of the trading post. It was time to be cautious again. He had not been this far up the Sun River before, so he had no knowledge of Alvin Peavy, or his trading post, other than the fact that Davey Crabb traded his pelts there. From what he could see from the trail, the store appeared to be fairly busy. There were three horses tied at a hitching rail out front and a wagon parked beside the porch, but there would have been more horses if he had caught up with Booth. *Maybe,* he thought, *Peavy must sell a little whiskey along with his other goods.*

He was a little anxious to find out if Booth had actually come this way, afraid that he might have spent half a day on a blind chase. He shrugged, remembering what Crabb had said, that he knew which trail Booth took, but he didn't know where he was heading. "Wonder if they sell supper," he said to Rascal. "Don't worry, I'm gonna let you take a long rest. I'll buy you some grain, if they've got any." He nudged the buckskin gently with his heels and rode down the path to the store.

"Howdy do, stranger," Alvin Peavy greeted him cordially when he walked in the store. "Don't believe you've stopped in before."

"Reckon not," Hawk replied while Peavy looked him up and down. "First time I've been this far up the Sun."

"Well, you've come to the right place to get whatever you're lookin' for," Peavy boasted. "If you're needin' supplies, I've got a good stock of most everyday needs. If you're lookin' to wet your whistle, the bar's on the other side of the store."

"I can see that," Hawk said, and he glanced toward the other side of the big room where there were customers sitting at a couple of the four small tables. "Looks like you do a pretty good business here. I expect you mighta seen a party of four fellers come this way in the last day or two, one of 'em sportin' a fancy mustache with the ends curled up," he said, thinking back on Donald Lewis's description of David Booth.

"Yep, they were here late yesterday evenin'," Peavy said. "Are you a lawman?"

"Nope, I'm just tryin' to catch up with 'em. Did you see which way they went when they left here?"

"I'm pretty sure they crossed the river and stayed on the trail to the Missouri River," Peavy answered.

"Like I said, I ain't been over this way before. Where does that trail strike the Missouri?"

"Wolf Creek," Peavy answered. "You goin' after 'em right away, or are you gonna stay with us awhile?"

"Well, I know where Wolf Creek is," Hawk said, then answered his question. "I think I'll camp here tonight. I rode my horse pretty hard today, so I'll let him rest up for tomorrow. If you've got any oats, or other grain, I'd like to buy some from you." He nodded toward the barroom side of the building. "I might like a drink of likker, but I'd better have some supper before I take a drink on my empty stomach."

"We can fix you up with both of those," Peavy was quick to reply. "My wife, Louella, has a big pot of beef stew on the stove and fifty cents will buy you a plate of it and a cup of coffee to wash it down."

"That sounds to my likin'," Hawk said. "It'll give me a little break from deer meat and bacon."

"Good," Peavy said. "Set yourself down at one of the tables over yonder and I'll tell Louella to get you some supper."

Hawk walked over to one of the empty tables next to the one where two men were playing checkers, and pulled a chair back. He returned the friendly nod from one of the two men before taking off his hat and hanging it on the back of an empty chair before sitting down. In a few minutes, a tall, bony woman with flaming red hair came from the kitchen with a cup of coffee for him. "You want bread?" she asked, her face expressionless. When Hawk said that he did, she turned around and went back to the kitchen. After a few more minutes, she returned with a bowl of stew with two biscuits sitting on top and placed the bowl on the table. She paused for a second as if to see if he had any comments or questions. Then, without a word, she turned around and went back to the kitchen.

He had finished almost all of the bowl of stew when the man who had nodded to him looked at him and grinned. "Ol' Red's a pretty good cook, ain't she?"

"I'd have to say so," Hawk replied. "Course, I ain't an expert on anything but the beef stew." He gave the gray-haired little man a friendly smile, then went back to work on the stew.

"That looks like a hawk feather in your hat there," the man said. It was obvious to Hawk that he just wanted to make a little conversation with a stranger.

"That's right," Hawk said. "It's a hawk feather." It prompted him to think about Winter Flower and wonder if she had recovered mentally from her ordeal at the hands of Luke and his partner.

"My name's Earl Belcher. Don't mean to be nosy, but does it mean somethin' special?" the man asked, still intent upon making conversation.

"No, I reckon not," Hawk replied. "I just thought I'd stick it on my hat." In fact, the feather held many meanings, all of them special to him, but none he felt like sharing.

"I think I'll try to find me a feather for my hat," the little man said. "Maybe it would bring me luck. Whaddaya think, Jack?"

His friend chuckled and replied, "You've already had all the luck in this game of checkers, enough to cost me thirty-five cents."

"Whoo, boy!" one of the three men drinking at the next table taunted. "How 'bout that, Lige? Those two old ladies have been playin' high-stakes checkers and the prissy one is holdin' thirty-five cents in prize money."

"He best be lookin' out for somebody wantin' to rob him, if he leaves here totin' all that cash," Lige responded. All three at the table enjoyed a big laugh. The two checkers players ignored the taunting, but Lige was liquored up just enough to amuse himself by intimidating two men who were obviously old enough to be his father. "How 'bout it, old man? You need somebody to walk you home, so no booger-bears don't get you?" He paused after he said it when he wondered, "Where the hell did you ladies come from, anyway? There ain't no houses around here."

It was obvious that the taunting wasn't going to stop, so Earl decided to respond. "All right, mister, you and your friends have had a little laugh, so why don't you get back to your drinkin' and mind your own business? And we'll mind ours. We'll be leavin' in a little while, anyway."

His response seemed to make Lige mad. "Did you hear what that old fart said, Clell? Told us to mind our own business." He turned a menacing frown on Earl and demanded, "I don't want you hangin' around in here where men are drinkin', so I reckon you'd best get your scrawny behind outta my sight right now. That's my own business."

Hawk, an interested observer to that point, said nothing, hoping for Earl and his friend's sake that it would amount to nothing more than talk. He looked back toward the general merchandise side of the store to see if Peavy was aware of the trouble. If he was, he showed no evidence of it. Although painfully outmatched, it was apparent that Earl Belcher was not one to slink cowardly out of a saloon. And judging by the determined look on his friend's face, neither was he. *This could be trouble,* was Hawk's immediate thought.

"Mister," Earl began, "I understand that the likker is doin' most of the talkin' comin' outta your mouth. But I'll decide when I wanna leave this place, and it won't be when some drunk tells me to."

Taken aback by the feisty little man's refusal to be intimidated, Lige paused a moment to make sure he had heard him correctly. "Well, old man, that's even better." He looked at his partners. "Ain't it, boys? I reckon we'll just have to throw you two out." He and his two partners got up from the table, prompting Earl and his friend to get up as well, preparing to stand their ground. Their show of resistance caused Lige to laugh, then remark, "Too bad for you that's it's gonna be three of us against two of you old sodbusters, ain't it?"

That was about as far as Hawk was willing to let the confrontation progress. "It'll be three against three," he said as he stood up. There was an immediate silence as both sides of the squabble were taken by surprise. Hawk took a couple of steps over to stand beside Earl and Jack, his imposing stature seeming to dwarf his two partners. "We might as well make it a fair fight," he said to Lige.

The third member of the troublemakers, Pete Whalen, had been a silent participant to that point. Of the three, he seemed to be the only one who recognized the lethal aura of the man with the feather in his hat. "No need to get stirred up over a little japin' here," he said. "Lige and Clell were just funnin' with you two old fellers. Ain't no need for this to go any further, right, Lige?"

"That's right," Lige said as he took a closer look at

the tall man in the buckskin shirt. "We was just funnin' with these two fellers."

"I think we was about ready to go, weren't we, Lige?" Pete asked, just noticing Alvin Peavy, finally aware of the potential for trouble, and standing at the doorway, shotgun in hand. When Lige looked toward him, he nodded in Peavy's direction.

"Right," Lige said at once. "I ain't got no reason to hang around here any longer." He glanced at Clell. "Let's get the hell outta here." Pete started for the door and Clell followed. Lige couldn't resist a side remark to Hawk as he followed his partners out. "Next time, stranger."

"Look forward to it," Hawk returned.

When the three walked out, Earl turned to Hawk and extended his hand. "Mister, I think you just saved me and Jack from gettin' our butts kicked at best, and maybe a shot in the head at worse. What is your name?"

"John Hawk," he said, and shook Earl's hand, then shook Jack's as well.

"Well, John Hawk, I'd like to buy you a drink, if we can get Alvin to put his shotgun down and pour us one."

"Much obliged," Hawk said, then asked, "You ever see those fellows before?"

"No, never seen 'em in here before. Have you, Jack?" Jack said that he had not, and Earl went on, "Me and Jack are tryin' to raise cattle back down the river a few miles from here, and if you're not in a hurry to get somewhere, you're welcome to rest up at our place."

"That's mighty decent of you," Hawk said, "but I am in kind of a hurry. Thank you just the same. And I expect my horse might come in here after me, if I don't get out there and take care of him pretty soon." He stayed long enough to have the drink that Earl wanted to buy him, then he took his leave. He wanted to find a spot to camp, so he could rest Rascal before much longer, so he stopped at the front counter only long enough to pick up a sack of oats and pay for his supper.

"Much obliged," Peavy said when he took the money for the oats but gave his supper money back. "Supper's on the house. That was a helluva thing you done for those fellers, and you likely saved me from gettin' mixed up in some real trouble with those three jaspers."

"I 'preciate it," Hawk said. "Seem like two nice fellows. It wouldn't have been a fair fight." Peavy looked puzzled when he drew his .44 from his holster and cocked it as he walked out the door. He stopped as soon as he was outside and stood for a few minutes in the shadow of the porch, waiting for his eyes to adjust to the gathering darkness. He stepped down from the porch just as Lige popped out from behind a tree at the corner of the building. With no more than an instant to react, Hawk fired a shot that caught Lige in the shoulder, causing him to yelp in pain and send his shot into the dirt at his feet. Hawk dropped the sack of oats and sank to one knee, his Colt cocked, and aimed at the corner of the store, but neither one of the other two appeared. In the quiet after the two shots, he could hear them frantically imploring Lige to hurry. So, he moved cautiously toward the corner of the store but arrived just in time to see the three of them galloping away. One of them was slumped over, hugging his horse's neck. He guessed that to be Lige.

He thought about taking a couple of shots at them but figured a bullet in Lige's shoulder was enough to settle it.

He walked back to pick up his sack of oats just as Peavy, Earl, and Jack deemed it safe to stick their necks outside. "Hot damn!" Earl exclaimed. "Are you all right?"

"Yep," Hawk answered as he tied the sack of oats on his saddle horn. "I keep loadin' this horse up with supplies and I ain't gonna have room to sit in the saddle."

"We heard two shots," Peavy said, then waited for an explanation.

"Yeah, one of 'em was waiting to take a shot at me when I walked out. I figure it was most likely Lige. I put one round in him, got him in the shoulder, I think. I kinda thought he might try something like that, but I expect that'll do it for him." He nodded once and smiled. "Well, maybe I'll be back this way sometime." He climbed up into the saddle. "Tell your wife she makes the best beef stew in the territory." He wheeled Rascal away from the hitching rail and rode up the path, back to the wagon track.

"I swear, I never thought that jasper would try to shoot that Hawk feller," Peavy remarked as the three of them watched him till he rode out on the road.

"He acted like that was the sorta thing that happened every day," Earl said.

"It's a damn good thing he showed up here for supper," Jack declared. "I was fixin' to stand with you, but I was surely expectin' a real ass-whuppin' from the likes of those three."

Hawk followed the road to the river and was relieved

to find a shallow crossing, so he didn't get his meat and other possibles wet. Once across, he left the road and set out along the riverbank until he came to a spot that suited him. Before doing anything else, he pulled the saddle off Rascal and let him go to water. Then he built his fire.

CHAPTER 10

He passed a peaceful night on the bank of the Sun River, waking with the first light of morning. He had taken the precaution of making his bed in a gully, away from his campfire, in case he'd guessed wrong about Lige and his two friends. He had felt that the three roughnecks were more accustomed to bullying people like Earl and Jack, and that the wound Lige suffered would be enough to discourage any more trouble to come his way. And since there was no visit from them during the night, he figured he was done with them. According to what Alvin Peavy had told him, it was about thirty miles from his store to Wolf Creek, not even a day's journey on horseback. But Hawk decided to delay his breakfast until he had ridden about halfway. It would be easier on Rascal, and he should still get there before very late in the afternoon. The big buckskin had enjoyed a hearty meal of oats the night before, so he should be ready to ride.

It was a clearly defined road leading to the Missouri at Wolf Creek, with plenty of tracks in both directions. When he started out that morning, he had walked a little way, so he could take a look at those tracks. But

he soon decided they could tell him nothing, except
that a good many horses had traveled south on the
road. He could not be sure he was looking at Booth's
tracks or somebody else's. So, he stepped up into the
saddle and started for Wolf Creek, thinking maybe
someone might tell him which way Booth went from
there. That thought automatically brought to mind
one Rufus Bodine, and he had to wonder if Rufus was
still alive. He couldn't help thinking that there was an
awfully good chance somebody had shot the ornery
son of a bitch. The last time he had been in Rufus's
trading post was probably at least four years before.
He and his Blackfoot friend Bloody Hand had gone
there to trade some deer hides, and it had not been a
genial transaction. It was the winter before Hawk
began his service as a scout for the army, the same
year Bloody Hand, along with all the other younger
men, left their village to escape life on a reservation.
He and Bloody Hand had spent the better part of a
month hunting in the Big Belt Mountains. It had
been a good hunt and provided a good supply of deer
meat and some elk for old Walking Owl's village.
Rufus Bodine's trading post at Wolf Creek was the
closest place to trade the many hides they had col-
lected. Hawk unconsciously shook his head when he
thought about it. Bodine was not willing to give a
fair price for the pelts. But more than that, he was
blatantly arrogant in his attitude toward the Blackfoot
hunters, as he thought both were. Before it was over,
Hawk had to restrain Bloody Hand from attacking
Bodine and adding his scalp to their supply of hides.
They managed to withdraw without spilling any blood
and took their hides thirty miles downriver, almost to
Great Falls, to trade them. "That was before you took

up with me," he told Rascal. "Maybe he's mellowed a little since that time."

After a ride of close to nineteen or twenty miles across an open prairie of rolling hills, devoid of any meaningful tree growth, he spotted what appeared to be a sizable creek ahead. "Just about right," he announced to Rascal. "We'll find us a good spot and I'm gonna eat some of that deer meat you're totin'." When he reached the creek, he saw obvious signs that more than a few travelers had stopped on the banks to rest their horses. He turned Rascal upstream from the road and rode about a hundred yards before finding the spot that suited him. The notion to check the ashes of the old campfires close to the road never entered his mind. There was nothing cold ashes could tell him. He already knew he was a day, maybe a day and a half, behind the four outlaws. So, at this particular point, his interest was directed toward a clean campsite with grass for his horse and easy access to the water. While the buckskin was drinking water, Hawk gathered wood for his fire and soon had his little coffeepot working away. With some strips of venison roasting over the fire, he felt a sense of real contentment, like that he had when he had hunted with Bloody Hand. For days prior to this morning, his mind had wrestled with the question of whether or not it was his responsibility to continue following Booth. He had not been appointed by any authority to follow the four murderers. But he felt that, if he gave up the chase, then Booth and his cutthroats would likely disappear, never to answer for their evil crimes against the defenseless Quakers. So he had made his decision, and now he was at peace with it, so much so that he drifted off to sleep watching his horse grazing close to the creek.

He was awakened by the sound of Rascal pulling up grass close to his feet. His first reaction was to wonder how long he had been asleep. He looked up at the sun before checking his pocket watch. His watch read half past twelve. He had slept away the morning. His next thought was one of disbelief, for he was never one to sleep in the daytime. Now disgusted with himself for sleeping, he announced to the buckskin, "It's a damn good thing there ain't nobody tracking me 'cause I expect you'd have a new owner right now."

Ready to ride again, he was pouring water on his fire when he was startled to hear the sound of voices. At once alert, he pulled his rifle from the saddle sling and listened. In a matter of minutes, he heard the voices again, and he was sure they came from the road. His first thought was that Lige and his friends had gotten on his trail, after all. So, leaving his horse where it was, he made his way back down the creek bank on foot in case they were following his trail from the road. When about thirty yards from the road, he could see the source of the voices. It was not Lige and his friends at all. It was a wagon, with one man driving, stopped at the edge of the creek while the horses were drinking.

Thinking he might get a closer look, Hawk moved up behind a bank of berry bushes and stopped to decide if he was going to announce his presence or simply return to get his horse. While he was deciding, he was distracted by a movement in the bushes several yards ahead of him. A moment later he was surprised by a man's voice. "If you're fixin' to shoot me, just let me finish takin' this dump, will ya? I ain't been able to get my bowels to move nothin' more'n deer pellets for a week, and I'd surely appreciate the time to enjoy this'un when I finally got an honest-to-God call."

Hawk couldn't think how to reply for a second. When he did, he found it hard not to laugh. "I didn't know you were squattin' there in the bushes. I just came to see who was talkin' over here 'cause I didn't hear you when you first drove up. If you're just takin' a dump, I ain't ever shot anybody for that, so you go ahead and take your time. I'll go back and get my horse."

"Much obliged," the man in the bushes said. Hawk turned around and went back to get Rascal.

When he returned, the two men were waiting for him beside the wagon, so he rode up before them and stepped down. The one who had been watering the horses was a young man, hardly more than a boy, Hawk decided. The other one, the one in the bushes, was a gray-haired old man whom Hawk guessed to be the boy's grandfather. "I wanna beg your pardon for walkin' in on your privacy, but damned if I knew you were there."

"No harm done," the old man replied. "I finished her off fine and dandy." He gave Hawk a good looking over, then asked, "What was you doin' back up the creek?"

"I just stopped to rest my horse and make a little coffee," Hawk answered, amused by the old man's bluntness. "And I wanted to get a little way up the creek, instead of stoppin' here where everybody else has camped." He grinned at the old man then. "Why did you go so far back in the bushes to do your business?"

"'Cause it ain't fittin' to do it where everybody camps." He looked at Hawk as if he couldn't believe anyone had to ask that question. "Which way you headin', north or south?"

"Figured I'd ride down to Wolf Creek," Hawk answered. "Looks like you fellows are headin' in the same direction. How far is it from here, say, to Rufus Bodine's place? That is, if he's still there."

"I hope to hell he is," the old man replied. "We ain't been there in a couple of months, and it's the only place we can buy flour and salt and such as that. Ain't that right, Thomas?"

"That's right, Grandpa," Thomas replied. Up to that point, those were the first words spoken by the young man. But like his grandfather, Thomas had looked Hawk over, from the hawk feather in his hat, to the toes of his boots. He and his grandpa most always saw drifters hanging around Bodine's store, and most of them looked to be someone the law might be interested in. He wondered if Hawk was another of the typical saddle tramps who gathered there. Answering Hawk's question, he said, "Bodine's is about eight miles from here. And I expect we'd best get goin', if we're gonna make it there in time for Mr. Pressley to take care of that loose shoe."

"It's been a long time since I was in Wolf Creek," Hawk said. "Who's Mr. Pressley?"

Thomas seemed reluctant to answer Hawk's questions, but he politely responded. "Reuben Pressley, he's the blacksmith. One of our horses is tryin' to throw a shoe and we was figurin' on gettin' Mr. Pressley to fix it while we're here. Our farm is too far for him to come out there, so we have to come to him. But he don't charge much, so he might just let us owe him till we get some money."

From the look of confusion on the old man's face

after Thomas's answer, Hawk realized what the young man was thinking. "Thomas, are you concerned that I might be gettin' ready to rob you and your grandpa?" Judging by the look of alarm on Thomas's face, he figured he had hit the nail on the head. Thomas didn't have an answer for him, so Hawk said, "You've got nothing to worry about from me. Robbin' folks ain't my callin'. I'm a scout for the army, workin' outta Fort Ellis, down on the Yellowstone."

"What's the matter with you, boy?" His grandpa spoke up then. "I knew right off this feller ain't one of them saddle tramps that hang around Bodine's." He stuck his hand out toward Hawk. "My name's Jacob Woodley, and that's my grandson, Thomas."

"John Hawk," he said as he shook Jacob's hand. "Pleased to meet you, sir."

Not totally convinced that he and his grandpa weren't in danger from this formidable-looking stranger, Thomas reminded his grandpa, "We'd best get goin' or Mr. Pressley might not get to our horses today."

"Then I reckon we'd best jump in the wagon," Jacob said, as cheerfully as if on his way to a county fair. "How 'bout it, Mr. Hawk? We'd be glad to have you ride along with us, seein' as how we're all headin' to the same place."

"Might as well," Hawk said, and stepped up into the saddle again. He figured it might be a good idea to ride into Bodine's beside the farm wagon, in case Booth might be watching for anyone following him. This was in spite of the fact that Tater could identify him, if he was the one who happened to spot him.

* * *

Hawk was surprised to see a few changes at Bodine's as he rode in beside Jacob and Thomas. He saw the blacksmith's shop next to the barn, as well as several outbuildings that weren't standing when last he was there. It reflected Rufus Bodine's prosperity at a time when the fur-trading business was no longer a major industry. It left little doubt in Hawk's mind that the largest part of Bodine's income had to come from outlaws on the run. And he fully expected to find that Booth and his three partners had come here. The question now was whether or not they were still here.

When they pulled into Bodine's, Thomas drove the wagon straight to the blacksmith's shop while Hawk left Rascal at the hitching post in front of the trading post. Taking note of the one horse tied there, a black gelding with a fancy hand-tooled saddle, he deliberately drew the Winchester from his saddle sling. Jacob stepped down from the wagon and left Thomas to talk to Reuben Pressley while he went to the store. "I'll be there directly, Grandpa," Thomas called after him. "Just go in the store part."

In the saloon, Bodine and his wife were standing at the bar talking to Booth Corbin, who had come to pick up a bottle of whiskey to take back to the cabin. The conversation was mainly about Booth's appearance. "I swear, I didn't know it was you when I first looked up," Dinah Belle claimed. She beamed broadly. "Did you, Rufus?"

"Well, he looked different, but I knew it was him," Bodine said. "Why'd you shave it off?"

"I don't know, just tired of messin' with it, I reckon." He reached up and stroked his upper lip. "Sure feels strange without it, though."

"I liked it," Dinah Belle said. "You shoulda left it."

"If I'da known that, I mighta left it on," Booth japed.

Bodine was about to complain that she never made a fuss over his mustache when he heard the door in the store open. When he turned to look, he saw Jacob and Hawk walk in the store, so he left his wife to tend the bar and walked over to greet them. "Well, Woodley, who's this you got with you?" He gave Hawk a hard looking over, especially noting the Winchester in his hand, before commenting, "It's been a while, but I remember you."

Before Hawk could say anything, Jacob blurted, "I'm needin' some things, if you ain't gone crazy with your prices again."

"Hell, old man, you'd bitch if I gave 'em to you for nothin'," Bodine said.

"Try me," Jacob responded immediately.

"You can always go somewhere else to buy your piddling supplies," Bodine suggested. "It ain't but about forty miles to Helena." He was participating in the usual debate about prices with the old man, but in his mind, he was still working on when he had seen Hawk. When it began to come back to him, he ignored Jacob and talked directly to Hawk. "I remember you now, you and that crazy Blackfoot Injun. Is he with you?" He strained to look around behind them, looking for Bloody Hand.

"Nope," Hawk replied. "That was four years ago. I don't do much huntin' for hides anymore. The only huntin' I do now is for something to eat. Right now, I'm tryin' to catch up with four men that musta come here. I don't suppose you recollect."

"Four men?" Bodine responded. "Yeah, I've seen 'em. They rode by here yesterday. They stopped long enough to have a drink of likker, then they headed on outta here, goin' to Helena." He said it, knowing even then that Booth Corbin was standing at the bar, talking to Dinah Belle.

"Reckon I'd best not waste much time here, then," Hawk said. "Stoppin' long enough for a little drink of whiskey sounds like a good idea, though. How 'bout it, Jacob? Could you use a little shooter? I'm buyin'—figure I owe you one for roustin' you outta the bushes."

"Never turn down a free drink of likker," Jacob said, "even if I ain't got time for one." He unconsciously looked back toward the door to make sure Thomas wasn't coming in, then handed Bodine a list that Thomas's mother had written for him. "There's some things we need," he said to him. Then he followed Hawk, who was already walking toward the bar on the other side of the store.

Hawk took note of the man at the other end of the bar, leaning on one elbow, a whiskey glass in his hand, having a conversation with Dinah Belle Bodine. They both paused and looked him over as well. He had to wonder if he was one of the men he trailed. He had no way of identifying any of them but Tater, whom he had seen—and he had a description of Booth. Donald Lewis had described him as a fairly impressive man with a thick mustache, groomed to curl up on the ends. This man at the bar had no mustache. "Howdy, stranger," Dinah Belle said. "What'll it be?" Unlike her husband, she didn't recall having seen Hawk before.

"I'll have a drink of whiskey," Hawk said, "and another one for my friend here."

She leaned aside to look behind him. "Jacob Woodley," she announced sarcastically. "The last time you was in here, your grandson had to come drag you out."

"Never mind your sweet-talkin'," the old man said.

"Pour my drink." He licked his lips in anticipation. Noticing, Hawk realized he may have made a mistake by inviting Jacob for a drink. Maybe Thomas was not going to appreciate the gesture. He remembered the boy telling his grandpa to just go in the store. Evidently, he meant for him not to go into the bar.

Thinking it was too late to stop the old man now, Hawk was to find it even more difficult when Booth greeted them. "Howdy, stranger," Booth Corbin said, still studying the tall man with the hawk feather in his hat. "What brings you to Wolf Creek?" Before Hawk could answer, Booth told Dinah Belle to pour them another drink. Jacob reached for his while she was still pouring.

"That better do for me and my friend," Hawk quickly told her. Then back to Booth, he said, "Much obliged. I'm just passin' through. You live around here?"

"No, I'm just passin' through, same as you," Booth said. He was thinking of the description Tater had given them of the man who shot Blue Davis—big man, wearing a buckskin shirt. Tater didn't say anything about a feather in his hat, but Booth doubted Tater was close enough to see that. Even without that detail, he felt this was Blue's killer, and the man who was now chasing him. The thing that didn't make sense, however, was the little old drunk with him. Maybe it just appeared they were riding together.

"I reckon a lotta people pass through Wolf Creek, don't they, ma'am?" Hawk asked Dinah Belle. "Your husband said a party of four men just rode through a day or so ago." He looked back at Booth. "You mighta seen 'em."

"Nope," Booth said with a smile. "I reckon I just missed 'em."

More convinced now than before, Hawk continued to probe the stranger. He did not miss the small show of alarm on Dinah Belle's face when he asked about the four men. "I'd say you're lucky you did. Word I hear is that those four cowards are the bunch that massacred about thirty folks that were headin' to Helena to build a new church." As he said it, he watched the stranger's eyes for any signs that meant he might have touched a nerve.

Booth calmly smiled even though he could feel all the muscles in his arms tightening. "Is that so?" he forced casually. "I hadn't heard anything about that."

"We have," Dinah Belle spoke up. "We heard about all them church folks gettin' shot down—women and children, too. It took some low-down son of a bitches to do somethin' like that." From what she had heard about Booth Corbin, she wouldn't have doubted he and his men were involved in something like that.

"You're absolutely right, ma'am," Booth said at once. "That was a terrible tragedy." He shook his head thoughtfully. "That kind of news makes it risky for any four men ridin' together, don't it? Even if they ain't ever been anywhere near that place it happened." He paused. "Where did it happen?" When Dinah Belle said it happened between Great Falls and Fort Benton, Booth said, "Then it was nowhere near us." Reasonably sure he was right about the stranger now, he asked Hawk, "You campin' here tonight, or are you goin' with your friend?"

"If you got any money, you oughta stay in one of them cabins ol' Bodine's got back down the river," Jacob piped up.

"I expect I'll just find me a place to camp where I can water and feed my horse," Hawk said. "I reckon

Jacob and his grandson will likely start back home."
He hadn't known about any cabins Bodine had built.
Thanks to Jacob he did now.

"Dinah Belle's gonna fix a big supper in a little
while," Booth said. "I guarantee it would be worthwhile
to stay for that."

"Well, now, that is mighty temptin'," Hawk said.
The conversation was interrupted then when Bodine
came from the store with Thomas behind him.

"Grandpa, it's time to go now," Thomas said when
he saw his grandfather standing by the bar. "We've got
to load our stuff in the wagon. Come on, I've paid for
the supplies and paid Mr. Pressley, too." It was obvious
in his tone that he was worried that his grandpa might
already be too far into the bottle to come without an
argument.

But Hawk came to his rescue. "Yeah, come on,
Jacob, it's time to get outta here." He took the old
man by the arm and pulled him away from the bar.
With one hand holding his rifle, he was ready to release Jacob's arm in an instant, if he needed his other
hand. Keeping his body half turned toward Booth as
he moved back to the store portion of the room, he
said, "Thanks for the drink. It was nice talkin' to you."

"Yeah, same to you," Booth returned. "Maybe we'll
run into each other again sometime." While he felt
reasonably sure he was looking at the man who shot
Blue Davis, he remained there, casually leaning on
the bar. His natural inclination would have been to
simply draw the Colt .44 he wore and shoot the man
down. He was discouraged from doing so by the wary
manner with which Hawk made his exit. Tater had
said the man was quick and accurate with that rifle.

Proof of that was in the lightning-like way Tater said he took Blue down. And Blue wasn't slow, so Booth reluctantly stood there and watched Hawk walk out, his rifle obviously ready for instant reaction.

"Who is that son of a bitch?" Booth demanded of Bodine, who, like his wife, was standing there watching Hawk leave the saloon.

"Hawk is his name," Bodine answered. "This is the first time I've seen him in a helluva long time. He came in here about four years ago with a Blackfoot Injun to trade some hides."

"That's where I seen him," Dinah Belle blurted. "I knew I'd seen him somewhere, but I couldn't place him." She flashed a wide grin in Bodine's direction. "I remember, if it hadn'ta been for him, that Injun he was with was fixin' to scalp you."

"I'll tell you somethin' that might interest you," Bodine said to Booth, ignoring Dinah Belle's comment. "He asked me if I'd seen four men ride through here in the last couple of days." Before Booth could ask, he continued, "I told him I sure did—told him they only stopped long enough to get a drink of likker and went right on, headin' for Helena."

"What the hell's he followin' us for?" Booth wondered aloud. He didn't say it, but he had to wonder if Hawk was after the money he and his partners were carrying. That was the only reason he could come up with, since Hawk was evidently not a lawman.

"Ain't no tellin'," Bodine answered Booth's question. "Was that you boys that done that piece of business on them church folks?"

"Hell no!" Booth answered at once. "Like I told that feller, every party of four men on the road will have folks thinkin' they're the ones that done for them Quakers." With his mind still working on Hawk's reasons for tailing them, he uttered one more statement, he wished he could take back. "Besides, there was five men that rode away from that massacre, and we ain't but four."

As soon as he said it, Bodine knew Booth and his boys had done that low-down job. Dinah Belle had come to the same conclusion when Booth had said he hadn't heard anything about it, then referred to them as Quakers. No one had said they were Quakers before that. As far as her husband was concerned, Bodine was not above such evil disregard for human life. Instead of compassion for the poor innocent victims, Bodine was quick to think about the money Booth and the others must have gotten. Talk was that those folks were going to Helena with the intention of buying land for all of their families plus building a meetinghouse. They must have been carrying a great sum of money to do all that. And Booth and his three partners were acting like they had plenty. Bodine was happy to see them so free with their money; it was good for his business. But he'd like to figure out a way to get more of it. In line with that thought, he made a suggestion. "Looks like to me the best thing for you boys is to stay right here in my cabin till talk about that massacre dies down a little. We got everything you need and then some. Josie's near 'bout done with her female sickness and she'll be rarin' to go. As far as Hawk is concerned, looks to me like, if he is tailin' you, he's a damn fool, 'cause he's by himself, unless he's countin' on help from old man Woodley and his grandpup. And in my way of thinkin', that ain't no help at all." He gave Booth a wink. "And if he's dumb enough to make a move on the four of you, you oughta be able to handle that."

"You might be right," Booth allowed, his mind already working on the best way to take care of Hawk. "We might stay right here for a while." Until Hawk was dead, or had moved on, which he didn't anticipate, he had to tell the others to stay together. He didn't want to give Hawk a chance to catch them alone, like he did with Blue and Tater, before Booth and his gang had a chance to hunt Hawk down and kill him. Satisfied with what he had to do, Booth shifted his attention to Dinah Belle. "When are you gonna have some supper ready? I'm workin' up a powerful hunger."

"In 'bout an hour," she replied. "I've got a ham in the oven that's just about ready to take out. And when it's out of the oven, I'll bake biscuits and cook the beans."

"That's good, maybe I'll just have another drink while I'm waitin' for the boys to come eat," Booth said. "Too bad Hawk didn't stay to eat with us."

"That would make your problem a lot easier to take care of, wouldn't it?" Bodine remarked.

"That's a fact," Booth answered with a smug grin. Then he walked through the store to the front window, just on the chance he might have a clear shot at Hawk, and get this business taken care of right then. He drew his .44 when he saw Hawk step up into the saddle, and quickly went over to the door, opening it just enough to see the yard. As he raised his pistol to aim at him, Hawk rode to the other side of the wagon with Jacob and his grandson on the seat. Then they moved out of the yard, toward the road, making it a harder shot with a pistol, but still worth the risk. Booth stepped quickly out on the porch and steadied his arm against the post. Setting his sight on the broad back of the rangy rider, he started to squeeze the trigger, only to have his target disappear. Startled, Booth hesitated, baffled by Hawk's sudden slide over on the side of his horse, leaving Booth no shot. It struck him then. "The son of a bitch knew I might take a shot at him," he muttered aloud. *You were lucky this time,* he thought. *You came walking in here with that old man and that threw me off. If you'd come walking in here by yourself, I would have shot you down, just on the chance you were following us.*

CHAPTER 11

"What the hell?" Jacob blurted. "I thought you was fixin' to fall offa your horse."

"Nope, I was just checkin' somethin' I thought I saw on Rascal's front leg." He straightened up in the saddle again as they rode up the path to the road. "It wasn't anything, though. I reckon I'm just seein' things." With a couple of trees blocking the line of sight between him and the front of the store now, he felt there was no danger of catching a .44 bullet in his back. It might have been an unnecessary move, rolling over behind Rascal like that, but he felt certain he had been talking to one of Booth's men in the saloon. And if he was, the odds were mighty good there would be a shot coming his way. He wasn't sure, but he also thought he had felt a little itch between his shoulder blades when he climbed on his horse.

Jacob and his grandson were both puzzled over Hawk's intentions when he got on his horse and rode out of Bodine's with them. Since he was heading back the way he had come when he first met up with them, Jacob wondered if he was going home with them. Finally, Jacob asked, "Where're you headin'?"

"I just thought I'd ride back a little way with you and Thomas. Then I'll swing over and ride down the river till I find a good place to camp."

"Oh," Jacob responded. "We was wonderin'. Thought for a minute you was fixin' to go home with us. Didn't we, Thomas?" Thomas just shrugged his shoulders. Jacob quickly continued, "You'd be welcome, if that's what you was thinkin'. We've got a little farm 'bout twenty-five miles from here. We'll be campin' tonight and get home in the mornin'. We'd be tickled to have you."

Hawk had to smile. Jacob's invitation didn't sound that sincere. He didn't know what the situation at their home was like—they had never talked about it during their short acquaintance. He guessed that he might not be a welcome guest, if their farm was as small as he imagined it to be. "That's mighty kind of you, Jacob, but I've got some unfinished business to take care of back at Bodine's. So I'd best make a camp a little closer than twenty-five miles." Having said that, he pulled Rascal to a stop. "I was glad to meet you and Thomas. I wish you luck with your farm." He wheeled Rascal then and set off downriver at an easy lope.

"Whadda you reckon he's up to?" Jacob asked, as Hawk rode away.

"I don't know," Thomas said, still a little undecided about the tall, broad-shouldered man. "I think ol' Bodine might be fixin' to get robbed."

"You think so?" Jacob responded. "He didn't strike me as a common outlaw." He shrugged and added, "'Course, I wouldn't grieve a lot if Bodine got cleaned out—the tight bastard." He chuckled at the thought. "You don't need to say nothin' to your grandma about them two little ol' drinks I had."

* * *

Guiding Rascal back closer to the river now, Hawk continued to ride downstream. While there was still plenty of daylight left, he hoped to find the cabins that Jacob had mentioned. If he was right, and Booth and his three partners were here, they would most likely be occupying one of the cabins. No doubt, if he had stayed in the saloon, the other three would have soon come in to join the one he had talked to. That might not have been a position he would have liked to be caught in, since Tater would recognize him. There would have been four guns blazing away at him at once.

It would have been easier to spot the cabin if he just rode along the banks of the river, but he didn't want to take the chance of being seen. If Tater spotted him, he would then be the hunted, instead of the hunter. So he kept Rascal just inside the outermost trees that lined the river. He had no real idea, but he assumed the cabins would not be very far from the trading post. That proved to be the case, because he caught sight of the first one after a ride of less than a quarter of a mile. He pulled Rascal up abruptly when he spotted a glimpse of a corner of the cabin and climbed down from the saddle. Then, leading the buckskin, he walked cautiously through the trees to a group of laurel bushes. He left Rascal there and continued on to a point where he could see the entire cabin, as well as a second cabin beyond it. They were located on either side of a shallow streambed that ran down the bluff to empty into the river. There was a small corral behind the second cabin and he counted nine horses in it. That seemed about right for five

riders, leading five packhorses, and there was still one
horse back at the store. The two extra horses had
likely belonged to the man he had shot at the deer
crossing. Everything seemed to indicate that these
were the four men he tracked from Choteau, but
the only way he could be sure was if he spotted Tater.
He wished he could get a little closer to that cabin,
but the cabin on this side of the stream was in the
way. It appeared the only way he could get closer to
the one where the horses were was to get on his horse
and take a wide circle around it and come up from
behind it. *Or,* it occurred to him, *if there ain't anybody
in that cabin on this side of the stream, I could sneak in it.*
That would put him close enough to get a better look
at what should be three men. Their partner, back at
the saloon, had talked about the big dinner Dinah
Belle was preparing. Odds were, the three in the
cabin were planning to be there. It was only about a
quarter of a mile back to Bodine's, but he was willing
to bet the three wouldn't walk it. If he was in that first
cabin, he might get a good look at them, and most
likely hear them talking.

He stared hard at the cabin. There seemed to be
no one in or around it. The one window on the side
was shuttered, and the door closed. The major problem was an open area of grass about twenty-five yards
wide between the trees and the cabin. He would have
to cross that without being seen. He decided it was
worth the risk. *Of course, if I'm wrong, then Rascal's gonna
be an orphan,* he thought as he crouched and ran
toward the side of the cabin. Once he reached it, he
was confident he couldn't be seen from the other
cabin or the corral. To be doubly sure, he peeked
through a crack in the window shutter and confirmed

that the cabin was empty. He would have liked to go inside to wait for the three men to appear, just for the protection of the cabin walls, but he didn't think it wise to risk going around to the front door to see if he could even get in. He would be a lot more likely to be seen if he was standing at the door. Further thoughts along that line were interrupted when one of the men walked outside the cabin across from him. Hawk quickly ran to the back corner of the empty cabin and got down on his belly. From there, he could see the man plainly. Of average height and lean as a knife blade, he wore his sidearm low on his hip in a fast-draw holster, and he carried his saddle on his shoulder. "Best get your ass goin'," he called back toward the cabin. "Ol' Dinner Bell oughta be settin' the table pretty soon."

"You ain't gotta tell me twice," a response came back as another man walked out behind him, carrying his saddle. Hawk felt his muscles tense. It was Tater! That was all he needed to confirm his belief that these were definitely the men who had slaughtered the people on the mule train. There should be one more now, and he anxiously awaited the appearance of the man with the fancy mustache, David Booth, as Hawk knew his name. After a few moments, he walked out, throwing momentary doubt into Hawk's mind. He wore no mustache! It was almost enough to make Hawk think he had been trailing the wrong gang. But there was no mistaking Tater. As the three of them saddled their horses for the short ride up to Bodine's saloon, Hawk was in for another surprise when Tater spoke again. "Ol' Booth's up there already, tryin' to get a head start, I reckon."

"Won't do him any good," Trip Dawson drawled.

"That gal, what's her name? Josie," he repeated when Jesse told him. "Anyway, she ain't hardly over the female sickness yet. Least, that's what Dinner Bell said this mornin'."

"Booth ain't got no interest in old wore-out whores like Josie," Jesse informed him. "He just wanted to get a drink and do a little thinkin' 'bout where we oughta be headin' when we leave here."

"How do you know she's an old wore-out whore?" Trip responded. "Bodine said she's younger'n she looks."

"'Cause what the hell would she be doin' at Bodine's if she wasn't?" Jesse answered.

Lying flat on his belly, listening to the idle conversation among the three outlaws, Hawk could hardly believe he had been talking to Booth in the saloon less than an hour before. It didn't register with him at the time that Booth looked freshly shaven. *And I'm supposed to be a scout,* he thought. *I had my rifle in my hand. I could have shot him down and cut off the head of this gang.* What to do now? That was the question. He found himself right in the middle of the vicious miscreants who had slaughtered whole families of innocent people. It left him facing a challenge that he had not anticipated when he first set out on this self-appointed mission. His original aim was to trail these killers, so the army or the marshals would know where to find them. He knew now that it was not a realistic endeavor. He could ride away, but by the time he left here and traveled to any law enforcement agency, these criminals would be gone to who knows where. They were still on the move. What it boiled down to was, he was the only recourse those massacred families had for vengeance. And it was his decision as to whether or not he was going to take justice into his own hands. It would not be the first time he had to make that decision. He thought about the two men on the Yellowstone who had kidnapped Winter Flower. When they came for her, he had killed them without hesitating. Booth and his partners would be no different. He would be their judge, jury, and executioner, because he was here. There was no one else to do it.

His decision made, he now tried to plan the best way to accomplish his role as an assassin. To begin with, he preferred to think of it as extermination, to rid the world of vermin like David Booth. To make the task more of a challenge, he was certain that the man in Bodine's, whom he now knew to be Booth, was very much aware that he was trailing him. So, it was going to be a question of *who gets who* in this game of assassination. He lay there, his rifle ready, but with no intention of shooting at any of them at this point. He had a good twenty or more yards of open area between the cabin he was hiding behind and the cover of the trees where he left his horse. He reasoned that he might get one, or maybe two, of them before they could retaliate. But he would be an open target when he tried to make it back to cover. And that would leave two, maybe three, of them to go unpunished, depending upon how many he was able to get before they got him.

He got up from the ground and went to the front corner of the cabin and watched the three men ride away. In a matter of seconds, they were out of sight, swallowed up by the dense growth of trees by the river. He realized that he wouldn't have had much time to shoot, even if he had decided to. Since he knew they

were going to Bodine's for supper, he decided to take
a look in the cabin before returning for his horse. He
was sure there would be none of the Quakers' money
left in the cabin, but he thought he might as well confirm that thought. More than likely, they each carried
their share of the stolen money in their saddlebags. It
seemed too large a sum to carry in your pocket. Part
of his plan was to recover as much of the Quakers'
money as possible and return it to Donald Lewis.

Jesse Corbin and Trip Dawson walked into Bodine's
saloon to find Booth sitting at a table, talking to Josie
Johnson, who, as Bodine promised, was on her feet
again—at least until she persuaded one of the gang
to part with some of the money he was carrying. "Is
that supper ready?" Trip asked upon seeing no food
before Booth.

"Won't be long," Booth replied. "Where's Tater?"
With Dinah Belle's promise of a big meal, he would
have expected Tater to be the first through the door.

"He went back to get his teeth," Jesse answered.
"He was so excited to eat, he went off and left 'em in
the cabin." That brought a laugh from them all and a
question from Josie.

"He's got store teeth?" she asked, thinking that only
rich people and maybe royalty, like kings and queens,
could afford false teeth. "He must be rich," she said.

That brought another laugh from the three customers. "Yeah, he's rich," Trip cracked. "He inherited
a lot of money." Josie looked puzzled by the chuckles
following that remark.

Booth interrupted then, already having had to try
to convince Bodine that the four of them had not

been the gang that robbed and killed those innocent families near Fort Benton. "They don't cost as much as you think," he said, then went on to explain the dentures made out of vulcanite with porcelain teeth. "He only uses 'em when he's got some meat to chew up, like that ham Dinah Belle put in the oven. He says he can gum just about everything else." Further conversation about Tater's teeth was halted by Dinah Belle's appearance at the kitchen door.

"It's on the table," she announced. "Better come and get it while it's hot." There was no hesitation by anyone, as they all filed into the kitchen, where she had set everything on the kitchen table. Bodine was already in place at the head of the table.

"Ol' Tater's gonna be fit to be tied, if he don't show up pretty quick," Trip commented, as Dinah Belle poured the coffee from a large gray pot.

Back at the cabin, Hawk looked around the front room, where the fireplace was located. There was nothing really to see, he decided, but he went into the back room just in case there might be a canvas money bag or something to make his investigation worthwhile. He looked around him. There was nothing but four bedrolls and scattered items of clothing. He had started to turn around and go back to the front room when something odd caught his eye. Sitting on the floor next to one of the bedrolls was something that looked like teeth. Not sure he wasn't seeing things, he drew his long hunting knife and poked at the teeth with the point of it. Hearing a noise behind him in the front room, he turned to find Tater standing in the doorway, dumbfounded. Startled as well, Hawk

had no time to think when Tater suddenly realized
who he was and went for his .44. In a split-second reaction, Hawk threw the hunting knife underhanded to
bury the blade halfway under Tater's rib cage. His gun
not clear of his holster, he released it and clutched the
knife lodged in his belly. Like a great cat, Hawk was
upon him and both men crashed to the floor. Hawk
would have preferred to finish the desperate man
with a quick shot from his .44, but they were too close
to the trading post. The shot would be heard. So, as
he had mercifully put many a deer out of their suffering, he withdrew the knife and drew it across the
struggling man's throat.

Tater held on to his life for only a few minutes
before his body relaxed in death. Hawk stood over
him until he did, not at all unfazed by the violent way
he had been forced to kill him. He had not considered the possibility that any of the three would return
to the cabin that quickly. He cleaned his knife on the
dead man's shirt, then thought to check Tater's pockets.
He was not surprised to find a large roll of bills in
Tater's vest pocket. Hawk took the money and went
outside, where he found Tater's horse standing. He
expected the money in his hand was probably a small
part of Tater's share in the robbery. So, he looked in
the saddlebags and found what he was looking for, a
canvas bag with a much larger sum of cash inside. He
put the money from Tater's pocket in the bag, hoping
that, somehow, he would be able to return it to the
church people. He picked the reins up from the ground
and looped them over the saddle horn, so the horse
would be free to wander. There was no thought of
taking the horse—he knew he was going to be too
busy to take care of an extra horse. But he took Tater's

weapons and cartridge belt. Then he took one quick look toward the path that Tater had come on and hurried across the open area to the woods beyond.

Back in the saddle, he turned Rascal toward the high hills to the north of the river. When Tater's body was discovered, the war would be officially on. So, he decided he had to find a camp he could operate out of, one that would be hard to find, because they would definitely be coming after him.

CHAPTER 12

"This is some mighty fine eatin', Dinner Bell," Booth commented, not realizing he had called her by her nickname and somewhat puzzled by the smug grin on his brother's face. "I'll take another one of those biscuits."

"'Deed it is," Jesse agreed. Then he glanced toward the kitchen door. "What I can't figure out, though, is what the hell happened to Tater? It sure ain't like him to miss a meal."

"Can't find them fancy teeth," Trip said.

"I expect he'll be here pretty soon," Booth said, his mind already working on things a lot more serious than the fact that Tater was late for supper. The mysterious Mr. Hawk would have to be dealt with. He had left Bodine's when the old man and his grandson left, but when Hawk had talked to Booth in the saloon before that, he just said he was going to find a place to camp for the night. He looked like a man who could handle himself, but Booth didn't think he was foolhardy to the point where he would take on four men like the four of them.

Almost as if he knew what his brother was thinking,

Jesse leaned toward him and asked, "What's on your mind, Booth? You look like you're gnawin' on somethin' in your head."

"As a matter of fact," Booth responded, "there is a little somethin' I was fixin' to tell you. I was waitin' for Tater to get here, but it looks like he changed his mind about eatin'." He paused to make sure Bodine wasn't listening in on their conversation. "While you boys were layin' around the cabin, I had a drink with the man who's been followin' us." That captured Jesse's attention at once. "His name's Hawk."

"Hawk? A lawman?" Jesse asked immediately.

"Don't think so," Booth replied. "I figure he's the same jasper that shot Blue. That's the only thing that makes sense to me. I don't know how he got on our trail to start with, but it's my guess he's comin' after the money."

Jesse shook his head slowly, concerned now. "He musta got on our trail right there where we done it." They had been so sure no one would find that hill where the slaughter took place until it was way too late to do anything about it. Then another thought naturally popped into his head. "Why didn't you shoot the son of a bitch?"

"I intended to," Booth said, "but he never gave me the chance." He told Jesse about the whole incident in the saloon and Hawk's cautious departure. "I thought I had a shot at him when he got on his horse, but he knew he was about to get it and he slid over on the side of his horse, Injun style. I didn't have nothin' to shoot at."

"We're gonna need to take care of him, and that's a fact," Jesse stated emphatically. "And we need to stick together, so he don't get another shot like he did with Blue." As soon as he said it, they both looked back toward the door as if looking for Tater.

Booth came out with the question that occurred to them both. "Where the hell is Tater?"

"I don't know, but we'd better go find out," Jesse at once replied. It had been long enough to conclude Tater wasn't coming to supper. Everyone had just about finished eating. "And we'd best all go together," he added, knowing there was safety in numbers.

Booth got up from the table and told Trip they were going back to the cabin, which was at first no concern to Trip. "You and Jesse can go back," he said. "I've already made some plans for some better company than you jaspers." He winked at Josie, who responded with her most enticing smile.

"You're gonna need to go back to the cabin with us," Booth said. "We've got a problem and we've got to fix it right now." When Trip started to complain, Booth nodded toward Josie and said, "That's gonna have to wait. We need to get back now and see what's keepin' Tater from comin' to supper."

"Who in hell cares why Tater . . ." Trip started to protest again, but one look at the stern expression on the faces of both brothers persuaded him to give in. "Ah, hell," he muttered, and looked at Josie, who was also disappointed. "I'll be back after I find out what's goin' on," he promised.

"Let's go," Booth prompted. They paid Bodine for the supper, plus a bottle of whiskey to take with them, and filed out the door.

Disappointed by their early departure as well, Bodine walked out on the porch and watched them ride off toward the narrow path by the river. "There ain't a doubt in my mind, those boys are the ones that done for that party of church folks. And they're settin' on a whole pile of money." He turned to Dinah Belle when he heard her come up behind him. "And I'm aimin' to get me a chunk of it before they ride outta here."

The path to the cabins led through a heavily wooded area and was only wide enough to ride single file. Booth led the others along the path, now shrouded in heavy darkness. Halfway back to the cabin, he pulled his horse up hard when he suddenly met a horse coming toward him, causing him to back into Jesse's horse. He saw a moment later that the saddle was empty. Then he realized it was Tater's horse, wandering loose. He immediately pulled his .44, which prompted Jesse and Trip to do the same. "Keep your eyes open," Booth warned. "That's Tater's horse!" They started up again, pushing Tater's horse in front of them until reaching a wide spot in the path where Tater's horse moved aside. "Grab his reins, Trip," Booth said as he rode by the riderless horse.

With no sign of Tater along the dark path, they spread out and pulled up when they reached the clearing and the two cabins, all three with guns aimed at the cabin. "Tater!" Booth yelled, but there was no response. He turned to Jesse and Trip. "Let's take a look around the cabin before we go walkin' in there. I don't like the looks of this." They did as he ordered but found no one.

"Hell, I'm goin' in," Trip declared, and stepped down from the saddle. With his six-gun in his hand, he walked up, gave the door a hard shove, and stepped quickly to the side in case his entrance was met with a few rounds from a .44. When there was no response after the door swung open and banged against the wall, he went inside. In a few seconds, Booth and Jesse heard him call out. "He's in here."

Booth and Jesse went inside the dark cabin to find Trip kneeling beside the body. "Damn," Booth swore when he saw him. "That son of a bitch shot him." He knew without doubt who the killer was. Then it occurred to him. "As close as this is to the store, we shoulda heard the shot."

"There weren't no shot," Trip said. "He didn't shoot Tater. He cut his throat."

"Damn," Booth swore again. "He's figurin' on gettin' us one by one. We've got to stick together, so he don't get a chance to catch one of us alone again. Light that lantern over there," he directed, pointing to a lantern on the table. They all bent over Tater's body then. "Looks like he caught him in the gut first," Booth observed. "Tater musta walked in on him when the bastard was searchin' in here." He looked at his brother. "He was lookin' for the money." He reached in Tater's vest pocket. "He got it, too. Look in Tater's saddlebags."

"I'll do it," Trip volunteered, and got up at once. He went outside where the horses were standing. After a quick search through the saddlebags on Tater's horse, he was back inside with the news. "He cleaned him out."

Booth looked at Jesse. "I told you he ain't no lawman. He's after the money, and he knows each one of us has got as much as he just took offa Tater. We've gotta go huntin'. We've damn sure gotta find him before he catches one of us alone again."

"Well, we can't do much huntin' tonight," Trip said. "Maybe we can pick up his tracks when it gets daylight."

"We're gonna have to track him down," Booth declared again, this time even stronger. "We can't wait around for him to get another chance to ambush one of us. He might be watchin' out there right now, but as long as the three of us are here inside the cabin, there ain't much he can do."

"I ain't gonna go far from the cabin when I have to get rid of this coffee I drank," Trip stated, "and everythin' else I ate is gonna have to stay right where it is till daylight." He looked down at the body and asked, "What are we gonna do about ol' Tater? We gonna bury him?"

"Not tonight, we ain't," Booth said.

"Well, let's drag him out the door," Jesse suggested. "We can leave him by the front door till mornin'." That was good enough for the other two, so he and Trip each grabbed one of Tater's boots and dragged him out the front door.

"Won't have to worry about Tater's snorin' tonight," Trip said when they came back inside and dropped the bar across the door.

While the three outlaws spent a watchful night inside a log cabin, the man who was the cause of their cautious fits of sleep was bedded down at the top of a steep ravine that ran up a heavily wooded foothill. He had been fortunate to find this campsite while there was still barely enough light to follow the tiny stream that ran down the ravine to join a larger stream at the bottom. He planned to make his base camp down where the two streams met. He estimated the camp to be about three and a half to four miles from Bodine's trading post. There was grass there for Rascal, and the water was good. But at night, he would sleep up at the narrow top of the ravine, so anyone who might attack him would have to climb up to find him. It would take a better tracker than he was to find him at night, and if they did, Rascal was there to warn him. He fell asleep knowing there was one less killer in the gang of five that coldly slaughtered women and children. He was at peace with his part in it.

He awoke the next morning to the sound of Rascal drinking from the tiny stream near his bedroll. He sat up and looked around him to see how secure his campsite appeared to be in the light of day. He decided it was as good as he could expect to find. "Come on, boy, let's go down to the bottom where you can get some good water," he said to Rascal.

Not sure what this day would bring, he decided to make coffee and eat some breakfast before he made his next move. While he ate his meal of venison, he tried to determine just what that move should be. He was still up against three hardened criminals, so he was not at all casual about how he intended to accomplish the task he had set before himself. The only thing he was sure he must do right away was to find out where they were and what they were doing, then hope they made costly mistakes. With that as his first objective, he lightened Rascal's load by hanging the rest of his meat supply, as well as his other supplies, in the trees by his camp. For his deer meat, he picked a small limb and hung the bundle as far out on the limb as he could without the weight of it breaking the limb. He didn't mind sharing a little meat with a hawk, but he hoped to avoid donating all of it to a mountain lion. It was high enough off the ground that he could reach it only on horseback while standing in the stirrups. Once that was done, he wheeled Rascal and headed back to Wolf Creek.

When he was within a mile of Bodine's, he guided Rascal to the east for what he figured to be about a mile and a half before cutting back in a more southerly direction. So, when he reached the river, he was quite a way downstream of Bodine's as well as the two cabins. From that point, he made his way upstream, so as to approach the cabins from below them.

While Hawk was having his breakfast and preparing to scout the cabin, the occupants of the cabin had been getting ready to track him. "How do you know he ain't out there in the bushes somewhere just waitin' to get a shot at one of us?" Jesse wanted to know.

"'Cause, if he was, he'da most likely took a shot at me when I was out there waterin' the side of the cabin," Trip replied.

"You walked around to the side of the cabin?" Jesse asked, thinking Trip wasn't showing much respect for the possibility that Hawk was waiting for just such an opportunity.

"Tater's still a-layin' right in front of the door," Trip said. "I didn't think it would be respectful to pee on him. Besides, I ain't talkin' about the side of this cabin. I went across the stream to the other cabin."

"That's crazy as hell. You'd best be thinkin' about the jasper we're dealin' with," Booth told him. "He's already took care of Blue and Tater."

"Well, I'll tell you why I ain't worried about steppin' outside this cabin," Trip said. "He ain't waitin' for us to come outta here 'cause he's gone."

"How the hell do you know that?" Booth asked.

"'Cause, after I walked around this cabin and he didn't shoot, I figured he wasn't here. So I took a look around that other cabin, and I found his tracks where he ran off into the woods," Trip crowed. "You said we was gonna track him down, so I can show you which way we need to start."

This captured both of the brothers' interest, so they followed him over to the other cabin, where he pointed out Hawk's tracks from the afternoon before. "Well, I'll be . . ." Jesse started when Trip pointed out the distinct boot tracks. "He came across that clearin', musta come up in those trees over there. He musta surprised poor ol' Tater when he was lookin' for his teeth." It looked to be the obvious answer and served to paint a picture of a determined assassin. Actually, it was Tater who surprised Hawk, not the other way around. The picture of a deadly night stalker was fixed in their minds, however.

"We've got to track this son of a bitch down and kill him," Booth said. "'Cause he's gonna keep comin' till he gets all of us and all the money."

"Let's get at it, then," Trip said. "I just wish I'd get a chance to take him on face-to-face. I'd like to see if he's as good when he's facin' me as he is when he's hidin' in the bushes."

After following the obvious tracks across the sandy clearing, they easily found the spot in the trees where Hawk had left his horse. There had apparently been no effort on his part to hide his trail as he rode out of the trees and into the hills beyond. The trail ended, however, when they came to a wide stream. From that point forward, Hawk had become careful about hiding his trail. They spent almost an hour riding up and down both sides of the stream, but to no avail. Booth reined his Morgan gelding to a stop and sat there gazing at the mountains before him, feeling the frustration of knowing Hawk would be hard to find in that wilderness. In a short while, both Jesse and Trip came from opposite directions and pulled up beside him. "I can't find a track where anything came out of the water," Jesse complained. "He's just disappeared."

"Well, I reckon that's one more thing we know about him," Trip said. "The son of a bitch can fly."

Booth made no comment as he continued to stare at the dark hills and the mountains beyond them. The loss of Hawk's trail led him into more serious speculation about the man who was stalking them. He had met and had a conversation with him, so he knew he was a white man. But he wore a shirt made out of buckskin, he wore a feather in his hat, and he had attacked Tater with a knife. All those things added up to make Booth think they were dealing with a half-breed, or at least a man who had lived with the Indians. *On the other hand,* he thought, *he didn't scalp Blue or Tater.* The more he thought about it, the less he wanted to play hide-and-seek in those hills with a man who might be at home in them. Sensing his brother's deep thoughts as usual, Jesse asked, "What's on your mind, Booth?"

"I'm thinkin' we're in that jasper's backyard and that ain't the best place for us to be," Booth answered.

"You think we oughta go back to the cabin and wait for him to come after us?" Jesse responded.

"No, I'm thinkin' we'd best go back to the cabin,

get our stuff, take it to Bodine's, and move into one of those rooms he's got over the saloon."

Hearing his comment, Trip blurted, "I thought we said we was gonna track him down."

"Yeah? Well, I've changed my mind," Booth replied. "Runnin' around out here in the woods, or holed up in that cabin, he's got us where he'd rather have us. If we were stayin' at Bodine's, he'd have a lot more to deal with, and it won't be so easy to get at us. He'll have to come out in the open."

"That'd be more to my likin'," Trip claimed. "I would surely like to stand face-to-face with that sneaky bastard." Then another thought entered his mind. "It would be a lot closer to the supper table at Bodine's." He grinned. "And Josie's room is over the saloon. Everything's handy."

In line with his brother's thinking, Jesse was inclined to agree. "I think that would be a smart move for us," he said. "He's gonna have to think twice before he steps into Bodine's to make trouble. Ain't no use to hide out in that cabin anymore, anyway. Hawk knows where we are, so we might as well make things a little bit easier on ourselves. I know we were planning to move on after a couple of days here, but I'd rather make sure that bastard's dead and not trailin' along behind us before we go."

"Good," Trip commented, and nodded to show his agreement. "And I'll bet ol' Dinner Bell is cookin' up some breakfast. I don't know about you boys, but I could use some coffee and biscuits right about now."

"Let's get our possibles outta that cabin first," Booth said. "Then there won't be no need to go back after breakfast."

Since they had not gotten very far before losing

Hawk's trail, it was a short ride back to the cabins. Even so, the three outlaws were not careless in approaching them, and once they were sure Hawk was not about, they quickly packed their things and were headed up the path to Bodine's and the prospects of a hot breakfast. Behind them was the body of their late partner, Tater Thompson, dumped in a gully behind the second cabin to await his final reckoning.

Forty yards downstream from the cabins, Hawk reined Rascal up short when he thought he heard voices through the trees. He paused there for a minute or two, listening, then he was sure. The voices had come from the cabins, and they had to be outside the cabin for him to have heard them. He nudged Rascal with his heels and the big buckskin gelding started walking slowly ahead until a glimpse of the cabins came into sight and Hawk stopped him again. Dismounting with his rifle in hand, Hawk moved cautiously through the growth of pines close to the river. He made his way to a spot where he could see both cabins clearly, just in time to see the rear ends of the packhorses as they were swallowed up in the darkness of the narrow path that led to Bodine's. *They're leaving,* he thought, *for good, if they're taking their packhorses!* He thought of his food and supplies hanging in a tree three and a half miles away. If Booth was heading out for who-knows-where, there was no time for Hawk to recover his supplies. He was going to have to survive on what he carried in his saddlebags, because he couldn't afford to let the three of them leave without him on their trail.

He hurried back to his horse. "It's your fault," he said to the buckskin as he picked the reins up from the ground. "If I hadn't tried to lighten your load, I wouldn't have to worry about starvin' to death." He climbed up into the saddle and rode on through the trees to the clearing where the cabins stood. With no thought that anyone was left behind to take a shot at him, he held Rascal to a fast walk across the clearing and onto the path to Bodine's. Once the trees enclosed on the narrow track, he slowed the horse down, so as not to catch up with the three men he knew were riding ahead of him, leading the horses.

As he approached the point where the path opened up to the shady bluffs where Bodine's buildings stood, he had to pull his horse to a stop to make sure he wasn't spotted following Booth and the others. When they rode through the willows and cottonwoods scattered around Bodine's little cluster of buildings, he could see them as they led their horses straight to Bodine's corral and began to unload their saddles and packs. While Hawk watched from his vantage point at the entrance to the river path, Booth and his two remaining gang members carried their saddles and packs into the barn. During the process, Bodine joined them when he was summoned by Tom Pointer, who took care of Bodine's barn and stable. Pointer seemed to have been surprised when Booth and his two friends showed up with their horses and belongings. Hawk guessed that their arrival was as much a surprise to Tom as it was to him. From the distance Hawk watched from, it appeared to him that Bodine was making them welcome. After a short conversation between them, Bodine and the three walked into the store, with their saddlebags on their shoulders and their rifles in their hands. The exception was Tom Pointer, who stayed behind to take care of the horses that had suddenly come under his care.

So they moved into the store, Hawk thought. *I wonder for how long.* He felt certain that Booth and his partners had no intention to stay at Bodine's for any great length of time. *Until they catch me sleeping,* he thought, answering his own question. This was going to change his plan of attack. They obviously felt they would be a great deal less vulnerable to his efforts to settle with them. On the other hand, they would have to come out of there, if they intended to kill him. Could he afford to wait them out? It could very well turn into a game of who became desperate enough to first take the big risk.

For the first time in the last couple of days, he wondered if his prolonged absence had already jeopardized his position as a scout for the army. He wasn't sure Mathew Conner could save his job again. As quickly as the thought occurred, it was just as quickly discarded. His friend Bloody Hand would tell him that he was walking the path that had opened for him. He wasn't sure about that, but he knew that he was already too heavily invested in the quest to avenge the families these men had destroyed. *Maybe I'll finish what I've started, then go up to Canada to find Bloody Hand.*

Thinking Booth would not be coming out of the trading post anytime soon this morning, since they had just moved in, he thought about going to get his meat and supplies while they were getting settled in their new quarters. He needed to set up a camp closer to the trading post, now that he would be watching it most of the time. And he knew that anytime the Morgan that Booth rode was gone, he was likely being hunted. Unless, he reminded himself, the Morgan and all the other horses they had were all gone. In that case, he would be trying to find their trail again.

CHAPTER 13

"I ain't got three rooms upstairs," Bodine said, "unless I move Josie outta hers. You wouldn't want me to do that, would you?" He was ready to do just that if Booth insisted on it. He had been mighty happy to hear they wanted to move in, happy to have all that money he was sure they were carrying that much closer to him. He would get a little more of it if they did insist on moving Josie to the pantry behind the kitchen.

"Ain't no need to move her, we don't need but two rooms," Booth said. "Me and my brother can share a room, and Trip can take the other one."

"If that's what you want," Bodine said. "Course, you know when I rent those rooms, I charge by the head, so you and Jesse would pay the same as Trip."

"I ain't surprised, you old skinflint," Booth replied. "I'll bet you don't rent those rooms out more'n five or six nights a year." When Bodine started to defend his policy, Booth stopped him. "Don't start your whining, we'll pay you for the damn rooms."

"Damn right," Trip spoke up, "We can afford it. Now, how's about we go back downstairs and get some

breakfast?" Without waiting for any response from
his partners, he started back down the steps with his
usual cocky swagger, even in light of the steepness of
the stair.

Behind him, Jesse hesitated a few seconds to speak
softly in his brother's ear. "I don't know about you,
but I'm gettin' tired of hearin' him brayin' about how
he can afford everything. He keeps it up and Bodine's
gonna think we're the ones that killed them Quakers
for sure."

"Yeah, I'm gettin' a little tired of it, myself," Booth
replied. "But I don't know if it makes a helluva lot
of difference, as far as Bodine's concerned. I think
Bodine's already figured we did that job and the only
thing on his mind is how much of it he can get his
hands on before we leave here."

"About that," Jesse responded. "How long you
think we oughta hang around here waitin' for that
jasper to take a shot at one of us? You know it ain't
gonna be long before a hard winter decides to roll
over those mountains and freeze this river valley up.
I'd sure as hell like to spend the winter in someplace
besides this tradin' post."

"I know what you're sayin'. I feel the same as you."
He paused at the top of the stairs to let Trip and
Bodine get a little farther ahead. "Let's stay in close
here for a couple of days and see if Hawk gets tired of
waitin' and decides to take a fool chance to get at our
money. And there ain't no doubt he's got his mind set
on gettin' every cent of the money. He got Tater's
share, and that's a pretty good payday for most low-
down killers. But not this bastard; he wants it all.
So, if he makes a play to sneak in here, he's in our

backyard. If we can catch him inside this place, he ain't got a chance against all three of us."

Jesse shook his head, unconvinced. "I don't know if he's dumb enough to do that, but I know I'm tired of him tailin' us." Frustrated, he followed his brother downstairs to breakfast.

The morning was not as frustrating to Hawk. His one goal for the moment was to relocate his camp closer to the trading post. He postponed the worry about how he was going to attack the three outlaws, now that they had holed up in Bodine's. He would worry about that later. So he went back to the ravine where he had made his camp and loaded Rascal again. Then he headed back toward Wolf Creek, but circled around the trading post, opposite the direction he had taken when he had approached Bodine's cabins. It was his opinion that the three he followed were most likely headed for Helena. That was the closest town of any size, and the trail Booth had taken from the Sun River led to Helena, some twenty-five or thirty miles from Wolf Creek. So Hawk circled to the upstream side of Bodine's until he struck the trail leading to Helena, about two miles from the trading post. The trail crossed the river at that point, and he selected his new camp on the other side, far enough down from the crossing so as not to be seen by anyone on the road.

While he went about the business of making his camp, he considered the idea that had occurred to him earlier. Since his present situation was akin to having Booth and his two partners secure in a fort, while he waited around on the outside, his possibilities were strictly limited. He felt strongly that they were ultimately going to Helena. He could gamble on that assumption and ride on to Helena to wait for them there. He knew people in Helena. It would be easy to know when three strangers rode into town, and they would not likely be as cautious in the town. Of course, it wouldn't be any easier than catching them crossing this river right here, he had to admit. "If I don't," he said aloud, "I'll end up followin' them to Helena, anyway." He was not ready to admit that he didn't know how he was going to accomplish the goal he had set for himself.

Unknown to Hawk, there was another influence working to become instrumental in his war with Booth Corbin. It started when Trip Dawson sat down at a table next to Josie Johnson. "I reckon you and me are gonna be seein' a lot of each other," Trip whispered in her ear.

"Oh, is that so?" Josie replied, at once coquettish. "And why is that?"

"'Cause I just moved into the room next to yours," Trip answered, "and I'm gonna be needin' a lot of your time."

"Put your money where your mouth is," Josie came back. "I don't waste my time on big talkers."

"You don't need to worry about the money," he said. "Hell, you oughta be payin' me."

"Ha! Why is that?"

"'Cause you're settin' beside the fastest gun in

Wyomin' Territory," he crowed. "There's a lot of women that'd pay for a chance to be with me."

"Well, you ain't in Wyoming Territory now," she said. "Anyway, if you're so fast with a gun, how come you and your two friends moved into the store 'cause you're scared of that Hawk fellow out there?"

Her comment was the perfect spark to light Trip's fuse. "The hell you say!" Trip blurted. "Who told you that? The only reason we moved in here was because Booth and Jesse were gettin' worried they might get shot at. That ain't me. I ain't scared of nothin'. Matter of fact, I'd dearly love to draw that jasper out in the open to face me. Then we'd see who was faster with a gun."

"Pshaw, that's just big talk," she said. "You just tell me when you're ready to come see me, and we'll see how much man you are."

"I reckon we'll see about that right after I finish my breakfast," he replied. "Then we'll see if you're worth spendin' my money on. After that, I think I'll take a little walk around the front yard to see if that jasper wants to take a shot at me."

"You hear what that fool's tellin' her over there?" Jesse asked his brother. Sitting at a table close by, it was impossible not to hear some of Trip's boasting.

More intent upon the tough strip of bacon on his plate, Booth paid little attention to Trip's boastful talk. "He's just tryin' to impress Josie, so she'll think he's somethin' special. I don't know why he cares, she's just a damn whore. You pay your money and she gives you a ride. She don't care about anything else. He thinks there ain't nobody faster'n him with that Colt he wears. He can walk around out in the yard all he wants. Hawk ain't likely to come ridin' up to face him to see who's the fastest with a handgun. He's more apt to take a shot at him with that Winchester he carries. Matter of fact, it'd be kinda interestin' if he was to draw Hawk out in a gunfight—might give one of us a chance to get a shot at him."

"Maybe it would be a good thing if he did draw Hawk out and got himself shot, as long as he wasn't carryin' his share of the money on him. Hawk's already got Tater's share, I don't wanna see him get Trip's, too." Jesse said it with recent discussions about Trip in mind. With the demise of two of their gang, the brothers had considered the possibility of ending their ties with Trip as well. The cocky gunman was promising to become more of a liability to them. He was fast with a gun, but the trouble was his hand was faster than his brain, and there were occasions when that had caused unnecessary problems. It was Trip who shot Brother Adams and started the massacre of the families on the mule train. Jesse and Booth had not planned to kill all those people, even though they agreed afterward that it might have made their escape easier. It was also Trip who had killed Grover Dean and his wife at that little trading post on the Teton River. The two brothers had talked about the possibility that Trip could go off half-cocked sometime and cause a real problem.

"We'll see if he goes struttin' around the yard out there like he's braggin' about," Booth said. "As long as he's keepin' that money in his saddlebags where Hawk can't get his hands on it, he can do what he pleases to impress that whore."

When breakfast was over, Booth and Jesse remained in the saloon while Trip and Josie went back upstairs. In no hurry to go anywhere, the two brothers took time to have a couple of shots of whiskey. "To settle that tough bacon down," was Booth's explanation for it. They were still sitting there when Trip came back down and sat down to have a drink with them. "Well, did you get your wild hairs smoothed down?" Booth asked, and winked at Jesse.

"I reckon," Trip replied smugly, "for the time bein', I reckon." He sat there for a few minutes after his drink, then got up out of his chair. "I'm feelin' a little cooped up in this place, like I'm in jail. I'm gonna take a little walk outside and get some air. I'll go over to the corral and make sure that feller is takin' care of the horses."

"It ain't bad for a jail, though, is it? You'd better watch yourself walkin' around out there," Jesse warned, with a wink for Booth. "That Hawk feller might be hidin' out in those cottonwoods, waitin' for a chance to catch one of us outside."

"I ain't worried about him," Trip declared. "Matter of fact, I hope to hell he is hangin' around out there someplace. I'd like to invite him to come on out and we'll settle this thing for good. Then we can get on down to Helena, where there's more goin' on."

When he walked out, Jesse looked at Booth and said, "Maybe that problem we talked about might get took care of."

A few minutes later, Josie came downstairs, on her way to the kitchen to help Dinah Belle. "You and Trip weren't upstairs very long," Booth said to her as she passed by the table.

She shrugged indifferently. "He was havin' some problems, said it was because he was in a killin' mood and that messed up his thinkin' about anything else.

Said he was gonna go huntin' for Hawk. He paid me double, though."

"That was probably to keep her from tellin' anybody," Jesse said after she left. He and Booth both had a good chuckle over it.

Outside, Trip sat down in one of the three rocking chairs on the porch. He reasoned that if Hawk was set up on the wagon track up on the bluff, he might take a shot at anyone who walked out of the store. Sitting in a chair, near the front door, he figured he wouldn't present an easy target, so he stared hard at the cottonwoods on both sides of the path down to the store. This would be the most likely spot for a sniper to hide, so he scanned the trees from one side and back to the other, straining to see any movement. After a quarter of an hour, he got up and stepped down off the porch, his whole body quivering from the anticipation of a sudden shot. There was nothing, no sign of anyone.

He turned to go to the corral when suddenly he heard a horse on the path behind him. His hand dropped at once to his Colt. He spun around as he did and fired a shot that barely missed the startled rider. To save himself from a second shot, the rider slid off his horse to keep the horse between him and his assailant. "Don't shoot! I give up!" Mose Avery yelled. "I just wanna go to the blacksmith."

Realizing at once the error in his judgment, Trip holstered his weapon. "You ought to know better than to slip up behind a man like that. You can damn sure get yourself killed."

"I'm sorry, mister," Mose explained. "I just rode down the path to the store, like I do every time I come to trade here. And it bein' broad daylight, I wasn't lookin' to sneak up on nobody."

By this time, the gunshot had summoned Bodine and the two brothers. Out on the porch by then, Bodine yelled, "Mose! What the hell's goin' on?"

Trip quickly answered for him. "Feller here slipped up on my blind side and I had to fire a warnin' shot to keep him from crowdin' me."

"Well, business ain't so good that I can afford to have you kill off my regular trade," Bodine said, more than a little irritated. "Some of the boys are a little touchy right now, Mose. I'm awful sorry about that."

"It was just a warning shot," Trip claimed again. He looked at Booth and Jesse gaping at him in disbelief, and he decided he didn't want to hear what they had to say about it. So, he turned and continued on his way to the barn and the corral.

While he was standing by the corral, he kept looking around him in case he might see some sign of a hidden sniper. Tom Pointer came from the barn. "What did you shoot at Mose Avery for?" Tom asked.

Trip turned to give him a hard look. "I didn't shoot at him. If I'da shot at him, he'd be dead." Not wanting to discuss it with him, he turned abruptly and started back toward the store. Before reaching the porch again, he stopped in the front yard and yelled out as loud as he could, "Hawk! If you're snoopin' around out there, why don't you come on and face me, man-to-man, fair and square!"

When he went back inside, Reuben Pressley walked over from his forge to talk to Tom. "What's wrong with that feller?" he asked Tom. "He acts like he's plum loco. He took a shot at Mose." He looked over toward the store, where Mose was still standing, apparently uncertain if it was safe to move. Reuben waved and called out, "Come on over, Mose."

Back to Pressley's remarks about Trip, Tom said, "I asked him why he shot at Mose and he claimed he wasn't shootin' at him—said it was a warnin' shot."

"My ass," Reuben scoffed. "He just flat-out missed." They both turned to welcome Mose as he led his horse over to them.

"I surely didn't mean to rile that feller up like that," the timid little man started to explain. "He liked to scared me half to death."

"He's got a burr up his behind about some feller that shot one of that bunch that rode in here the other day," Tom said. "He's wantin' to shoot somebody, and that's a fact."

"I was thinkin' about gettin' me a little drink of likker while I had you take a look at the right-front hoof of my horse," Mose said. "But I ain't so sure I wanna go in the saloon now."

"Come on," Pressley said to him, "and I'll take a look at that hoof for you." He turned back to Tom when he walked toward his shop and declared, "Matter of fact, I plan to stay away from all three of them jaspers."

About two miles upstream from Bodine's trading post, Hawk paused when he heard the report of a pistol. At two miles, it was faint, but he thought it sounded like that made by a Colt .44. He continued to listen for a while, but decided it was nothing meaningful, so he went back to work disguising his camp. The crossing was shallow enough, so he could keep Rascal in the water and ride parallel to the bank for close to seventy-five yards before coming out downstream from the crossing. By doing that, he left no tracks from the road when coming from or going to his camp.

Once he had finished his camp to his satisfaction, he turned his mind back to the task of settling with the three outlaws. His aim was still to recover as much of the money as possible and return it to the survivors of the massacre. But he was not dumb enough to think he could walk into that saloon again without being shot at on sight—by Booth and his partners, and possibly Bodine as well. So, he finally accepted the fact that he had to play a waiting game, watching for any opportunity that came his way. With that in mind, he figured it time to go back to make sure they were still there.

Since his camp near the Helena trail was upstream from the trading post, he would approach it from behind the buildings, reaching the corral and barn first. Under cover of the trees that lined the river, he was able to ride close to the corral before thinking it necessary to dismount and leave his horse. So he dropped Rascal's reins underneath the branches of a large bur oak tree and advanced the rest of the way on foot. Right away he was able to confirm the fact that Booth and the other two were still there, for all their horses were in the corral. That was actually all he could expect to find out. Then he got a glimpse of someone moving about in the barn, so he moved a little closer. He was handicapped by the fact that he had never seen the two men with Booth up close, and he didn't know their names. But he had seen them when he had hidden behind the empty cabin next to the one they had occupied. It was in poor light, but he felt confident that he would recognize the man who had been jawing back and forth with Tater. He wore his pistol low in a fast-draw holster. In a few minutes, he recognized Tom Pointer coming back out, carrying a bucket. There was no sign of any of the three he sought, nor did he really expect to see them outside the saloon.

He watched Tom walk back to the store and go inside. There was no one else outside the store. There was someone over at the blacksmith's shop. He recognized Reuben Pressley, but not the man with him. A second look at the little fellow told him he was not one of Booth's men. He wondered then about the pistol shot he thought he had heard. There was no evidence of anything having happened in that calm setting. He decided at that moment that he was not willing to sit and wait for the three to come out of Bodine's. *It's time to bring them outside,* he thought, got up from his kneeling position on the riverbank, and went directly to the corral. While keeping an eye out for anyone coming toward him, he opened the gate wide and walked in among the horses.

Sitting at a table on the saloon side of the trading post, Bodine's three special guests were passing some time in a three-handed poker game. Trip Dawson's streak of winning hands was beginning to wear on the nerves of the two brothers. So, when he spread a ten-high straight before him on Jesse's call, Jesse threw his two pair in disgust. "You ain't that lucky! I swear, if I knew for sure you've been cheatin', I'd shoot you!" Seeing Tom Pointer walk in the door, he invited him to make it a four-man game. Tom wisely declined, saying he had chores to do, and went back outside.

Jesse's frustration served only to fan Trip's confidence. He threw his head back and released a gleeful cackle. "You just ain't used to playin' cards with a real poker player," he taunted.

"The sun don't shine on the same dog's behind all the time," Booth declared. "Deal the cards."

It was Jesse's deal, so he gathered up the cards and started to shuffle. "It's gonna be different this hand," he informed Trip. Laughing in response to Jesse's complaining, he was about to make another boastful prediction when they heard the shots outside.

"What tha hell . . . ?" Booth blurted, and all three stood up immediately, their hands finding their six-guns, all eyes toward the door when Tom Pointer came running back inside.

"The horses!" Tom exclaimed. "They're stealin' the horses!"

"Who is?" Bodine demanded.

"I don't know," Tom said, "but the horses are outta the corral and they're scattered all over the bluffs.

"Injuns, I bet!" Bodine responded. "We ain't had no trouble with Injuns in I don't know when. Most likely them damn Blackfoot. I shoulda knowed when that Hawk feller showed up here, some of them Blackfoot was snoopin' around."

While Bodine ran to get his shotgun, and Tom and Trip stood ready to move to defend themselves, one remained calm. "That ain't no Injuns," Booth declared. "That's Hawk. He's tryin' to get us to come runnin' out there to save our horses. He's tryin' to get us out in the open."

"That son of a bitch!" Trip blurted, still fired up over what he saw as the coward who refused to answer his challenge earlier. "I'll sure as hell come out there to meet him!" He ran for the door, in spite of Jesse and Booth warning him that he was running into an ambush. He ran by Tom, who was crouching just inside the door, his six-gun drawn.

"I don't see nobody out there!" Tom exclaimed when Trip went past him.

"He's out there, all right," Trip called back over his shoulder, "and I want him before he runs off and hides again." Certain now that Hawk would not stand and face him in a shoot-out, he had his Colt .44 in hand with just one thought in mind. That thought was to kill the man who was keeping the three of them from riding on to Helena.

Standing in the open gate of the corral, Hawk saw Trip running from the house. He recognized him as the thin man wearing the quick-draw holster. He was an easy target, but Hawk waited to see if the other two would come out of the store. Hawk could tell when Trip spotted him standing at the corral, for he jerked back to a quick stop, then continued to run straight toward him. His pistol was in his hand, but he didn't shoot. Hawk figured he wanted to get closer because of the inaccuracy of a pistol at long range. *He's crazy*, Hawk decided, drew his Winchester up to his shoulder, and squeezed the trigger. Trip ran half a dozen more steps after the .44 slug struck his chest before crashing to the ground, dead. *That leaves two*, Hawk thought. He continued to wait, but no one came out of the building to check on Trip, no one made any move to save their horses. He had figured Booth and the other man would make some effort to get him, but they remained inside the store. He could not see the blacksmith shop from where he waited, so he moved closer to the corner of the barn in case Reuben Pressley suddenly showed up.

The only show of retaliation came from Rufus Bodine, who was not willing to stand by and see his horses stolen. Out the back door, he came, ran to take cover behind the smokehouse, and promptly began blasting away at the corral with his shotgun. Hawk quickly took cover behind the corner of the barn. He had no sooner taken cover when a chunk of the corner post was chipped away by a shot from a rifle fired by Tom Pointer from the front porch. The return fire placed Hawk in a position he didn't want to be in and should have thought about before he stampeded the horses. He had no reason, and no desire, to shoot at Bodine and Tom Pointer. In spite of the fact that he had extremely low regard for the dishonest old bandit, he had no reason to take his life. And he couldn't blame him and his employee for trying to stop someone who appeared to be stealing their horses. Then he thought of Reuben Pressley again, and the possibility he might join in the fight. As it was with Bodine and Pointer, he had no desire to kill the blacksmith. With all this in mind, he had no choice but to withdraw before he was forced to kill to save his own life.

There was still no sign of Booth or his brother when Hawk retreated to the bank of the river, keeping the barn between him and the gunfire from Bodine and Tom. Moving quickly along the bank, using the trees as cover, he returned to find Rascal patiently waiting

beneath the large oak where he had left him. He
stepped up into the saddle and headed back up the
river for about fifty yards before turning Rascal back
toward the west to make sure there was no chance
anyone at Bodine's could see him. He was heading
to a low ridge close by the trail from Sun River. The
ridge would be the best place to watch the whole trading post, some one hundred yards away. So after he
left his horse on the back side of the ridge, he climbed
up to the top and knelt there while he waited to see if
Booth and the other member of his gang were going
to help gather their horses.

By the time he reached his position on the ridge,
the shooting had stopped. It had taken that long
before Tom and Bodine realized that he was gone.
There was a wait of considerable length before he saw
Bodine run from his cover behind the smokehouse to
a new spot behind the outhouse. While he couldn't
understand what he was saying, Hawk could hear him
yelling some instructions to Tom. And after a few seconds more, Tom left his position at the corner of the
porch, jumped down, ran to the front of the barn, and
disappeared inside. It was only a few minutes more
before he heard Tom shouting from inside the barn,
which Hawk guessed was to tell Bodine he was gone
for sure. To confirm Hawk's guess, Bodine came out
from behind the outhouse and walked to the back
corner of the corral. He was joined there moments
later by Tom, who came out the back door of the barn,
and Pressley, who had taken cover behind his forge.
Glancing back at the forge, Hawk could see the
mousy little man still crouched behind it, but there was
still no sign of the two men Hawk was watching for.

Luckily for Tom Pointer, most of the horses had

not strayed very far from the trading post. Some were wandering back to the barnyard, while some others gathered at the edge of the river. With a little help from Booth and his partner, it wouldn't be a great deal of trouble to round them up and herd them back into the corral. To Hawk's disappointment, Tom was charged with the job of herding them back in all by himself when Bodine went back inside the store. Reuben volunteered to help him, however, knowing it would be difficult for one man to do it. When the sudden stampede of the horses had happened, Reuben had been in the process of shoeing Mose Avery's gray mare. When the shooting started, he and Mose had taken cover behind his forge. And when the shooting was over, Mose chose to stay with his mare while Reuben helped corral the loose horses.

"I'd be glad to give you a hand, Tom, but I reckon that might be a little too risky for me," Hawk muttered to himself, disappointed that Booth had not seen fit to appear. It seemed apparent that he had no intention of leaving the safety of the building, so Hawk decided he might as well return to his camp to cook some more of his venison. At least he had eliminated the one who looked like a gunslinger. He might have been a real threat in a duel, but he hadn't shown much sign of being smart. With only the two of them left to deal with, Hawk considered going into the saloon after them, relying on surprise to give him the chance to take one of them out, so as to face off with only the one left. What he could not count on, however, was for Bodine, Reuben, and Tom to stay out of it. And that was too great a risk. Even if Hawk was successful in getting Booth and his partner, who was still nameless to him, there was the possibility he might hit someone he had no quarrel with.

CHAPTER 14

Bodine was not in a friendly mood when he walked back into the saloon and saw Booth and Jesse seated at one of the tables, both men with chairs angled toward the door, a bottle on the table as well as their handguns. His mood was not improved when Booth asked, "Did you get him?"

Bodine paused before answering, in order to keep from saying what he felt like telling him. "Well, Booth, no, we didn't, didn't even get a good look at who it was. Trip mighta got a better look at him before he got shot in the chest. But you and Jesse don't have to worry, your horses didn't get run off. Me and Tom and Reuben saved 'em for you. Tom and Reuben are roundin' 'em up out there now, if you wanna go out there and take a look."

He was not successful in keeping the sarcastic tone out of his reply and Booth picked up on it. "He got Trip, huh? Well, there wasn't nothin' we could do to keep him from goin' after Hawk. We tried to tell him, didn't we, Jesse?" He looked at his brother to get his nod of confirmation, then looked back at Bodine.

"I tried to tell you that Hawk wasn't after your horses. He got what he came for—Trip—but he didn't get all he came for, and that's because me and Jesse have got better sense than to run right into an ambush."

His indifferent attitude about the death of one of his men did not escape Bodine, who was not known for his compassion for the unfortunate victims of violence. But even he felt a sense of loyalty to one's own gang. "Like I said, we didn't get close enough to get a good look at him. I don't know if it was Hawk or some Injun tryin' to steal a horse." Actually, he was pretty sure it was Hawk, he just wanted to aggravate Booth.

"I know damn well it was Hawk," Booth insisted, rising to the bait.

"I'da thought you and Jesse mighta wanted to get out there and help 'em round up your horses." He paused, then said, "I mean, after you knew he was gone—whoever it was that done it—and it was safe outside."

Again, he was not successful in hiding his sarcasm, and again, it did not go unnoticed by Booth. "Let's get one thing straight, old man," he informed him, no longer willing to play word games. "We're spendin' a helluva lot of money in this dump of yours. We're payin' you to take care of our livestock, so you damn well better make sure those horses ain't gone. From what you've charged us to rent two rooms, I sure as hell ain't plannin' to get out there to round up horses I'm payin' you to take care of."

Bodine didn't like the dressing-down, but he took it because of the violence he knew the two brothers were capable of. He didn't respond at once, and when he did, it was in a calm voice. "What about your friend? Whaddaya wanna do about Trip's body?"

"Hell, I don't care," Booth at first replied, then reconsidered. "Have your man bury him somewhere. Bring his weapons and other personal stuff to me, whatever he's got on him." He glared at him, a smug smile on his face, waiting to see if Bodine wanted to push his luck any further. An amused witness to the discussion, Jesse sensed the tone in Booth's voice that usually signaled an explosion about to happen. Bodine recognized it as well and decided not to push the dangerous man any further. He nodded and turned to go back outside. "Before you go out there again, tell ol' Dinner Bell to make us a fresh pot of coffee. I need something to settle this rotgut whiskey you sell." Bodine didn't reply but turned toward the kitchen door to do Booth's bidding and stopped once more when he spoke again. "While you're at it, tell her she needs to empty those damn chamber pots in our rooms. The air's gettin' downright rank up there."

Thinking that was a little too much to put up with, Bodine replied, "Dinah Belle don't perform no maid work. She does the cookin'."

"What about Josie?" Jesse asked. "She ain't doin' nothin'."

"We ain't had nobody in them rooms before you that used a chamber pot," Bodine answered. "Everybody else just went outside to find a tree, or used the outhouse for serious business."

"We ain't like everybody else," Booth informed him. "Ain't you got it in your head yet that there's a back-shootin' son of a bitch with a rifle hangin' around out there just waiting for one of us to step outside? You saw what happened to Trip, didn't you? Besides, we're payin' you to do it."

"All right," Bodine gave in, "I'll get somebody to empty it, or I'll do it, myself." He went into the kitchen to tell his wife to make the coffee.

"I heard," Dinah Belle said as soon as he walked in. "It's already on the stove. I'll cook and make 'em some coffee, but I ain't emptying no slop jars for the lazy cowards." She glared at her husband as if daring him to object. "I swear, since those bastards came here, it's like we're livin' in a fort or somethin'. It's as bad as it was back when the Injuns were raidin' us," she huffed. "Least that Hawk feller ain't tried to burn the house down yet."

Bodine shook his head, perplexed. "I might have to do that, myself, to get them two outta here. We're gonna make good money off of 'em, but I'm ready to see the last of those two." He started toward the back door but stopped long enough to tell her not to worry about the chamber pot, he would get Tom to take care of it.

Back in the saloon, Booth and Jesse remained seated at the table, the six-guns of each man lying on the table, aimed at the door. They were discussing the split of the late Trip Dawson's estate, mainly the saddlebags in his room upstairs. "What about that roll of bills he likes to carry in his pocket?" Jesse asked, thinking of Booth's orders to Bodine to take care of Trip's body and bring his personal effects to him. "You know damn well Bodine's gonna pocket that and tell us Trip wasn't carryin' any money."

"That's what I think," Booth agreed calmly. "I figure it outta be enough to pay Bodine for our stay here, don't you? 'Cause he ain't gettin' one red cent out of me and you when we're done here."

"That's the next question," Jesse said. "When are we gonna break outta this place? It's startin' to get on my nerves. I'm about ready to shoot my way out. The longer we stay, the more I'm afraid I'll get as loco as Trip was."

"I've been thinkin' about that," Booth said. "And I believe this feller is plannin' to wait us out as long as we stay here, so we're gonna have to take a chance to ride out in the middle of the night. He's got himself a camp close by, and he won't stay away from here long enough to let us get the horses packed up, ready to ride, before he'll be back to see us leavin'. I say, hell, let's stay right here for a couple more days and let him get used to seein' those horses in the corral every mornin' after he's laid awake all night keepin' his eye on 'em. I'm willin' to bet he gets pretty doggone sleepy, tryin' to watch us day and night. I'll bet he thinks, if we're fixin' to leave, we'll most likely start out in the mornin'. After a couple nights, he's gonna figure our horses are gonna be there in the mornin', so he can get a little sleep. That's gonna be the night we slip outta here and head for Helena. We've got a place to go to in Helena where we can stay while we wait to see if Hawk shows up."

Jesse looked surprised. "Is that so? Where's that?"

"The Capital City Saloon," Booth crowed, "owned and operated by Mutt Crocker." He waited for Jesse's reaction. He wasn't disappointed.

"Well, I'll be damned," Jesse swore. "That's right. I forgot all about that. That is where Mutt went—Helena, Montana—to open a saloon."

"Financed by a gunpoint loan from the First Bank of

Wyomin'," Booth reminded him. It had been a source
of envy by the Corbin brothers when Mutt pulled off
one of the biggest bank holdups in Wyoming history
after he left them. Mutt had ridden with Booth and
Jesse until he decided he wanted to be the boss of his
own gang. There had really been no hard feelings
when he left because Mutt was getting a little long in
the tooth to continue riding with them. He was older
than Tater. If things didn't go like he planned, they
figured he'd eventually want to come back. But it
didn't happen. He made that one big bank job and
decided it enough to retire from the bank business.
"Helena ain't but about twenty-five or thirty miles from
here," Booth continued. "We can drive our horses hard
all night, without stoppin'. It'll be a different game in
a town. He ain't gonna be able to hide in the bushes
and pick us off one at a time."

Jesse considered Booth's plan and decided the two
extra days might work like Booth figured. But once
they were successful in escaping, he was more inclined
to find a good spot on the road to Helena and wait
for Hawk to come after them. "It would be him that
wouldn't know somebody was waitin' for him, and I
think he'll get a little careless while he's bustin' his ass
tryin' to catch up with us. I'd like to settle that jasper's
hash before he ever gets to Helena."

"All right," Booth said without hesitation. "We'll do
it that way. We'll each take one packhorse and make
ol' Bodine a present of the rest of 'em. I don't aim to
be trying to drive those extra horses to Helena."

"What we need is for that son of a bitch to get up the
nerve to come walkin' in here to settle it face-to-face,
like ol' Trip was always jawin' about," Jesse said. "That
would make things a helluva lot easier, wouldn't it?"

He had no sooner said it when the outside door to the saloon came swinging open and he stood in the doorway. Without a second's delay, both brothers grabbed the six-guns lying on the table before them and pumped four shots into him. Mose Avery clutched at the doorjamb for support, only to slide slowly down to the floor, dying. Both men got to their feet, guns still in their hands, and ran over to look at their victim, who was softly muttering incoherently. "Damn," Jesse cursed, surprised when he looked at the little man. "Is that him?"

"No," Booth said, and holstered his weapon. "That ain't Hawk."

"Reckon what he's tryin' to say?"

Booth chuckled and replied, "Most likely that he ought notta come in that door." His answer caused Jesse to chuckle as well.

Frightened moments before, when the gunfire went off, Dinah Belle and Josie had taken cover in the pantry. Now that it was over, and everything was quiet in the saloon, they came out and peeked around the kitchen door to see the two men standing over the body. Frightened to see who it might be, they hurried to the saloon door. "It's Mose!" Dinah Belle shrieked. "You shot Mose!" She dropped down on her knees to see if she could do anything for the unfortunate victim. "Mose," she begged. "It's me, Dinah Belle. Can you hear me? I'll try to help you, just try to hang on."

Failing fast, the little man tried to apologize. "I was just wantin' a drink," he managed to sputter weakly through the blood in his mouth, and then he lay still.

Josie glared at Booth. "What did you shoot him for? Mose ain't never done nobody any harm. Why'd you have to shoot him?"

Booth answered her with an indifferent smirk. "I don't know," he said, "maybe because he didn't knock before he walked in." His retort triggered another laugh from his brother.

By this time, the sound of the gunfire had brought Bodine and Tom running to see the cause of it. "What tha . . . ?" Bodine blurted as soon as he saw Mose crumpled up on the floor.

"I swear . . ." Tom started. "Old Mose . . . He just got his horse fixed up."

"What happened?" Bodine addressed his question to Dinah Belle and she told him how the harmless old man came to be gunned down when he walked in the door. Bodine looked first at Booth and then at Jesse, shaking his head slowly in disgust. "Hawk has got you two so spooked till you're shootin' at shadows. Who you gonna shoot next?"

"Maybe you, old man," Booth answered, "if I take a notion."

"Maybe it's time for you and your brother to pack up your mess and get outta here," Dinah Belle blurted since her husband was reluctant to do it. "See how you do outside where there's somebody to shoot back at you. One man's got the two of you so scared you can't walk out the door."

Her remark brought an angry glare from both brothers and a warning from Booth. "You'd best put a bridle on that wife of yours, Bodine, or I'm gonna do it for you."

Bodine was as disgusted as his wife, but her angry remarks had placed him in a bad spot. He took her by the arm and pulled her away from Mose's body. "Go on back in the kitchen, you and Josie, before one of 'em decides to shoot you." Though reluctant to do so, Dinah Belle did as he said, and Josie went with her. Once they were gone, Bodine decided it was time to stand up to the notorious outlaw. "I reckon my wife is my business and none of yours," he told Booth. "I 'preciate the business you and Jesse brought me, but you also brought a world of trouble I didn't have before you came."

It was obvious to Booth that Bodine was trying to work up to the point where he told them to get out, so he interrupted him before he got that far. Calm now, he said, "You want us to leave, and we wanna leave, so I'll make you a deal. Me and Jesse will stay two more days. We'll pay you for everything we owe, plus we'll leave you the extra horses that belonged to Trip, Tater, and Blue. Now, that's a pretty good deal for you. You just make sure your wife does the cookin' like she's supposed to, and we'll be gone in two more days."

"All right," Bodine said, relieved to think he wasn't about to get shot after all. "I'll see you get your money's worth." He turned his attention back to Mose's body. "Come on, Tom, gimme a hand. We'll carry old Mose outta here." He and Tom picked up the body and started out the door when Bodine called back to Booth. "We got all Trip's stuff at the barn. I'll bring it to you. He wasn't carryin' any money."

"Right," Booth said, and winked at Jesse.

Two miles away, Hawk paused to listen when he heard the faint sound of shots fired. They were in a quick series of four and had come from the direction

of Bodine's. He continued listening for a while, but
no more shots followed. He looked at the cup of
coffee he had just poured and hesitated, but he knew
he had to investigate the cause of the shots. "Damn,"
he swore, took a few quick gulps of the hot liquid,
and whistled for Rascal. After he put his fire out, he
climbed up into the saddle and rode back around to
the ridge where he had watched the trading post
before.

The first thing he checked after climbing up on the
ridge was the corral to make sure none of the horses
were missing. This, even in spite of the fact that they
would not have had much time to pack up and go
since he was last there. He decided he had rushed off
and left his coffee for nothing. But then he saw
Bodine and Tom carrying a body out the saloon door,
obviously the reason for the shots he had heard.
From the ridge where he knelt, it was difficult to see
who the dead man was. Hawk watched them as they
carried the body across the yard and laid it down near
the blacksmith's shop. He recognized the body then.
It was the little man who had hidden behind the forge
with the blacksmith during the shooting before.
More senseless killing, Hawk supposed. What, he
wondered, could the insignificant little man have
done to warrant his death? The thought made him
even more impatient to end Booth's trail of terror.

Hawk sat down on the ridge and prepared to keep
watch on the trading post for the rest of the day, leaving only when he thought it too late for Booth to start
out for anywhere. It was to be his routine for the next
two days, until the third day, when he climbed to his
lookout on that morning to discover there were horses
missing. Not all had gone, but the one critical one, a

black Morgan, was not there, and he guessed three others were gone as well. Two riders and two pack-horses, he thought. They had left in the middle of the night while he was sleeping, padded quietly by on the road near his camp, unaware of its existence. And he had not heard them, nor had there been any alert from Rascal. He considered the possibility that they might not have gone to Helena and that was the reason he had not heard them. He quickly discarded that likelihood. Helena was where he was sure they were originally heading, and it was unlikely they would turn around and go back toward Great Falls or Fort Benton. *The fact is,* he thought, *in the middle of the night, we were within seventy-five yards of each other, and none of us knew it.* "I guess I'd best count myself lucky I didn't get shot while I was asleep," he said.

He got to his feet and went back down the ridge, where Rascal was waiting. With no thought toward going into Bodine's to make sure they were gone, he went back to his camp to pack up all his belongings. Soon, he was in the saddle again, on the road to Helena.

CHAPTER 15

He had not traveled more than about nine or ten miles when he came to a wide stream. He paused before crossing to let Rascal drink. Sitting there while he waited for the buckskin to satisfy his thirst, he suddenly became alert, distracted by a noise made by something disturbing the leaves of a serviceberry bush on the other side of the stream. He immediately drew his rifle and backed Rascal around, so he would be facing that way, ready to shoot, if necessary. He cocked the Winchester, even though he suspected he might be preparing to shoot a possum or maybe a large snake. It was difficult to determine in the late afternoon there in the shadows of the trees. Staring at the berry bushes, he was suddenly startled to see a young Indian boy get to his feet with his hands raised in the air. "Don't shoot," the boy spoke in the Blackfoot tongue. "We can do you no harm. We have nothing left to give you."

We, he thought. "Who is with you?" He answered the boy, also speaking in the Blackfoot tongue.

"My father," the boy answered.

"You have nothing to fear from me," Hawk said.
"Tell your father to come out where I can see him."

"He can't. He is wounded, a very bad wound in his
side. I pulled him back to hide behind the bushes
when I heard you coming. I thought you were one of
the men that attacked us."

"What kind of wound?" Hawk asked, not entirely
ready to believe the Blackfoot boy's story.

"They shot him with a gun," the boy said, "and left
him for dead. They shot at me, but I ran in the trees."

"I might be wrong," Hawk said in English, "but I
reckon you sound like you're tellin' the truth." In the
Blackfoot tongue again, he said, "Let me look at him.
Maybe I can help." He rode across the stream, eased
the hammer back down on his rifle, put it back in the
saddle sling, and dismounted. Just in case he was getting played, he rested his hand on the Colt on his
side. He soon saw that the boy was in earnest. Looking
helplessly up at him, the boy's father was lying on his
back, holding a bandanna tightly against his side in an
effort to slow the bleeding from a gunshot wound.

As Hawk bent over him and gently moved the
Indian's hand from the wound, the suffering man's
eyes suddenly became wide open and he uttered one
word. "Hawk?"

Taken by surprise, Hawk did not respond immediately. A picture of the little goblinlike man the Quaker
survivors had called Frog came to mind. He wondered
if the wounded man was commenting on the feather
in his hat, like Frog had. "Yes, I am John Hawk," he
said, bringing a weary smile to the man's face.

"Hawk, friend of Blackfoot," the man said faintly.
"Swift Runner," he said to the boy, "Hawk is friend of

Blackfoot." He closed his eyes as if in peace, alarming the boy.

Hawk felt for a pulse and told the boy his father was just resting. He was not dead. "Swift Runner, is that your name?" The boy nodded. "Who shot your father?"

"Two white men," Swift Runner replied. "They waited in ambush and shot my father and shot at me. Then they took our horses." He studied Hawk's face as the tall scout made a bandage from an old sheet he carried for that purpose. "I pretended I was hit, then when they were chasing our horses, I got up and ran."

"You're lucky to have gotten away, if it's the two men I'm thinking about," Hawk said slowly, thinking before forming his words. It had been some time since he had talked in the Blackfoot tongue. "You speak any white man talk?" he asked in English. When Swift Runner nodded, Hawk asked, "What is your father's name?"

"He is Black Elk," the boy replied, also in English.

"Tell me about the white men who shot you. Why did they shoot at you?" Hawk asked.

"They were waiting in ambush to kill us and steal our horses, I think," Swift Runner replied. He went on to tell Hawk the entire circumstances that brought him and his wounded father back to this stream. He and his father were on their way to Lost Creek, hoping to find deer there. They were on the road that leads to Helena, and as they approached the creek, they were suddenly shot at by the two white men hiding in ambush. Black Elk was hit and told Swift Runner to play dead until the shooting stopped and their attackers went after the horses. When they were chasing the horses, he got up and ran to hide, hoping the white men would leave, and he could come back to help his father. "We had only our bows," he explained. "We could not shoot back." Black Elk managed to get to his feet with his son's help and tried to walk back to their camp in the mountains. But it was too much for him, and he was barely able to get to this stream before he collapsed. "When I saw you coming, I pulled my father up under these bushes. I thought you were one of them."

Hawk was beginning to get a clear picture in his mind of what was supposed to have happened. The two men he pursued had set up an ambush that was intended for him. Thanks to Black Elk and Swift Runner's unfortunate luck, they unwittingly might have saved his life. There could be no other reason for Booth and his friend to wait on that road in ambush. "Where is your camp?" he asked then.

"In the mountains the white man calls Big Belts."

"Ain't that a long way to go huntin'?" Hawk commented. No matter which part of that mountain chain their camp was located in, it was a long way from here.

"We have to go where the deer are," Swift Runner answered.

"Reckon so," Hawk said. He studied the wounded man now seeming to rest easily. And just by Black Elk's reaction when he recognized him as a friend, he guessed that Black Elk felt that he would help them. Hawk thought about the two men who had been waiting for him in ambush, and he was more anxious than before to catch up with them. He knew he was not far behind them now. Maybe they had even set up their ambush again and he might not have a better chance to circle around it and get behind them. This business with the wounded man and his son would greatly delay any chance he had to settle with Booth right away. He knew he had no choice, however. "How far is your camp from here, seein' as how you have to walk it?" Swift Runner said it would be more than half a day. Hawk took another look at Black Elk and shook his head. "I don't think he can sit up in the saddle. We'd best make him a travois and my horse can haul him home." The boy's immediate reaction told Hawk how thankful he was for his help.

The next hour was spent chopping down two small trees to use as poles for the travois and some stout limbs to tie across them for the platform. The crude conveyance took all the rope Hawk had, plus some vines that Swift Runner found, to hold it together. When it was finished, however, Hawk spread his piece of canvas and his bedroll on the platform, then laid Black Elk on it. Rascal was a little uneasy at first, when the two poles were tied on each side of the saddle, but as soon as he understood what Hawk wanted, he was all right with it. With Swift Runner pointing the way and Hawk leading Rascal by the bridle, they set out on a journey that would ultimately take them a full day's walk. It would result in the necessity to camp overnight before they would reach their destination. Hawk could have ridden Rascal, but he elected to walk with Swift Runner to make Rascal's job easier.

While they walked together, Hawk learned a great deal about the Blackfoot man and his son. Like Hawk's friend Walking Owl, Black Elk and his wife and son lived with a small village of mostly older people who were not willing to go to the reservation. The younger men had all gone north into Canada, but Black Elk and the other elders were not up to the bold attempt

to live free again. Their only alternative was to keep a
low profile so as not to attract the army's attention.
Hawk was very compassionate toward this group of
people and had willingly steered army patrols away
from old Walking Owl's village more than once.

At the end of that day's walking, they stopped beside
a small stream to make camp. Hawk and Swift Runner
lifted his father off the travois and settled him as
comfortably as they could. Then Swift Runner gathered wood for a fire while Hawk relieved Rascal of his
burdens. Their patient seemed in reasonable condition, all things considered, even to the extent of eating
a little of the smoked meat Hawk was carrying. A
special treat was the coffee Hawk provided. He had
only two cups, so Black Elk and his son shared one.

As they sat by the fire after eating, Black Elk, in
spite of his pain and discomfort, was curious about
the man called Hawk. "I have heard of you," he said.
"There was talk among the tribes about the white man
who lived with Walking Owl's people many winters
ago. He wore the feather of a hawk in his hat, and he
came to help the people. It was said that this man's
medicine was very strong, and that the feather he
wore was given to him by a great hawk, to be a symbol
of his great medicine. And now the hawk has come in
my and my son's hour of need."

Hawk knew that Black Elk was looking for valida-
tion of stories he had heard from others because he
believed, as all Indians did, in the mystical powers of
the earth's wild creatures. It was not the first time he
had been questioned by both Blackfoot and Crow
about stories of the white man with the hawk feather
in his hat. This was the first time, however, that he had
heard that an actual hawk had plucked one of his

wing feathers and given it to him. He didn't have the
heart to tell Black Elk that he usually found a feather
lying on the ground, most likely the result of a fight
with another bird. And he only stuck it in his hat because his name was Hawk. So he neither denied it or
confirmed it, but said, "A man's medicine may come
from many things. Only that man can know from
which it comes." He thought that sounded pretty mystical, and evidently so did Black Elk, for he nodded
solemnly and sank back on Hawk's bedroll.

When morning came, Black Elk seemed to be some
better, but Hawk thought he was still too weak to walk,
especially since they would now be climbing up into
the mountains. At this point, they were only a few
miles from the village, according to Swift Runner, and
he wanted to run on ahead of them to tell the people
what had happened to Black Elk. "That would be a
good idea," Hawk said, "so they can be ready to help
him. But I'm gonna feed you some breakfast first,
so you can run fast." So, after some coffee and deer
meat, the boy helped Hawk settle his father on the
travois and they set out on the last leg of their journey.
After telling Hawk that the trail he had led him to
would lead to the village, Swift Runner started out
ahead of them and was soon out of sight. "I reckon I
can see where he got his name," Hawk commented to
Black Elk, who nodded, smiling.

The entire village, which consisted of no more than
four tipis, stood waiting for Hawk and Black Elk. It was
a sight Hawk had seen on other occasions, one that
always saddened him. Gaunt, gray-haired men and
tired-looking women, standing at the edge of a clearing,
staring at him as he led the travois toward them. He
could see right away that Black Elk was the youngest

man in the village, and little wonder it was primarily his responsibility to hunt for food to feed the village. It was also obvious that Swift Runner had told them that his father had been saved by the white man who wore the hawk feather in his hat, for their eyes were full of wonder. But Hawk imagined he could also see the disappointment in them as well for the fact that Black Elk and Swift Runner had not returned with fresh meat. He looked beyond the tipis to see half a dozen horses that, in spite of ample grass, looked to be in as poor shape as their owners. His thoughts returned to the mission he had accepted as his own, and the time he was spending away from that mission. It was poor timing, this encounter with a group of poor-devil Indians, who looked to be starving. Once again, he told himself he had no choice. He could not turn away from them without offering some help.

The people gathered around the travois when he led it into the clearing, anxious to see if Black Elk was all right, but equally curious to see the man Swift Runner had said was Hawk, friend of the Blackfoot. A woman Hawk learned later to be Black Elk's wife came immediately to her wounded husband's side and helped move him from the travois and into her tipi. When that was done, Hawk came out of the tipi to find Swift Runner standing beside an elderly man, waiting to introduce him. "This is Wounded Bear," Swift Runner said. "He is our chief."

"Wounded Bear," Hawk greeted him. "My name's John Hawk."

"Welcome to our village," Wounded Bear said. "I have heard of a man called Hawk who once lived with the Blackfoot."

"I reckon that's me," Hawk said.

"Thank you for bringing Black Elk back to us." He turned to smile at Swift Runner. "And Swift Runner, too. They do what they can to provide food for our village, but they have no weapons to hunt with but bows. And it is not always easy to get close enough to the deer and antelope to use their bows."

Hawk didn't have to pause to consider that. "Well, they have now." He walked over to Rascal and untied the buckskin straps holding the Winchester '66 rifle that had belonged to Tater Thompson. He handed it to Swift Runner, then took the Colt .44 and holster from his saddle horn, along with an extra cartridge belt, also property of the late Tater Thompson, and hung them on the boy's shoulder. "You won't have to get so close with these, the rifle, anyway. The handgun ain't bad for small stuff, like rabbits and squirrels and such." Swift Runner said nothing, but his eyes were wide with joy and surprise as he carefully turned the rifle over in his hands as if it were a magical thing. "You might notta fired a Winchester before," Hawk went on. From the look in the boy's eyes, he figured he probably hadn't fired any kind of rifle or gun. "I can show you how best to use it. Your father oughta be up and be gettin' around pretty soon, and then you can show him how to use it."

Seeing the signs of joy in the faces of the people gathered around him, Hawk knew that he could have made no other decision—Booth would have to wait. A smiling Wounded Bear stepped forward to thank him again. "I am ashamed that I cannot prepare a feast to honor you. The hunting has not been good here, and Black Elk has had to travel farther and farther to find game."

"No problem a-tall," Hawk replied. "I've got a little

bit of food with me. We'll just cook that up. I expect my horse will be glad to get rid of it." He untied the bundle of smoked venison Rascal had been carrying and set it on the ground. It caused a wave of excitement to rise among the small gathering of people when he spread the hide out to reveal a still sizable pile of smoked meat. He realized the people were on the verge of starvation as they hurried to prepare the meat. It caused him to make another time-consuming delay in his anxious pursuit of Booth and his partner. He looked at Swift Runner, still holding the rifle as if it were a living thing. "Why don't you and I head out in the mornin'? I think I know where we can find some deer." He was thinking about the herd of deer the cavalry patrol had frightened near Hound Creek between this chain of mountains and the Little Belt Mountains. "The place I'm thinkin' about is less than a half day from here, and you can get a chance to see how that rifle shoots without wastin' a lot of cartridges." His announcement was too much for them all to contain and a happy cheer resulted, bringing the women tending Black Elk's wound out of the tipi to see the cause.

It was impossible for Hawk not to share their joy as every one of the Indians gathered around him stepped up to touch his arm or shoulder, nod happily to him with most repeating the one word, "Hawk." Black Elk's wife left her husband's side to express her thanks for bringing her husband and her son back to her. She introduced herself as Walks Along. Before it was over, Hawk had contributed almost all the supplies he had with him and apologized for not having more. He donated flour, salt, and coffee, keeping only enough strips of jerky to keep him alive until he got to Helena, or some trading post along the way. When he asked if there was a trading post closer to them, he was told there was only one, Bodine's. Wounded Bear said that the man, Bodine, was not very friendly to his people, even when they had money or hides to trade. Hawk didn't tell them of his experiences with Bodine.

A big fire was soon burning in the center of the clearing and before long there were strips of smoked venison roasting over it. With the flour Hawk furnished, the women made pan bread. There was enough for everyone to get a share. Afterward, Hawk was invited to sleep in Wounded Bear's tipi, so he spread his bedroll inside and passed the night there. Up early the next morning, he found Swift Runner waiting for him with two horses that belonged to Wounded Bear, one to ride and one to pack meat. With Wounded Bear and several others there to see them off and wish them good hunting, they set out at once for the east side of the Big Belt Mountains.

After a ride that Hawk estimated to be close to ten miles, they came out of the hills near Hound Creek. There were no deer to be seen, but there was plenty of sign that suggested it was a regular feeding and watering spot for them. Hawk decided to put the horses out of sight and wait in hopes deer came out of the mountains to the creek, thinking there was a good chance of it. While they waited, he gave Swift Runner a little training on sighting and firing his new rifle, so if deer did show up, the boy would be ready to actually shoot at one. Swift Runner had no problem holding the rifle properly and aiming it. After Hawk was satisfied that the boy wasn't likely to shoot him or himself, they settled back and waited. As the sun came up and it grew later and later, Hawk was afraid they had not picked a good spot. But just before he suggested they should move farther around the mountain, one lone buck came out of the trees above them and stopped to sniff the air. Hawk counted ten points on the antlers. He was not a young buck. Swift Runner immediately raised his rifle to his shoulder, but Hawk took hold of the weapon to stop him from shooting. "Wait," he whispered. "There should be more." Swift Runner understood and nodded apologetically. At the boy's young age, he was an experienced hunter. But he was so eager to fire his new weapon that he forgot to wait for the does that were waiting in the trees for the all clear from the buck.

After a few minutes, the buck squealed his signal, and he was joined by a party of four does and one young buck. "Wait till they stop to drink," Hawk whispered, raised his rifle, and set his front sight on one of the does. "You take that young buck. All right?" Swift Runner nodded. When the deer went down to the edge of the water and stopped to drink, both hunters pulled their triggers. Hawk knocked one down, cranked another cartridge in, and downed a second one, while Swift Runner's shot hit the young buck in his haunch, crippling him. The rest of the deer bolted across the creek with the wounded buck trying to hobble after them. With a third cartridge already in the chamber, Hawk quickly brought the buck down.

"I did not kill him," Swift Runner cried out, disappointed with his performance.

"You did good," Hawk said. "You hit him and that's real good for your first shot with that rifle. You just haven't gotten to know that rifle yet. I'da most likely done the same thing if I was shootin' that rifle for the first time. Let's go put 'em outta their misery."

Since the deer hunters were but a few hours' ride from the Blackfoot camp, Hawk decided to throw the carcasses on their horses and take them back there to skin and butcher. He figured they might as well go where there was plenty of willing help to prepare the meat. He had in mind delivering the supply of fresh meat, then saying a quick farewell, anxious to get back on Booth's trail. With Swift Runner's help, he loaded the buck and the smaller doe on the extra horse. The other doe was loaded onto Rascal with him.

When they rode into camp, the reception was as he expected from the near-starving people. Everyone was eager to help, so all he had to do was unload the deer and Wounded Bear's people did the rest. He stood and watched for a few minutes while Swift Runner talked excitedly about the place to find deer so near their village. Ready to leave, Hawk prepared to say good-bye to old Wounded Bear, but he was delayed when the women of the camp came to thank him. Each one was eager to thank him for his help. Waiting for the other women to thank him, Walks Along, Black Elk's wife, wanted to thank him again for bringing her husband and son back to her. "I wish that I could cook you a really fine meal to show you how much I appreciate your kindness." She shook her head sadly, then said, "But we have had no flour, or salt, or sugar, or cornmeal for a long time. And we used what flour you had last night."

Before she could go further, he interrupted. "You

shouldn't feel bad about that. I'm just sorry I didn't have more to give you."

She looked as if she was about to cry, and he knew he would be uncomfortable if she did. So, he quickly told her it was time for him to go; he had to get to Helena right away. Everyone else seemed to be caught up in the skinning and butchering of the three deer, so he said, "Take care of Black Elk. I hope he will soon be on his feet again, so he can hunt with Swift Runner." He turned and went directly to his horse, climbed up into the saddle, and wheeled him back toward the path he had first entered the village on.

So busy were the others that they took no notice of him as he rode down the path, with the exception of one. Wounded Bear raised his head in time to glimpse the tall man on the buckskin as he disappeared into the trees. Then his attention was captured by the sight of a hawk flying across the clearing to a perch in the top of a cottonwood tree. He knew it was a sign—the medicine of the hawk was strong as iron. A random thought crossed his mind, and he wondered if he were to go to the trail now, would there be a man on a horse? Or was it the hawk he had seen overhead, no longer in the form of a man?

"Damn . . . damn . . . damn," Hawk kept repeating as Rascal found his way back down the narrow path. "I've got business to attend to. I can't waste any more time in these mountains. There's no tellin' if Booth and his partner are in Helena or gone on somewhere else without leavin' a trail for me to follow." Rascal understood his dilemma, but as usual, made no comment. "Here I am only halfway done with what I set out to do, and I've only recovered one fourth of the money that belongs to Donald Lewis and his people," he went on, knowing he was losing the argument. "Oh, to hell with it," he finally cursed, wheeled Rascal off the path, and rode up through the trees until he reached the back side of the clearing where the horses were grazing. Without getting out of the saddle, he rode into the small herd, grabbed the bridle of the horse Swift Runner had ridden on the hunt for deer, and led it back the way he had come. Then he continued on down the path, leaving the Blackfoot village to enjoy their celebration.

CHAPTER 16

"What tha hell . . . ?" Rufus Bodine blurted. He found it hard to believe he was seeing the man who had just walked in his store. "Hawk!" he blurted again, and started to reach for a shotgun leaning against the end of the counter.

"Now, why in the world would you wanna do somethin' as stupid as that?" Hawk asked as he leveled his rifle at him. "How long would you stay in business if you greeted every customer like that?" He glanced up to see Dinah Belle coming in from the kitchen, curious to see what had caused her husband to bellow. "Good evenin', Mrs. Bodine," Hawk said. "I just came in to buy a few supplies, and your husband went for his shotgun." She paused in the doorway, just as astonished as her husband, not knowing what to say.

"You got your nerve, comin' in here," Bodine growled, waiting for what he feared was coming.

"Why do you say that?" Hawk replied. "You run a store, don't you? Ain't my money good enough for you?"

"You know why," Bodine shot back, his astonishment rapidly turning into anger. "You come in here, stampede my horses, and shoot one of my customers down. You're lucky I didn't see you ride up. I'da shot you down before you got off your horse."

"Now, whatever gave you that idea?" Hawk asked, still holding his rifle ready to shoot. He gave Dinah Belle an inquisitive look, as if he couldn't understand what was possessing her husband. "Do you think I did what he said, ma'am?"

She was not sure how to respond right away, but then answered him. "Well, somebody sure as hell did what Rufus just said." She looked at her husband then. "Nobody ever really did get a look at who done the shootin'." She reminded him then, "You told Booth nobody got a look at the shooter but Trip, and he was dead. It was Booth that said it was Hawk, and Booth wouldn't go out the door. So he didn't see who it was."

"You came in here askin' me if four men came through here," Bodine said. "Said you was tryin' to catch up with 'em."

"I sure did," Hawk said, "and you told me they were here, but kept on goin' on their way to Helena. So I never had any reason to doubt you and I kept on goin'. They didn't come back here, did they?" Bodine was too flustered to answer at that point. "Anyway, I ran into some friends of mine. They're short on supplies and you're the closest store, so that's why I'm here—to buy supplies." He looked from one of the Bodines to the other, both of them standing dumbfounded from the conversation just ended.

Bodine and his wife exchanged puzzled glances, then Bodine asked, "Whaddaya need?"

"To start, I need some flour. I'd say about a hundred pounds," Hawk answered.

"A hundred pounds?" Bodine repeated, surprised. "That's half a barrel of flour."

"Right," Hawk said, then proceeded to call out a few other things, like salt, sugar, beans, and coffee, all in large amounts.

"You got the money for all this?" Bodine asked, still expecting a holdup about to occur. "Startin' with the flour, at twenty cents a pound, that's gonna run you about . . ."

He paused to look at Dinah Belle then, who replied, "Twenty dollars."

"Right," Bodine repeated. "Twenty dollars."

"Now, I'm buyin' a lot of supplies from you, so when I buy a hundred-pound bag of flour, I expect to get a better price than that. I know things are higher out here than they are back East, but I'm thinkin' more like a nickel a pound."

"Hell, I'd have to get more'n that for it. That's damn near what I pay for it. How 'bout ten cents a pound?"

"How 'bout eight?" Hawk countered. And so it went, with bargaining continuing with every item on his list. A fascinated bystander, Dinah Belle watched the trading, halfway excited about the size of the order and halfway expecting to be robbed of it and maybe more. When the list was completed, she added up the total cost on a paper sack and pushed it across the counter in front of Hawk. He took a moment to look it over, then said, "Looks right to me."

Bodine and his wife each took a step back from the counter, with Bodine inching a little closer to the shotgun at the end of the counter. Expecting some such move, Hawk walked directly to the end of the counter, picked up the shotgun, took the shells out of it, and propped it back against the counter. Then he pulled his money out of his pocket and counted out enough to pay for his purchase, a move that took both husband and wife totally by surprise. Amazed by what had just happened, Bodine's manner was immediately converted to that of a grateful merchant. "You're gonna need a hand loadin' all that on your horses," he volunteered, and came around the counter to help.

"Much obliged," Hawk said, and put his rifle aside so he could pick up a fifty-pound sack of flour. Dinah Belle picked the rifle up, giving him pause when he wondered if he had taken his bluff too far. But she merely followed him outside and handed it to him after he dropped the sack of flour beside his packhorse. He replaced the rifle in his saddle sling and turned to see Tom Pointer coming from the barn.

When Tom saw who it was and both Bodine and Dinah Belle out in front of the store, he had to stop to think what to do. When Bodine, who was standing there, his arms loaded with smaller sacks, saw Tom, he said, "Don't just stand there. Give us a hand. There's another fifty-pound sack of flour in there." With eyes wide with confusion, Tom went to get the flour.

With Tom's help, Hawk tied the two sacks of flour on the extra horse, one sack on each side, to balance the load. Then the smaller sacks were tied on, some on the packhorse and some on Rascal's saddle. Hawk stepped up into the saddle and nodded politely to Dinah Belle, then told Bodine, "Pleasure to do business with you," wheeled his horse, and rode out of the yard.

"Come back to see us," Dinah Belle suddenly called out as he rode away, for no reason she could explain.

Bodine looked at his wife and exclaimed, "Now, ain't that somethin'?" He unconsciously took Hawk's

money out of his pocket and stared at it, as if it might
not be real.

Totally confused, Tom looked first at one face and
then the other, searching for some explanation.
When none was offered, he asked anxiously, "Am I
goin' loco? What just happened here? I thought he
was the one who . . ."

That was as far as he got before Bodine interrupted
him. "Yeah, he's the one, all right, but I don't know.
Maybe he ain't." He looked at his wife and said,
"Didn't none of us get a good look at who was doin'
the shootin' when Trip Dawson got killed."

"And you remember," Dinah Belle reminded him
again, "Hawk was the one that kept that Blackfoot
Injun from scalpin' you when they was in here four
years ago."

Wounded Bear's eyes opened slowly. Something
had awakened him. He looked over at his wife, sleeping peacefully, so he knew it was much too early to get
up. He lay back and closed his eyes again, hoping to
go back to sleep, but then he heard it again, and he
realized it sounded like the snuffling of a horse as it
grazes. Concerned then that it might be a raccoon or
a possum trying to get into the tipi, he roused himself
up from his blanket. "What is it?" his wife asked, when
she awoke to find him getting up.

"Go back to sleep," Wounded Bear said. "A varmint
is trying to get in the tipi." He picked up a hand ax
and went outside. When he did not return, and she
heard no sound from him, his wife got out of her
blanket and went outside to find him standing beside
a horse. He turned when he heard her come out

behind him. "It is the Hawk," he said softly with a voice trembling with reverence, then he stepped aside so she could see the horse, loaded down with supplies. "This is the horse that was missing. Hawk has sent it home."

With the first light of morning, a little more than ten miles away from the Blackfoot camp, Hawk came out of his blanket, anxious to get back on the road to Helena. It had been pretty late when he led the paint gelding into Wounded Bear's sleeping village and tied it to one of the chief's tipi poles. He knew the supplies he had left them would last only a little while, but he thought that maybe they would enjoy them for that short time. Maybe, now that they owned a rifle, they might be able to provide meat for the tiny village. He hoped they would be wise enough to trade the pelts for more ammunition. In his heart, he hoped the village would be able to survive as free men and women, but in his mind he knew that to be highly unlikely. They would soon die if they didn't go to the reservation, but they preferred that to living on the reservation. *I can't blame them,* he thought as he saddled Rascal. He felt free to take care of the business that caused him to be this far up the Missouri River, now that he felt he had done what he could for Wounded Bear's people. Once again, David Booth was his main target to concentrate on. And the sooner he could track down Booth and his partner, the sooner he could get back to a normal life as he knew it. There was only one priority that stood in the way of that ambition, and that was a hot breakfast at Sophie's Diner in Helena, next to the Davis Hotel. While he tightened the cinch on his saddle, he paused to think about the attractive owner of the dining room. *Sophie Hicks*, he thought, and wondered if she would even give him the time of day when he showed up there again. Every time before, there had been circumstances that prompted him to leave almost as soon as he had arrived. It appeared that this visit to Helena would be no different in all likelihood. It might be better not to even go to see her until his business in Helena was finished. But he was only fifteen miles away, at best, and he was craving a good hot breakfast with eggs and biscuits that someone else fixed. He'd been living off smoked venison for too long, and now he didn't even have any more of that. He had given all of it he had on his first day in Wounded Bear's camp. The decision made, he climbed into the saddle and started off to strike the Helena road.

They were clearing tables left by the early customers when he walked in the door. Sophie paused and stared at him for a few seconds before announcing loud enough for him to hear, "I do declare, Martha, look who just walked in the door. Are my eyes deceiving me, or is that really John Hawk?" Martha didn't reply, but paused in her work to form a big grin on her round face.

"Mornin'," Hawk offered sheepishly. "I hope I ain't too late for breakfast." He wasn't sure why he always turned bashful in the presence of Sophie Hicks. He wasn't bashful around any other woman.

"Well, I reckon not," Sophie allowed, still in a mood to tease. "Whaddaya think, Martha? You think you could take the time to scramble up some eggs for Mr. Hawk?"

"Course I can," Martha said at once, not inclined to bedevil the tall young man who always wore a feather in his hat. After all, she thought, he had told her that she was the best cook in the whole territory. "You set yourself down right here and I'll get you some coffee and have some breakfast for you in a jiffy."

Sophie had to laugh. "You go ahead," she said. "I'll get his coffee for him." He sat down at the table Martha had just cleared, and in a minute or two, he was joined by Sophie with his coffee and a cup for herself. "What brings you to our fair city this time?" she asked, remembering the last time he was in Helena he was involved in a shooting and left town almost as fast as he arrived. "Are you gonna be here awhile this time?"

"I don't know," he answered her question honestly. "I reckon I'll have to wait and see." She didn't have to say anything; he could see in her expression that she decided he hadn't changed. "I'd sure like to stay awhile, but I just can't say yet. I'da been back sooner, but I had to do some scoutin' for the army." He hoped his face didn't reveal what he was thinking when he looked at her. *If ever I was to get married, it would be to a woman just like you, if she'd have me.* Whenever thoughts of that nature entered his mind, he told himself he would never get married. He couldn't. He had no steady job, he didn't own a farm or a cattle ranch. He was just a drifter, so he attempted to put the idea out of his head. "I reckon I had to get back in town to see if you'd gotten married yet."

"Ha!" she exclaimed. "Fat chance of that. I'm a little more particular about who I get tied to." Too impatient to play the game any longer, she finally asked, "What are you really in town for?"

"I'm tryin' to catch up with a couple of fellows that have caused a world of hurt to a lot of folks," he said.

He didn't have to say more before she interrupted. "Why are you always chasing outlaws and murderers? You're not a lawman, are you?" When he shook his head, she continued, "Then why don't you leave the job of catching outlaws to lawmen who are paid to do it?"

"It ain't by choice," he was quick to protest. "It just happens to fall in my lap."

"Well, when it falls in your lap," she insisted, "take it to the sheriff or some other lawman and dump it in theirs."

"Sometimes there just ain't any lawman handy," he tried to explain, but she obviously didn't accept that. So he told her more than he had anticipated telling her. He told her about the vicious massacre of the religious group near Fort Benton and the fact that, were it not for him, no one would be after the men who did it. "When we started out, I was scoutin' for the cavalry patrol that was after those outlaws. After a while, the patrol had to return to Fort Ellis. There wasn't anybody to keep after the outlaws but me. I didn't have any choice."

"And you've followed them to Helena?" she asked, still of the opinion that it was not up to him to do so. "And if they are here, what are you going to do, shoot them down?"

"Well, that ain't the best way of handlin' it," he answered, while thinking that was exactly what he had in mind. "Is Porter Willis still the sheriff? Maybe I can get him to help if I see those outlaws in town."

"Porter's still the sheriff," Sophie said. "But he's not

fully recovered from the shot he took in his belly." She paused and raised an eyebrow as she added, "The last time you were in town."

"I don't reckon you've seen any new fellows in the dinin' room in the last couple of days, have you?" he asked just in case Booth might have stopped in the hotel.

"Sure," she replied. "We see new people in here all the time, don't we, Martha? It's hard to tell which ones are mass murderers. Maybe we should start asking." She got up from the table then and went into the kitchen. Martha watched her till she went in the door, then shook her head solemnly as she filled Hawk's coffee cup.

"I don't mean to do it," Hawk said to Martha, "but I always seem to get her riled up."

"You sure do," Martha agreed. She could have told him what she was thinking but decided not to. *She gets riled up at you because she cares for you. You're just too blind to see it.*

He finished his breakfast, paid Sophie, and told her he was hoping to get back for supper. She realized she had been a little less than gracious when he came in, so she offered some cheerful conversation to send him off. "Good, I'll look forward to it."

He went to the sheriff's office next, only to find the door locked and a sign hanging on the doorknob that said the sheriff would be back in an hour. Since he didn't know when Porter had hung the sign there, he decided not to wait and headed for the Last Chance Saloon instead. As a precaution, he stood just inside the doorway and scanned the room before entering. Dewey Smith, the bartender, sang out as soon as he stepped inside. "Hawk! When did you get in town?"

"'Bout an hour ago," Hawk replied. "Thought I'd stop in to see if you folks were still in business."

"We're in business, all right," a voice from the storeroom door called out, "and gettin' busier every month." Hawk turned to see Bertie Brown coming to meet him, her face one big smile. She walked up to him and extended her hand. "I was wonderin' when you were gonna ride up this way again."

"Howdy, Bertie." Hawk took her hand and they shook, as was Bertie's style. "I figured you'd be managin' this saloon by the time I got back here."

"I'll say she is," Dewey said. "It's got to where Sam don't hardly ever come in but once in a while to count the money."

"We treat the customer right," Bertie boasted. "Makes 'em wanna come back." Always thinking of business, she asked, "You ridin' scout for a bunch of soldiers? We're real partial to our brave boys in uniform."

"No," Hawk said. "Hate to disappoint you, but I'm by myself this time." Dewey and Bertie both waited to hear what brought him to town, but that was all the explanation he offered until Bertie pressed him for more. "Well," Hawk told them, "I'm tryin' to catch up with a couple of jaspers that headed this way. Fellow name of Booth, I don't know the other one's name. You ain't seen anybody like that, have you?"

"Not that I know of," Bertie said. "Can't say that I haven't, though. I don't ask every saddle tramp that comes in here what his name is. What did these fellers do to get you on their tail?"

Hawk told them what Booth and his gang of

murderers had done and how it now happened that he alone was still on their trail. "My stars in heaven," Bertie exclaimed. "We heard about them church folk that got killed. You sayin' the bastards that done that are here in town?"

"I don't know if they are or not," Hawk explained. "There were five of 'em that did the killin'. Three of 'em are dead, and the last sign I got of the other two was leadin' to Helena. I'm a couple of days behind 'em now. I got sidetracked back at Wolf Creek." He didn't bother to elaborate on the reason.

Totally concerned at this point, Bertie looked at Dewey. "You see anybody like that come in here the last couple of days?" Before he could answer, she looked back at Hawk. "What did you say that feller's name was?" When Hawk told her the one name he knew was Booth, she looked at Dewey again for his answer.

"Not that I know of," Dewey replied. "Like you said, though, we don't usually ask them their names. What do they look like?" he asked Hawk.

"I don't know, just regular-lookin' jaspers," Hawk answered. "The one named Booth rides a black Morgan with a fancy saddle. That's about all I can tell you."

They talked awhile longer, then Bertie's daughter, Blossom, came down the stairs, a young cowhand preceding her by about ten minutes. Like her mother, her face lit up when she saw Hawk standing there at the bar. Unlike her mother, however, she ran up to him and locked him in a warm embrace. John Hawk had helped her and her mother when they were in desperate need of help and she would always be indebted to him.

CHAPTER 17

"How 'bout it?" Mutt Crocker bellowed. "That room suit you all right? You ain't gonna get nothin' much fancier up at the hotel." He grinned at them as they came down the steps to the saloon.

"I've seen worse," Booth Corbin answered. "I reckon it'll do. What do you think, Jesse?"

"I've slept in fancier jail cells than that, but I reckon it'll do," Jesse japed the onetime member of their gang and now owner of the Capital City Saloon. "How'd you come up with the fancy name for this place?"

Mutt shrugged. "Since they moved the capital of Montana to Helena, it's the capital city, so I thought that's what I oughta call it."

"How's business?" Booth asked. "I mean, since you're not exactly in the center of the town."

"I was lucky to get this spot on a back street, as it was. I didn't have the money to buy anybody out on Main Street. But I'm doin' all right since I got Loretta workin' the floor," Mutt said with a nod of his head to the bored-looking woman sitting at a table watching them. "She does all right when the evenin' crowd comes in, sells a lotta whiskey for me." Having ridden with the two brothers before, he was sure they were this far from Wyoming for a good reason, so he asked point-blank, "Who's after you boys?"

"What makes you think anybody's after us?" Booth said, and winked at Jesse. "Me and Jesse just wanted to see how an old bandit like you was makin' out tryin' to run a saloon, knowin' you as good as we do."

"Is that a fact?" Mutt huffed. "You boys wouldn't be up this way if you wasn't on the run. Who can I expect to be showin' up here lookin' for you? You ain't had a fallin'-out with the rest of the boys, have you? When I left Wyomin', Trip Dawson, Tater Thompson, and Blue Davis was ridin' with you. Ain't they with you no more?" He looked from one brother to the other, waiting for the truth. His suspicion was that Booth and Jesse had somehow double-crossed the rest of the gang.

Booth shrugged. "I know what you're thinkin', but it ain't like that. All three of them boys are dead, and they all got killed by the same man. Trip was the last one he got, and that was Trip's fault. He went plum loco, wantin' to shoot it out with him, so the son of a bitch shot him."

Mutt shook his head, thinking of the fast gun that Trip was. "Where was that?" Booth said it was at Bodine's on Wolf Creek. "Bodine's?" Mutt responded. "Ain't nobody killed that ornery old goat yet?"

"Not since a couple of days ago," Jesse quipped. "But there ain't no tellin' now, since me and Booth ain't there to protect him."

"Who the hell is this feller that's got you on the run? A marshal or some other lawman?" Mutt asked.

"No, he ain't no lawman," Booth answered. "Me and Jesse figure he found out about a job we pulled that was a pretty big payday, and he's thinkin' he wants to get some of it."

"Just one man?" Mutt found that hard to believe. "And the two of you can't take care of one man?"

"He had us pretty much holed up at Bodine's, so that's the reason we came here," Booth said. "To get him out in the open. We set up an ambush, figurin' he was gonna follow us. We were gonna take care of him for good, but the bastard never showed up. So we ain't sure if he's give up on tailin' us or not. I reckon we'll find out if he shows up here."

Mutt was working his mind on the piecemeal story he was getting and the one thing that struck him was that Booth and Jesse must have made a big score on some job. They were pretty tight-lipped when it came to talking about it, so that told him it must have been so big they didn't want him to know how much they stole. Maybe, he figured, there was a possibility he could cash in on it as well. "This jasper that's tailin' you, has he got a name?"

"Yeah, his name's Hawk," Booth said. "He's easy to spot, big feller, wears a buckskin shirt, and has a feather in his hat."

"Hawk," Mutt repeated. "I've heard somethin' about a feller named Hawk. He had some kinda trouble here, in the Last Chance Saloon. I don't know what it was, but I think that Hawk feller is a big friend of Sam Ingram's, who owns the Last Chance." Thinking now about getting his hands on some of Booth and Jesse's money, Mutt made a suggestion. "What you need is a man who's an expert at gettin' rid of people like that."

"We don't need nobody to do our killin' for us," Jesse responded, his dander up at the suggestion. "We just need to catch him when he's out in the open, face-to-face, then we'll see who kills who."

"You're startin' to talk like Trip Dawson," Booth said. "It would be a lot easier for somebody Hawk ain't ever seen to get the jump on him." Turning back to Mutt then, he said, "You talk like you've got somebody in mind."

"I do," Mutt replied. "Billy Crocker—he's the fastest man with a gun this town's ever seen."

"Your son, Billy?" Booth responded in surprise. When last he had heard of Mutt's son, he was serving time in prison for holding up a stage out of Cheyenne. "Has it been that long? I wouldn't have figured he'd served his time yet."

Mutt chuckled when he replied, "Neither did the territory of Wyomin', but Billy figured he'd served as much time as he wanted to. He's been layin' low since he came out here, pickin' up cash any way he can. So far, ain't nobody complained about his work. You oughta talk to him, let him take care of that little problem of yours. Hell, if you pay him, Billy'll go find him, even if he didn't follow you here."

"Maybe you're right," Booth said, "if he ain't lookin' for too much to do the job—save us a little trouble." He glanced over at the bored woman sitting at the table. "Is it all right to talk about it with her sittin' right here, listenin' to every word?"

Mutt chuckled. "Ain't nothin' to worry about with Loretta. She's heard a lot of talk in here since I opened up and she knows not to open her mouth about it. I think you'll be satisfied with Billy to do the job. He'll be in to get some grub around suppertime."

* * *

At the other end of the street, Hawk pulled Rascal up in front of the stable and dismounted. Seeing no one in the blacksmith's shop next door, he figured to find Grover Bramble at the stable. Grover took over the stable after Frank Bowen was shot down by a fellow named Zach Dubose. He remembered Hawk because it happened that he was his first customer when he became the stable owner. On this day, Grover was cleaning out some stalls when Hawk walked in. "Well, John Hawk," he declared when he saw who it was. "When did you get back in town?"

"Grover," Hawk greeted in return. "This mornin'. How's business goin' for ya?"

"I reckon I can't complain, and even if I do, it don't seem to make no difference. You wantin' to board that buckskin?" He took a look out the stable door. "You ain't got a packhorse?"

"No, I don't, and I've regretted it every day on this trip. I'll leave Rascal with you at least for tonight, and if you don't mind, I'll just sleep with him. I don't know if I'll be here longer'n one night or not. I'm hopin' I'm on the trail of two men I think came to Helena. Any chance you've seen two strangers, one of 'em riding a black Morgan with a fancy saddle with a lot of handwork on it and both of 'em leadin' a packhorse?"

"Nope, I ain't seen nobody like that come by here. What are you followin' them for? I thought you was ridin' scout for the army. You ain't gone to work as a lawman, have you?"

"No," Hawk answered. "Things just turned out that way." He went on to explain to Grover what had happened near Fort Benton, and how it was that he was left with the job of running two killers to ground. "And the trail I've followed tells me they came here."

"My Lord," Grover gasped after hearing what crimes these men had committed. "We don't need men like that in Helena. Whaddaya gonna do if you don't run across 'em here?"

"Damned if I know," Hawk admitted. "'Cause I reckon I'll have to admit I've lost 'em for sure." He was sure the ambush that Black Elk and Swift Runner had stumbled into was meant for him. And when that failed, he assumed the two outlaws would continue on to Helena. He had no tracks to confirm it, however. They may have set out in a different direction. "Well, I'm gonna walk around town to see what's what," he said after he took Rascal's saddle off. "Are you gonna lock up that tack room when you leave to go to supper?" Grover said that he usually did, so Hawk said, "I'd like to leave my saddlebags in there. I've got a little money in 'em that I don't like to carry around." He didn't tell Grover how much he was carrying in his saddlebags. He was sure that Grover was honest, but if he told him he had Tater Thompson's share of the Quaker robbery in the tack room, and how much it was, it might worry him to death. "I'll get some supper at the hotel dinin' room, then I expect I'll stop by the Last Chance for a drink and that'll about do me for the night."

When he left the stable, it was way too early for supper, so he took the time to stop in the general store to pass the time of day with Betty Benton, Chad Benton's widow. Chad had been killed by the same man who shot Frank Bowen. Betty was glad to see him again and introduced him to her brother, Phil, who had come to help her run the store. Like Grover, they could not remember having seen any strangers during the last several days. He left them without telling them the whole story behind his trailing the two men, only that they were dangerous. He made one more call before going to supper and that was in the Gold Nugget Saloon. He was met with the same response as everywhere else he had checked, with one exception, and that was the fact that there was a new saloon in town. Back off the main street a little way, the saloon was called the Capital City Saloon. The folks at the Capital City were not friendly with all the other merchants in town, he was told. He decided to pay them a visit in the morning, for it was suppertime by then and he had told Sophie Hicks he hoped to show up.

Sophie was engaged in a casual conversation with two young men at a table near the front door of the dining room when Hawk walked in. She laughed delightedly at something one of them said. Hearing the door open, she turned to see Hawk and interrupted her chatting only long enough to greet him politely and say, "Sit anywhere you like, Hawk."

He didn't know that he had any right to expect anything more than that, so he had to question why it seemed to disappoint him. It registered in his mind that she hadn't called him John, calling him simply Hawk, like everybody else. It seemed blatantly impersonal. Then he scolded himself for thinking they were better friends than that. At first glance, he guessed the two young men she was talking to might be cowhands from one of the ranches close by. Suddenly feeling out of place, he quickly found a chair at an empty table and sat down with his back to that table. Seeing him from the kitchen door, Martha poured a cup of coffee for him and brought it to him. "Evenin', Hawk," she said. "Glad to see you came back to eat with us. You're in luck tonight. Betty Benton got in a barrel of dried apples and Sophie got enough of 'em to make a couple of apple pies."

"Well, that surely sounds to my likin'," Hawk said. "I'll have whatever you're pushin' for supper tonight."

"Beef stew," Martha said. "I'll fix you up a plate," she called back over her shoulder, "and I'll set a slice of that pie aside to be sure you get some."

"Much obliged," Hawk called after her. He sat there, sipping the hot coffee, trying to get his mind back on the business that caused him to be in this town. He was still irritated with himself for letting irresponsible thoughts take control of his mind when he suddenly felt a hand on his shoulder, causing him to start.

"Whoa, horse!" Sophie said. "You're as jumpy as a cat. What were you thinking about?"

"Nothin'," he quickly insisted. "I just wasn't expectin' it, that's all."

"Glad you made it back for supper. Is Martha fixing you a plate?"

"Yes, she is," Martha answered for him, coming through the doorway at that moment, carrying a plate heaped high. She placed it on the table before him and checked to see if he needed coffee.

"If you pile everybody's plate up that high, we're not gonna have enough to make it to closing time," Sophie teased.

"Hawk appreciates my cookin'," Martha said, "so I like to see that he gets plenty of it." She turned her head toward him and gave him a little smile. "Besides," she went on, "if you hadn't been flirtin' with those two cowboys over there, you mighta waited on him and fixed his plate the way you wanted it."

"That's just doing business," Sophie replied. "Those boys come in here to eat every week. Mr. Hawk, here, doesn't come in but once in a blue moon." She turned quickly toward him then. "But we're still mighty glad you come in when you are in town."

Sitting there with his fork raised halfway to his mouth, he was astonished by the inane bantering between the two women. Noticing, Martha said, "Look, we've got him so confused he can't enjoy his supper. Let's let him eat." Another customer came in the door at that moment, so Martha said, "Go take care of that customer. I'm going back to the kitchen, and we'll let Hawk eat."

When they left him, it felt to him like he had been struck by a lightning bolt of reality, his own, in particular. And he realized the absurdity of his thinking there might be something between him and Sophie. His life was not compatible with any woman's. When he was not working for the army, his home was a cabin, far up the Boulder River, on a stream three hundred yards up the side of a mountain where nothing but wild animals lived. He had no future to offer a woman. With that discouraging truth fixed firmly in his brain, he signaled Martha to bring his apple pie, which he made short work of. Gulping the last of his coffee down, he left his money on the table and headed for the door. *What I need is a drink of whiskey,* he said to himself.

* * *

Booth glanced at Jesse when the stranger walked in the door. He didn't have to be told that the man was Billy Crocker. Jesse nodded in response to Booth's unspoken signal. Billy paused to look the room over. His gaze stopped for a moment on the two men sitting at the table in the back corner next to the kitchen door before continuing. Fred Futch, the bartender, nodded and said, "Evenin', Billy." Billy responded with a nod, then proceeded toward the kitchen with the swagger of a man confident in his ability to master any challenge anyone might offer. Both Jesse and Booth gave him a nod when he walked past their table. His manner was typical of most gunslingers who believed themselves faster than any other man with a six-gun. He was reminiscent of Trip Dawson, with the exception in the way he wore his .44. Billy wore his in a double holster with the handles forward.

He didn't return the nods from the two brothers as he stepped inside the kitchen door to inform the cook that he was ready for his supper. His father was in the kitchen, talking to Cora, and he answered for her. "She'll fix you a plate," Mutt said. "First, I want you to talk some business with those two fellers settin' at the table."

"What about?" Billy asked. "I'm hungry."

"Won't take but a few minutes, and it'll damn sure be worth it," Mutt said. "That is, unless you've come into a lotta money I don't know about." Billy responded with nothing more than a bored shrug of his shoulders. "Come on in here for a minute," Mutt insisted. When Billy walked on into the kitchen, Mutt took hold of his elbow to make sure he had his attention. "That's Booth and Jesse Corbin settin' at that table out there. You've heard me talk about ridin' with them before I went on my own. They're two of the meanest men the devil ever put on this earth, so you need to keep that in mind. I think they're settin' on a lotta money from some job and they've got some jasper on their trail they need to get rid of."

"If they're so mean, why don't they get rid of him?" Billy was inclined to ask.

"This jasper's pretty slick, so they ain't been able to corner him, but he's already shot three men that was ridin' with 'em. I told 'em they'd be smart to hire you to do the killin', figurin' somebody he don't know could get close to draw him out. Oughta be a nice payday for you."

"All right," Billy said. "I'll talk to 'em."

He followed Mutt back into the barroom, where he was introduced to the Corbin brothers. "This is my boy, Billy," Mutt said. "I ain't never seen nobody faster with a six-shooter than Billy." He paused only a moment before saying, "And I've seen Trip Dawson draw." He paused again to gauge the interest generated so far in his selling of his son's services, then continued, "Billy killed two men at the same time in a gunfight in the Trailsman Saloon in Cheyenne. That's why he's out here in Montana now, waitin' for things to cool off in Wyomin'."

"It's a wonder we ain't ever heard of you," Booth said, talking directly to Billy. "Maybe it's because you're so young." Billy shrugged indifferently. "How old are you, anyway?"

"What difference does that make?" Billy responded.

"He's goin' on nineteen," Mutt quickly replied for him, afraid that his gruff indifference might queer the deal.

"Old enough to know what the consequences are

if you ain't as good as you claim, I reckon," Booth said. "I've gotta warn you, if we was to give you this job, you won't be comin' up against some drunk in a saloon. This cat ain't nobody to fool with."

"Is he fast?" Billy asked, starting to get interested.

"With a handgun?" Booth replied. "I don't know. He seems to favor a rifle from a distance, but he killed Tater Thompson with a knife. I've met him, although at the time I didn't know who he was, and he didn't know who I was. If I had, I'da shot him. He's a big feller, tall, wears a buckskin shirt and a feather in his hat, like a damn Injun."

"I'd like to see how fast he is when he's standin' in front of me," Billy said. "A big man ain't nothin' but a big target. How much is it worth to ya?"

Booth glanced at Jesse before answering, in case he saw any signals guiding him one way or the other. There were none, so Booth made an offer. "This is more a matter of convenience because sooner or later one of us will get a chance to shoot the son of a bitch. He's just a damn annoyance right now. He won't show if you call him out to a face-off. Trip tried to call him out, and he shot Trip with his rifle before he got close enough to use his six-shooter. So it's worth two hundred dollars cash money to have somebody take him out." He glanced at Jesse again and Jesse nodded. So they waited for Billy's response.

Mutt was disappointed with an offer less than what he believed he could get, but Billy accepted the two hundred before he could speak. It was big money to Billy, who had never been paid to kill, in spite of his father's attempt to put that image into Booth's mind. *Maybe it doesn't make any difference, anyway,* Mutt told himself. *He might not even show up in town.* To Booth, he said, "Well, I believe you boys made a good deal, if that feller does show up, he's as good as dead. Right, Billy?"

"Right," Billy answered. "Now, I want my supper. I'm hungry. Tell Cora to bring me a plate."

"You can sit down with us, if you want to," Booth offered, but Billy declined, saying he liked plenty of elbow room. So he sat down at a table across from them. *Suits the hell outta me,* Booth thought. Mutt's son was not a likable young man, that was for certain. There was no more conversation between the Corbin brothers and their hired assassin.

Although Billy devoured the plate heaped up with ham and potatoes, beans and corn bread, he was not finished before a topic of interest to all of them came in the door with one of Mutt's drinking customers. He passed the time of day with Fred, the bartender, for a few minutes before Fred suddenly left the bar to get Mutt's attention. Mutt was engaged in conversation with Booth and Jesse, but he stopped abruptly to hear what Fred was anxious to tell him. "That Hawk fellow you've been talkin' about is in the Last Chance right now," Fred told him. "Barney Meadows saw him goin' in the door. He remembered him from when he was in town before."

Mutt turned at once to see if Booth and Jesse had heard. From the startled expressions on both their faces, he knew they had. Billy had heard as well. He paused long enough to release a loud belch, then finished the last couple of bites of ham before getting up from the table. He walked over to stand before their table and asked, "Two hundred dollars, cash money, as soon as he's dead?" Both brothers nodded. "Then I reckon I'll go have a little drink at the Last Chance instead of drinkin' your likker, Pa." He started toward the door.

Mutt hurried to walk to the door with him. "You mind how you go about this, son. Don't give nobody a chance to say you just walked in and dry-gulched him. You do that and there'll be a posse out lookin' for you. Make it look like a regular face-off if you can."

"Hell, it'll be a face-off," Billy boasted. "I'm gonna call the son of a bitch out right there in the saloon, where everybody can see I gave him a chance. Those two back there better damn sure come up with my money, or this Hawk feller ain't gonna be the only one gets shot tonight."

"Don't you worry none about that," his father assured him. "They've got the money. I know they have."

CHAPTER 18

"John Hawk!" Sam Ingram called out from a table in the rear of the saloon. He motioned for Hawk to come join him. Seated at the table as well was Bertie Brown. Hawk signaled with his hand, then stopped at the bar to order a drink, which he carried back to the table. "Have a seat," Sam said. "Bertie told me you'd been in earlier today, and the reason you're back in town. Damned if trouble don't have a way of findin' you. You didn't pay Dewey for that drink, did you?"

Hawk propped his ever-present rifle against the wall next to an empty chair and sat down. "Not yet," he replied to Sam's question. "I thought I might have a couple more before I'm done." He was still thinking about his thoughts in the dining room and considered going over his usual limit of two shots of whiskey.

"That drink's on the house," Sam said, "and you can take the next ones outta this bottle on the table."

"You must be something special," Bertie said, beaming at Hawk. "I don't think Sam ever offered anybody drinks on the house before."

"I owe Hawk," Sam said. "If it wasn't for Hawk, I

wouldn't have you or Blossom workin' here." He looked at Hawk and said, "I ain't forgettin' that."

"Well, I'm much obliged," Hawk said, "but we'll just call it even after a couple of drinks, all right?"

"You oughta take 'em free as long as ol' Sam offers 'em," Bertie said. "He might wake up any minute and find out what he's doin'."

"Looks like a party goin' on here," Blossom declared as she walked back to the table. "I leave just long enough to go to the outhouse and come back to find somebody settin' in my chair," she joked. "I reckon it's all right, long as it's you." She smiled at Hawk.

"I won't be in it long," Hawk responded as she sat down in the empty chair on his left.

The conversation was light and jovial, in spite of the serious nature of Hawk's visit to Helena. These folks were friends of his, a friendship forged after a dangerous time for Bertie and her daughter when Hawk was able to help them. He poured his second drink from the bottle on the table and tossed it back. He could still feel the burn after he was sure it was mixing with the heavy supper he was carrying in his stomach. It was sign enough for him to call it enough after only two drinks. When Sam picked up the bottle and started to fill his glass again, Hawk held his hand over it. "No thanks, Sam. I 'preciate it just the same, but I think I'm gonna call it a night. Rascal's waitin' down at the stable for me to come to bed."

Blossom placed her hand on his arm and leaned closer to him. "You ever think about sleepin' with somebody besides your horse? You know, all the time we've known you, you ain't ever asked me for a ride.

And I figure I owe you one." She gave his arm a little squeeze. "I'm free right now."

He was immediately uncomfortable. Her suggestion was the last thing on his mind. He glanced at Bertie, who had obviously overheard her daughter's proposition and graced him with a smile of approval. He would not for the world insult them, so he paused while he tried to think of what to say. Finally, he came out with it. "Blossom, you don't know how much I appreciate what you're offering to do for me. Any man would. But I think of you as a true friend and never any other way. And I just can't make it right in my mind to take advantage of a friend." Blossom looked confused. She looked at her mother, who also looked confused. "I'd best just thank you and get on back to the stable," he said, and pushed his chair back.

Before he could get up, Sam blurted, "Who the hell is that?" They all looked toward the front door and the menacing-looking stranger standing just inside. Dressed in black, from the Stetson "Dakota" hat to his stovepipe boots, he wore a double brace of Colt Peacemakers, with the handles forward. With heavy dark brows, he stared out from under the brim of his hat as if searching for someone. "Is that one of those men you're looking for?"

"Nope, never seen him before," Hawk replied, unaware that he was just about to get his second proposition of the evening, this one not so much of a romantic nature.

Billy Crocker scanned the back of the room, his gaze stopping at the table in the corner where two men and two women sat. One of the men wore a buckskin shirt. No one else in the busy saloon caught his eye. To be certain he had picked out the two-hundred-dollar man, he walked over to the bar, where Dewey was already eyeing him with interest. "Gimme a shot of whiskey," Billy ordered. When Dewey poured it, Billy picked up the glass, but didn't drink it as he continued to stare at the table in the corner. It was then that Hawk put on his hat, picked up his rifle, and stood up. That was confirmation for Billy when he saw the feather in the hatband. To make doubly sure, he asked Dewey, "That's Hawk, ain't it?" Dewey said that it was.

When Hawk started toward the front door, Billy, still holding his drink, moved away from the bar, as if to walk toward the back of the room, thereby passing Hawk. Just as they were passing, Billy lurched over and bumped Hawk's shoulder. The whiskey glass in his hand dropped to the floor and he jerked back as if he had been attacked. "What the hell's the matter with you?" Billy demanded. "You need the whole damn room to walk in, you damned drunk?"

Startled, Hawk took a step back and replied. "Sorry, friend," he said. "I must notta been watchin' where I was walkin'." The man seemed to be awfully steamed up about it. So, he offered to buy him another drink, even though he was sure the man walked into him and not the other way around. Judging by the scowling face that met his offer, he decided the confrontation was deliberate, although he had no idea why.

"You damn saddle tramps think you own the saloons, don't you?" Billy blared. "You ran into me on purpose. Everybody in here saw it, and you're a damn liar if you say you didn't." The room suddenly became very quiet as the noisy crowd became aware of an altercation about to happen.

Certain that he was being deliberately baited now, Hawk asked, "Have you got some kinda problem with me? If you do, why don't you tell me what it is and maybe we can straighten it out."

"I got a problem with you, all right. You knocked my drink outta my hand, then tried to tell me I bumped into you. You're a liar, and I hate liars, almost as much as I hate cowards. And I'm callin' you out to settle it man-to-man, unless you ain't got the guts to stand up to me. So, I'm givin' you a choice. Get ready to use that .44 you're wearin' or get down on your hands and knees and crawl outta here like the yellow dog you are."

Overwhelmed by the absurdity of the assault, Hawk decided he had had enough. The only reason he could come up with for this bizarre confrontation had to do with Booth and his partner. "Who put you up to this? Was it a fellow named Booth? How much did he pay you?"

"Ain't nobody put me up to it," Billy snarled. "I don't know nobody named Booth. I just don't like your looks, and you knocked my drink outta my hand. So you back up and we'll see how fast you are with that gun you're wearin', or get down on your hands and knees and crawl outta here." He stepped back a couple of steps and took a wide stance, poised to draw his weapons as soon as Hawk backed up. Instead of backing up, Hawk stepped forward, matching Billy step for step, so they were still only a couple of feet apart and standing face-to-face.

"You wanna have a face-off, do ya?" Hawk asked a now-confused Billy Crocker. "Are you real fast with those six-guns?"

"You're about to find out," Billy sneered. "So back up and draw when you think you're ready."

"All right," Hawk said. "Or you can walk outta here and we'll forget the whole thing." The grin on Billy's face was answer enough. "No?" Hawk continued, "Well, have it your way 'cause I'm fast with a rifle." Still holding his rifle in his right hand, he suddenly brought it up from the floor between Billy's legs as hard as he could manage, rendering the startled gunman helpless. He doubled up in pain and collapsed to the floor. "And I was ready," Hawk added as he walked past the crumpled-up would-be assassin and went out the door.

Outside, Hawk started walking down the street toward the stable, trying to decide if Billy was telling the truth when he claimed not to know anyone named Booth. He couldn't think of any other reason for the confrontation. He had never seen the man before. He could be some young gunslinger trying to work up a name for himself. But why would he target him? *I sure as hell don't have a reputation,* he thought. No telling how fast Billy was, and Hawk wasn't interested in finding out, because he didn't think of himself as being especially fast with a handgun. He had underestimated Billy's resolve to get his revenge for the humiliating show in front of the patrons in the Last Chance. He found out the extent of Billy's need for revenge, however, when a bullet ricocheted off the siding of the barbershop Hawk was walking past. The next shot smashed the window of the shop. With no option other than to shoot back, Hawk spun around, dropped to one knee, and pumped two rounds from his Winchester into Billy's chest.

He waited for a couple of minutes, watching the

body sprawled facedown in the middle of the street to make sure Billy was no longer a threat. Hawk got up from his knee when the patrons filed out of the Last Chance to look at the body. He walked back to the saloon just as the sheriff arrived on the scene. Porter Willis looked up at Hawk when he came up to stand before the body. "I heard you were in town, Hawk. I mighta figured there'd be a shootin' pretty soon." He bent down and took Billy by the shoulder and pulled him over far enough to see his face. He looked back at Hawk then. "Who is he?"

"I don't have the slightest idea," Hawk answered, "and I ain't got any idea why he came after me."

"Hawk's right," Sam Ingram spoke up. "That fellow tried to pick a fight with Hawk in the saloon, tried to get him into a gunfight, right in my saloon, but Hawk wouldn't do it and walked out."

"After Hawk gave him a lick where he was most vulnerable," Bertie piped up, causing a few snickers among the spectators.

"Well, how did the shooting out here in the street get started?" Porter asked.

"I was on my way to the stable," Hawk said, "and he threw a couple of shots at me. I reckon he still wasn't walkin' too steady, 'cause he missed me and hit the barbershop. I had to stop him before he got his aim straightened out."

"I reckon you didn't have much choice," Porter decided. "There's been a lot of nameless drifters passin' through town since summer. Most of 'em don't cause this kind of trouble." He looked around the circle of spectators. "Anybody know who he is?" No one did. He looked at Fred Carver, the undertaker, who had happened to be in the saloon when the trouble started.

"Reckon you oughta go get your cart and haul him over to your place. When I get back to my office, I'll look through my notices and see if there's any paper on somebody that fits his description."

Another spectator, who unfortunately had an interest in the incident, stepped forward then. "How about checking in his pockets to see if he's got any money?" Alan Greer suggested. "He oughta have to pay for the window he shot outta my shop."

"That ain't a bad idea," Fred Carver answered before Porter could. "I'll check him out when I get him ready for burial. Course, I'll have costs to cover as well."

Unable to resist, Sam Ingram spoke up. "And he owes the Last Chance for that drink he never paid for." His comment brought a chorus of chuckles from the people gathered round the body.

"I expect I'd best take charge of searchin' the deceased," the sheriff decided. "If he's got any money, I'll see if he can repay what he owes."

"You need anything else from me, Sheriff?" Hawk asked.

"Nope, not right now, I reckon," Porter replied. "I'd appreciate it if you'd come by the office and fill me in on those two fellows I heard you followed into town. I need to know when I've got wanted men in town and exactly what you've got on your mind to do about 'em." He looked down at Billy's corpse again. "I'd like to know if this jasper's got anything to do with them."

"I'd like to know that, myself," Hawk replied.

"Well, come see me," Porter said. "You're lucky this jasper's aim wasn't any better."

"He warn't walkin' very steady when he went out

the front door after Hawk," one of the spectators offered, bringing another round of chuckles, as Hawk turned and headed for the stable.

The sound of gunshots captured the immediate attention of three particular people of interest in the Capital City Saloon. "Hot damn, he found him!" Jesse Corbin sang out.

"It musta been one helluva shoot-out," Booth Corbin commented after the night went quiet again. "I counted four shots—sounded like two from a hand-gun and two from a rifle."

The third vitally interested party, Mutt Crocker, was concerned about the order of the shots heard. Just like Booth, Mutt could easily tell the difference in the sounds made by a Colt pistol and a Winchester rifle. The pistol shots were the first heard, two of them, which told him that Billy got off the first shots. It bothered him that the two rifle shots came last. It could mean anything, good or bad. "Fred," he called to the bartender, "run over there to Main Street and find out about them shots." When Fred untied his apron, Mutt said, "I'll watch the bar. Find out if Billy's all right."

"Since you're tendin' bar now, you can pour us a drink," Booth said to Mutt. "We might have some cel-ebratin' to do, if your boy did the job he went to do. Ain't that right, Jesse?"

"That's a fact," Jesse answered. "But I'll wait to kick up my heels when I find out for sure that son of a bitch is layin' toes-up."

Thinking it a good time to solicit some business for herself, since everybody seemed to be ready for a celebration, Loretta moved up close to Booth. "If you're wantin' to kick up your heels, you might wanna go upstairs with me," she said in her most seductive tone.

Booth answered her with a sneer. "I'd sooner go upstairs with the itch," he replied, causing Jesse to laugh at the humiliated woman.

"Pay 'em no mind, Loretta," Mutt said. "They ain't ever been with a real woman. They wouldn't know what to do." She tried to give him a smile for his effort to console her.

Soon the discussion was back to the question of whether Billy was capable of doing the job he had been hired for. "Ain't nobody faster with a six-shooter than Billy," Mutt commented, more to reassure himself than to give the Corbins hope. He still couldn't lose his concern for the four shots. If the shoot-out had gone the way it should have, there would have been one shot, and that was all—possibly one more if Hawk had managed to clear his holster before Billy shot him down.

Fred was gone for only thirty minutes, but it seemed like hours to Mutt. Concerned as well, though not to the extent Mutt was, Booth and Jesse passed the time in a two-handed poker game. When Fred finally returned, the expression on his face told them the news was not good. He had the immediate attention of all three, but he directed his report to his boss. "It's bad, Mutt. He killed Billy."

"Hawk?" Booth asked anxiously.

"Yeah," Fred answered. "It was the feller called Hawk, two shots to the chest. The undertaker took him to his place."

"What about Hawk?" Mutt asked. "I know I heard Billy shoot twice." Fred related the whole story of the confrontation in the saloon as he had been told, and the shooting that followed outside. "I can't understand how Billy missed him twice," Mutt insisted.

"Well, what they told me was Billy weren't too steady on his feet on account that Hawk feller hit him where it counts," Fred explained, although reluctant to subtract from the dignity in the way Billy died. Seeing the look on Mutt's face, he quickly said, "Nobody knew who Billy was, and I didn't tell 'em. You can go to Fred Carver's shop, if you wanna claim Billy's body."

Mutt didn't have to think about it. "No, I reckon I won't," he said at once. "I wouldn't bury him much different than the undertaker will—just dig a hole and put him in the ground." He shook his head then in a moment of reflection. "Good thing his mama ain't here to see how her boy ended up. She cared about things like that." His moment of compassion passed, he said, "No, don't tell nobody who he was—it wouldn't be good for business."

"You're doin' the right thing," Booth said to him. "It's best not to have any connection between Billy and your saloon." He was thinking the same thing that Jesse was thinking. If Hawk knew there was a connection between Billy and this saloon, he might put two and two together and come looking for the two of them. Booth would never admit it to his brother, or to anyone else, but this man called Hawk was beginning to seem invincible. No matter who confronted him, he just kept on coming after them. Booth had little respect for Mutt's son, Billy, but he was supposedly a fast hand with a gun. And he had met the same fate as everyone else who had attempted to stop Hawk. "Who is that son of a bitch?" He suddenly blurted it, not realizing he was thinking out loud. When Jesse gave him a questioning look, Booth went on with what he was thinking. "How the hell did he find out we had a little money? He got all of Tater's share of the money. Ain't that enough for him?"

Jesse gave his brother a look of astonishment, thinking if he continued, he might verify Mutt's suspicion that they had made a major score. Booth didn't seem to pick up on his signal, so Jesse said, "There ain't no tellin' how he found out about that bank job." He hoped Booth realized Mutt was already thinking they were carrying a sizable amount of money. If he found out just how sizable it really was, he would be thinking up ways to cut himself in on it. "But he found out somehow," Jesse went on. "He's hunted us long enough, it's time we started huntin' him." Even as he said it, he wasn't sure how best to go about it, so he asked Booth what to do.

"First, we gotta find him before he finds us," Booth said in response to Jesse's question. "If we can catch him out in the open, don't matter where it is, we shoot him down."

"That sounds like the best thing to do," Mutt put in. "If he sets foot in here, that's what he'll get, both barrels of my shotgun. I ain't gonna bother sayin' howdy do. I'll let my shotgun do the talkin'." Billy had suddenly become dear to him in death, replacing the indifference he had felt when he was alive.

"Where is Hawk stayin'?" Jesse asked Fred. "Is he at the hotel?"

"I don't know," Fred answered. "I didn't hear anybody say where he was stayin'."

"I'd say the hotel would be a good place to start lookin'," Booth suggested. "I know for sure the son of a bitch has got enough money to stay there, and we might be able to catch him when he ain't expectin' it."

That sounded good to Jesse. "When ya think we oughta go after him?"

"Now's as good a time as any," Booth said. "Now's when we want him dead, ain't it? He ain't at the saloon no more. Ain't that what you said, Fred?" He paused to hear Fred confirm it. "Might be we could catch him in his bed, or in the washroom," Booth continued. The nagging concerns he had begun to experience about Hawk's seeming to be invincible were fading away, since he and Jesse were now going on the offensive. He looked at his brother and grinned. "Whaddaya say we take a little ride over to the highfalutin part of town and pay our respects to Mr. Hawk?"

Jesse responded at once, happy to see a little fire back in his brother. He was tired of staying cooped up in a trading post or saloon and running away from one man. Without further delay, they went upstairs to their room to get their saddlebags. It was not that much of a walk over to Main Street, where the hotel was located, but they could not chance leaving saddlebags filled with money for Mutt to plunder. "Besides," Booth said, "it ain't a bad idea to have a saddled horse handy in case you do need one."

Mutt followed them out to the small barn behind his saloon to encourage their efforts while they saddled their horses. "When you find him, put an extra bullet in him for me," he said as they rode out of the corral, heading for Main Street and the Davis Hotel.

Actually little more than a rooming house with the added convenience of a dining room built alongside, the Davis Hotel was a favorite stop for travelers passing through town. A large, rambling house, it was owned and operated by Gracie Davis, since her husband's death some years back. With rifles cradled across their arms, the Corbin brothers rode cautiously up to the picket fence in front of the hotel. With no sign of any outside activity, they replaced their rifles in their saddle slings and stepped down, figuring handguns were better suited for close work. Gracie, who was folding sheets in the linen closet, heard the tiny bell announcing their arrival and hurried to the parlor to find the two men standing near the small table she used as a desk. "Are you looking for rooms?"

"No, ma'am, we ain't," Booth answered politely. "We're lookin' to find a friend of ours. He said he usually stays here, and I wonder if he's in his room right now."

"Well, I can certainly find out for you," Gracie responded. "What's your friend's name?" When Booth replied that his name was Hawk, Gracie shook her head. "John Hawk doesn't stay with us when he's in town. Maybe he told you to meet him in the dining room next door. I know he usually eats there when he's here. My sister, Sophie, operates the dining room. If you don't see him there, she can tell you if he's been in."

Jesse and Booth looked at each other, not sure if she was covering for him or not. "Sometimes he tells people not to let on he's stayin' here, but it's all right to tell us. We're friends of his."

Baffled by his statement, Gracie said, "No, Mr. Hawk isn't staying with us. I don't know why you think he is. Now, if there's nothing more I can do for you, I have work to do."

"There's one more thing you can do," Booth said, and grabbed her by the arm. "I hate to think a pretty little lady like you could be lyin' to save a no-account bastard like Hawk. So, we're gonna take a little tour of your hotel to see who is in your bedrooms. He might be usin' another name."

"Take your hands off me!" Gracie cried indignantly. "I know what John Hawk looks like, and he's not here."

"We'll see," Booth said. "If you've got a master key, you'd better get it, else I'm gonna kick open any locked doors."

Realizing how dangerous the two men were, she did as she was told, fearing for her safety. "All right, I'll get a key, but please, can I at least knock on the occupied rooms, so we don't terrify anyone else?"

"Yeah, you can do that," Jesse said. "But if you say anything besides your name, give any kind of warnin', it's gonna cost you your life. You understand that?"

"Yes, yes," she gasped. "I understand, but I'm telling you the truth, Hawk isn't staying with us."

Holding her arm tightly with one hand, the other holding his pistol ready to fire, Booth held her in front of him and Jesse as they checked each room on both floors of the house. As she had tried to tell them, there was no trace of Hawk. Six of the nine rooms available for rent had tenants, but there were only three people in those rooms at the time of the search. Gracie went back to these three guests after the Corbin brothers left to explain why she had knocked on their doors. The cause of their confusion paused outside the hotel to decide where to look next. From the looks of the dining room next to the hotel, supper hour was over, for they could see no one through the windows. "Might as well check," Jesse said. "Maybe they can tell us where he was headin' when he left."

"Sorry, boys," Sophie greeted them when they

stepped inside. "We're closed. Supper hour is over. We've already cleaned up the kitchen."

"We're lookin' for Hawk," Booth said. "Was he here for supper?"

At once becoming concerned, Sophie answered, "No, Hawk didn't come in for supper tonight, did he, Martha?" Martha, clearing a table on the other side of the room merely shook her head as she stared at the two strangers, looking as if they were ready to shoot someone. No one said anything more as Booth and Jesse seemed as uncertain as the two women. After what seemed an extra-long moment, the two men left the dining room. "That looks like trouble for sure if those two ever find Hawk. If I had to guess, I'd bet Hawk ain't looking for company of their kind. I think I'll run down to the sheriff's office. It might be a good idea if Porter knew they were looking for Hawk." Martha nodded her agreement, and Sophie moved to the door. "Damn," she swore, "they're still out front." She waited, peeking out the edge of the front window until they finally turned their horses away from the picket fence and rode toward the center of town.

As soon as she felt the two riders were far enough ahead not to notice her, Sophie hurried down to the sheriff's office, where she found Porter Willis drinking a cup of coffee, his feet propped on his desk. When he saw her at the door, he quickly put his feet down and sat up straight. "Sophie," he acknowledged, "what can I do for you? Something wrong?"

"I don't know," Sophie answered, "but I thought it'd be a good idea to let you know there's a couple of strangers looking for Hawk."

"Well, that ain't against the law," Porter responded. "Maybe they're friends of his."

"I doubt that," Sophie stated firmly.

"Why? Did they say somethin' that sounded like they might be lookin' to do him some harm?" He kept asking her pointless questions, even though he knew they could only be the two men Hawk followed to town. He was reluctant to get into the middle of it and was halfway inclined to let Hawk handle it. He'd already had one shooting to deal with and that was enough trouble for one night.

"They didn't have to say anything," she insisted. "I've seen enough troublemakers in this town to recognize one when I see one. And I'm telling you, Porter, these two are looking for Hawk for no good reason."

Porter put his coffee cup down on his desk and tried to turn a concerned face to her, reluctant to respond to a young woman's intuitions. "Where are these two men now? Are they still in town?"

"They're right down the street at the Last Chance," Sophie said.

This was not good news to the sheriff. He had just returned to his office after having to respond to a shooting in the street involving Hawk. No one knew who the victim was or why he went after Hawk. And if Hawk knew, he wasn't saying. If there were two strangers in town looking for Hawk right after he shot that man, chances were they were looking to avenge their friend's death. "It might not be anything at all, but I'll go on over to the Last Chance just to look into it," he said. He would like to hope they were just in town to pick up the body, but he knew they wouldn't be looking for Hawk if that were the case. He got up from his desk and strapped his gun belt on and walked to the door with her.

Outside, Sophie pointed toward the saloon and said, "Those two horses nearest the end of the hitching rail. Those are their horses."

"I'll see about it," he assured her. She thanked him and watched him until he had crossed the street and stepped up on the boardwalk in front of the saloon, as if she wanted to make sure he did as he promised.

CHAPTER 19

Bartender Dewey Smith noticed the two strangers as soon as they walked in the door. It was their manner that caused him to give them a second glance. *Cautious* was how he would have described it. Before walking into the crowded room, they scanned it from front to back. He was immediately reminded of the reason Hawk gave for being in town, and in Dewey's opinion, these two looked like they might be the men Hawk was looking for. His next thought was that it was good that Hawk had left the saloon early, or there might possibly have been a second altercation in the saloon that night. As he expected, when the two decided they didn't see what they were looking for, they walked on inside and headed for him.

"What'll it be?" Dewey asked, making an effort to greet them as he would any stranger, when they stepped up to the bar.

"Give us a shot of your best whiskey," Booth said. He figured they would get more of their questions answered if they tried to take a friendly approach. While Dewey poured a couple of drinks for them, Booth said, "It's been a good while since we've been up this way. I expect it's been a couple of years or more. Wouldn't you say, Jesse?"

"Yep, I expect it has," Jesse replied, aware of Booth's friendly approach. "The town sure has changed a lot."

"It sure has," Booth commented. "This is the capital of Montana Territory now, ain't it?" Dewey said that it was. The conversation continued through a second drink of whiskey. There were aimless questions about the town and the surrounding farms and ranches, until Booth got around to the issue they were concerned with. "We've got a friend who's supposed to be up this way. I hear tell he might be in town now. It'd sure be somethin' if we could run into him while we're here. Wouldn't it, Jesse?"

"It sure would," Jesse agreed. "I bet he'd be tickled to see us."

Booth waited for Dewey to ask who that friend was, but Dewey was already suspicious of the ominous pair's intentions. And when he failed to take the bait, Booth went on. "Our friend's name is Hawk, big feller, wears a feather in his hat. I'll bet he's been in here."

Dewey hesitated. About to declare that he didn't know anyone by that name, he thought again and decided against it. If they had been in town any time at all, they would surely know about the shooting only a little earlier that evening. And chances were they knew it was Hawk that did the shooting. "Yes, sir," he finally answered. "That feller named Hawk was in here earlier, but he left. Too bad you missed him." He was aware at once that Booth was looking at him as if suspecting he was holding something back. He took a step back from the bar, in case Booth's next move might be to grab him by his collar and threaten him. At that moment, however, he was relieved to see

Porter Willis walk in the door. "Well, well," he said. "Here's the sheriff, come in for his nightly visit." That captured the immediate attention of both men.

Forgetting Dewey for the moment, Booth and Jesse turned their attention toward the sheriff. After looking him over, they silently agreed that he would offer them no problem, if it came to that. Turning back to Dewey, Booth asked, "Where did Hawk go when he left here?"

When Dewey replied that he had no idea, that Hawk didn't say, Jesse asked, "Where does he stay when he's in town? Maybe we can catch him there."

Dewey, who had been trying to signal Porter with his eyes to no avail, answered, "I'm awful sorry. I got no idea where he stays."

Booth gave him a hard look then. "Is there some reason you ain't tellin' me?"

"No, friend," Dewey exclaimed. "Why would you think that?"

"'Cause of the way you've been blinkin' your eyes at the sheriff," Jesse answered him.

"Ah no, friend," Dewey quickly replied. "I didn't know my eyes were blinkin'. I would sure help you find Hawk if I could, I just don't know much about him. He don't hit town very often." He felt a measure of relief then when the sheriff finally walked over to the bar. "Evenin', Sheriff," he greeted him. "These two gentlemen are askin' about Hawk. I told 'em I don't have no idea where he stays."

"That's right, Sheriff," Booth said. "My brother and I are just passin' through your town and we heard that Hawk was up this way. Maybe you know where we might find him. I think he'd be disappointed if he found out we were in town and didn't even stop to say hello."

Just as skeptical as Dewey had been, Porter was immediately suspicious that these were the two men that Hawk had tracked from Wolf Creek. His problem was, he wasn't sure what to do about it, even if there was anything he could do about it. There were no "wanted" papers out for two men meeting their description. All he had was Hawk's story about the two men, and Hawk was not a representative of the law. He couldn't arrest them, because there was no law against asking where someone was.

"Well, I'm afraid I can't help you any more than Dewey has," Porter said. "John Hawk doesn't come through here very often. And when he does, he never stays long. He was here this evenin', got into a shootin' with some stranger, and killed him. It wasn't his fault, the stranger came after him, but I told him it would be best if he was to leave town. I ain't got no idea where he went when he left town." He glanced at the pained expression on Dewey's face before looking back at Booth to judge whether or not they believed him. He wasn't sure, so he hoped Hawk didn't decide to come back to the saloon for a drink.

Undecided at this point whether to suspect the sheriff and the bartender of lying about the whereabouts of Hawk, Booth wondered why they would want to protect him. He suspected they might have some reason to, otherwise, they would have given him up without concern. It was then that a woman behind the bar caught his attention. He had paid her no mind when he and Jesse first walked up to the bar. She had been at the other end of the long bar, seeming to pay no attention to them. He realized now that she had gradually moved up closer to them, and when the sheriff came over to the bar, she moved closer still. He was sure it was so she could hear the conversation between them and the sheriff. He suddenly had a hunch she could be of some help to them. He surprised Jesse then when he abruptly declared, "Well, I reckon we won't get a chance to visit with our old friend this trip. Maybe we'll just have to have a drink and get on our way." He motioned to Dewey to pour another drink. "How 'bout a drink, Sheriff? I'm buyin'."

"Thanks just the same," Porter declined. "I reckon I'd best keep a clear head."

Bertie Brown moved back down the bar and walked toward the kitchen. Booth followed her with his eyes until she disappeared into the kitchen. "Come on, Jesse, we need to go." He didn't wait to find out if Jesse was ready to leave but grabbed his arm to get him started. As soon as they were out the door, Jesse asked, "What in the hell lit a fire under your behind?"

"Just follow me," Booth said, and went directly to the corner of the building, leaving Jesse to follow, still waiting for an explanation. Within seconds, they saw Bertie go across the alley between the saloon and the barbershop, walking behind the buildings. "That's what I thought. We need to follow that woman," Booth said to Jesse. "I think she's gonna lead us right to Mr. Hawk."

They hurried down the alley to the back corner of the barbershop in time to see Bertie striding deliberately behind the buildings. "She's goin' to the stables," Jesse said when Bertie continued past the blacksmith's shop. "That's where he is!" They left the corner of the building and ran toward the stable, anxious to get there before Hawk could get away. Fueled by the fact that they were no longer running away from the relentless hunter, they were confident they would put an end to this problem for good.

"Hold up!" Booth whispered when she disappeared into the barn. "We go runnin' in there wide-open, we're liable to walk right into an ambush."

"Circle around to the back of the barn," Jesse said. "If he's in there, she's told him we're comin' by now. He'll be waitin' for us to come chargin' in the front door of the barn."

"You're right," Booth declared, and pointed toward a stand of pines behind the corral. They angled off toward the trees at a fast trot, their eyes on the back door of the stable in case Hawk decided to make a run for it. Once they reached the pine trees, they stopped to make sure they hadn't been seen. When there was no indication that they had been spotted, they moved through the trees to the corral behind the barn, then took cover at the back corner. Kneeling by the corner post, they watched the back door of the barn. There were more than a dozen horses in the corral, and as dark as it was, they provided a screen of sorts. Anyone looking out the rear barn door would not likely see the two men kneeling behind the back rails. After a few minutes with no sign of Hawk sneaking out the back way, their concern turned to wondering if he had gone out the front while they were sneaking around the back. "Maybe he's gone, maybe he ain't," Booth speculated. "He might be hunkered down in there waitin' for us to come bustin' through the front door."

"If we set here, we're gonna come up empty, that's for sure," Jesse said. "Let's go in there and get him."

"Take it easy," Booth told him. "Remember how he got Trip."

"Yeah, but I ain't talkin' 'bout chargin' in there, out in the open, yellin' my head off, like that dumb son of a bitch did," Jesse said. "I say we can use these horses for cover and work our way all the way through 'em till we get right to the barn door. As dark as it is, it'd be pretty damn hard for anybody to see us. Then we can slip inside one of the back stalls till we find out where he's hidin' in there. If he's hidin' in there," he added. "The longer we set here, the more I'm thinkin' he ain't in there at all."

"I don't know, Jesse." Booth hesitated, thinking that might be pushing their luck.

"I'm goin'," Jesse insisted. "I'm tired of that bastard on our tail everywhere we go. If he's in there, he's gonna have to shoot it out with me. Can I count on you to back me up, in case I have to come back out that door?"

"You know you can," Booth assured him, "like I always do."

"All right, let's get the bastard," Jesse said, and crawled through the rails of the corral, then started working his way slowly through the horses.

Booth followed a few yards behind him, trying to calm the horses as he went, afraid their milling about would alert anyone inside the barn. His six-gun in hand, he took cover behind a big buckskin gelding to watch Jesse crawl between the rails and quickly press his body against the wall of the stable. He signaled for Booth to come ahead. Still reluctant, Booth left the cover behind the buckskin and made his way to the corral rails and crawled through. When he moved up behind his brother, Jesse pointed to the back stall, which he could just see in the darkness through the open doors. "I'm gonna make a run for that stall," he said. "When I get in there and make sure everything's all right, I'll signal you. Then we'll work up to the front of the stable, stall by stall."

"Watch yourself," Booth cautioned. "He's a tricky bastard." He was not sure this was a good idea, and gradually, that nagging feeling that he and his brother had crossed paths with an avenging disciple of the Quaker religion returned to trouble him. *More likely he's just another outlaw who wants that money for himself,* he thought, *just like we figured all along.* "I'll be right behind you," he said to Jesse as his brother inched closer to the edge of the barn door.

"Wait for my signal," Jesse whispered, then pushed away from the edge of the door and ran across the open doorway. He made it to the middle of the opening before the blast of a shotgun broke the silence and knocked him down. Frozen by the shock of seeing his brother flat on the ground, Booth was unable to move for a long few seconds, the explosion of the shotgun blast seeming to continue ringing in his ears. The Colt .44 he held in his hand felt heavy and cold, and he thought he heard Jesse calling his name. After another moment, he heard it again.

"Booth," Jesse cried out in agony as he struggled to pull himself up on his hands and knees. "I'm hurt bad," he wailed painfully, bleeding from his face and chest, as he tried to pull himself back out of the open doorway. "Help me, Booth."

Booth had no intention of exposing himself to the same reception Jesse had run into. Undecided what to do, all thoughts turned to saving himself from the same fate. Still, he stood beside the back wall, frozen, while he heard Jesse's pitiful pleas for help. Then there was another shotgun blast and Jesse's cries were no more. Terrified at that point, he turned and ran as fast as he could, down the side of the corral, expecting a bullet to find him at any second. When he reached the pine trees, he remained in them, running until he thought he could safely leave them. Only then would he cut back to the alley that ran between the saloon and the barbershop, his fear driving him until he reached the horses tied at the rail. He untied the horses, climbed into the saddle, grabbed the reins of Jesse's horse, and galloped off down the street toward the Capital City Saloon.

Back at the stables, Grover Bramble broke his double-barreled shotgun and reloaded with two new shells. He suffered no qualms for having taken the man's life. He might have given any intruder a dose of buckshot if they came sneaking into the back of his stable under the cover of darkness. But this time, he had been warned by Bertie Brown about the two men who were hunting Hawk. And Hawk was a friend of his. "You can come out now," he called back over his shoulder. "The other one ran off behind the corral. I reckon I'd best shut this door now, seein' as how it's attractin' vermin when it's open."

Bertie came out of the tack room, where she had taken cover when Grover told her to hide. After Grover pulled the two doors together and dropped the bar to lock them, he took a lantern that was hanging on a post and lit it. She walked over beside him to look at the body. "That's one of 'em, all right." She felt a shiver over her whole body as she gazed down at the mutilated corpse. "That shotgun made a real mess out of him."

"At that range, buckshot usually does," Grover commented. "Wonder how they knew Hawk was stayin' here with his horse." He thought about it for a moment, then said, "You didn't hear Dewey say anything about it when he was talkin' to 'em, did you?"

"No," she answered. "Dewey didn't tell 'em anything. They musta followed me when I ran over to warn Hawk. Where is Hawk? I thought he was sleeping in the stall with his horse."

"He is," Grover said. "He was here a little while ago, but he said he needed to go talk to Porter about somethin'. I reckon I need to talk to Porter now." The words had no sooner left his mouth when they heard Hawk calling his name from the front of the barn. "Speak of the devil," Grover quipped, then yelled in answer, "Back here in the stables."

In a few seconds, Hawk hurried into the stables with Porter Willis right behind him. "You all right, Grover?" Hawk asked. "Bertie?" he questioned, surprised to find her there. "We heard the two shots and came runnin' to see if somebody shot Grover." Then he saw the body lying just inside the back door and went at once to see who it was, even though he already had a good idea who it might be. "It's one of the two I've been followin'," he said. "I wonder how they knew I was here."

"I reckon you can thank me for that," Bertie volunteered. "I ran down here to warn you that him and the other one was in the Last Chance askin' Dewey all kinda questions about you. They were tryin' to find out where you were." She looked at him with a sheepish expression on her face. "I reckon I oughta learn to mind my own business."

"Who is this feller, Hawk?" Porter asked, still looking at the mess Grover's shotgun had made of Jesse's face. "And why was he after you?"

"I don't know who he is, for a fact," Hawk said. "I just know what he's done, him and the four outlaws that rode with him. And I expect he came after me because him and this Booth fellow finally got tired of runnin'. He's definitely one of the two I was tellin' you about when we heard Grover's shotgun. I ain't got no idea what his name is."

"Jesse," Bertie volunteered. "That's what the other one called him, and I heard him say this fellow was his brother."

"That's right," Porter said, just recalling. "He did say he was his brother."

This was Booth's brother? Hawk's mind was turning rapidly, thinking it critical that he get after Booth right away. According to what Grover just told them, Booth took off running, leaving his brother behind to die. "I need to saddle my horse," he said. "If Booth is off and runnin' again, I need to try to find him before he leaves town. He and his brother had to be stayin' somewhere here in town."

"The Capital City Saloon," Porter said quietly. "That feller you just shot was Billy Crocker. He was Mutt Crocker's son, fellow that owns the saloon." When Hawk looked a little startled, Porter quickly claimed, "I was gonna tell you that when we were talkin' in my office, but that's when we heard the gunshots and came runnin'."

"How long have you known that?" Hawk asked, more than a little irritated.

"Not long," Porter said. "Jim McDonald just told me. Said he was in the barbershop the other day when Billy Crocker came in to get a shave and a haircut. He was braggin' to Alan Greer, said he was the fastest gun in the territory. I knew that Mutt Crocker mighta been on the wrong side of the law, but I never had any trouble with him. There mighta been some shady-lookin' drifters that did business with him. But I didn't know he had a son, and I sure didn't know he was in town till today." Porter could see that Hawk was thinking hard and fast, so he asked, "What are you fixin' to do?"

"I'm fixin' to saddle my horse," Hawk replied. "I hope to hell I can find him before he skips town." Based on what Porter had just told him, he figured if he didn't see that black Morgan gelding tied up anywhere on Main Street, it was a good bet Booth had been staying at the Capital City. Already a step ahead of him, Grover opened the back doors again and hurried to the corral to get Hawk's horse. If it had not been for the visit from Jesse and Booth, Rascal would have already been inside his stall.

Porter walked beside Hawk when he went into the tack room to get his saddle. "Maybe I'd best come along with you," he said, "since I'm the sheriff. And maybe we can make an official arrest. Avoid more killin', you know. Whaddaya think?"

Hawk was short of patience at the moment. When he had gone to talk to Porter earlier, it was with the thought in mind that maybe he should ask for Porter's help in apprehending the last two members of Booth's gang. He was not at all comfortable as the self-designated assassin of Booth's gang. He had been

thinking that now that he might have the last two of
them in a town with a sheriff, maybe it was time to
bring an official lawman in and arrest them. And
now, with Porter's weak suggestion to do just that, he
changed his mind. He was not confident in Porter's
ability and feared he might just be in the way.

"I think you've got the responsibility of protecting
the town from any more harm from this one man,
and you might be best utilized by keepin' a sharp
watch on the town. Why don't you deputize me and
I'll do my best to arrest Booth."

"Well, I hadn't thought about that, but I reckon I
could," Porter said. "Like you said, it would be better
if I keep my eye on the town. After all, that's what I'm
paid for. If I was to go with you, chasin' after this
fellow, somebody else might think they can get away
with somethin' 'cause I wasn't here." Feeling a great
deal more comfortable now, he said, "I've got a deputy's
badge in my desk. We can make it official."

"Never mind the badge," Hawk said, and stepped
up into the saddle. "I've already wasted too much
time." He rode Rascal out of the stable.

Porter called after him, "Don't forget, arrest him if
you can."

"Right," Hawk bellowed. "But it'll be up to him."
I hope to hell he refuses to be arrested, he thought as he
cut Rascal toward the back street and the Capital
City Saloon. First, he reminded himself, he had to
find Booth. It was nothing more than an assumption
that Booth and his brother were staying at the Capital
City. But it was a good bet since the saloon seemed to
be the usual hangout for any outlaws passing through
town. Had he known that when he first got to town,

he would have checked that saloon first, instead of the two on Main Street.

As he rode up to the two-story frame building sitting back on the lower side of town, he held Rascal to a fast walk while he looked the saloon over. There was a barn and a small corral behind the saloon, but there were no horses at the hitching rail out front. *Doesn't look like he's got much business,* he thought, which was a good thing in his opinion. A crowded bar wouldn't be a good place to do what he had to do. David Booth was not his only problem, however. There was the matter of facing a father whose son he had just killed. *Maybe I shoulda brought Porter,* he thought.

CHAPTER 20

Mutt Crocker heard Booth's horse when he rode around the house to the corral. He went to the back door in time to meet Booth just as he was coming in. "Did you get him?" Mutt asked. "I heard a couple of shots. Sounded like a shotgun to me. Where's Jesse?"

"He's layin' back there in the stables, dead," Booth answered as he brushed on past Mutt, in a hurry to get upstairs to his room.

"Jesse, dead?" Mutt blurted. "What the hell happened?" He followed Booth up the steps, scarcely able to believe what he had just heard. In all his years riding with the Corbin brothers, it was always somebody else who got killed. "You takin' off?" he asked then when Booth hurriedly started gathering up his belongings. "How'd he get Jesse?"

"It don't matter," Booth replied, still busy tying his extra shirt and socks up in his bedroll. "He got shot and he's dead."

"Two shots from a shotgun," Mutt insisted. "That's all I heard. Didn't you get a shot at him, at all?" He was forming a picture of Booth that he didn't like, and he suspected Booth should have told him what

a wildcat this Hawk fellow was. He wouldn't have
sent Billy in there to call Hawk out. He could have
told Billy to set up somewhere and dry-gulch Hawk.
He still hadn't accepted the story as told to him by
Fred, who also got it secondhand. Hawk must have
tricked Billy somehow, just so he wouldn't have to
square off against him man-to-man. Now it sounded
like Jesse tried to stand up to Hawk and he ended up
like the three members of Booth's gang before him.
"How come you didn't stand up to Hawk after he shot
Jesse? Sounds to me like you turned tail and ran and
hung ol' Jesse out to dry."

That remark brought Booth's head up abruptly. He
dropped his bedroll on the bed and straightened up
to his full height. "You'd best be careful, old man.
You're about to let your tongue get you in trouble.
You weren't there. You don't know what happened.
You'd do well to just leave it at that."

Mutt wasn't satisfied to leave it at that. His first
thought had been that Booth had a yellow streak
down his back. But on second thought, it occurred to
him that Booth was now the sole possessor of whatever score the gang had made that put them on the
run. It must have been enough money to cause this
fellow, Hawk, to stick on his trail like stink on a sow.
He recalled Booth's remark that Hawk had Tater's
share and should have been satisfied with that. Mutt
decided that he should be compensated for the loss
of his son. "You fixin' to leave?" Mutt asked again.

"I reckon I ain't got much choice," Booth said.
"Hawk's got too many friends in this town. Every place
I go the people alibi for him, don't nobody know a
thing about him, so they say. It was just bad luck we
picked a town to light in where he had so many

friends." He smiled smugly and said, "Don't worry, I'll pay you for what me and Jesse both owe you."

"I'm figurin' you owe me a helluva lot more'n that," Mutt replied. "And I'm pretty sure you can afford it. You owe me a cut of that money you're settin' on, now that there ain't nobody left to split it with."

"What in the hell makes you think that?" Booth responded. "What money I've got is mine alone, same as it would be if I was the one got killed and Jesse ended up with the money. I don't owe you squat. You're lucky I'm willin' to pay you for what we used in this rattrap you call a saloon."

"You owe me for the life of my son," Mutt insisted. "It was on account of you and Jesse wantin' somebody to do your killin' for you 'cause you were too yeller to do the job yourself. You coulda told me how dangerous that man is." He paused and waited for Booth's reply. When there was none other than the same contemptuous smile, he asked, "How much money did you boys take from that bank? It musta been a helluva lot."

With a calm voice and a smile still on his face, Booth said, "It wasn't a bank holdup. It was a mule train with a bunch of Bible-thumpin' Quakers. They were carryin' thirty-one thousand and three hundred dollars with 'em, to be exact, hopin' to get to the promised land."

"That was you," Mutt exclaimed, "killed all them folks!"

"Every damn one of 'em," Booth replied, arrogantly, "'cause there wasn't any reason to let 'em live—same as you." As he said it, he drew the .44 from his holster and aimed it at Mutt. "Say hello to Billy for me when you get to hell." He pulled the trigger as Mutt tried to back out of the room.

Mutt stumbled out into the hall before doubling up and collapsing to lay helpless on the floor. Booth walked out in the hall and stood over him as he casually cocked his pistol again. "Me and Billy'll be waitin' for you, you son of a bitch," Mutt gasped before the fatal shot to his forehead quieted him forever.

In a hurry to get out of the saloon now, what with the delay just caused by having to deal with Mutt, Booth picked up his few belongings and walked out the door. At the top of the stairs, he stopped when he saw Fred coming up, having heard the gunshots. Fred stopped at once, his head just about even with the second floor. He glanced at Mutt's body lying on the hallway floor, then back at Booth gazing down at him, and backed slowly down the steps without saying a word. "Looks like you just inherited a saloon," Booth sneered, and started down the steps. A frightened bystander, Loretta stood by the bar, her eyes wide with the sight of Booth, a mocking smile still firmly in place, as he came downstairs. She didn't have to guess the explanation for the two shots just heard. Fred continued slowly backing away until he was stopped when he bumped into the end of the bar. The two of them stood frozen with fear as Booth casually came down and started toward the back door.

Relieved that Booth had no intentions of killing him and Loretta, Fred finally permitted his brain to free him up. Mutt had speculated more than once about the large amount of money he was sure Booth and Jesse had amassed. It occurred to him that the money was now walking out the door, with Booth's back turned toward him. He had no need to think further. He spun around the end of the bar and grabbed the shotgun propped there. Before he got the butt of it up to his shoulder, Booth turned and fired. For one instant, Fred looked down in disbelief at the hole in his shirt before he crumpled to the floor. Anticipating just such a move, Booth had pulled the extra six-gun from his belt before he reached the back door. Looking now at Fred to make sure he was no longer a problem, he then glanced at Loretta. "How 'bout you?" he asked. "You got any ideas?"

Loretta immediately threw her hands up. "No, sir!" She exclaimed, "I've got no part in this." He stuck the pistol back under his belt and went out the door.

Making his way cautiously up to the front corner of the corral, Hawk stopped when he heard gunshots from inside the saloon. While he paused to wonder what they might mean, he glanced at the black Morgan tied there. *He's planning to leave,* he thought, since the horse was still wearing the saddle with the fancy etched designs on the skirts. While he thought to decide how best to approach his target, he then heard a third shot, this one from a different part of the saloon. He took another second to ponder what that might imply. It was still in his mind that he would have to deal with Mutt Crocker as well as possibly the bartender and anyone else who worked for Crocker. He decided his odds were better if he waited to ambush Booth when he came for his horse, instead of going into the saloon after him.

There were other thoughts that interfered with his mission to put a permanent stop to the cruel life of David Booth. He had given Porter Willis half a promise to capture Booth if at all possible, with all intent that it would not be possible. Porter was no doubt thinking of the prestige he might gain in his town by the arrest of the boss of the gang that massacred the Quakers. Aside from that, Hawk now had thoughts that it might be a better lesson for other outlaws of Booth's nature to see him tried and hanged. *I'll give him a chance, but if he doesn't surrender right away, he's dead.* With that decided, he waited.

The wait was not for long. In a few minutes, the back door from the kitchen opened and Booth stepped out on the low porch. About to step down he was stopped when he heard Hawk's warning. "You can hold it right there." Gripped by the fear that had caused him to run, even as his brother was calling for his help, Booth was unable to move. Even more frightening was the fact that, due to the darkness behind the building, he could not see the man who haunted him. Then the voice came again from the dark. "I'm gonna give you a chance to surrender, so decide now. If you don't surrender, you're a dead man. So, what's it gonna be?"

Facing sudden death only a moment before, Booth realized that Hawk's intention was not to shoot him down as he expected. Hawk wanted to arrest him. Although Booth's situation was still desperate, he figured the odds were now in his favor. "Don't shoot, don't shoot! I'll give up!" he blurted, dropped the belongings he was holding, and raised his hands.

Hawk walked out of the shadows and ordered, "Turn around." When Booth turned around, with his back to him, Hawk stepped up and removed the .44 from his holster. Then he stepped back again and ordered, "All right, unbuckle that gun belt and let it drop." While Booth's back was still turned toward

him, Hawk took a few steps to his right. Even though
it was dark, he had seen the extra handgun Booth had
stuffed under his belt. Expecting a desperate move on
Booth's part when he told him to turn back to face
him, Hawk moved to make Booth's attempted shot
more difficult. He stood ready to execute the heart-
less killer when he made his move. Booth dropped his
hands and unbuckled his gun belt and let it drop.
Then his hand dropped to the extra gun and pulled
it out of his belt. Behind him, Hawk leveled his rifle at
him, ready to cut him down. He never got the chance.
In the next instant, the blast from both barrels of
Fred's shotgun, through the open kitchen door,
knocked Booth off the porch and dumped Loretta on
her backside on the kitchen floor.

Startled, Hawk took a quick look at Booth to determine he was dead. Then he moved quickly up the
steps and through the kitchen door, in an effort to get
there before there was time to reload the shotgun. His
haste was unnecessary, however, for he was met with a
now-frightened Loretta, still seated on the floor, the
shotgun lying several feet away. She started explain-
ing before he said a word. "I killed that son of a bitch
before he could shoot anybody else," she uttered excitedly. "I saw him pull that gun he had stuck in his
pants, the same way he killed Fred. He shot Mutt, and
Mutt and Fred were the only men who ever gave a
damn about me. And that son of a bitch killed everybody who took care of me. Now what am I gonna do?"

"What are we both gonna do?" The voice came
from the pantry door, which had been firmly closed
until that moment. Cora walked out of the hiding
place she had chosen when the shooting started and
walked over to comfort Loretta.

At a loss for something to tell them, Hawk came out with the first thing he could think of. "I reckon the two of you are partners in this saloon now."

His suggestion struck a chord in Cora's brain. "Hell, why not?" She helped Loretta to her feet. "Anybody can run a business better'n Mutt Crocker." The idea was already taking wings in her mind. "Hell, Loretta, Billy was Mutt's only heir, so that means he's left the saloon to me and you. Too bad about poor Fred, though, we coulda used his help. Whaddaya say we give it a try?"

"I don't know," Loretta answered. Nothing could be farther from her mind. She looked at Hawk. "I reckon it has to do with what he has to say about it."

"Ain't none of my business what you ladies do with this place," Hawk said. "My business is with Booth, and it looks like that's been pretty much taken care of. I will take charge of his possessions, because he's got some money that belongs to a church group up at Fort Benton. That's the only interest I have here. I wish you luck in your new business."

While the women were talking seriously about the possibility of the two of them operating a saloon, Hawk went back to the porch to pick up Booth's belongings, dropped there. With no interest in anything but the saddlebags and a canvas bag, he left the personal items for the women to deal with. He was relieved to find the saddlebags filled with money and the canvas bag carrying what cash couldn't be stuffed in the saddlebags. He didn't take the time to count it but took it to the corner of the corral and tied it on his horse. He admitted to feeling a small sense of fulfillment of a promise he made to himself. But he knew his mission was not complete until he returned the money to Donald Lewis and his church.

Ready to depart, he went back inside the kitchen. "You said Mutt Crocker was killed, too. Where is his body?" Loretta said it was upstairs, so he went upstairs to find it sprawled on the floor in the hall. *Lucky,* he thought, *he ain't a big man.* He managed to stand the body up long enough to let it fall across his shoulder. Then he carried it downstairs and out the back door and continued on to drop it by the stable door. He made a second trip with Fred's body. As he walked back to the porch to get Booth's body, he thought about the two women already planning for their business. *Ain't much chance,* he thought, *but miracles happen.* It was difficult not to think about the large sum of money he had just recovered and how much the two of them needed money. He couldn't in good conscience donate any of that church money to help them get a saloon started. In the first place, it was for a saloon, and in the second place, it wasn't his to give. When he got to the porch, he stopped and looked at the body of the man he had come so far to kill. It gave him an idea. *On your way to hell, I hope you can help out a couple of desperate women.*

He looked inside the kitchen door and called out, "You ladies wanna come on out here for a minute?" They promptly came out the kitchen door, both looking somewhat concerned. "I'm fixin' to drag his body over by the stable with the other two. It's kinda late now, so I expect I'll have to see Fred Carver in the mornin' to have him pick 'em up. I'll pay him for it, so don't you worry about payin'. Before I drag this one away, you might wanna go through his pockets to see if he's carryin' anything valuable. I expect you're gonna need some cash if you're really gonna run this saloon." They eagerly jumped to the opportunity. As Hawk expected, Booth was carrying several hundred dollars. He figured the Quakers could spare that contribution. As the women were gleefully counting the money, Hawk said, "I think he's got a pocket watch. That'll be worth something. I'm gonna take one of those horses in the corral for a packhorse, but I'm leavin' the rest of 'em with you. They oughta be worth a little money, especially that big black one he rode. The saddle oughta bring a good price, too."

He walked in the dining room soon after it opened in the morning. "Good morning, John Hawk," Martha greeted him. "Looks like you're getting an early start." She had glanced out the window when he rode up and noticed the packhorse. "You leaving town again?"

"I expect so," Hawk replied, "after I make a few stops here this mornin'." He gave her a smile and added, "The first one, and most important, was to stop here for some coffee and the best breakfast in the territory."

She left to fetch his coffee, passing Sophie on her way out of the kitchen with a stack of plates. "Well, good morning," Sophie sang out. "I wondered who Martha was talking to." She placed the plates on the long table in the center of the room, then came back to visit with him. "Whatcha got good to say for yourself?" she asked playfully.

"Nothin' much," he answered, "except I'll be leavin' town after I make a few stops after breakfast."

The smile on her face seemed to freeze in place

and she shook her head as if perplexed. "Gone again, skip to my Lou," she slowly recited the words to a popular children's song. "You think you'll be back this way anytime soon?" This time her tone was serious. At least, it seemed so to him, but he wasn't sure. He never was about her.

"To be honest, I don't know for sure. I get up this way every chance I get. I just don't get as many chances as I want."

The smile returned to her face and she said, "John Hawk, I don't reckon you'll ever land in one spot and stay there, will you?"

"I don't know," he answered honestly. "It doesn't look like it, does it?" He would like to have told her that he was quitting the army and settling down, but he didn't know what he could do to support a family.

"No, I guess not," she answered his question. "Well," she sighed, "I'd best see if Martha has your breakfast ready." With that she turned and went to the kitchen.

Martha read her face when she took Hawk's plate from her. "You don't look too happy to see him," she couldn't help commenting.

"He's not ever gonna settle down in one spot," Sophie said. "No use wasting time thinking he will."

"A man like that might be a lot better than one that's hanging around under your feet all day. If you're giving up on him," Martha joked, "can I have him?"

Sophie shook her head. "Not quite yet."

After a quiet breakfast, Hawk reported to Porter Willis at the sheriff's office and told him the whole story about the happenings of the prior night. After that, he went to the undertaker and paid him to pick up the three bodies behind the Capital City Saloon. It was well after noon when he bought the supplies he needed and settled up with Grover Bramble at the stable. But he started back up the Mullan Road to Fort Benton, anyway, anxious to make this final journey to finish this quest. A journey of over one hundred miles, he planned to make it in two and a half days, barring any trouble along the way. There was none, and he made his camp on the Missouri River just twenty miles short of Fort Benton at the end of the second day of travel. He rode into the town of Fort Benton shortly before noon and went directly to the First Baptist Church. At first, he started to pull up in front of the church, but upon noticing a small collection of army tents behind the church, he rode around behind it. As he had thought, it was a temporary camp of the survivors. One of the men recognized him and ran to fetch Donald Lewis.

"John Hawk, right?" Lewis asked as he walked to meet him. "I didn't expect to see you again. Lieutenant Sessions told us the Fort Ellis patrol had returned to base without finding the outlaws. What brings you up this way again?"

"I just wanted to drop off a little something you and your folks lost," Hawk replied. He went to his pack-horse and untied the extra saddlebags and the canvas bag. "I know this ain't all of what you lost, but I think it's most of it."

Not certain what Hawk was talking about, Lewis untied the laces holding the canvas bag closed and peered inside. His knees almost buckled when he saw what the bag held. "My Lord, My Lord," he uttered, thinking it couldn't be true. Hawk opened one side of the saddlebag, so Lewis could see that, too. It was almost too much for him.

"Brother Lewis!" the man who had first greeted Hawk, cried out. "What is it?" Seeing Donald in distress, or so he thought, he ran to help him."

Lewis waved him off. "It's a miracle," he said, then shouted it out for all the tent camp to hear. "It's a miracle!" Soon the little group of survivors of the massacre were gathered around them. Lewis held the sacks up for them to see. Remembering Hawk standing watching the celebration then, he said, "You must have caught the men who did this. I hope they did not have to be killed." When Hawk made no comment, Lewis asked a direct question. "Did you kill David?"

Knowing the Friends' position on the taking of another man's life, Hawk answered truthfully, "No, I didn't, but him and the rest of his gang have all gone where they won't bother anybody no more." That seemed to satisfy Donald's conscience.

Although eager to start back to Fort Ellis, Hawk agreed to stay and share a meal with the overjoyed Friends. He figured they might be hard up for food, but Donald told him the people of Fort Benton had been more than generous in supplying them. During the dinner, plain but filling, there was much talk about going on with their original plan to journey to Helena to find the land to start their own congregation of Friends. At one point, Donald asked Hawk if he would be available to lead them there. "Ah, I don't reckon so," he started. "I've gotta get on back to Bozeman and Fort Ellis to see if I've still got a job. You shouldn't have much trouble gettin' there without a guide, just follow the Mullan Road. But thanks just the same."

"Well, it's gonna take us a while yet to get organized again," Lewis said. "This time, I expect we'll go in wagons, instead of a mule train. Is there some way I can get in touch with you when we're ready—just in case you change your mind?"

Hawk shrugged, not wishing to be rude. "I reckon you could wire a message to me at Fort Ellis. I expect I'll be there." *If Lieutenant Meade hasn't got me fired again,* he thought.

"Good." Donald beamed. "The Lord has been most gracious to us when he sent you to cross our path. Who knows? He might have one more miracle in store for us."

"Well, I don't know about that," Hawk stammered, "but I wish you folks all the luck in the world. Thank you for the dinner, but I best be on my way." He nodded good-bye to them all as they followed him out to his horses. Aboard Rascal, he wheeled the big buckskin away from the hitching rail and headed for Fort Ellis. He had to pick up his pay for the patrol just finished and he had work to do on his cabin. He didn't get a chance to plug that hole near the back door and the last time he was away for a while he found a raccoon in the cabin. If the critters kept working at that hole, he might find a bear in the cabin one day. After he crossed the river and pointed Rascal toward the Big Belt Mountains, he caught sight of a hawk as it flew across his path and lit on the limb of a tall pine. The sight brought a smile to his face and he thought about Donald Lewis's interest in having him lead the Quaker survivors to Helena. *You ain't trying to tell me something, are you?* He reached up and touched the feather Winter Flower had exchanged with him. Trying to be sensible about the possibility of accepting Lewis's offer, he thought, *I've got a lot of friends in Helena.* But when he concentrated on it, all his mind could conjure was the image of Sophie Hicks, and that brought another smile to his face.

Keeping reading for a special excerpt . . .

MASSACRE AT CROW CREEK CROSSING
A COLE BONNER WESTERN
by Charles G. West

FIRST COMES BLOOD
Cole Bonner will never forget what happened
to his family at Crow Creek Crossing.
His wife, her parents, and their three young
children—brutally slaughtered by outlaws.
The horror of the massacre drove him into the
wilderness. Drove him nearly mad. And drove him
to seek an equally brutal revenge . . .

THEN COMES CARNAGE
Now, against his better judgment, Bonner is
returning to the place that almost destroyed him.
While hunting in the mountains, he discovers that a
man has been murdered and his wife abducted.
He manages to track the killers and free her. But to
bring the widow to safety, he will have to face his
own demons. Return to his old homestead.
And relive the violence—and the vengeance—
of another massacre at Crow Creek Crossing . . .

**Look for *Massacre at Crow Creek Crossing*
on sale now.**

CHAPTER 1

Cole Bonner stood up again after having put the mortally wounded deer out of her misery. He looked back when he heard Harley Branch pushing through the willows beside the busy stream behind him.

"I swear," Harley offered, "she got farther than I thought she would." He was breathing heavily from his efforts to catch up to the deer and his younger friend. "Fine shot, though," he continued as he walked up beside Cole and peered down at the doe. "Right behind her front leg—you're gettin' pretty good with that bow. I reckon that's what you were aimin' at, tryin' for a lung shot."

Cole snorted, amused. "Hell, I was just aimin' at the deer. It just happened to hit her there."

Harley snorted in reply, knowing Cole had hit the deer exactly where he had aimed. His young friend seemed to be handy with just about any kind of weapon, so Harley had not been surprised by the short time required for him to become quite efficient with a bow. Cole had deemed it important to learn to use the weapon since money for .44 cartridges was not in great supply.

"I reckon we'll butcher it and smoke it and pack it if we've got any more room on the horses to tote it," Harley said. "If we run up on any more deer, we're liable to have to train some of 'em to use as packhorses to tote the rest of the meat." He paused to chuckle at the thought of it. "I reckon old Medicine Bear will be surprised to see us show up with all the meat we've cured—happy, too. He ain't lookin' for us to come back before spring."

"Reckon so." Cole had not planned to return to the Crow village on the Laramie River before spring, and maybe not until summer, depending on how he felt. The time he and Harley had spent in the mountains had served to entice him to push on to explore the ranges beyond the Bighorns. It was a period in his life when he needed to find a peace in his soul, and the high snowy peaks seemed to speak to him. There were things he would like to forget, and people he would always remember. The solitude of the Rocky Mountain ridges and valleys came to him as a place to heal. But as winter deepened, he realized that Harley was past the point when the mountains spoke to him. Cole owed a great deal to the short, bowlegged little man the Crow people affectionately called Thunder Mouse. Harley had come along at a time when Cole needed someone who knew the country and would stand with him when the going got rough.

Although Harley never complained about the rough dwelling they had fashioned at the bottom of a long narrow ravine, Cole decided to pull out of the snowy Bighorns and take Harley back to a warm tipi. "This oughta just about do it," he said, nodding toward the carcass. "We'll start back in the mornin'."

"Whatever you think best, partner," Harley said as

casually as he could manage, still trying to disguise his eagerness to return to the Crow camp. They worked the rest of that day, smoking the largest portion of the fresh kill to preserve it, while keeping a generous amount of it to eat on the way back to the village.

On the second day of travel about a mile short of the South Fork of the Powder River, Cole pulled his horse up short when he discovered a thin column of smoke rising on the far side of a treeless ridge up ahead. He waited for Harley to pull up beside him on the low rise before commenting. "If I had to guess, I'd say that oughta be comin' from beside the river."

"I expect you're right," Harley agreed. They both studied the smoke that etched a thin dirty yellow line on the cloudy gray sky. "About right for a campfire, providing there's a sizable party campin' there," he added.

Cole was thinking the same as Harley. They had seen signs of a hunting party in the foothills, and on one occasion, had gotten close enough to identify it as Sioux. They could play it safe and swing around far enough to strike the river south of the camp and avoid it altogether. With no wish to encounter the Sioux hunters, that would be the wisest choice to make. Cole could not ignore the natural urge to take a look, however, in case it was not the hunting party's camp. Some innocent travelers might be under attack by Sioux warriors, although if that was the case, he and Harley were close enough to hear any shooting, and there was no sound of that. Also, if that was the case, it probably meant they were too late to help. It was not likely to be settlers traveling this time of year in that country, anyway—maybe a cavalry patrol that found itself outnumbered by the hostiles.

Still, Cole decided it couldn't hurt to find out who was burning what, if only to determine any threat to Harley and himself. "We might best take a look."

"I reckon," Harley agreed, knowing his friend well enough to have been certain they would all along.

The snakelike course of the river was easily traced by the trees and bushes that lined its banks as it wound its way through the open prairie on both sides. Their concern was that they would have to cross that rolling treeless plain before reaching the cover of the cottonwoods beside the river. Anyone who might be watching from the river could easily see them before they got within one hundred yards. Consequently they decided to angle off toward the east to strike the river farther downstream and then work back to the point where the smoke originated. Hindered a great deal by the string of packhorses behind each rider, they knew it would not be to their advantage to be spotted by anyone in the event they were forced to run. They planned to tie the horses in the trees when they approached the camp and proceed on foot from that point.

It took almost half an hour to reach a spot on the riverbank approximately two hundred yards short of the place from which the smoke emanated. They dismounted and Harley remained there to guard the horses while Cole made his way along the bank on foot.

"Make sure don't nobody spot you," Harley said. "We might have to leave in a hurry if that is a pack of

Sioux and they come after you. I'll have a helluva time tryin' to manage this big bunch of packhorses by myself."

"I don't plan on gettin' caught," Cole assured him. "But if I do, I'll try to get off at least one round to warn you. If you hear it, don't wait for me." He didn't care much for alerting a Sioux hunting party of his and Harley's presence and losing the supply of meat they had cured to take to the Crow village, as well as the horses that were carrying it. There was also concern for the hides he was packing. He sorely needed them to trade for the ammunition and supplies he was running short of.

In spite of those concerns, however, he could not ignore the column of smoke and ride on, not knowing if someone there was in a bad situation. "I'll whistle if it's all clear."

"Just be careful," Harley reminded him once more as Cole started out along the bank of the river.

Within fifty yards of the smoke, he still heard no sounds that would indicate the presence of anyone. Another ten yards took him to the edge of a low bank of berry bushes where he got his first glimpse of the source of the dirty yellow smoke. In a small clearing near the water's edge, a typical farm wagon was still smoldering, the wagon box and its contents having been mostly consumed by the flames beneath it. He paused for a few moments, scanning the campsite carefully, then looked back at the burning wagon. To set it on fire, the Indians had simply pulled the wagon over their victims' campfire and parked it there. He scanned the campsite again to make sure, but it was obvious that no one was left in the camp, at least no one alive. Cole shifted his gaze back closer to the edge of the river when the dark shape of a body caught his eye. Someone, he thought, prospector or settler, has rolled the dice and lost. It was a shame, but it was not that rare an occurrence at a time when Sioux war parties were raiding all along the Yellowstone and its tributaries. Satisfied that there was no longer any danger, he stood up and whistled for Harley to bring the horses.

Cole walked out of the cottonwoods and went straight to the body lying near the water, paying close attention to the tracks in the light snow on the ground. By the time he reached the body, he knew it was not Indians who had attacked the unfortunate victim. There were no tracks left by unshod ponies, as there would have been had the man been killed by Indians. And there were footprints left by men in boots, not moccasins. The men who did this rode shod horses. And from what he could see, there were no more than two or three men. He turned the body over and stared down at the victim, a youngish man, possibly no more than twenty-five or thirty. Dressed in the simple garb of a farmer or prospector, his scalp had not been taken, a further indication that the evil business was conducted by white men. There were two bullet holes in his chest and a more obvious one in his forehead, that one evidently to make sure he was dead.

Cole was looking around at what remains he could find near the smoldering wagon when Harley entered the clearing, leading the horses.

"I swear . . ." Harley muttered when he saw the corpse,

"some bad business here." He looked over at Cole, still close by the wagon. "Whaddaya figure?"

"Well, it wasn't Indians," Cole replied, concerned more than he had been because of the pieces of woman's clothes he'd found that had not been completely consumed by the flames. He held a scorched skirt up for Harley to see, all that was left of a gingham dress.

"I swear . . ." Harley muttered again, shaking his head slowly. "What in the world was they doin' out here in the middle of nowhere, all alone?" He looked around him as if searching for another body.

Sharing the same thought, both men began a scout of the clearing, hoping to find the woman still alive. After a thorough search, they concluded that she had been taken by the men who had killed her husband.

"They headed out this way," Harley called from the opposite end of the clearing. When Cole joined him, Harley added, "Yonder," and pointed toward a line of low hills to the southeast.

Cole studied the line of tracks that led into the river. "Might be three men, but I'd bet there was just two of 'em and the woman, and maybe two pack-horses, with the woman ridin' a mule." He pointed to the smaller hoofprints mixed in with the others. He stepped up in the saddle then and forded the river to see if they had continued in the same direction once they crossed.

He returned to join Harley, shrugged, and said, "I reckon we'd best find out what happened to the woman." His comment seemed almost casual, but the picture of what the woman might be enduring was not something he could ignore. Her husband looked to be a fairly young man, causing Cole to speculate on the woman's fate. Had she been older, she would more than likely be lying dead beside her husband. "I can't waste any more time," he said to Harley. "I don't know how much head start they've got, but there ain't much daylight left before they'll be thinkin' about making camp."

Harley understood what Cole was about to say. He was thinking the same thing, so he cut him off. "That feller layin' over there is just startin' to get real stiff, so maybe they ain't got too much of a lead. I figure it'd be best if you was to go on after 'em, and I'll come behind you with the horses. If they hold to that line the tracks started out on, they're pretty much headin' the same way we are. I hope I won't be that far behind you." He knew what Cole was capable of on his own and that he would just slow him down. "You just be careful you don't go ridin' into no ambush."

"Right." Cole turned the big Morgan back toward the other side again. "It ain't gonna be a hard trail to follow," he called back over his shoulder. He hated to leave his friend with the job of protecting their horses, but in good conscience, he had no choice. He just hoped that he could find the woman before she was harmed too badly.

"I'll wait here till the horses have had a chance to drink before I start after you," Harley said. "While I'm waitin', I'll put this poor feller in the ground."

Cole waved his hand to acknowledge, then set out following the obvious trail in the light snow. Harley paused a few minutes, watching his young friend as he rode off after the men who had done this evil business. He had not mentioned it, but he was sure that memories of Cole's past had come rushing back to remind him of the tragedy that had destroyed his family—also at the hands of murderers like these he was bound to go after today. Harley could tell when the occasional memory came back to haunt his friend, but Cole never spoke of it. Maybe time will eventually heal his sorrow, Harley thought.

As he had told Harley, Cole had no trouble following the trail, which led to the southeast in the general direction of the little settlement of Casper. He encouraged Joe to a fast walk, and the big Morgan gelding responded willingly. Cole had planned to rest Joe at the river even though he had not shown signs of exhaustion, but he was going to have to ask a little more of him. If the men he pursued were heading to Casper, it was unlikely they planned to reach that town with a woman hostage in tow, so he could not waste any time in the chase. Maybe they would stop a little earlier than usual to make camp. That would be good for him, but might not be good for their captive. The thought increased the urgency he already felt for the woman's situation.

Malcolm Womack pulled his horse to a halt and waited for his brother to pull up beside him. He pointed to a pocket of trees a few hundred yards ahead, where a stream wound its way through a shallow valley. "That looks like a good place."

"I was startin' to wonder if you was gonna stop anytime soon," Travis said. Younger than his brother by a year and a half, he was accustomed to waiting for Malcolm when it came to making decisions—at least when their eldest brother, Troy, was not present.

That was the case on this trip, Troy having elected to remain in Laramie.

Malcolm chuckled in response. "You ain't gettin' itchy, are you, brother? Hell, we ain't rode more 'n five miles from their camp." He turned in the saddle to look back at the woman on the mule behind him. "How 'bout you, Buttercup? You gettin' itchy, too?" He chuckled again at the joke he had made, amused by the lack of response from his hostage.

In mortal fear for her life, Carrie Green was not certain whether or not she might prefer death to the horror she feared was awaiting her. Her eyes downcast, she sat astride the mule that had pulled her wagon, her mind's eye still blinded by the picture of her husband's brutal slaying. Since there was no saddle and no reins, she had kept from falling off by holding on to the mule's stubby mane, her wrists firmly bound together. She wished now that she had been killed with her husband, and the thought of letting go of the mane had tempted her. But she feared a fall from the mule would only cause her more pain to add to that from the deep bruise on her face, the result of a stunning blow from Malcolm's fist. It came as a clear message of her helplessness at the hands of her abductors.

"Yonder in that sharp bend looks like the best spot," Travis suggested, the hint of excitement obvious in his voice. "There's still a good bit of daylight left. I reckon we're just gonna stop long enough to rest the horses, ain't we?" His mind was already heating up with thoughts of what he might do to pass the time while the horses were resting.

His brother's impatience caused Malcolm to chortle.

"Why, hell no. We might as well camp early—give us a little time to enjoy some of that ham Buttercup and her husband brought with 'em, and maybe see if she's worth the trouble it took to take her with us. They sure as hell weren't carryin' anythin' else in that wagon worth two cents." The lecherous grin plastered on Travis's face told him it was good news to him. Too bad ol' Troy stayed back in Laramie, Malcolm thought. He'd sure enough get a kick out of this.

Travis was a little slow between the ears. It was not noticeable right off, but his lack of common sense exposed itself within a short time in any company. Malcolm was looking forward to seeing Travis's reaction to having a tussle with a respectable woman, even if it was against her will.

Malcolm grinned. That would be after he had his tussle with the unfortunate woman, of course. He laughed to himself, thinking that Travis would probably try to pay her afterward. Malcolm shook his head when another thought occurred to him. *She's a right handsome little filly. Too bad I'm gonna have to kill her before we hit town.* "Come on," he blurted. "Let's get on down there and get us a fire goin'. I'm hungry." He gave his horse a kick and started off down the rise, leading Carrie's mule.

Travis followed, leading their two packhorses, the foolish grin of anticipation still in place.

They weaved their way through the stand of pines that bordered the stream and pulled up just short of the water. Travis slid off his horse immediately, drew his knife to cut the rope binding her wrists, and rushed to pull Carrie off the mule. Kicking at him furiously, she tried to resist his efforts, and for a few moments it appeared to be a draw, since he only had one free hand. Finally in frustration, he dropped the knife, grabbed her ankle, and jerked her roughly off the mule. Landing hard on the ground, she nevertheless kicked at him before sliding on her backside under the mule to escape him. The mule naturally jumped sideways to avoid the frantic woman under its belly, almost knocking Travis down in the process.

Highly entertained by his brother's clumsy attempts to subdue the terrified woman, Malcolm threw his head back and laughed. "Damned if you ain't got a strange way of courtin' a woman," he chided. "Just hold off a bit before you get all lathered up and I have to throw you in the water to cool you off. Take care of the horses first, then we'll get a fire goin', so we can get somethin' to eat. We got all night to see that the lady gets all she deserves. Don't that make more sense?"

After a moment, Travis settled down and stepped back to stand beside Malcolm. They stared down at the frightened woman for a few moments as she continued to slowly push herself away from them until she was stopped when she met with the trunk of a young cottonwood at her back.

"That's as good as any," Malcolm smirked. "Fetch me that rope," he said to Travis. When his brother stepped quickly to get the coil of rope from his saddle, Malcolm took it from him and proceeded to tie Carrie to the tree she had unintentionally selected. "There," he declared, "now you just pull yourself together and we might give you a little somethin' to eat to keep your strength up. And, Buttercup, you're gonna need it. That boy's as rank as an unbroke mustang."

Like a calf roped and tied for branding, Carrie

stared up at him with eyes wide with fear. For the first time since her abduction, she spoke, pleading for mercy. "Please don't hurt me," she sobbed.

Enjoying evil satisfaction from the doomed woman's helplessness, Malcolm replied, "Why, we ain't gonna hurt you much. You might even have a good time." He left her then to contemplate the ordeal awaiting her while he went to help Travis unsaddle the horses.

A multitude of thoughts collided inside her brain, thoughts of terror and the recurring image of her husband as he lay dying, seconds before the sickening sight of the final shot to his head. Friends in Bozeman had advised against starting back to Cheyenne alone, but Robert had been determined to get back before hard winter set in. She sobbed when she thought about it, ashamed that she could think of blaming him for delivering her to this fate. She even envied him, now dead, with no suffering left to face.

From the tree where she was tied, she could see the two men thirty yards away by the side of the stream, joking and teasing each other as they unsaddled the horses and began to collect firewood to build a fire. After they have had their way with me, she thought, they will kill me, just as they did Robert. It was enough to cause the tears to flow down her cheeks again. The thought of the assault upon her body was more horrifying than the death that was sure to follow. She could think of only one way to deprive them of their wicked pleasures. Even though she truly believed that it was a sin to kill oneself, she felt sure that God would be forgiving in this case. Resolved then to try, for she was not sure she had the strength to accomplish it, she strained to reach under her heavy skirt for the knife knocked from Travis's hand when the mule bumped him. He had evidently forgotten it in the excitement. It had fallen between her legs, and she had managed to drag it with her on her skirt tail as she had backed away from the two men.

In his hurry to make camp, Malcolm had not deemed it necessary to bind her securely to the tree since he was planning to untie her again in a matter of minutes. Consequently, Carrie was held to the tree by several loops of the rope around her upper body and her arms down to her elbows. Even though her wrists were still tied, she found she could just reach the knife by straining as hard as she could. Once she secured the handle in her hands, she drew it up to her to see if she had enough freedom to make the move necessary to plunge the blade into her breast. The question she could not answer was whether or not she could summon enough strength to force the knife into her bosom. Determined to do it, however, she hesitated a moment to ask God for forgiveness. Then she closed her eyes, and calling on all the strength she could muster, she snatched the knife toward her breast. She was immediately stunned when her arms were blocked by an unyielding force and a hand was clamped tightly over her mouth.

"Don't make a sound," a voice behind the tree ordered. Her eyes fluttered open and she could still see the two brothers down near the stream. "I've come to help you." The arm that had blocked her knife thrust was cloaked in a buckskin sleeve, leaving her to believe her rescuer was an Indian. Thinking she had been saved from one fate only to be threatened by another, she was too terrified to decide which would be worse.

As the hand covering her mouth was slowly withdrawn, she thought to scream until the voice said, "My name's Cole Bonner. I'm gonna try to get you outta here." He took the knife from her hand and cut one strand of the rope around her shoulders. When he had freed her, he pulled her back behind the tree with him.

Less fearful now, she quickly scrambled back to him, eager to do anything he ordered.

"Any minute now, they're gonna look over here and see you're gone," he said, speaking softly. "Are there just the two of 'em? Anybody else with 'em?"

She shook her head anxiously, her tears flowing freely, as she uttered, "They killed my husband! They murdered him!"

"I know," he said, doing his best to calm her as he cut the ropes binding her wrists, for she looked as if she might lose control of her emotions. "And I'm gonna try to get you somewhere safe while I take care of them. Just do what I tell you. Can you do that?"

She nodded.

"Good." He led her a few steps away, keeping the tree between them and the two, so far, unsuspecting outlaws. Pointing toward a small gap in a bank of laurel, he said, "Run just as fast as you can through that hole in the bushes. Twenty or thirty yards on the other side of 'em you oughta find my horse standin' in the trees. Wait for me there."

Before he could say more, the sharp report of a handgun rang out, and a chunk of bark flew from the tree behind them at almost the same instant. It was followed in rapid succession by three more shots, each one impacting with the tree trunk.

"Go!" Cole ordered, and Carrie did not hesitate. He watched her briefly to make sure she gained the bank of bushes and disappeared beyond, then he turned his attention back to the two men inching their way toward the tree, firing wildly as they approached.

Lying flat on his belly, Cole inched up closer to the trunk of the tree, wishing they had picked a bigger tree to tie the woman to. The unfortunate cottonwood was suffering a major assault as the two brothers concentrated their fire at the foot of it. The rain of bullets made Cole reluctant to expose his head and half his body to get off a shot in return. Knowing he couldn't remain there much longer before one of their shots found him, he pulled a piece of a dead limb out from under him. With almost one movement, he tossed the limb at some bushes to his right, then quickly rolled to his left, his rifle held tightly up against his chest. There was little time to aim, but the moment's distraction caused by the limb he had thrown afforded him the opportunity for a quick shot. He pulled the trigger before the butt of the Henry was even close to his shoulder. The shot caught one of the men in the shoulder, knocking him to the ground.

"Travis!" Malcolm Womack cried out when he saw his brother fall. He dropped immediately to take cover behind a rotten log. "You all right?"

"I'm hit!" Travis answered.

"Can you move?" Malcolm asked. When Travis replied that he thought he could, Malcolm said, "Crawl back to the riverbank. I'll keep this son of a bitch busy till you get there." Seeing Travis making his way backward toward the cover of the low bank,

Malcolm raised his head to take a shot at the rifleman, only to receive a face full of wood splinters when a slug from Cole's rifle tore into the rotten log. It was enough to cause him to push himself backward while keeping as flat on the ground as he could, hoping to reach the riverbank, firing in the direction of the rifle blast as he did. He dropped below the low bank just as the hammer of his pistol clicked on an empty cylinder. Using the cover of the bank, he quickly reloaded the empty cylinders. Ready to fire again, he raised up to find his adversary standing no more than fifty feet away, his rifle aimed, waiting for Malcolm to show himself.

In the next instant, the .44 slug from the Henry struck him in the center of his chest. The loaded pistol dropped from his hand as he slumped to the ground, never wondering why his brother had not shot the tall figure in buckskins as he stood unprotected, waiting to take the fatal shot.

Cole walked cautiously to the edge of the bank to make sure Malcolm wasn't playing possum. The blank, wide-eyed look of surprise frozen on Malcolm's face told him he was no longer a threat. He looked then toward the north when he heard the sound of hooves, just in time to see a horse and rider disappearing beyond the bend of the river. The thought of pursuit crossed his mind, but he discarded it. It would take too much time, and he had the woman to think about. It would be best to do what he could for her, wait for Harley to catch up, and move on. It seemed unlikely to think they'd see any more of the outlaw that had escaped. He was wounded, how badly Cole wasn't sure, although it appeared to be no more than a shoulder wound. From the way the outlaw had run off, leaving his partner with no backup, told Cole the man had no stomach for a face-off.

Beyond the bend in the river, Travis Womack urged his horse for more speed. When he had been shot and retreated to the cover of the riverbank, he had not been sure how many were in the party that attacked them. His first thought had been to get away, with only a brief concern for Malcolm, thinking it his brother's choice to run or stay. There had been no time to saddle his horse or grab his saddlebags. Before galloping away along the river, he looked back to see the one lone man, standing in the open, waiting for Malcolm to pop up from the riverbank. In mere seconds, he saw Malcolm raise up to be immediately shot down. He felt bad for his brother, but his death only served to convince him that he had been wise to run. Too bad Malcolm didn't. He would retain that vivid image of a wild man in buckskins, Indian or white, he wasn't sure.

CHAPTER 2

Tense with fright after hearing all the shooting on the other side of the thick laurel bushes, Carrie was not sure what she should do. What if the mysterious man who had come to help her was killed by the two murderers who had taken her? When the shooting finally stopped, she wondered if she should take the stranger's horse and flee. When she looked at the dark horse tied to a laurel branch, it looked so big and powerful that she questioned her ability to ride it. She was no rider by any means, having barely been able to hang on to the mule's mane to keep from falling off. Flustered by indecision, she decided not to try riding the horse and chose to hide instead. She ran farther back in the trees to find a place to hide. A deep gully that ran back toward the river seemed the best place, so she stepped down into it and huddled up against one side of it.

Pushing through the bushes again, Cole found Joe where he had tied him, but there was no sign of the woman. He called out, "Ma'am?" But there was no answer. Surely she didn't run off, he thought. Maybe she just tried to find a place to hide. Thinking that to be the most probable thing, he looked around him at the ground. He couldn't help shaking his head in wonder when he looked at the obvious footprints in the thin layer of snow. He proceeded to follow them, pausing several times when they led in one direction, then back in the opposite, first right, then left. It was plain to see that the woman had run in fright, unable to find a place to hide. Finally finding a deep gully leading down to the water, she had evidently settled on it to take refuge. With the tracks in a straight line toward it, Cole stopped some distance short of the gully and called out again. "You can come outta that gully now. Ain't nobody gonna hurt you."

A few long moments passed, then finally she peeked up over the edge of the gully. Seeing him standing several yards away, patiently waiting, she sheepishly climbed up out of her hiding place, realizing she had not thought about the obvious trail she had left in the snow. Seeing him standing tall and powerful, she wondered if she could trust his intentions any more than those of the two he had just freed her from. As soon as he spoke, however, she sensed an honest quality about the man. Although dressed like a savage, he obviously was not, and she felt safe almost immediately.

"I'm real sorry about your husband, ma'am," Cole said. "What were you doin' out in the Bighorn Valley by yourselves? Where were you headed?"

"We were on our way to Cheyenne," Carrie said. "My husband's father has a store there. We were going to try to make a new start there."

"Farmin'?" Cole guessed.

Carrie nodded.

"Where did you start out from?" Cole asked.

"The Yellowstone. About six miles from Bozeman. We had a piece of land near the river, but it was a sorry piece of land, so we decided it best to go to Cheyenne. Robert's father told him he could help in the store while he looked for some decent land to work. But now this has happened, and with Robert gone, I don't know what else to do but to go on to Cheyenne. I've got nobody to go back to in Bozeman."

"Yessum, I can see that you're in a real bind," Cole said. "I reckon if you're still wantin' to go on to Cheyenne, though, I can take you there." He had no desire to see Cheyenne again. There were too many memories in the little town that was originally called Crow Creek Crossing. So many of those memories were bitter ones. But he didn't see that he had much choice, now that he had rescued this woman. He felt responsible for her, at least as far as seeing her safely to Cheyenne.

"I would certainly be beholden to you," Carrie said, although without her husband she was not sure Cheyenne was the best place for her. She had never met his parents, and she could not be certain she would be welcome there now that Robert was gone. How would they react, she wondered, when a strange young woman appeared, claiming to be their daughter-in-law?

"Maybe you got family somewhere else," Cole suggested when she confessed her concerns.

"No, no family," she replied. "Robert was all the family I had."

"What's your name?"

"Carrie," she replied, Carrie Green."

"Green," Cole repeated. "Your married name?"

She nodded.

"That'd be Douglas Green then. Is that your husband's father?" He remembered the owner of the dry goods store in Cheyenne.

She nodded again.

He stroked his chin as he thought over the circumstances in which he now found himself. After a minute, during which Carrie watched him anxiously, he sighed and said, "Well, Carrie, I've had dealin's with Douglas Green and I've met Mrs. Green. They both strike me as nice folks. They'll most likely welcome you in their home. Tell you what. I'll see that you get to Cheyenne to your in-laws, but we're gonna have to make a stop at a Crow village on the way. We're packin' a right smart load of meat that'll look mighty good to those folks in that village. My partner's comin' along behind me with the packhorses, so we'll wait for him to catch up. He's seein' that your husband's body gets a decent burial. While we wait, why don't you come on back and sit by that fire those fellows started? Maybe I can fix you something to eat, if you're hungry. First I'll see if I can round up the horses they left behind."

Already, Carrie felt she was in safe hands, even though she felt as limp as a rag now that the tension in her body was reduced. "I'm not hungry right now, but I could sure use some coffee." She was trying, but it would be a while yet before she could recover from the events that just happened. And she wasn't sure she could eat, even if she had been hungry. "Thank you for taking care of Robert," she said softly.

* * *

Before Harley showed up with the packhorses, Cole had caught the sorrel that Malcolm Womack had ridden as well as their two packhorses. Carrie's mule wandered back on its own. Seeing the body before Cole had dragged it out of the clearing, Carrie identified it as the one called Malcolm. She told Cole they were brothers, and the one who had fled was Travis Womack, the youngest of three.

When Cole had stripped Malcolm's body of weapons and ammunition, he had found forty-seven dollars in his pockets and he promptly handed it to Carrie. "Ain't much in the way of makin' up for the loss of your husband," he had told her, "but if anybody's got a right to it, it oughta be you."

There was also the matter of the outlaws' packs and some clothes for Carrie, since hers, other than what she was presently wearing, had been destroyed along with everything else in her wagon. The dress she had on was torn in several places, the result of the rough handling she had suffered at the hands of the two brothers. Travis had been closer to Carrie's size than his brother, so she found some of his things that would work for her. The biggest complaint was the fact that they needed a good washing. She was resolved to endure the smell, however, the alternative being to freeze to death. Since the brothers had pulled the saddles off their horses, they were both left behind. Travis had not had the time to saddle his horse before he fled. Consequently, Carrie would no longer ride without a saddle, and she would be riding the sorrel instead of a mule.

By the time Harley arrived, Cole and Carrie were

seated by the fire drinking coffee from the pot the
Womack brothers had used.

"Save me a cup of that," Harley called out as he led
the horses into the clearing by the stream. "We gonna
be here a while?" he asked before stepping down from
the saddle.

"Yeah, reckon we'd better," Cole answered. "I expect
the horses need some rest. I know Joe does. I pushed
him pretty hard to catch up with the lady, here."

Harley stepped down from the saddle and nodded
politely to Carrie. "I'm mighty glad to see you're all
right, miss." Then he looked at Cole for the story.

When Cole brought him up to date on the shoot-
out, and the identity of the woman joining them,
Harley had only one question. "The feller that took
off, you reckon he'll be back? Looks like we've got
everythin' he owns and you killed his brother, to boot."

"There's a chance, I reckon," Cole replied, "but I
don't figure he'll come back for more. I put a bullet
in him. I don't know how bad he's hurt, but I think he
would have already been back, if he was of a mind to."

"Might not be too good an idea to stop here for the
night, anyway," Harley advised, still concerned. "Just
in case that other one ain't hurt as bad as you think.
Might be he'll take a notion to sneak back here." He
waited for Cole's reply, but when he did no more
than shrug, Harley continued. "Whaddaya say we
take advantage of the hour or so of daylight we got
left and push a little farther on?"

Cole shrugged again, not really worried about a
visit from the wounded outlaw. He had not taken even
one shot after he had been hit in the shoulder. Cole
wasn't even sure if the man had waited to see his

brother killed before climbing on his horse and running. But if it would make Harley more comfortable, Cole didn't object to the suggestion.

"You're right," he said. "We haven't started cookin' any food yet, so we won't even unload the horses. We oughta find some water between here and the North Platte, so we'll camp when we come to a good spot." The North Platte River was probably no more than twenty miles from where they stood. But there wasn't enough daylight left to count on making that distance, and the horses were too tired to be pushed another twenty miles that day.

After they took time to drink their coffee, they started out again, holding the horses to an easy walk. After what Cole estimated to be a distance of about eight or nine miles, they came to a small creek. He figured that was as far as he wanted to push his horse. It was almost dark, anyway, so they made their camp beside the creek.

Feeling a sudden relief, now that she was removed from the campsite where he had found her, Carrie was able to dispense with any lingering fears she might have had. For it was obvious to her that the hands she found herself in were sent by the angels and she was safe. Why the Good Lord had sent them to save her, but not her husband, was not for her to ponder. It was just one more sorrowful event in her lifetime to add to those that had preceded it. She would just give thanks for her salvation and vow to be strong in facing what the fates had in store for her. With her confidence restored, she insisted that she could take over the cooking, since they provided the food. She found that it helped take her mind

off the loss of her husband when she busied herself
with the mundane chore.

Harley agreed with Cole when it came to the
property of the Womack brothers. Carrie should be
given anything that she might sell or trade. That in-
cluded the three horses and the contents of the packs.
Carrie insisted that Cole certainly deserved something for rescuing her, and in the end, he settled for
the weapons and ammunition. Harley was struck
with admiration for the fancy Spanish-style saddle that
had belonged to Malcolm Womack and immediately
offered to buy it from Carrie. Cole wondered what
Harley was going to use for money, but Carrie, grateful to them both, insisted that Harley should take it.
She was perfectly comfortable with Travis's saddle.
The fancy trimmings on the other saddle held no
special interest for her, but Harley was overjoyed. He
had never seen it in his means to afford a saddle so
elegant with its high cantle and handsome designs
embossed on the skirts and back jockey.

When they broke camp the next morning, Cole was
certain that his old partner appeared to be sitting especially straight and tall in his new saddle as he led
them out toward the crossing at the Platte. He looked
back at Carrie, riding the sorrel, dressed almost entirely in garments owned by Travis Womack, looking
more like a child in hand-me-downs than a recently
widowed woman. *We ought to make quite an impression
when we ride into Medicine Bear's camp*, he couldn't help
thinking.

* * *

For Travis Womack, the cold cloudy morning that greeted him promised nothing but pain and hunger. His shoulder had stopped bleeding, but it was still throbbing with pain. He had nothing to eat or drink, save water from the Platte River, where he had been forced to stop for the night. Confident at least that the tall, fearsome-looking man wearing buckskins was not on his trail, he was thinking about finding something to fill his stomach. Unfortunately, his Winchester '66 rifle was still on his saddle, back on the South Fork of the Powder River. Somehow, he had managed to hold on to his pistol when he was shot, however, so he was searching the banks of the river, hoping to get a shot at a muskrat. He was not looking forward to the long ride ahead of him to Laramie to join his brother. It was sorry news he had to deliver. Troy would be furious to hear of Malcolm's death at the hand of the buckskin-clad killer. To make matters worse, Travis had been forced to return with nothing to show for their trip to Bozeman. His luck improved, however, with the arrival of two trappers at his camp.

"Well, I'll be . . ." Zeb Worley exclaimed softly to his partner as they sat on their horses on a rise near the bluffs of the river. "Whaddaya make of that?"

"Damned if I know," Smiley Bates replied. "Looks like he's lookin' for somethin' in the river."

They looked back again at the small fire near the trees beside the river. They could see a horse down near the water's edge, but there was no evidence of a saddle or bedroll, and no packhorse, either.

Smiley remarked, "Ain't much of a camp."

"He sure as hell travels light, don't he?" Zeb commented.

"Maybe he's run into some trouble somewhere, and that's the reason he ain't got nothin'," Smiley said.

They watched the movements of the lone man for a while longer as Travis made his way along the bank. Finally it struck them that he was walking a little awkwardly, almost stumbling a couple of times.

"Damned if I don't believe he's been shot," Smiley observed.

"Could be," Zeb replied. "Maybe he got caught in a bind somewhere. Sure looks like he could use a little help."

"I reckon we oughta ride on down there and see what's what," Smiley said.

"I reckon," Zeb replied, "but it wouldn't hurt to keep an eye on him, just in case." He urged his horse forward with a light pressure of his heels and the bay gelding descended the bluff at a slow walk, a pack-horse trailing behind him.

Smiley followed along behind Zeb, leading a pack-horse as well.

Intent upon trying to find something to eat, Travis was not aware he had visitors until his horse nickered a greeting. Startled, he turned quickly to defend himself, his pistol in hand, thinking the buckskin-clad killer had found him. But the two trappers approaching were brandishing no weapons and appeared to be peaceful enough. Travis realized that they were a sign of good luck and welcome after just having sampled a dose of the other kind. He holstered his weapon and walked up the bank to meet them.

When Travis's pistol was back in the holster, Zeb

and Smiley felt no need to remain wary. They had pulled up abruptly when Travis turned to first discover them and immediately brought his pistol to bear on them. With the weapon holstered, they proceeded to approach. Close enough to confirm what they had suspected, they could plainly see that the man was favoring a wounded shoulder.

"Looks like you've had a little spell of trouble, young feller," Smiley said.

"You could say that rightly enough," Travis replied. "More 'n I figure I needed."

"Maybe it was a good thing we come along," Zeb said. "It sure 'pears you could use a little help."

"Mister, that's the God's honest truth," Travis said, doing his best to appear respectful, a trait that did not come naturally to any of the Womack men.

"We might oughta start by takin' a look at that shoulder," Zeb said. "Smiley, here, is pretty good at doctorin' bullet holes and knife wounds. Looks like you was tryin' to find somethin' to eat. While Smiley tends to that shoulder, I'll see about fixin' you somethin'. We've got some fresh deer meat, just kilt last evenin'."

"Well, I surely do appreciate it," Travis said. "When you first rode up, I thought you were the same fellers that ambushed me." He watched while the two trappers dismounted. "Killed my brother," he went on while they took care of their horses. "Took everythin' I own, my saddle, and my rifle. I was mighty lucky to get away with my horse."

"I swear. That sure is sorry business. Set down on that there log and I'll see what that wound looks like."

While Smiley worked on Travis's bullet wound, Zeb

busied himself over the fire, roasting some venison and boiling some coffee. Travis continued to create a story for them of how he and his brother were bushwhacked by outlaws, so convincingly that they began to be concerned for their own safety.

"Where 'bouts was this spot where they jumped you and your brother?" Zeb asked. "Maybe we oughta be lookin' out for ourselves. We was more worried about Injuns than a gang of outlaws."

"I don't think you've got anythin' to worry about from those fellers," Travis assured him. "That was back this side of the South Fork of the Powder, and they were travelin' toward the east."

"How you know that?" Zeb asked. "I thought you said they was hid and jumped you when you rode down to water your horses."

His question caused Travis to pause for a moment while he tried to think of an answer. "That's right, I did say that, didn't I? Well, I reckon I just figured they were headed that way. It don't matter none, anyway. They ain't nowhere around here and I ain't worried about 'em no more because I've got supplies and horses to take care of what I'm needin'."

Zeb and Smiley exchanged puzzled glances. "Where are your horses?" Zeb asked. "We didn't see but that one by the creek."

Travis chuckled, amused by their blank faces. "You rode in on 'em," he said and continued to grin at them.

A little slow to grasp the meaning of the young man's casual remark, Smiley stared in astonishment at the .44 Colt suddenly aimed at his stomach. A fraction of a second later, he recoiled with the impact of the slug as it tore into his gut. Equally slow to react, Zeb was frozen for a moment, caught with a coffeepot in his hand. He dropped the pot, turned, and ran for his horse, only to be stopped by a bullet in his back before he was halfway there. He staggered on for a few more feet before falling facedown on the ground.

Travis got up from the log he had been seated on while Smiley tended his wound. He paused to gaze at the wounded man writhing in pain on the ground. "You son of a bitch," Smiley rasped painfully.

"You done a right handy job on my shoulder," Travis said, "so I reckon the least I can do is put you outta your misery." Another shot from his .44 in Smiley's forehead silenced him forever. "That oughta do the job," Travis commented and walked unhurriedly toward Zeb to check on him. He found the unfortunate trapper mortally wounded, but still clawing at the light covering of snow in an attempt to pull himself over the ground. "I reckon I oughta tell you how tickled I am that you and your partner came along, 'cause I was in a fix," he said as he placed another round in the back of Zeb's head.

He looked around him then while he casually replaced the cartridges he had used, pleased with the good fortune that had come his way. There was still the regrettable news he was bound to report to his brother, Troy. But instead of arriving in Laramie with nothing to show for the trip to Bozeman, it would be tempered a bit with four extra horses and whatever possessions the trappers had. With that thought in mind, he went to work searching the bodies and the packs of his victims. He soon found that he had gained very little of value other than some decent hides he could sell, a couple of Civil War surplus Sharps rifles, and two .44 caliber pistols. The horses looked to be in pretty good shape, though. It was enough to permit him to return to Laramie with a modicum of pride—even if it was without his brother. "Hell," he snorted, "Malcolm oughta not been caught with his head down behind that bank, anyway." His brother's death was certainly a disappointment, but not to the extent that would cause him to feel guilt for not backing him up. To the contrary, the only emotion he felt was one of relief that he had managed to escape getting killed, himself. Add to that the good fortune that sent him Zeb and Smiley, he felt in good spirits as he set out for Laramie, leading the horses he had just acquired.

The journey to the Crow village near the confluence of the Laramie and the North Laramie Rivers would take the pack train three and a half days. During that time, Carrie developed a deep trust in the two men who had happened into her life at the precise moment she needed them. It was much too soon for her to get over the loss of her husband, but the easygoing nature of her two traveling companions, and their polite consideration toward her, made her suffering bearable. Her two rescuers appeared to be a perfect team. The older man, called Harley, was an elf-like little man, no taller than Carrie herself, although she wondered if he might not be a head taller if his legs were straight. They were so bowed that he looked as if he had come from his mother's womb ready to ride a horse. Judging by the heavy solid white beard that covered most of his ruddy face, however, she had to speculate that that event must have been many years ago.

In contrast, the younger half of the partnership was

as straight and tall as a lodgepole pine. A serious man of few words, Cole Bonner made her think of a mountain lion. Dressed in animal skins, as was Harley, he was clean-shaven. His hair was worn in two braids after the style of the Crow Indians he lived with. Whereas Harley could rattle on about any subject, Cole used his words as if they were too expensive to waste. A perfect set, Carrie thought. Robert could rest in peace knowing that she was with them.

"Do you think we'll reach that Indian village tomorrow?" Carrie asked as she brought Harley a cup of coffee.

"Yes, ma'am," Harley answered. "We'll be home tomorrow, all right." He chuckled and added, "Leastways, me and Cole will be home tomorrow. Crow Creek Crossin's a good eighty miles or more from there," he said, referring to Cheyenne by its original name. "You gettin' kinda anxious to get on down to your in-laws?"

She hesitated before answering. "To be honest, I'm not really looking forward to it. I've never met my late husband's folks, so I'll be a complete stranger in their home. I don't know if they'll be glad to see me or not, especially since I'll be bringing such bad news." She sat down beside the fire near him. "I might be thinking about going someplace else if I had someplace else to go to."

"Why, I'm sure they'll be tickled to meet you," Harley said, although he fully understood her apprehension. "And I know they'll wanna take care of you since their son picked you for a wife. How long was you and Robert married?"

"Not quite a year and a half," she answered with a sad smile, thinking what a short time it had been. She and her husband were still only beginning to get to know each other.

"So you two hadn't got around to havin' young'uns yet, I reckon."

"There was one. A boy, but he was stillborn," she said, looking down at her lap as if ashamed. "We would have named him Douglas, after his grandfather."

"I declare," Harley said, "that's sure enough bad luck." For one of the few times in his life, he found himself short of words. "Well, you're young yet," he finally consoled. "You've got time to start out with somebody else. Why, the way I hear talk of Crow Creek Crossin', I mean Cheyenne, and the way it keeps growin', I expect there's a gracious plenty young men there that'd stomp all over each other to get to a pretty little gal like you."

She responded with another sad smile, causing him to declare, "I'd best go see if Cole needs any help with the horses. We gotta be ready to ride come sunup." The conversation was getting a little too uncomfortable for him, so he swigged his coffee down and got to his feet. He realized that she was sincere when she said she wasn't looking forward to meeting her husband's folks. But according to what she had told Cole and him, she had no other place to go.

Before retreating to join Cole with the horses, he offered one other suggestion. "You might wanna stay a little while in Medicine Bear's village, till you feel like ridin' on down to Cheyenne. I expect you'd be welcome for as long as you wanted to stay."

Once again, the sad smile appeared. "Maybe," she

said. "I guess we'll see." In truth, she could not see any possibility that she would be comfortable in an Indian village for any length of time. The thought brought a picture to mind of savages dancing around a roaring fire, brandishing tomahawks and bows, and chanting songs with no distinguishable words. Since both of her rescuers looked like they'd be right at home in a tipi, she declined to express her opinion.

As Harley had said, they were up and in the saddle at sunup, planning to stop for breakfast when the horses needed rest. Carrie wished she felt the enthusiasm to reach the Indian village that was so evident in Harley's attitude. To the contrary, she didn't expect her experience to be as comfortable as the one she now had with just Cole and Harley. She tried to tell herself that it would at least postpone the meeting she was to have with Robert's parents. These were the thoughts troubling her when they rode through the trees to get her first glimpse at the Crow village by the river.

Connect with Us

Visit us online at
KensingtonBooks.com
to read more from your favorite authors, see books
by series, view reading group guides, and more.

Join us on social media

for sneak peeks, chances to win books and prize packs,
and to share your thoughts with other readers.

facebook.com/kensingtonpublishing
twitter.com/kensingtonbooks

Tell us what you think!

To share your thoughts, submit a review,
or sign up for our eNewsletters, please visit:
KensingtonBooks.com/TellUs.